A Man of Character

THE PERFECT FANTASY MIGHT JUST BE REALITY

MARGARET LOCKE

For Brett.
My very own knight in shining armor.

PROLOGUE

Charlottesville, Virginia – Spring 2001

rank Schreiber examined the book in his hands, a satisfied grunt escaping his lips as his fingers trailed over the spine. "A pretty good job, if I do say so myself," he murmured, pleased at how well the binding job had come out. The plain black cover with its simple lettering disguised the inner contents well.

"You doing okay, Dad?"

He glanced up. His youngest daughter, Catherine, stood at the entrance to the bookstore, humor lighting her face.

She nodded toward the stack of books at his elbow. "Lost in your treasures again, huh?"

You have no idea, honey. "I'm great! How could I not be, surrounded by so many goodies?"

She laughed as she pushed her hair out of her eyes. "Why did I even ask? Hey, I'm picking up Mom and we're going to grab something to eat. Wanna come?"

"No, no." He waved her on with his hand. "I already ate. You guys have fun. I'll see you when you get home."

"I'm betting you won't notice we're gone."

"You know me too well. But I'll notice. It's a lot quieter in here without you chattering females around. Perfect for reading." He laughed out loud when he caught Cat's faux outraged expression. "You know I speak the truth."

Her eyes softened as she turned the doorknob. "Yeah, whatever. Love you, Dad," she called, as she walked out into the late afternoon sunshine.

"Love you, too, Catey. Always."

Turning back to the book in his hands, he opened it and surveyed the inside pages. *Gorgeous. Simply stunning.* He didn't believe the legend his grandmother had told him about the book; that was clearly nonsense her grandmother must have told *her*, a myth passed down through generations. But given its age, he didn't doubt the value of its contents. He'd dutifully guarded it, rebinding the pages when the ancient bindings gave way. Better to have it in a secure house, he reasoned. He liked the idea that such an ordinary exterior could house such riches. Just like people.

"Give it to Cat when she's twenty-five," his grandmother had said all those years ago. "Promise me. She's the one."

Frank had nodded. His second-born daughter, although only seven then, seemed the most likely to share his passion for the written word.

"Why twenty-five?"

Her eyes had twinkled. "It's how it's done."

He'd pressed his grandmother for more information, but she'd remained tight-lipped, saying only that Cat would eventually understand.

He couldn't believe his youngest child would hit that magical age in a few months. Twenty-five. His baby, grown up and out in the world.

He frowned. At least he wanted her out in the world, more than she currently was. Submerging oneself in books wasn't a bad thing, of course—he was guilty of that himself. But he had his beautiful Grace. He had someone with whom he was sharing his life, someone who reminded him to come back to the real world once in a while.

"I hope you find love, my Catey girl," he whispered. "It's the greatest treasure of them all."

God, had he really just said that? He was going soft in his old age.

Whistling, he set the book down, jotted a quick note, and stuck it inside the cover. Then he wrapped the book in the plain brown mailing paper they kept near the cash register and scrawled her name across the front. Setting the book back into the box, he carefully stacked other titles around it for safekeeping until her birthday.

"I'll tell her, Grannie." He'd even tell Cat the absurd claims his grandmother had made about it. For now, at least, it was well protected, as she'd asked.

He hauled the heavy box to the storage closet under the stairs.

Heading back to the main room, he wiped his hand across the beads of sweat that had formed on his forehead. *I'm getting old, if one box of books has me breathing this hard.*

As he walked to the staircase to head upstairs, sharp pain shot across his ribcage. He grabbed the stair railing to steady himself, his other hand flying to his heart. Large dots floated at the edge of his vision. Daggers ripped through his chest as his lungs seized.

No. Oh, no, no, no. He collapsed on the floor, gasping for breath. *I should have told you, Catey. I should have told you.* All went black.

CHAPTER 1

Charlottesville, Virginia - Fall 2011

The last thing Catherine wanted to do was talk about men. She didn't need to think about anything except the bookstore, especially on today of all days. But she'd promised to rehash her roommate Eliza's date from the night before, so with a sigh she placed her standard coffee order and prepared herself for what was to come.

"Vente latte, skim milk, with a shot of butterscotch." Cat stood back to let Eliza order.

"Double espresso and, um, a slice of that crumb cake. Although I shouldn't." Eliza smoothed her hands over her round hips. She flashed a self-conscious smile at the barista as she fumbled in her large, floppy shoulder bag for cash.

After paying for their drinks, the two women sat down in their usual booth next to the front window. Normally Cat loved the open view, but the steady gray October rain wasn't doing anything to help her attitude this morning.

"So, how'd it go with Jeff?" Cat asked, forcing a smile. She shouldn't let her own rotten mood dampen Eliza's spirits. It wasn't Eliza's fault. Nobody was to blame but ... She closed her eyes, determined to rid herself of any thoughts of *him.* "I couldn't sleep and heard you come in late. I'm assuming that means things went well?"

Eliza wrinkled her nose. "He was nice. We ate at that new Italian place on the Ped Mall. It was wonderful, and the tiramisu was to die for." She took a quick bite of cake before continuing. "We talked about grad school. Did I tell you he's getting his masters in history?"

Cat shook her head, savoring the warmth of the coffee mug cradled in her hands. She breathed in the heavenly scent, grateful for its calming effect.

"We had a great time talking. And he *was* nice. He just wasn't ..." Eliza paused to lick bits of cake off her fingers.

"Just wasn't Darcy?" Her friend's passion for all things English included a love affair with Jane Austen, especially *Pride and Prejudice.*

Eliza stiffened. "Don't we all want a Darcy? Besides, is hoping for a British accent such a bad thing?"

Cat shrugged. "Not at all," she said in the best Queen Elizabeth impression she could muster. Losing the accent, she added, "You might be looking for love, but *I* am not. You know I haven't had the best of luck in that area. Men aren't exactly beating down my door."

"That's because you're not willing to open it. You let one bad relationship sour you on the whole idea," Eliza retorted. "I know what today is, Cat. I know it marks six years." She took another sip of her coffee, gazing with sympathetic eyes over the cup's rim. "I'm sorry about Ryan. He was a jerk."

Cat's stomach tightened at his name. She hated how she still reacted to the mention of him, how she struggled through this day every year. He'd ruined October for her, once her favorite month. Hell, he'd ruined everything.

Most of the time she was fine. Weeks passed, sometimes months now, in which that part of her life didn't register. But he'd left her scarred, a deep emotional branding. Fear of having to endure that kind of hurt again kept her from opening up. She'd had enough loss in her life, thank you very much.

If she were honest, though, she'd admit loneliness crept into more and more of her days … and nights. Fear couldn't hold her hand. Fear couldn't rub her shoulders when she was tired or snuggle with her in the early morning. And fear didn't silence the longing scratching at that part of her she'd locked away. She wasn't quite sure what she was longing for. It wasn't a man. Was it? No relationship was worth risking what was left of her heart, right?

"Six years is a long time," Eliza added in a soft voice. "Aren't you the tiniest bit interested?" She motioned around the room. "I bet there's at least one guy in here right now who'd love to go out with you, if you'd just make yourself approachable."

Cat surveyed the room. She loved this old coffee shop with its eclectic furnishings and low-key atmosphere. Today it housed a mostly younger crowd: college students buzzing up on caffeine before classes, a few moms sipping coffee while trying to entertain babies in strollers. The hum of conversation surrounded them, a sound that always soothed her. An older woman read a novel in the corner, and at a stool near the side window, a man typed on a laptop.

"No, I'm most definitely not interested. I don't want to go through it all again, and I've got bigger concerns, anyway."

She gestured toward the man at the laptop. "Plus, he's the only one here close to my age. Not a lot of choices for women in their thirties, you know. Single choices, at least."

Eliza turned to assess him. Whipping her head back toward Cat, she whispered, "He's cute. And now he's looking at you."

Sure enough, the man had raised his head and was watching Catherine with a quizzical expression. He was rather handsome, Cat conceded. His rich chestnut hair cropped close to his head emphasized his cheekbones and nicely shaped lips. From this distance, she could make out a slight cleft in his chin. As she tried to surmise the color of his eyes, his eyebrows raised in silent inquiry.

"Do you think he knows we're talking about him?" Eliza shoved another bite of cake into her mouth.

Heat raced to Cat's cheeks. "He does now." She shot him a small, embarrassed smile.

He offered a quick grin in return, but then looked over at an auburn-haired woman who'd stopped next to his table. His face lit up as he sprang from his seat, enfolding the woman in a tight embrace. The fleeting streak of jealousy that coursed through her caught Cat by surprise. *No.* She didn't want anyone. She didn't need anyone. Her books were enough. Well, her books and Eliza.

"And apparently he's already taken." She jumped from her seat, pushing thoughts of men—all men—firmly away. "We should get back. You know the crowds will be rioting with pitchforks if we don't open."

Eliza nodded and stood up. "Let me just get a quick refill."

As Eliza moved off to the counter, Cat stole a peek at the laptop man. He was laughing at something the woman said. She envied the easy sense of familiarity the couple exuded. What would it be like to have that again?

The man's eyes darted toward her, and his eyebrows wrinkled in puzzlement. He watched her for a second before turning his attention back to his companion. The woman didn't seem to notice.

Cat wanted to die of embarrassment, having been caught for a second time staring at the man—by the man. She was grateful for Eliza's cheery chatter as her friend returned. They headed out, opening their umbrellas against the downpour.

Across the street sat a large brick Victorian-era home with numerous turrets and a wide, welcoming staircase leading to a wrap-around porch. It was a gorgeous home, a mansion in its day, but it showed its age. Paint peeled off near the upper left window frame, and the steps needed refinishing. The small sign hanging over the staircase read Treasure Trove Booksellers. The name and the grinning pirate next to it were rather corny in her opinion, but Dad had insisted, "There be no greater treasure than a book—unless it be yer imagination, me Catey! Arrr!"

Oh, how she missed him. It'd been far too long since he'd stood at the top of the steps, inviting all pirates and landlubbers inside to seek their fortune in a book's pages.

Her mind on the store, she didn't notice the Camaro zipping down the road. As she was about to step into the street, the car hit a large puddle, drenching her in water. Cat sputtered as dirty streams dripped from her hair and down her legs.

Eliza burst out laughing. "I'm sorry. I know I shouldn't. But oh my God, you should see your face. You look so … so …"

Cat glared down the road at the taillights retreating in the distance. "What a *jerk*!" She brushed water from her jacket. "Be thankful you were behind me."

"Hey, wait, he's backing up."

Cat peered through her dripping bangs as the car made

its way in reverse towards them. "He'll be lucky if he doesn't cause an accident. Come on." She grabbed Eliza's arm and tugged her across the street.

"Excuse me," a voice called after them.

Cat turned halfway up the stairs to the bookstore as a man hopped out of the Camaro. He jogged across the street and up the bottom steps.

"I'm so sorry. I didn't see the puddle before it was too late to avoid it." He held his hand out to Cat. "I'm Derrick. Derrick Gibson." When she ignored his hand, he stuck it in the pocket of his leather bomber jacket. "I'll pay to get your clothes cleaned."

His longish dark brown hair fell into earnest hazel eyes. No doubt that charming, apologetic grin on his face allowed him to get away with murder. Tiny lines around his eyes suggested he was somewhere in his thirties. *Wasn't that too old to be driving a Camaro? Who drove Camaros anymore, anyway?*

"That's not necessary." Her wet skin left her feeling itchy and wanting nothing more than to get inside and change.

"Then let me take you to drinks and dinner to make up for it. It's the least I can do."

Cat's eyes widened. Even when she didn't resemble a drowned rat, she wasn't the kind of woman who generally turned men's heads. Eliza was, for all she complained about that extra twenty pounds. Eliza's blonde hair, deep blue eyes, and bubbly personality drew men left and right.

But Cat? She liked her own face with its strong angles and her gray eyes so like her mother's, and her brown hair, which gained red highlights in the sun. But she was never going to win against Eliza in a beauty competition. Plus, according to her friends, Cat gave off a distinct touch-me-not air.

"No thanks. I'll dry out just fine."

"Oh, come on, Cat," Eliza broke in. "You can at least accept dinner off the man. What could it hurt?"

Derrick flashed a grateful grin toward Eliza. "Wonderful." He looked back at Cat. "How about Friday at 7:00, Miss…?"

"Catherine Schreiber. And no. No, thank you, I don't care to go out with you, Mr. Gibson." She grabbed a clump of hair and squeezed the excess water out of it. "Maybe you should ask Eliza here."

Eliza's cheeks turned pink even as she frowned.

"What?" Cat said. "You're looking. I'm not. Now, if you'll excuse me." With that, she raced up the remaining steps, unlocked the front door, and sailed through it into her escape.

CHAPTER 2

Cat pushed the door closed behind her, desperate to shut out all that had happened in the last few minutes. What was up with Eliza, pimping her out like that? Her friend had made her sound desperate for a date. Which she most decidedly wasn't. She didn't want to date *anyone*, much less a man who'd nearly drowned her.

The image of the laptop guy darted through her mind. Ugh. What was *wrong* with her today?

The door opened and slammed closed.

"*What* was that?" demanded an angry voice from behind her.

Eliza stood in the doorway, glaring at her. Cat's shoulders slumped. "I'm sorry. I shouldn't have said that. But you shouldn't have tried to force the issue, either."

Eliza grimaced. She hung her umbrella on a hook behind the door before walking over to Cat. "You're right. I shouldn't have. I'm sorry. But I was excited for you. I mean, really, he was good-looking. And interested."

Cat sighed. "He felt guilty. Not interested."

"Oh, no. He was definitely interested. Once you fled, he asked me what he could do to get you to agree to a date, that he felt like he had to get to know you."

"He did?" A small part of her wanted to preen from the unexpected attention. *Where had that come from?* "It doesn't matter. I don't want a date." She shrugged off her coat and hung it with the umbrella next to Eliza's.

"Why don't you grab a quick shower?" Eliza said. "I'll hold down the fort for a bit before I have to go to class."

With a grateful nod, Cat trudged to the back of the store and up to the second floor. She paused at the top of the stairs for a minute to glance back at the gleaming wooden bookcases and gorgeous oak floors, before opening the door to the upstairs apartment.

Dad had bought this grand old house on a thirty-year mortgage, knocking down the inner walls to create wide-open spaces. He'd built and finished the cherry bookcases himself. Being so close to the university, the Treasure Trove had been a college hangout in the '80s and '90s before the coffee shops popping up all over pulled most students away. He'd worked hard to draw in families and kids with his pirate motif, often greeting them personally in a salty pirate brogue.

And then he was gone.

Cat still couldn't believe it at times. She'd thought he'd always be here. He'd been her rock, her dad. The store should still be his.

She walked back to the bathroom and stripped off her soaked clothes. Hopping into the shower, she turned the water up as hot as she could stand it. Maybe she could scald away all thoughts of men.

She washed her hair. How much longer would she be able

to hold on to the store? Losing her father had been awful enough; she didn't want to see the Treasure Trove die, too. But sales were down. It'd been hard enough once people had started ordering books online—now more and more people had Kindles and Nooks. Everyone wanted e-books these days, it seemed, not print volumes.

Turning the shower off, she stepped out onto the rug and rubbed herself dry with a towel. She paused, examining herself in the mirror.

When had those lines across her forehead appeared? She ran her fingers over her belly. When had it lost the tautness she'd once so admired? When had she stopped caring what she looked like?

Since I gave up and walled myself off.

Her eyes flew back up to meet those of her reflection. *When did I lose myself? And how do I get me back—whoever 'me' is?*

Pushing those thoughts out of her mind, Cat blew her hair dry as quickly as she could, then ran to her room and threw on a clean pair of jeans and a green blouse. Eliza had to get to class, so she headed down the stairs without bothering to put on any make-up. Not that she wore it regularly, anyway. *Maybe tomorrow.* She reentered the main area to find a family playing with the plush puppets in the kids' section. After checking on them, she waved as Eliza waltzed out the front door.

Standing behind the register, which sat on a large, old oak desk at the back of the room, she surveyed her bookstore. She'd loved it as a child, and still loved it today. Floor-to-ceiling bookshelves lined the open room, most pushed up against the paneled walls, with a few shorter ones sectioning off various areas. Well-padded, strategically placed chairs invited readers to relax for a while, and a small table on the right provided a spot for working or studying, although few customers used it. A faded but comfortable pale green couch rested in front of the fireplace on one side of the room.

It wasn't a huge bookstore, but Dad had put his soul into making it a homey place to visit. After he passed away, she'd moved back into the upstairs apartment. The bookstore truly was her home in every way.

Reaching for the book she'd unearthed from the box that had arrived early that morning, she muttered, "Pull yourself together, Schreiber, and get back to work."

Her mom had sent the box along with a note:

Found this while I was working on cleaning out the upstairs room. I guess it got put in with my things during the move, but it's obviously full of stuff that's yours. Sorry it took me so long to get it to you, sweetie! Love, Mom.

Cat hadn't explored the box fully yet. She'd found a bunch of her old college papers, and a few of her favorite childhood books: *Weeny Witch, Charlotte's Web, The Secret Garden*. Of course her parents had saved those; as if Dad could ever give up a beloved book.

The brown paper package had caught her attention immediately, especially since it had her name written on it in Dad's handwriting. She'd run her fingers over each letter, longing once again for his presence. Undoing the wrapping, she'd been surprised by its contents: a simple black book. Touching it sent goose bumps racing up her arms, almost as if she'd been shocked. Probably a reaction to knowing it was from Dad. One last gift from a man ten years dead. She hadn't had time to examine it further, since Eliza had come down, ready for coffee.

Happy to get back to it now, she traced her fingers over the letters on the book's cover, which read *De Arte Amoris et Litterarum. On the Art of Love and Letters.* She'd translated it easily that morning with her rusty Latin skills. Her Classics major wasn't completely useless after all.

"Excuse me, ma'am? We're ready to buy this mouse puppet and this book," broke in a voice.

Cat set the book down to ring up the purchase, and then handed the bag with the puppet to the woman's excited young daughter. "Thank you so much. Please come back soon."

The mom smiled and waved as she ushered her kids out into the rain. Silence flooded the now-empty store. Unless the rain let up, it might be some time before anyone else ventured into the Trove. Great, just what business needed. Well, more time to explore the box.

She picked the book back up. The cover itself was nondescript: a simple black binding with the title rendered in small, silver-embossed lettering. Why had Dad wrapped it? What was it?

As she lifted up the front cover, a folded piece of paper fell out. Cat opened it with shaking fingers. Inside she read,

Happy Birthday, Catey! Your great-grandmother considered this her greatest treasure and asked me to bestow it upon you on your 25th birthday. I rebound it for you. I can't wait for you to tell me what it actually says. And then I'll tell you what Grannie told me about it. You'll get a kick out of that. With love, Dad.

Tears filled her eyes. She sniffed but fought them back. *Oh, Dad.* She forced her feelings aside as she opened the cover fully.

She gasped at the sumptuous illustration on the cover page. Sizzles of excitement flooded through her. A woman sat at a small writing desk, holding a quill. She was garbed in a floor-length dress of bright blue with a red belt encircling her waist, and a green cap nestled atop her long blonde hair. Around her, in smaller enclosed circles, were pictures of various couples acting out what appeared to be courtship scenes. All were dressed in what Cat surmised to be a late medieval or early Renaissance style.

The detail of the pictures was most extraordinary. She could read the expressions of every man and woman on the page. Some were happy, some adoring, others wore expressions of lust. That particular expression wasn't reserved for the men, thank goodness. Not everyone's affections appeared to be requited, though. One man's face bespoke a great sadness, while a woman from another frame anxiously observed the male figure standing next to her, who was watching a woman from a different frame.

Ha. I know how that feels. Cheaters apparently weren't reserved for the modern era.

It looked like an authentic medieval illumination. She longed to touch the shiny gold frames around each picture. Her fingers hovered above, refraining in case it truly was original, since oil from her hands could damage the page. Carefully, she turned to the next page. Latin text had been handwritten on real parchment in a script that resembled the Uncial font she sometimes used on her computer to create signs for the store.

It can't be. Surely it can't be.

She closed the cover, breathing deeply, unnerved by the conviction that she held in her hands a genuine medieval manuscript. "Oh my God, Dad," she whispered, as if speaking louder would wake her from a dream. Who had created the book? For whom had it been made? And how much might it be worth?

Cat stared at the volume. Dad had gifted it to her as a family heirloom. No way she'd part with it, no matter how much she needed the money.

She scanned through its pages briefly. It wasn't a long book, but she could see a number of additional illuminations interspersed with the text. They almost always featured a woman writing—although at times it was a different woman—and couples embracing.

She'd never been so happy she'd learned all that blasted Latin. She turned back to the opening page of text. And to have taken that paleography class. She actually had a shot at deciphering the handwriting.

Hearing the door chime, Cat looked up as a middle-aged woman entered the store and walked over to the Mystery section. With a sigh, she set her dad's gift back in the box and followed her customer.

The book would have to wait.

CHAPTER 3

*E*liza walked through the door that evening as Cat was tallying the day's receipts.

"Ooh, could you lock that behind you?" Cat called. It had been surprisingly busy that afternoon, given the rain. Then again, gloomy days were excellent for reading. She couldn't wait to finish the daily accounting so she could get back to examining the manuscript.

After securing the door and flipping the sign to *Closed*, Eliza approached her friend. Once at the desk, she handed over a brown paper bag from which the delicious odor of beef with broccoli wafted.

"What's this for?" Cat's eyebrows knitted together. "Not that I'll ever turn down Chinese."

"It's my way of saying I'm sorry for this morning. I should have been more sensitive, especially today."

Cat offered her friend a smile, touched by the gesture. "I overreacted, too. I wasn't expecting it. No one has asked me out in ages. Much less someone who's drenched me from head to foot."

Eliza chuckled, popping a bite of egg roll into her mouth.

"And, to be honest, I was feeling defensive, not only because I was irked at the guy, but because I feel as if I *should* be ready."

Eliza stopped chewing the egg roll and looked at her.

"I mean, you're right," Cat continued. "It's been six years. Six years is a long time. Don't they say it's supposed to take you half the time a relationship lasted to get over it? Not three times as long." Cat frowned as she speared a piece of broccoli. "What's wrong with me, Lizzie?"

"*Nothing* is wrong with you. You're awesome. And I don't know which 'they' you are talking about, but I'm guessing this 'they' wasn't abandoned at the altar after receiving a note saying 'their' fiancé had run off with another woman."

Cat gave a painful snort.

"Besides, no one says you need a guy to be happy, right?" Eliza continued.

At that, Cat burst out laughing. "Except you! You're even parlaying your obsession with finding your Darcy into your career."

Eliza was in the midst of writing her doctoral dissertation on Jane Austen. She narrowed her eyes. "That's not the *only* reason. I happen to love the Regency time period. The glamour, the titles, the balls ..."

"The diseases, the lack of Internet, the likelihood you would have been a servant, not a duchess or princess or whatever you fantasize you'd be."

Eliza ignored those observations. "Jane Austen is an amazing author, as you well know. Most of us could look around today and pick out people who'd match the crazy characters she dreamt up two hundred years ago."

"Yes, who could forget your own Mr. Collins? I couldn't

believe his last name really *was* Collins. I thought that guy would never leave you alone."

"He was rather obsessed, wasn't he?" Eliza said. "Until he decided his other instructor might be more beneficial to his aspirations of graduating. Which was unlikely, considering the guy couldn't write a decent paper if he tried." She reached for the chicken with cashew nuts Cat had pulled out of the bag.

A frown settled on Cat's face. "But don't you think I should be ready, Eliza? I mean, part of me thinks I'd be fine growing old with you and running this store until the end of my days."

"Um, as fun as that sounds, and as much as I love you, dear friend, I'm hoping for a different happily-ever-after."

Taking a sip of her hot tea, Cat mulled that over. She didn't want to think about Eliza moving on, but it was likely someday, especially since Eliza was more than halfway through writing her dissertation. She couldn't expect her to stagnate with her forever, just because Cat wasn't able to move forward. She sighed.

"You all right?"

"Yeah, I guess. I'm wondering if I should have said yes this morning."

Eliza choked on a piece of chicken as she gaped at her friend. After she caught her breath, she blurted out, "Really? Hallelujah!"

"You're that desperate to get rid of me?"

"No, no. I'm ecstatic to hear you're finally considering getting back up on the horse. Now if only that horse were pulling a barouche."

"A ba-what? Never mind. I don't want to ride a horse."

A gleam entered Eliza's eye. "Fine. No horses. But what about a Camaro?"

Cat chuckled. "That ship has sailed. Or driven off. Or

whatever. I still maintain he asked me out because he felt guilty, but regardless, with how rude I was, he won't return."

"You never know, you never know."

They continued to eat, each lost in their own thoughts for a bit. The bookstore ought to be her priority, Cat reminded herself. She owed that to Dad. Didn't she? And to herself. She didn't have the time or energy to worry about a relationship. Oh well. She'd shut the door that morning on the one option she'd potentially had.

Her mind drifted back to the man in the coffee shop, the one with the chestnut hair. She could still see him watching her. Before his girlfriend had shown up, at least. No chance there. There was no way she'd ever make a move on a taken man.

Shake it off, Schreiber. Get back to what's important. Get back to …

Suddenly Cat dropped her fork. "Oh my God, I can't believe I forgot to tell you about the box!"

"What box?"

"From Mom. It arrived this morning, but I didn't have time to go through it before you left." She reached under the desk and pulled out the box, setting it on the desk.

"Aren't you going to open it?"

"Nope. Not until we're done eating. No messes on these contents. You're not going to believe what's in here." Cat's skin tingled with excitement.

Eliza shoved another bite of egg roll in her mouth, chewing it quickly and swallowing.

"Ha, ha. You can slow down. We've got all night."

Eliza glared at her. "I'm done."

"Okay," Cat said. "Me, too. Let me go wash my hands."

When she returned, she quickly wiped off the desk before lifting the lid from the box and pulling out the medieval book. As her fingers clutched its cover, a frisson of electricity raced through her, just as it had that morning. God, she was a geek. Her whole body was reacting to a book. Her heart racing, she held the book up, a wide grin stretching across her face.

Eliza gave it a cursory glance. "Looks like a regular book. What is it?"

"I don't know exactly."

"What do you mean, you don't know—doesn't it have a cover page?"

"Yes, but it's like nothing I've ever seen. Look!" Cat opened the book to reveal the elaborate frontispiece.

Eliza's eyes widened. "Wow. That's stunning."

"I know! And it's real parchment. Look at the hand lettering. This book is *old*, Lizzie."

"Your mom sent you that?"

"Dad, actually." She showed Eliza his note. "Do you know what it feels like, to see his handwriting after so many years? To know he meant this as a gift for me?" Cat's eyes blurred with tears.

Eliza stood up and gave her a long hug before sitting back down. "Is it a religious text? Isn't that what most medieval writings were?"

"I don't think so. It's called *On the Art of Love and Letters*."

Eliza giggled. "Sounds like a book of medieval pornography."

"No, Ms. Dirty Mind. Everybody's clothed. But I *am* thinking love stories, given the way most of the people are looking at each other." She pinched her lips in amusement. "Maybe they're medieval versions of those tawdry romances you like to read."

Eliza fixed her with a cool stare, broken only by a slight upturn of her lip. "Be careful what you say. Those allegedly 'tawdry' romances sell better than almost anything else in here. Plus, a lot of them are really good."

"Sure, if you say so. But can you believe this book? I wonder what we can figure out about it."

"You're not going to sell it, are you?"

Cat studied the front illumination for a minute. "Lord knows we could use the money. But, no. Not a gift from my dad." Her finger hovered over the figure of the blonde woman. "I'm going to read it, find out more about it, more about this lady. Maybe she wrote it."

"Wouldn't that be unusual? I thought mostly men wrote in the Dark Ages. If anyone was writing at all, that is."

"It's not the Dark Ages," Cat huffed. "Middle Ages. Not Dark. And yes, mostly men wrote, but we do have writings penned by women. Hrotsvitha of Gandersheim, Hildegard of Bingen, Julian of Norwich, Christine de Pizan, to name a few."

"Wow. You know your female medieval authors."

Cat smiled. "Yeah, I guess the brain hasn't fully rusticated in my years as a shop owner."

Eliza elbowed her. "That's not what I meant. I'm just impressed."

"Why, thank you." She winked at her friend.

"So what's it say?"

"I've been working on reading it—slowly, since I'm out of practice and all, plus I didn't have much time today. Here's the preface:

"In her hands she holds
The greatest power of them all.
The ability to create
That which all want but few attain.

28

*Helped by God, she writes the letters
And the Word becomes Flesh
Bringing Love to all who seek it.'"*

Eliza's brows puckered. "Who's 'she?' It sounds like she's writing about Jesus, with the Word becoming Flesh."

"That's what I thought, too, but the stories that follow have nothing to do with Christianity, from what I've been able to surmise. The first one tells about a woman named Thea. Her family locked her away in a room to keep her from marrying. I haven't figured out why yet. It doesn't seem to say. But after a few years a strange man appeared in town, 'brought into Flesh,' the text says, and helped her escape. They ran off to the neighboring land and lived happily ever after."

Eliza peered at the illustration on the page Cat held open. "It actually says 'happily ever after?' What is this, an early Disney storybook?"

"Says the romance novel lover? I thought you'd be eating this stuff up."

"It is pretty awesome, actually. I'm amazed you can read that."

"It's slow going, that's for sure. If I come across a recipe for finding the perfect date, I'll let you know." Cat snapped the book shut. "I'm going to take it to Jill, see if she can scan it for me. I don't feel I should be touching it so much." Their friend Jill worked in the Rare Books department of Alderman Library.

Eliza nodded. "Sounds smart. What else is in the box?"

Cat pulled out a pile of papers, setting them on the desk. "Hmm. Mostly looks like school essays from high school and college."

"You saved those?"

"Not me. My dad. He was always proud of anything I wrote."

Eliza grabbed the top paper. "*The Coolest Guy in School,*" she read out loud. "Really? That was your title?"

"Come on, I was probably in tenth grade."

She grabbed for the paper, but Eliza twisted away quickly, chuckling as she read. After a few minutes, she said, "Ha, this guy drives a Camaro, just like Derrick. The names are similar, too. In this story the guy's name is Ricky."

Cat's eyebrows furrowed. "I vaguely remember naming him after Rick Springfield, because I loved that *Jesse's Girl* song."

"Me, too." Eliza strolled back and forth as she read. "Hey, you say he looks like John Cusack." Her head snapped up. "You know, Derrick looks a little like him, too."

Cat rolled her eyes. "What's your point?"

"I don't know. It's … weird. The similarities."

Cat shuffled through the papers on the desk. "Um, similarities is too strong a word. And I don't think Derrick looks anything like John Cusack. Can I see that?"

Eliza handed over the paper, grabbing a second one off of the desk.

Cat skimmed the story, which felt familiar and unfamiliar at the same time. In it, Ricky, a high school senior who worked with his dad on cars, was dating a girl named Abby, who was kind of a misfit, always with her nose in a book, though he was the quarterback and the most popular guy in school. Abby. She'd named her that because Abigail was Cat's own middle name. "Ha. He ditches her for the cheerleader here at the end. See, even then I had a hard time believing in happily-ever-afters."

When Eliza made no response, Cat looked at her. Eliza's eyes were glued to whatever she was reading. Cat leaned in, trying to catch the title. *Carreling.* "Oh my God! *Give me that!*"

"No way."

Cat tugged on the pages, but Eliza refused to let go, her eyes dancing as she looked up at her friend. "*His lips move down the side of my neck, pressing kisses the whole way. I can smell the books around us, but mostly I can smell the intoxicatingly manly essence of him,*" she read out loud. "Manly essence?"

She giggled as Cat pulled at the paper again. "No way. Imagine my delight to discover that my best friend, the one who's teased me for years about reading romance novels, not only wrote smut, but was also pretty good at it. Except maybe that manly essence part."

Cat groaned, embarrassment careening through her. She prayed her dad had never read that particular story.

"And, my goodness," Eliza continued. "I know I, uh, read this kind of stuff all the time, but this is quite the vivid visual image. In the stacks at Alderman? I will never think of that library the same again!"

Cat's face burned. She wouldn't be surprised if it burst into flame. "That was supposed to be private."

"Oh, I'm sure. I don't suppose it's a true story? You *did* spend an awful lot of time in that library, after all."

"Yeah. *Studying.*"

"A girl can dream. The guys from these two stories both sound great. Well, except for that ditching you for a cheerleader part."

"Not ditching *me,*" Cat huffed. "Ditching the *character.* And that's exactly what those stupid stories are—dreams. Fantasies of people who aren't real."

Eliza waved the *Carreling* story in the air. "You don't think you can find a guy like this?"

"Haven't yet, obviously. Such men don't exist."

"They do in my novels."

"Exactly. Novels. Made-up stories. I've never understood why you read romances, actually. You know from page one the hero and heroine will end up together. What's the point?"

Eliza paused for a minute, her face taking on a serious expression. "I know it makes no sense to you, but that's precisely why I love these novels. No matter what happens— and believe me, some crazy things happen—they *will* end up together. And it's not about mere sex, though of course there's some pretty hot sex. It's about love. Real, undying, forever love. With some fun between the sheets for good measure." She sighed. "That's what I want, Cat—someone so devoted to me that there will never be another. Isn't that what you want, too?"

"I thought I had that once, remember? I was wrong." Cat ran her fingers over the cover of the medieval manuscript. "I'm not sure it exists outside of your novels, anyway. Sorry to burst your bubble, but look at the divorce rate. And I read somewhere that eighty percent of married men cheat. Guess it was fortunate Ryan cheated *before* we got married, huh?"

Eliza frowned, closing her eyes. "He was an ass. But not all men are like that. Greg wasn't."

Greg. Eliza's high school sweetheart—and husband.

Cat wished she could take away the pain that snaked across her friend's face. It was strange to think of her friend having been married. Eliza rarely talked about him, and had shared only a few photos. They'd eloped in 2001, Eliza had told her, right after high school graduation. Eliza hadn't wanted to marry so young, but Greg had enlisted in the army and they hadn't wanted to take chances—who knew how long they'd be apart or what could happen if he got sent overseas? Eliza never thought she'd lose him. Certainly not after only a few months, not stateside.

He'd gone to visit his brother in New York before shipping out to Germany. On the morning of September 11th, he'd called to tell her his brother was showing him his office in the World Trade Center before he caught his flight. It was the last she ever heard from him.

Cat reached over and grabbed her friend's hand. "Oh, Lizzie," was all she could think to say.

"I'm fine. I'm good." A small smile edged across Eliza's face as she reached for a fortune cookie. "Everything happens for a reason. And I still believe God has someone else in mind for me."

Cat envied her eternal optimism. Eliza had lost her husband and then her parents within the space of five years, and yet still believed in the goodness of the world, still thought that life was wonderful and full of possibilities.

Was it hard-wired, that rosy view of things?

Cat liked to call herself a realist, but she tended toward a more Eeyorish attitude. Heck, most days she wanted to hide. She'd joked to Eliza on more than one occasion during their Harry Potter-obsessed phase that her patronus—her protector—was an ostrich. Instead of defending her against the Death Eaters, it'd stick its head in the sand.

Eliza always laughed, pointing out that ostriches didn't actually do that. "A book," she'd said once. "Your patronus has to be a book. And mine's a … a …"

"Jane Austen?" Cat had quipped.

"Yes! My patronus is Jane Austen."

"Ha, check this out." Eliza's comment broke into Cat's reverie, and Cat looked to see her holding out the fortune from her cookie. *Powerful changes are coming*, it read.

"That's exactly what that fortune teller we saw over the summer said, remember? She said powerful changes were coming in your life and she could see a great romance in your future."

"Eliza, she said the same thing to you, and to Jill. I'm pretty sure she says the same thing to everybody." Cat waved her hand. "I don't believe in that stuff anyway. I only went to humor Shannon. Who was disappointed the fortune teller told her all was going to stay as it was, if you remember."

"See? She told Shannon something different." Eliza shrugged. "I'm choosing to believe it's true."

"And that's one of the many things I love about you, dear friend—your undying optimism."

"Try it sometime. You might like it." Eliza hopped up from her seat. "Hey, how about we go see the latest Hugh Jackman movie? I can call Jill and Shannon and see if they want to come."

"Are you kidding me? Isn't that one all testosterone-fueled?"

"Ever since *Kate and Leopold*, I'll take any movie with Hugh Jackman in it. He'd make one fine Regency duke," Eliza said, a dreamy expression in her eyes.

Cat gathered up the take-out boxes and threw them in the trash. "Fine. It'd be good for me to get my mind off of everything, even if it is to watch a flick intended for teenage boys."

"I'll buy the popcorn!"

"My, you really *do* feel guilty about this morning, don't you?" Cat teased.

Eliza smirked. "No. I just like popcorn."

Cat laughed as she collected the papers together, tucking them back into the box.

The doorbell chimed. Cat and Eliza both looked at each

other. Who'd be ringing at this time? The sign clearly said *Closed*, as they'd been for more than an hour.

"I'll get it," Eliza called. She crossed the store and opened the door.

Derrick Gibson stood on the porch.

Chapter 4

lustered, Cat smoothed her hair out of her eyes.

"Hi." His voice was uncertain.

"Come in," Eliza said.

Derrick gave Eliza a nod, and then crossed the room to where Cat stood. After closing the door again, Eliza followed behind him.

"Hello," Cat said. Derrick stood in front of her, shifting his weight onto one leg as if he were nervous.

With a wink, Eliza dashed toward the back room, calling out, "I need to go get something. I'll be back in a … while."

Cat watched her friend go, and then turned to face Derrick again. "Listen, I'm sorry—"

"I'm not trying to stalk you—" he began at the same time.

They both chuckled, the tension broken.

"Ladies first," he said.

Cat tucked her hair back behind her ears. "I'm sorry I was rude to you this morning."

"You had every reason to be. I drenched you in filthy water, then asked you out, then tried to accept your friend's answer for yours. I'm the one who needs to apologize." He shuffled his feet, hesitating. "I couldn't stop thinking about you. I felt like I had to try again. Will you reconsider? Since I haven't dumped anything on you yet?" He hooked his fingers through his belt loops.

This guy came all the way back here to apologize again, in spite of how you treated him. Take a chance, Schreiber. Her second chance had just walked through the door. How often did that happen?

She set her hand on the desk, and her fingers grazed the edge of the medieval book. With one look at Derrick's hopeful hazel eyes, tendrils of electricity snaked through her fingers. Surprised, she glanced down at the book. What was up with that? The book had zapped her when she'd first taken it out of the box, and again when she'd showed it to Eliza. She'd figured the combination of fall air and her dragging feet had produced an ungodly amount of static electricity, resulting in one powerful shock. But zinging her again now, when she'd just been handling it? Goose bumps scampered up her arms and the back of her neck. Maybe the book was communicating with her, encouraging her to take a chance.

She shook her head. *Books don't talk, idiot. Or try to electrocute people.*

Derrick's face fell. "Oh. Um. Sorry to—"

"No, no, that wasn't about you. Sorry—it was a crazy thought in my head."

A cautious smile crossed his face. "So …?"

"Yes. Yes, I will go out to dinner with you." *Oh my God, did I really just agree to a date?* Cat squared her shoulders. Yes, she had. And she'd follow through with it. It was about time.

His smile turned into a wide grin. He was cute in a puppyish sort of way. This could be fun.

"Great! How's Friday? Pick you up around six?"

"Sounds great. I'll see you then, Derrick."

"Awesome. 'Til Friday."

"'Til Friday."

With a final nod, he turned and strode toward the door. As he walked out, Eliza emerged from the back. "Way to go, friend."

Cat stared at the book, tracing its title with her fingers once more.

"I can't believe it's Friday already!" Eliza gave an excited clap of her hands.

Cat was a lot less enthusiastic as she searched her closet for a dinner-date outfit. Why had she agreed to this again?

"Hold on a minute." Eliza raced out of Cat's bedroom.

"I need something that says 'attractive, but not easy.'" Cat spoke to their cat, Elvis, who sat on her bed, staring at her with his big yellow eyes. "Can't have him thinking he's going to get lucky, Elvis. You know I'm not that kind of girl."

She gave him an affectionate scratch under the chin. He purred, watching as she pulled out a pencil skirt and tossed it aside, then a clingy green dress. After discarding two more options, she shimmied into her favorite long khaki skirt and light plum sweater.

"There. This says 'Interested, but not slutty.' Right, kitty boy?"

Elvis just blinked.

"Yeah, some help you are."

"Not that." Eliza dismissed her choice as she skipped back into the room. "It makes you look too matronly."

Cat sighed. "I *am* practically matronly. But all right, how about this one?" She pulled another outfit out of the closet.

Eliza eyed the sleeveless white blouse and floral skirt. "I guess. It's not too suggestive, not too mom-like. But don't order spaghetti with that white top. I did that once and it pretty much ended any chance of romance after I spilled big glops of sauce down the front."

"I'm not looking for romance, Lizzie. I'm not sure why I'm going out on this date. I still don't think I'm ready." She'd battled the urge to call the date off from the moment Derrick had walked out the door. She knew nothing about the man. What if he were a serial killer?

Eliza had scoffed at that, saying Cat watched too many crime shows. She'd made Cat promise to call and check in, however.

Cat pulled on the skirt, her hands shaking slightly. *It's just a date. It's not life or death. I hope.* She reached for the blouse, thinking again of the mysterious book, of her bizarre notion it'd been trying to tell her something.

As if. Next she'd be thinking Elvis really understood her, or that Santa Claus actually existed, or that fairytales could come true.

"Come on. He was cute. And he wants to make it up to you for, you know, drenching you, which means he'll try extra hard, right? Here, how about this barrette of mine for your hair?"

Cat tucked her hair back behind her ears. "No, this is fine with me."

She hooked a pair of silver hoop earrings through her ears as she studied the photo hanging beside the mirror of Dad and her in front of Monticello, taken when she was eight years old. Framed drawings of buildings had long replaced the boy band posters on her bedroom walls, images of places she'd been and places she wanted to go. Her favorite was the large print of the buildings of Florence. *Someday.* She walked into the living room for her jacket.

Eliza followed her, settling in on the old overstuffed couch with her latest romance novel. "This is my hot date for the evening." She waved the book in the air and grinned. "A viscount and the governess."

The doorbell for the outside landing rang. Cat smoothed her skirt down as she stood up from the couch. She looked at Eliza. "You okay here on your own?"

"Yeah, I'm good. I've got Elvis to keep me company." Eliza petted the cat, which had hopped up onto her lap. "Not to mention a man with rock-hard abs and the ability to self-reflect." She held up the romance. "Off you go. Have fun!"

Cat laughed. "Thanks, friend. You, too."

She crossed the room and opened the door.

Derrick grinned upon seeing her. "Hi there. You look great! How're you doing?"

"Fine. No drive-by showers lately—so far."

He chuckled. "Good to know. I'd hate to have to share you with another offender."

They descended the apartment stairs to the Camaro. He held the door for her while she settled into the front seat. She had to admit she enjoyed being treated in such a manner.

"I've never ridden in one of these," she said. "But I always wanted to in high school."

Derrick slid into the driver's seat and turned the engine on. "I've actually had this car since high school."

"Seriously?"

"Sure. My dad bought it for me my senior year. He's a

mechanic. He's helped me keep it in tip-top shape all these years."

"All these years? High school wasn't *that* long ago, was it?" They backed out of the driveway and started down the road.

"It doesn't seem like it to me, either. But our twentieth reunion was this past summer."

"Wow."

He grinned at her sideways. "Disappointed to be out with an old fogey like me?"

"If you're an old fogey, I don't want to hear what you'd call me."

"You can't be older than I am." He looked her up and down, an appreciative gleam in his eye. "I'd guess ... twenty-nine?"

"Flatterer. Try thirty-five."

"Oh, well, in that case, get out of the car."

She gasped before she caught the cheeky grin.

"Kidding, gorgeous. I'm glad you changed your mind."

Cat's cheeks warmed as they pulled into Scooter's Sports Bar and Grill. Gorgeous? He thought she was gorgeous? It was true, what they said: a little flattery never hurt. She was enjoying this more than she'd thought she would.

"This place all right? I love it here—they have the best burgers."

"Sure," she replied, surprised but pleased at the casualness of the locale. At least she wouldn't have to worry about which fork to use.

As they walked through the doors, nearly everyone greeted him. It was clear he came here often.

"Hey, Donny," he said to the guy standing by the front counter. "Table for two, please."

"Sure thing." Donny led them across the room.

As Cat sat down in the chair Derrick held out for her— another point in his favor—she looked around. It was a typical sports bar: big screens everywhere showed the latest games, and sports equipment and jerseys hung wherever there was space.

"There's mine." Derrick pointed to the back wall where a football jersey with *Gibson 7* emblazoned on it hung. "We won the state championship two times."

"Impressive!"

Derrick grinned. "Those were the days, weren't they? I played football, wrestled. Baseball in the spring. Man, I miss that."

"Wait, were you at Charlottesville High? I think I would have heard about a jock like you, even if I was a few grades younger."

"Nah, Albemarle. We lived out in the county." He paused. Was he lost in thought or watching the football game? She followed his gaze to the screen.

"Hey, you." The petite waitress flashed Derrick a flirty smile. "What can I get you?" she asked him, without greeting Cat. *Must be some history there.*

Derrick gave Cat an apologetic smile. "Sorry, I was checking out the score. Britney, I'll have a cheeseburger with onion rings and a Bud."

Britney looked over at Cat without speaking. "Um, I'll have the chicken sandwich with a side salad, please. And, what the heck, throw in a frozen raspberry margarita."

After caressing Derrick's shoulder, the waitress walked off without acknowledging Cat's order. *Nice. Hope she doesn't spit in my food.*

Derrick fidgeted in his seat. "Sorry about her. I've told her I'm not interested."

Cat pushed her hair behind her ears and smiled, determined not to let the rude waitress affect her mood. "So, what do you do when you're not drenching strange women with water?"

"Ha, ha. I work with my dad, helping him run his shop. We buy, fix up, and sell old cars. How about you?"

"The bookstore you nearly mowed me down in front of? That's mine."

Britney returned, dropping off their drinks. When Derrick ignored her, she flounced off.

"Wow, you own it? Awesome." He sipped his beer.

"Yeah. It used to be my dad's. When he passed away, I took over. I've been running it ever since."

"Oh, sorry to hear about your dad. I can't imagine."

She nodded curtly, wanting to move past discussing her father. "It's been ten years." Cat took a sip of the margarita. "I've thought about closing the store, maybe going to grad school," she ventured, not sure why she was sharing that. It wasn't something she'd mentioned to Eliza.

"Why?"

"Business is tough. Sales are down, what with everyone buying online now. Plus, as much as I love books, I never thought I'd be a bookseller forever." She nursed her drink. "But it's hard considering shutting down what was my dad's dream."

"I know what you mean. It was my dad's dream for his sons to work with him in his shop. He was so disappointed when my brother insisted on going off to study law. Of course now Chad's an attorney and makes the big bucks, so Dad doesn't mind so much anymore." He took a sip of his beer. "It's one of the reasons I never went to college; I already had a job with Dad."

"You didn't go to college?" Cat said without thinking.

Derrick's eyes narrowed. "That a problem?"

"No. I'm sorry. I just don't know many people in this university town who haven't."

At that moment their meals arrived, and Cat couldn't have been more grateful to ease over that point. She hadn't meant to hurt his feelings. He didn't seem too bruised, however. He smiled at her before taking a big bite of his burger.

"Gibson!" called an enthusiastic voice a minute later. A man carrying a large bin full of dirty dishes approached them.

"Davis," Derrick replied. "What's up, dude?"

"Not much. Working here to pay the bills." He set the bin on the neighboring table. "What do you think of the Cowboys' chances this season?"

"C'mon, man, the Cowboys suck. Redskins all the way."

The men lapsed into a heated discussion about football, and Cat's attention wandered around the room. Her mind drifted back to the man in the coffee shop again, and the intense concentration he'd given his girlfriend.

She looked back at Derrick. He was paying no attention to her. Apparently he and Davis, whoever he was, had moved on to an intense debate over NASCAR.

Cat sighed. Was this how first dates went nowadays? "Excuse me, can you tell me where the restroom is?"

Derrick turned to her. "Oops. Get me talking on sports and I don't stop. Junior Davis, this is Cat Schreiber. Cat, this is Junior. Running back in high school."

"Hi." She tipped her head at him.

"Hi," he said. "The restroom's back that way."

"Thanks." She stood up and wandered off to find it. When she walked back to the table a few minutes later, the men were still arguing in a friendly way.

"Hi, again," she interjected.

Junior picked up the bin of dishes and clutched it against his hip. "I better get back to the kitchen. Nice to meet you, Cat." He moved away from their table.

After he left, Derrick reached over and ran his thumb over her hand. "Sorry. That was rude of me." Chagrin was evident in his voice. It was a sweet gesture, but didn't erase her irritation.

As she took another sip of her margarita, a boisterous group of men and women burst through the door.

"Yo, Spiller! Teal! Wakeham!" Derrick called out. Three guys separated themselves and came over, greeting him with high fives.

"This is Cat." He gestured to her. "This is Jason, Brett, and David."

The men nodded briefly at Cat. "Howdy," Brett said.

"You staying for the dancing, Gibson?" Jason asked.

Derrick turned to Cat. "It's '80s night." He checked his watch. "Music starts in about fifteen minutes. I was hoping you might want to dance."

"Sounds fun." She loved to dance, but it'd been years since she'd done so. Outside the privacy of her apartment, at least. Maybe it would help rescue the evening.

"Cool," Jason called as they headed off to find a table of their own.

After finishing their meals, Derrick settled the bill with Britney, who shot Cat repeated sullen looks. He didn't pay the waitress any attention, instead standing up to help Cat out of her chair as loud '80s music began emanating from speakers on either end of the room.

"Yes!" she exclaimed. "I love Wham!"

"Are you kidding?"

"Of course not. *Wake Me Up Before You Go-Go!* is a classic."

"If George Michael is what floats your boat. Personally, I prefer INXS or Duran Duran."

"Duran Duran? Meh." She pinched her lips in distaste. "I never liked them as much as my sister Marie did. *She* was a Duran Duran fanatic. She always announced she was going to marry Roger Taylor."

"How'd that work out?"

"She *did* marry a man named Roger, believe it or not. But he's an accountant out in Columbus, Ohio, not a rock star. They live there with their two girls. My mom moved there a few years ago, too."

"You miss them?"

"Yeah," Cat admitted. "But Mom wanted to be close to her grandkids. And since it wasn't looking like I was going to provide any ..."

"I never wanted kids, either," Derrick said. "I like my life the way it is."

"I didn't mean I don't want kids. I don't know. I don't really know what I want half the time." Why had she admitted that? Must be the margarita. Tamping down those uncomfortable thoughts, she pulled Derrick onto the dance floor. "Let's dance."

"A woman who isn't afraid to get out there and dance, now that's awesome."

He danced well, moving with the sensual physicality of an athlete. Cat wondered if he'd be good in bed. *Where the heck had that come from?* She hadn't thought about sex in some time, at least not with anyone she actually knew. Fantasizing about celebrities didn't count, right?

Catherine glanced around. A number of women were watching him. It didn't surprise her. He seemed the type to hang with the in-crowd, a group around which she'd never felt comfortable. She'd fantasized about having such a boyfriend as a teenager, but had always assumed she was too nerdy for guys like him.

A slow song came on and he moved in closer, wrapping his arms around her. "May I have this dance?"

"Sure," she said, giving in to the moment. They moved together, bodies lightly touching. It was jarring to realize how much she was enjoying the rush of desire, something she hadn't felt in forever. Her hormones were jumping all over the place.

He murmured in her ear, his warm breath sending shivers up her neck. "You remind me so much of one of my high school girlfriends. The one I shouldn't have let get away."

"What?"

"My girlfriend, junior year. God, I loved her. She was one of the smart kids, always with her nose in a book. I don't know why I was attracted to her. We just had this spark."

He grimaced. "I broke up with her to stop the constant ribbing from my friends. Started dating this other girl. Tiffany. Everyone said we made the best couple, the quarterback and the head cheerleader." He shook his head. "We got married right after high school, but it only lasted three years."

Cat froze, every nerve ending instantly on edge. The quarterback? He'd been the quarterback? Who'd dated a nerd? Whom he'd then dumped for a cheerleader? *He worked on cars with his dad?* All the details matched the story Eliza had read earlier, the one Cat had written as a teenager.

"What was her name?" she choked out, as her stomach twisted.

"The girlfriend? Abby. Why?"

No. It couldn't be. It wasn't possible. White squiggles swam in front of Cat's eyes.

She was sure she was going to pass out.

CHAPTER 5

*D*errick grabbed her arm, concern evident on his face. "Hey, you okay? You don't look so good."

"I'm fine." *It's all a big weird coincidence. That's all.* "I … it … that margarita was more than I'm used to." Swallowing hard, she pasted a grin on her face. "What happened to her? The bookworm, I mean?"

"Don't know. I've always wondered. You sure you're okay? You look a little green."

"Yeah. Give me a minute." Cat clutched her arms around her stomach. Maybe it was roiling on account of the margarita, not the oddness of the situation. Except this guy was exactly like the one in her story, though that was impossible. She wanted to throw up. What was going on?

A voice broke in from behind him.

"Hey, sexy. How are you?" A woman pressed her enormous breasts against Derrick's arm. She had her blonde hair up in a ponytail and wore shorts and a close-fitting shirt that accentuated the leanness of her body.

"Hey, Candy, great. You?" Derrick answered. He took a small step back, which Cat noted with satisfaction.

Candy? Her name was Candy? Cat's skin rankled at the woman's manner—those boobs had to be fake—although she was grateful for the interruption. She needed time to pull herself together.

Candy was somewhere in her thirties, probably similar to Cat's age. One could see the beginnings of lines across her forehead and around her eyes, but she was still stunningly beautiful.

Candy inspected Cat for a moment, challenge radiating from her eyes, and then turned all smiles for Derrick. "Better now."

"It's been a while. How's Joe?"

"No clue about that asshole. We got divorced six months ago."

"Sorry to hear that," Derrick said, frowning. He settled his arm around Cat's shoulders. "Hey, this is my date, Cat."

"Hi, Candy," Cat said with a politeness she didn't feel. Derrick's arm felt heavy across her neck, but she appreciated him setting a clear boundary with Candy.

"Yeah, hi," Candy bit out. She made one last attempt with Derrick. "Can I get you a beer or anything?"

"Nah, I better not. Gotta drive Cat home later."

Candy walked away without a further word to either of them.

"There's some history there, I presume?" Cat said.

"Not really. We dated for a month in high school, but that was it. She dumped me for Joe, actually, sophomore year."

"Guess she's reconsidering that now."

Derrick laughed. "You jealous?"

Cat clenched her teeth. She wasn't. She'd just never liked

women like Candy; women who made her feel as if she couldn't compete.

"You've got nothing to worry about. You're the only one here I want to be with." He lowered his eyelids, piercing her with an unmistakably sultry gaze. "You're who I'm supposed to be with."

Cat giggled awkwardly. How was she supposed to respond to that? She had no experience in dealing with cheesy come-ons, which was exactly what that was.

Another slow song came on, and he moved in closer, lacing his arms around her waist. He set his forehead against hers, leaving his mouth inches from her own. Cat cast a surreptitious glance around. Candy, and a number of other women, glared at her from near the bar. How strange it felt to be with the most desired man in the room and to have him focused solely on her. It was exciting, but also uncomfortable. It felt wrong.

"I'm sorry, Derrick, but I need to get home. I, um, have an early morning tomorrow."

He frowned. "Did I do something?"

"No, no, it's me. Not you. My stomach's still a little upset." That was the truth, at least.

"Okay, then. Let me say goodbye to the guys."

He crossed the room, exchanging a few words with a number of people as he went. Her insides still roiled. It was a coincidence, all of those similarities. It had to be. She chewed the inside of her cheek as he walked back toward her. What else could explain it?

The radio eased the tension on the way home. Derrick hummed along to the songs, apparently fine with Cat's silence. Occasionally he'd glance over and flash her a grin.

When he pulled into the driveway next to the bookstore, he turned toward her with a soft smile. "I had fun with you tonight."

"Thanks. I had a good time, too." *Well, kind of. Except for the part when you ignored me at dinner. And, well, the part where I freaked out about the old girlfriend-coincidence thing.*

Derrick reached over and stroked her hair. "I don't know what it is about you, Cat. To be honest, you're not the kind of girl I normally go for. But I feel so pulled toward you."

Before she could answer, he leaned in and kissed her. She didn't break it off. It felt nice to be wanted. It'd been a long, long time.

After a minute or so, he stopped, breathing heavily. "Can I come in?"

Cat trapped her lip with her teeth. He was a nice guy. Certainly attractive. And her hormones were sparking in a way they hadn't in years. Casual sex had never been her thing, though.

"I'm sorry, Derrick. I have a three-date minimum before I invite anybody in." Most women probably jumped in bed with him the first chance they got. "And I'm really not feeling well."

Disappointment cooled his eyes, but he nodded. "Guess I'll have to hope for more dates, then, huh?"

"I guess so. Good night." She reached for the car door handle.

"Let me get that." Hopping out of the car, he ran around to open the door for her. "I know you think I was being chivalrous, but that was really just an excuse to do this." He pulled her against him as he kissed her aggressively. He kept his arms loose, though, letting her know she could break out of them at any time.

Cat pushed away after a few seconds, desperate to keep from changing her mind. "Good night, Derrick."

He gave her that cheeky grin again. "Call me Ricky. All my friends do. When they're not calling me Gibson, at least."

Cat's eyes widened as the blood drained from her face.

He frowned. "You okay?"

"Yes … margarita … sorry." Turning on her heel, she fled up the stairs.

"I'll call you," Derrick yelled, as she fumbled to unlock the door. She gave him a meager wave—it was the best she could manage—grateful when the door opened.

She ran to the toilet, her stomach heaving. She sat there for a few moments, the coldness of the bathroom tile seeping through her thin skirt. Breathing deeply and slowly, she worked to corral her spinning thoughts.

Light snoring coming from the next room meant Eliza was already sleeping. Should she wake her up?

And tell her what? That the guy in the story had come to life? A harsh snort of laughter erupted from her nose. She rose, catching a glimpse of herself in the mirror as she did. She stood there, staring at her bloodshot eyes, her paler-than-usual skin. It figured. She'd finally worked up the nerve to go on a date after six years, and this happened. Whatever this was. She groaned, covering her eyes with her hand.

A meow at her feet startled her.

"Oh, Elvis." She scooped up the cat, carrying him with her into her room. "Everything will make more sense in the morning, right?"

The cat purred and settled down in his usual spot on the covers.

She shed her clothes and climbed into bed with him, one thought resonating over and over as she drifted off.

That's all they were, right? Coincidences?

The next morning, Cat sat on the sofa, waiting for Eliza to wake up. She hadn't slept well and her eyes were heavy with exhaustion. Images of Derrick and story pages and her high school self had woven themselves through her dreams. The medieval manuscript had been in there, too, for some reason.

She wondered idly when Jill would be able to scan it. She'd taken it over to UVa's Rare Books department yesterday morning, but Jill had warned her it would take a bit to get to it, since there was a backlog because of some ancient medical treatise they were working on.

Cat was anxious to get back to translating it. Anything to get her mind off the bizarre coincidences of the previous evening.

When Eliza finally plodded out of her room, Cat heaved a heavy sigh.

"Was it that bad?" Eliza's eyebrows went up.

"Yes. And no. You need to sit down."

Eliza stopped. "Can I get breakfast first?"

"Sure. But bring it in here."

A few minutes later, Eliza settled herself next to her friend, munching on cereal. "What's up?"

"You're not going to believe it." Cat skipped over the first part of the date, jumping right to the story Derrick had told her about his high school girlfriend. "Her name was Abby, Eliza. *Abby*. He works on cars. His friends call him *Ricky*."

Eliza said nothing for a bit, holding her bowl of cereal on her lap. "Yeah, that is weird," she finally conceded. "But you said the guy was a local, right?"

"Yeah, so?"

"Maybe you knew him in high school."

"You can't be serious."

"Why not? I'm sure there were stories in the paper about

his athletic achievements, him being a star quarterback and all. And maybe you heard other details from friends or something."

"Oh, come on. You have to admit the details are uncanny." Was it possible? *Could* she have heard about Derrick/Ricky back then, and spun a story about a guy like him? Wouldn't she have remembered? On the other hand, she hadn't even remembered she'd written stories until they'd shown up in that box.

"Yeah. But I can't think of a better explanation. Can you?"

"Nope." Cat clutched her forehead with her hands.

Eliza stood up. "I'm ready for coffee. How about you?" She carried her bowl into the kitchen.

"God, yes," Cat said, standing up herself. She yawned. "It's the only thing that's going to get me through the day."

"Once we're over there, I want to hear more about this date. And not the kooky stuff. The intimate stuff. Details, baby."

"Who says there's intimate stuff?"

"I was merely hoping, but the color on your cheeks tells me I'm right," Eliza teased. She sprinted into her bedroom, closing the door seconds before the sofa pillow hit it.

CHAPTER 6

"He kissed you? That's it?"

Cat added creamer to her coffee and swirled the little stick. "Yup. That's it."

"Hmm. You going to see him again?"

"I doubt it. He's a nice guy, for the most part." She shifted on the chair, casting a longing glance toward their usual booth. A college couple had taken it before Cat and Eliza could sit down, and were busy making moony eyes at each other. She and Eliza had had to settle for a smaller table near the far wall.

"But?"

"You mean I need more than those freaky coincidences? Wouldn't those make you run?"

Eliza arched an eyebrow.

"Okay, fine. At times he seemed interested, but he often paid more attention to the people around us than to me. Not a good sign on a first date. And, in truth, I don't think we have much in common. Most of his friends seem to be the same ones he had in high school."

Most of her high school friends had drifted away over the years. Not that that surprised her; Cat was such a different person than she'd been then. In some ways, at least. She was more confident, less insecure. Happier in herself.

She frowned. Or at least she had been. Good Lord, had her ex-fiancé really stolen so much of her six years ago? She wanted it back, that spunk she'd found in her twenties. The loss of her father had put a huge dent in it, to be sure. Ryan's betrayal had destroyed it. Anger flared in her briefly, but she doused it as she turned back to the conversation with Eliza.

"It's clear he was part of the popular crowd, a social circle in which I certainly never ran. And he didn't go to college." Cat snorted to herself in disgust. "Listen to me, to how elitist I sound. I can go out with someone who didn't go to college, right?"

"Sure," Eliza enthused. "At least for a fling."

Cat sipped her coffee before answering her friend. "I have to admit it felt wonderful to be desired again. To *feel* desire again. And, well, a fling—or something—does sound appealing. Lord knows it's been long enough." She cast a sly glance at Eliza. "For a minute there I actually considered inviting him up."

Something crashed onto the floor with a loud thump, startling them out of their conversation. Cat turned toward the noise and saw someone at the table next to theirs leaning down to pick up a book that had fallen. It was the man from the previous week, the laptop guy. Today, no laptop was in sight. No girlfriend, either: just a mug of steaming tea and the book. Cat sneaked a peek at its cover.

"That's a fantastic book," she commented, hoping he hadn't been able to hear her previous conversation. She didn't like the idea of anyone hearing details of her sex life. Well, potential sex life, anyway.

"Is it? I started it this morning," came a deep voice in

reply. He ran his fingers over the cover. "It was a gift from my parents. They delight in sending me anything related to Benjamin Franklin."

"Really? Why?"

A sheepish expression crossed his face. "Because they named me after him. My parents are obsessed with colonial America. My mom's a proud member of the D.A.R., and claims a number of our ancestors served during the Revolutionary War."

Cat grinned. "Do you have a brother named Jefferson?"

"No." His lips thinned, and his eyes squeezed shut for a moment. "He was George Washington, actually."

Recognizing that all-too-familiar look of loss, Cat impulsively reached over and rubbed his hand to soothe him. When his eyes dropped to her fingers, she pulled them away. What had come over her, touching a stranger like that?

"Sorry," she said. "The look on your face reminded me of how I felt when I lost my dad."

He gave her a brisk nod. He looked as if he were going to say something else, but didn't. His eyes remained fixed on hers, however. Brown, Cat noted absentmindedly. His eyes were a milk-chocolaty brown.

"It's been ten years," she said. "I still miss him every day."

He paused a moment before admitting, "Wash passed away last year. I miss him, too. Terribly." He exhaled, as if releasing the painful memory. A smile curled the corner of his lips. "My sister didn't escape the name game, either," he said, changing the subject. "She's Martha. After Jefferson's wife."

"Are you serious?" Cat laughed openly now. "You poor guys. Those names are a lot to live up to." She fingered the rim of her coffee cup as she observed him. Was that a hint of a dimple when he smiled?

His eyes twinkled. "Believe me, I know. People always expect me to be out flying kites."

Eliza broke in with a sideways glance at Cat. "Hi. I'm Eliza James, and this is Catherine Schreiber. It's nice to meet you."

"Ben Cooper. Or should I say Benjamin Franklin Cooper?" he added with a wink toward Cat. "Nice to meet you, as well. Sorry about the book. I didn't mean to interrupt your ... conversation."

Cat peeked at him curiously, noting his brief hesitation before that last word. Was that a pinkish tinge infusing his cheeks? *Oh, good Lord. He* had *been listening.* Her own cheeks burning, she said, "Not a problem. It wasn't anything serious."

Why was she embarrassed that he'd overheard her talking about Derrick? It wasn't like anything had happened. Or like a stranger's opinion should matter. Although since they'd now been introduced, she guessed Ben Cooper wasn't exactly a stranger anymore.

She smoothed her hair back from her face, casting a quick glance at Eliza, whose lips were pursed in amusement as she raised an eyebrow at Cat.

What?

She looked back at Ben. He was still watching her, his eyes open and friendly. Suddenly flustered, her gaze dropped to his lips, then his chin, lingering on the cleft there.

What was wrong with her? She'd gone from ignoring men to being thrown off-kilter by two of them, all in the space of a week. And this one was not available, whether or not she wanted him to be.

Did she want him to be? *Augh.*

Dipping her eyes, she took a quick sip of her coffee, relishing its sweet-yet-bitter taste. Away. She had to get away from this Mr. Cooper and his strange effect on her.

"We should get back to the bookstore now, right, Eliza?"

"The Treasure Trove?" He gestured out the window at the house across the street. "How long have you worked there?"

"I own it," Cat replied, a sharp edge to her voice. Eliza stared at her, surprise at Cat's tone written all over her face. Cat didn't know why she was so testy, either. She just knew she needed space from Ben Cooper and his chocolate eyes; space from everyone.

Ben didn't seem to notice. "Oh, that's wonderful. I like the pirate sign."

"That's great," she replied in her business voice, standing up to signal to Eliza she was ready to go.

He stood up, as well. "I've got to go, too. I'm meeting someone shortly."

Cat's thoughts flew to the woman she'd seen with him before, and she bit the inside of her cheek. Was he meeting her? She squared her shoulders, chiding herself. What did she care if he were meeting someone? She didn't.

"Pleasure meeting you, Ben," Eliza said quickly.

"You, too," he answered as they walked out the door.

"What was up with that, Cat? And why are you walking so fast?" Eliza said, running a few steps to keep up with her friend, who was stalking across the street.

Cat slowed when she reached the other side. "I don't know." She blew out a breath. She didn't want to admit she envied Ben's companion the tiniest bit. Because that made no sense. "I guess I was embarrassed he'd heard me talking about sex. And it annoyed me that he assumed I just work here."

"Like me?" Eliza tipped her head to the side.

"No, no. This is a part-time job to you, Lizzie. You're a grad student and you're going to be—"

"I was kidding," Eliza interjected. "I know what you meant. And I know what I am. I don't mind 'just working here,' as you put it. For now."

Cat fumbled in her purse for the keys as they climbed the steps. Unlocking the door, she said, "You're far from 'just' anything, Eliza. You're amazing. I don't know what I'd do without you."

"Nor I you. But hopefully someday we'll find out."

Cat whipped her head back around. "What?"

"You know I love you, Cat. You're the best friend I've ever had and, now, my only family. But I do want to get married again. To have a family of my own."

Holding the door while Eliza walked through, all Cat could do by way of answering was nod. *What would she do without her best friend?*

They'd met six years ago, less than a month after her wedding fiasco, when Eliza had come in looking for a particular Jane Austen biography for her senior thesis. They'd had such fun chatting about Darcy, Cat teasing her that Eliza's last name ought to be Bennet instead of James, that they'd gone across the street for lunch, arguing over coffee and cake about what it would have really been like to live in nineteenth century England.

Eliza had spoken longingly about riding in carriages, walking through beautiful gardens, and the fashions women wore. Cat had countered with reminders of no running toilets, no central heat, and no clue how women dealt with their periods, but it couldn't have been as convenient or pleasant as modern tampons.

Eliza had laughed, calling Cat a pessimist without a romantic bone in her body. Cat had retorted that Eliza's head was in the clouds, and then, to her own surprise, had told Eliza about Ryan. Eliza had shared about Greg. The two bonded instantly, and had continued their almost-daily coffee tradition ever since.

Five years ago, after Eliza's parents died in a horrific automobile accident, Eliza had moved in with Cat. She'd needed the support. So had Cat, who secretly hoped Eliza would stay with her forever.

"I can't lose you, Eliza!" Cat said in a half-joking, half-panicked voice as they crossed through the store.

Eliza tucked her bag behind the register desk and glanced at herself in the wall mirror, smoothing her hair down and lifting her chin to make it appear firmer. "Oh, silly, you'll always be my best friend. But I still believe, still have to believe, that the right guy is out there waiting for me. The next right guy after Greg, at least."

"You're such a romantic, Eliza. You need to stop reading all those romance novels."

"Says the woman who writes them."

Cat huffed. "I don't write smut! Those were silly scribblings from fifteen years ago."

"Methinks thou doth protest too much. And no, I don't need to stop reading them. They're what keep my hope alive, that someday my duke will come."

"Then I hope for that, too. But not *too* soon, please."

Eliza raised an eyebrow.

Cat squeezed her close. "Because knowing me, I'd end up dueling him for your affections. And I'm no good with a pistol."

Later that morning, Cat was walking back to her desk when she heard a soft, low voice. "You've got a wonderful poetry section here."

Startled, Cat turned to her right, where the poetry books were shelved. A tall, lean man with dark, charmingly disheveled hair stood leafing through a book.

"Thank you," she said. "My mother is a poetry fan and enjoys adding to our collection. Is there anything in particular you're looking for?"

He glanced up from the book. His face rendered her mute—here was a beautiful man. He had chiseled cheekbones, the kind you only saw on models, with full lips and stunning blue eyes. Cerulean, or maybe azure. Definitely something beyond simple blue. Only the slight crookedness of his nose saved him from Greek god status. The stubble gracing his face and the casualness of his hair suggested he didn't much worry about his appearance, though. She guessed him to be somewhere in his twenties.

"Your mother has good taste. Listen to this."

He began to read, but Cat wasn't really listening. She watched his lips move and wondered what it would be like to touch them. She marveled at the beauty of his features and the melodic tone of his voice. God, she wanted to listen to him all day. Or kiss him. *But if I kiss him, he'll stop talking.* She tried to tune back into the words, but everything in her remained focused on those magnificent lips.

He stopped. "Isn't that awe-inspiring?" His face lit up as he talked.

His voice hypnotized her, lulling her as if by some secret spell. She attempted to focus on what he'd read, something about having no fear. She locked eyes with the mysterious stranger. "It's wonderful," she mumbled. "Who wrote it?"

"W.S. Merwin." At her blank expression, he added, "Former poet laureate of the United States. It's called *A Contemporary*. I've loved that poem for years." He looked back at the book, flipping pages as if searching for a specific piece. Cat struggled to think of something more intelligent to say, as her pulse raced and her nostrils flared at the clean, delicious scent of him.

What was *wrong* with her? A week ago she'd insisted to Eliza that she wasn't the least bit interested in a man, and here she was, having gone out on a date with one—although said date turned out to be a bust—and now fantasizing over another, thinking thoughts that reminded her of the smutty story Eliza had found. She hadn't paid attention to men for six years; what had her reacting to two in such a short time period?

Make that three. You can't deny Ben Cooper caught your attention, too.

The door opened and an older couple walked through. At the sound of their voices, the man looked up and then checked his watch.

"Oh, I'm late." He gave her a wolfish grin. "Gotta scoot." Tucking the book back onto the bookshelf, he winked and sauntered out the door.

Cat stood there, breathing slowly to calm her flaming senses. Anyone would react to that man, right? Right? That mouth. She'd wanted to touch it, to feel those lips on hers. Goose bumps prickled her skin.

She didn't understand what was happening to her, why she was suddenly so aware of men, when before she'd managed to convince herself they were just part of the scenery. No doubt her sister would say it was her biological clock, tick, tick, ticking away.

Cat wasn't so sure. Maybe it was her stories, the ones Eliza had unearthed from that box. She *had* written them, after all. Perhaps reading them again had sparked something within her, made her realize that at one point, at least, she'd been very, ahem, interested in men and sex. And love.

She glanced around the store, noting the couple bent over a book together, their heads nearly touching. The woman was chatting excitedly about something in the book, her finger pointing at it. The man gave her a quick kiss on the forehead.

He looked up, noticing Cat watching them. He tipped his head in greeting, and Cat could see his brown eyes sparkling. "Still the love of my life," he said, as his wife tittered beside him.

Cat smiled in return, but it was forced. A wave of loneliness engulfed her. *Would someone love her like that when she was their age?*

Chocolate brown eyes swam before her.

The next afternoon, Cat handed Eliza a stack of fluorescent-colored papers. "Help me hang these up, will you? We'll put a few here in the store. I was hoping you could also tack them up around your department and the university libraries. The coffee shop, too."

Eliza took the papers and skimmed the top one. "Poetry Night. Sounds fun. I bet we'll get all sorts of interesting types in here. Some people will use any excuse to get up in front of a mic."

"Yeah, well, we'll see. I got the idea from my mystery poetry guy. I thought maybe it'd help pull in the college crowd."

"Oh, yeah, Mr. Merwin."

"Not Mr. Merwin, silly. He *read* me Merwin."

Eliza studied her. "Are you hoping he'll come?"

"You'd be hoping he'd come, too, if you'd seen him, Lizzie. He is *that* good-looking."

Cat moved over to the table, setting a Poetry Night table topper at its center. The door opened and a man walked through. Cat glanced at him briefly, and then her eyes flew back to him in shock. It was the poetry guy, the man about whom she and Eliza had just been speaking. How was that possible? Her cheeks tingled, though she knew he hadn't heard them.

"Hello, again." He addressed Cat, coming to stand before her.

"Hel-lo!" interrupted Eliza, eyeing her friend as she hurried over to them both.

The man turned toward Eliza. "Hi," he said.

Cat was surprised when his gaze came right back to her. Usually men lingered on Eliza. "Do you have any works by Anne Haselhoff?" he asked her.

"Hrm. The name is not familiar. Is she a poet?"

"Yes. I'm considering including some of her works in my dissertation."

"Dissertation? So you're in the English department here, too? How have I not seen you before?" Eliza interjected. Cat regarded her friend with surprise, as if she'd forgotten Eliza was there.

" … Right." Eliza held up the papers in her hands, giving Cat a knowing grin. "I'll take these flyers on over to the library, then. It was nice meeting you …"

"Grayson." He stuck his hand out in introduction.

Eliza shook it. "Right. Grayson." Then, with a wink at Cat, she walked out the door.

Grayson turned back to Cat. "I should have introduced myself earlier. I'm Grayson Phillips. You can call me Gray."

"Catherine Schreiber. Or, as most people call me, Cat. Nice to meet you. I could check the computer, but it's probably faster to look this way." She walked over to the rows of poetry books. "Haselhoff, Haselhoff," she muttered as she ran her fingers along the book spines. "Hey, we do," she noted with surprise. "My mom must have ordered it for us."

"Great." He pulled the volume off the shelf and started scanning through its pages. Cat stood there awkwardly, unsure whether to try to make more conversation as he immersed himself in the text.

After a moment he looked up at her and smiled. The force of his grin nearly made her heart skip a beat—a notion she'd only read about in books, and which she'd mocked Eliza about plenty of times in the past. But there was something about him. He was so … intoxicating.

"Here, listen to this," he murmured.

> *"'An arm passes a leg in darkness.*
> *I feel you move over me, slowly, carefully.*
> *I brush your face and your stubble kisses my fingertips.*
> *Your mouth descends onto mine in soft hello.*
> *I move my hand across your back, feeling the muscles*
> *turn as you dip to greet my stomach with your lips,*
> *your beautiful lips.*
> *Your hair whispers across my chest, telling me of love.*
> *I am listening.'"*

"That's nice," Cat mumbled lamely, not sure what to say. "I like '*your mouth descending onto mine …*'"

Gray's eyebrows went up and a slow, suggestive smirk

spread across his face. Realizing what she had implied, Cat wanted to sink into the floor as her cheeks burned a Code Red. "I ... uh ... that's not what I meant. Um ..."

"I know," he said, still grinning. "But the imagery is striking, isn't it?"

Cat wasn't sure if he was referring to the poem, or to what she'd inadvertently said. She smiled weakly and turned to walk back to her desk. Anything to get away from the mixture of embarrassment and desire that was flooding through her veins.

"I'm researching various twentieth century female poets," he continued as he followed her, once again the intellectual. "I'm writing about their takes on sexuality and feminism and how these views have evolved and changed in their works over the course of the last fifty to one hundred years—the kind of pre- and post-feminist movement view, as it were."

"Really?" Cat asked, her voice echoing her surprise. "I wouldn't think that topic would interest most men. The feminist part, at least."

"What a sexist statement!" He chuckled as she nearly dropped the remaining flyers she still held in her hands. "Do you mean men can't be interested in feminist thought? Or that men are only interested in sex?"

His eyes raked her as he waited for her answer.

Good Lord, when he looks at me like that, I feel as if he's about to devour me. She folded her arms and the papers across her belly in a defensive position. "You really want me to answer that?"

"You just did," he retorted. "But it's fine. You're certainly not the only one to think that. Any modern magazine would say the same."

Cat relaxed a bit.

"I blame my mother," he went on. "She was quite active in the feminist movement in the 1970s. She never thought she'd get married. Didn't have me until she was in her forties. Said she was too old to have more, so I ended up an only child."

He turned back to the book without seeming to want a response.

"Well, um, maybe you'd like to come to our first Poetry Night?" Cat thrust a flyer into his hands, wanting him to look at her again with those gorgeous azure-colored eyes.

He took the flyer and examined it. "Sure. It's a date."

"It is?" she said. "Oh, I mean, yes, we're hoping to have lots of people there. It'd be great if you could read something."

He grinned again, seeming to enjoy her discomfiture. His eyes dropped to her lips, and then rose back to her eyes. "It's been a pleasure seeing you again, Cat. I'll take this book. And I'll see you next Tuesday."

CHAPTER 7

"So, would you sleep with him?" Eliza said the next morning, as she and Cat settled into their regular booth. "I might, if I got the chance."

"Shh!" Cat choked out, nearly tipping over her coffee mug. "Someone might be listening." She peeked around the room. No one seemed to be paying any attention.

"Well, they wouldn't have much to hear, would they, if neither one of us sleeps with him. I thought you said you wouldn't mind a little action," Eliza shot back. "It's exciting to see you finally noticing men again. It's been a long time."

"What do you think I am, a Cat on the prowl?" She snickered at her own bad joke. "I know most people will sleep with whomever whenever these days, but I'm not like that."

"Despite what you wrote in that *Carreling* story, huh?"

Cat gritted her teeth. "That was a story."

"Ha, ha, I know. But, hey, Grayson *is* a grad student, right? What's wrong with hoping a little fantasy can come to life?"

Cat tensed. She'd thought of the similarities between the grad student and her story, too. She couldn't help it, not

69

after her crazy thoughts about Derrick and that high school story. Of course, meeting a grad student didn't mean she was destined to sleep with him. Grad students were a dime a dozen in Charlottesville. And her story had been about a guy named Nick. In the library. *Not* about a guy named Grayson in her bookstore.

She wanted to laugh at how presumptuous it sounded, to think a man like that might want to sleep with her. Her body flamed at the thought, imagining those lips trailing down over …

She shook her head. *Stop it, Schreiber! That's never going to happen!*

Still, it was odd that she'd met a quarterback mechanic and a sexy doctoral student within days after reading stories— stories she'd written—about people who bore more than a passing resemblance to those main characters. Wasn't it?

Eliza grimaced. "Well, *I* like the idea."

Cat was grateful Eliza had misinterpreted her headshake —no need for her bestie to know she was drooling over a man. Any man. Or that she was having bizarre thoughts about those stupid stories.

"I want you to live a little," Eliza said. "Let passion in your life again. Let love … heck, let lust!" Her eyes bore into Cat's. "Don't let Ryan win. He didn't deserve you then, and he certainly doesn't deserve the power he still holds in your life now."

"Power now? What are you talking about? I've moved on." Cat set her coffee mug down defiantly. "He was a deceiving jerk, and I wouldn't give him the time of day if he walked in here right now."

"Maybe not," Eliza conceded. "But you haven't moved on. You're treading water, just trying not to drown. And you're convinced no one will help you, that you can't trust anyone to throw you a line, because he hooked you so deep, reeled you in, and then left you gasping for air."

"Oh my Lord, drama queen. No wonder you're an English major. Enough with the swimming-fishing analogies. And enough about men. I don't want to talk about it. We've got more important things to worry about."

Cat took a bite of an enormous blueberry muffin. She usually didn't indulge in sweets in the morning, but a downed computer system meant she didn't give a fig for moderation. "Did you do anything on the downstairs computer last night?"

Eliza looked up from swirling her coffee. "Me? No. I was in bed by 9:30. Exciting life I lead, I know."

"Ugh. Guess I'll have to call Mike. I don't want to shell out for computer repairs, but I think we're going to have to. An order came in last night for that *Winnie the Pooh* book, but I can't get the Internet working to see where to send it. That's an $11,000 sale. Lord knows we need the money."

She sighed as she took another bite of the muffin.

Eliza had suggested a couple of years ago that they branch out into the online market. Cat had resisted at first—wasn't that everything her father had fought against?

"There's nothing like a real book," he'd stated. "You've got to touch it, to feel it, to be able to absorb its essence."

How could one do that buying off a screen? But knowing such sales could save the store, they'd started offering rare and antique books on the Web—they couldn't compete against Amazon with the popular stuff, anyway. Sales were infrequent, but did boost revenue. They certainly had enough inventory; Frank's favorite pastime had been buying crates of old books from auctions and estate sales—his own form of treasure hunting, he'd joked.

"Did you call the cable company?" Eliza asked.

"Yeah, that's the first thing I did, but they say everything's fine on their end—that it must be something with our computers." Cat nervously shredded her napkin.

"Excuse me. Did you say eleven grand for a *book*?" came a male voice at her right side, causing Cat to knock over her coffee.

"I'll get some napkins," Eliza exclaimed, leaping up and heading to the sidebar.

"I'm sorry. I didn't mean to startle you." The man leaned over the table and started sopping up the mess with his own napkin.

Cat turned toward the source of the voice. "Oh, it's you. Hi, Ben," she said, swiping at the coffee with her napkin, as well.

He was so close Cat caught the surprisingly delicious smell of his skin. She inhaled, trying to determine the scent. It was pleasant. Masculine. With undertones of something she couldn't quite identify. She ducked her eyes when he looked at her questioningly.

"Someone will really pay that?" he continued. It was a relief he was asking about the book, seemingly unaware of her olfactory fantasies.

"It's a 1926 American first edition, one of only two hundred copies, signed by both Milne and his illustrator," she rattled off. "So, yeah, collectors will pay for something like that. But I can't ship it if I can't get on the site."

"You can't check the website somewhere else, like on your phone?"

Cat sat there, nonplussed. Eliza, who'd returned with a pile of new napkins, stared at her, wide-eyed.

"Why didn't we think of that?" Eliza said. She grabbed her phone and pulled up the store's email. "Here it is," she yelled, hopping up and down.

"Thank God." Cat sighed in relief. "That never occurred to me."

"Yeah, because you don't like technology," Eliza interjected.

Cat bristled. "It's not that I don't like it. It's that it doesn't come naturally to me." She picked at the edge of her muffin. "Your phone doesn't solve the problem of our non-working Internet, though. How are we going to ring up customers today when the card processing software can't connect?"

"I could come over and check it out if you'd like," Ben offered. "I'm a professor, not a repair person, but I might be able to figure it out."

Cat gaped at him. "You're a professor? Here? At UVa?"

"What kind of professor?" Eliza demanded at the same time.

"Computer science," he said to Eliza, and then looked back at Cat, his eyes twinkling. "I take it you don't think I look like one?"

"Um, not really. You're not wearing a sweater vest. Or glasses," Eliza put in.

"And you're actually cute," Cat blurted out. *Oh my God, I can't believe I said that.* She was sure her cheeks were going to fall off, they burned so badly.

Ben's cheeks colored as well, but he gave her a warm grin. "Why, thank you."

Cat stared at him. "I thought you were a grad student or something. You're always wearing sweatshirts and jeans."

"You've noticed what I wear?"

Cat briefly considered sliding under the table. "Uh …" she hedged.

Thank goodness he didn't notice how flustered she was—or at least he was gracious enough to ignore it. Her cheeks sizzled as he left to throw away the soggy napkins. Even her ears felt as if they were on fire.

Walking back to the table, he said, "In any case, shall I see if I can figure out the problem?"

"That would be great. I'd really appreciate it."

"Do you need another coffee?" he asked as he picked up his bag. "Or you, Eliza?"

"No, no, I'm good. Thanks, Ben," Eliza answered.

"Me, either. I can't think of anything else but getting this all sorted out," Cat said, pulling on her jacket.

Ben held the door for both Eliza and her as they all headed out. Suddenly, he sang out, "Here I come to save the day!"

"Mighty Mouse!" Cat answered, laughing as they crossed the street.

"You know Mighty Mouse?" His face lit up in surprise.

"Sure, my sister and I used to watch the old cartoons at my grandma's house," Cat said as they climbed the steps to the house together.

Eliza held the door while Ben walked through. As Cat followed him, Eliza gave her a knowing grin.

What? Cat mouthed.

Eliza snorted as she followed her friend through the door, but said nothing further.

"This place is beautiful," Ben said, pausing as he surveyed the store. He strolled down an aisle, touching the shelves and perusing book titles. "I love the cherry bookcases. Real wood warms up any space, doesn't it?"

"My dad always said the same thing, that there was nothing like true wood to show off books and bring coziness to a library," Cat said, following him. "The only thing better, according to him, was a fireplace. A real wood-burning one— none of this modern artificial flame stuff from today."

Ben looked around, and then walked over to the fireplace near the sofa, running his hand along the top of the mantel. Cat followed him. "Wow, is this original?" he asked.

"Yeah. From the 1880s, Dad said."

Eliza called out from the back of the room. "It's over here, Ben. The screen is on, but it's not letting us get on the web."

"OK," he replied, heading back to the oak desk. He pointed at the computer monitor. "This icon shows there's no Internet connectivity. Where's your modem?"

"Uh, I think it's under the desk with all the other cords," Cat answered as she crossed to the desk. "I haven't done anything with all that stuff since Mike from C'ville Computers set it up for us."

Ben got down on his knees and crawled under the desk. "Yup, here it is," came his muffled voice.

Eliza cast an appreciative glance at his backside, then waggled her eyebrows at her friend. Stifling a giggle, Cat moved around to the back of the desk to stand next to her.

"Can you tell what the problem is?" she asked, trying hard not to ogle Ben's nicely formed derriere herself. She always had liked a man in jeans.

She heard a bit of rustling, and then Ben called out, "Try it now."

Leaning over, she clicked the icon on her screen for checking her email. "It's working! What did you do?"

Ben backed out from the desk and stood up. "I plugged the cable back into the modem. It had been jiggled loose and almost fell out. And I think I know the jiggler."

He held up a clump of fur, arching an eyebrow. "In my estimation, the culprit was someone of the feline variety," he intoned, Sherlock Holmes-style.

Cat and Eliza both burst out laughing. "Elvis!" they exclaimed at the same time.

Ben's eyebrow remained arched in an inquisitive fashion. "No, ladies, I'm pretty sure Elvis is dead. This was the workings of a cat."

"Elvis *is* our cat." Eliza giggled. "He likes to seek out warm places to hide, especially in this colder weather. I guess under the desk seemed like an ideal spot."

"Thank you so much, Ben. I'm glad we didn't have to pay someone to come out and discover a cable was loose," Cat said. She reached out to dust fur off of his arm. "Obviously I need to sweep better under the desk."

"Not a problem. Any time. Listen, I need to head over to my office for office hours, but I'll stop back in again sometime." He looked around the store once more. "Ever thought about serving coffee in here? It's got a great atmosphere."

Cat and Eliza looked at each other. "Not really," they answered together.

"We always go across the street for that," Cat added.

"I'd bet lots of people would hang out in here if they could get their caffeine fix as well as their literary one. Works for Barnes and Noble, and this place has more character than your run-of-the-mill chain bookstore. I'd far prefer to hang here."

He cast a quick glance at Cat, and then looked back toward the front door, letting out a small sigh. "I have to go. My students will be crushed if I don't show up, I'm sure."

Cat walked with him to the door. "Thanks again. You're a lifesaver!" she said as she flipped the sign from *Closed* to *Open*. Impulsively, she clasped him in a quick hug. When he didn't return it, she stepped back, tucking her hair behind her ears. "Sorry. I'm just so grateful." She opened the door for him.

He paused a moment before answering. "Not a problem." His eyes twinkled. "Anything for a damsel in distress," he added, raising a pretend sword as he walked out the door.

Cat could hear Eliza's footsteps as her friend approached her.

"You know, coffee's not a bad idea," Eliza said. "It would at least save us the cost of our daily lattes."

Cat's eyes remained fixed on the retreating form of Ben Cooper. "True. But do we want people spilling coffee all over the books? And what if they hung out but didn't buy anything?"

"Ever the pessimist, darling Cat," Eliza chided. "Let's think it over. Maybe we could lure our favorite barista away from across the street."

"We can't afford a barista. And I'm not a pessimist." Cat crossed her arms. "I'm a realist."

Eliza rolled her eyes. "If you say so." Strolling back toward the desk, she called over her shoulder, "So, what do you think about Ben?"

"Ben?"

"Yeah, Ben. You know, the guy that was just here? The one who saved the day? The one who I'm pretty sure has the hots for you?"

Cat snorted. "For me? I don't think so. He was being helpful." Images of Ben's well-formed, jeans-clad rear popped into her head.

Eliza eyed her. "I'd take that kind of helpful any day."

"He's taken."

"Really? I didn't see a ring."

"You were looking for one?" Cat laughed as Eliza's cheeks flushed.

"A woman notices these things. What makes you think he's taken?"

"Don't you remember the woman he was with that day we first saw him in the coffee shop?" Recalling how Ben had looked at that woman brought an ache to her rib, a sharp stab of envy.

Eliza's brow furrowed. "Vaguely. Do you know for sure she was a girlfriend? I mean, did they kiss?"

"Uh, not that I recall. Regardless, I'm not about to go near a taken man. Not that I would have cheated before, but knowing what it's like being on the other side of that issue? Nu-huh, not gonna happen."

"You could always ask him."

"No way," Cat choked out, her face burning once again.

"So you *are* interested …"

Cat wished she had something to chuck at her friend. "Give it a rest, Eliza. You're making it sound like I'm desperate."

"Ha, definitely not desperate. I can't keep up with you these days, with all these men in your life."

"All these men? I've gone out with one guy, and mildly flirted with another—meaning Grayson, *not* Ben. I hardly think that counts as a lot of men."

"Let's see. How many men have you paid attention to in the last six years? Zero. So I would say two in the space of a month is a two hundred percent increase. Plus, I still think Ben is a possibility. *Your* possibility." Eliza gave her friend a wicked grin. "What's your secret?"

"Secret?"

"Are your ears clogged? Yeah, secret. You go for years ignoring men and, without wanting to hurt your feelings, not having them pay any attention to you. That armor you've been wearing is pretty thick. So what's changed?"

Cat walked over to the Nonfiction section and pretended to straighten books, her posture exuding a defensive tone. "Armor?" she scoffed. "I think you have me confused with a medieval knight."

"No, I'm pretty sure your knight just walked out the door."

"Stop it!" Cat protested, laughing. "Pretty soon you're going to be trying to hook me up with whatever male passes the least bit near me."

"Hardly, dear friend. I'll only accept the best for you."

Cat gave her a smile, surprised to feel tears well up in her eyes. "You are so good to me, Eliza. Thank you."

Eliza waved her hand dismissively. "Back at ya, friend. But I'm waiting to hear the secret, because my last few dates have been busts, and I'm not getting any younger."

Cat's mind jumped immediately to the medieval book, the one she was hoping to pick up from Jill soon. She'd called her last night to ask about it, but Jill said it would be another day or two, that she had to scan it in between other official work projects.

Why did she keep thinking about the manuscript? Or those stupid stories she'd written? Because of the similarities to Derrick and Grayson? Alleged, superficial similarities, that was.

At least I never wrote one about a computer science professor for Eliza to rib me about. She snorted at the thought. Computer guys weren't what leapt to mind when one thought of romantic heroes. Not that she was thinking about Ben in that way.

"If you'll recall, my date with Derrick wasn't exactly a match made in heaven. I'm betting Grayson Phillips flirts with every woman he sees. And Ben Cooper is not an option, whether or not I want him to be." Which she didn't. Did she?

Eliza was right. She could ask Ben outright if that woman was his girlfriend. Simple enough. But doing so would make him believe she was interested, wouldn't it? And something about that made her very nervous, more nervous than she'd been around Derrick, or even Grayson. *Why?*

She left the bookshelf and strolled toward Eliza, determined to change the subject. "As for serving coffee, we can consider it. I could use another cup after this bizarre conversation. But for now, since it's slow, let's get everything prepped for Poetry Night. I found an old wooden podium under the stairs I thought people might like to use. It's over near the storeroom."

Eliza retrieved the oak podium and wheeled it in front of the sofa. Standing behind it, she said, "This is great. It makes me feel positively professorial." Pulling her hair up into a severe bun, she pointed to an imaginary blackboard with a ruler she'd found on the podium's ledge, calling out "For example!" in as pompous a voice as she could muster.

Cat cracked up, laughing so hard her sides hurt. Thank God for her best friend. Eliza said her mom had often called her 'Spunky Sunshine,' and Cat could see what she meant. It was nice to have someone temper Cat's own often less-than-optimistic outlook.

She moved to the entrance and opened the door to usher in an elderly couple who had just made their way up the front stairs. Eliza was still pontificating behind the podium. Cat asked the wife if she could help them find anything, then offered a Poetry Night flyer.

"She's warming up over there," Cat commented, as the elderly man's eyes fixed on Eliza.

"If she's the main attraction, we'll be sure to return," he said, waggling his eyebrows.

"Oh, Norm." His wife rolled her eyes, an amused smile teasing at her lips. Clearly she was used to such comments.

"No one can hold a candle to you, m'dear." He reached for her hand. "But that doesn't mean it isn't fun for an old man to watch them try."

Cat smiled at the obvious affection between the couple, even as a bolt of jealousy zapped her. She wanted someone to look at her like that when she was eighty. The face that flashed through her head, however, was not Derrick's, nor Poetry Guy's, but that of a man laughing as he waved his imaginary sword to defend her from dragons. Or cats.

CHAPTER 8

as that Ben Cooper? It was.

"Fancy meeting you here." Cat pushed her shopping cart closer as Ben looked up. He quickly set the box of Twinkies he'd been clutching back on the shelf. *He looks like the cat caught eating the canary.*

"I, uh," he stammered. "I only eat those once in a while."

She scrunched her cheeks in amusement. "I don't have anything against Twinkies." She glanced at his cart, which was filled with a decent number of fruits and vegetables, nary a junk food item in sight. Embarrassment flooded her at the legions of frozen dinners she'd chucked into her own cart.

"I hear they're virtually indestructible," Ben said, his face relaxing. "So perhaps they're good to have in case of emergency."

"What kind of emergency?"

"Oh, you know: plague, flood, nuclear annihilation, sugar cravings."

Cat laughed.

Ben stuck his hands in the front pockets of his jeans.

"What are you doing here in the middle of the day? I would think you'd be at your bookstore."

"Mondays are my weekend." At his confused expression, she clarified. "Saturday and Sunday are my busiest days. I close the Trove on Mondays so that I can get everything else done. You know, laundry, bills, grocery shopping."

"Ah, makes sense."

"It must be nice to be a professor." She moved her cart so that others could get by. "Your schedule is much more flexible. And you get summers off."

Ben ran his fingers through his hair. It made the front stand up in an adorable fashion. Cat was oddly sad when he brushed it right back down. "Kind of. You're right that I choose my hours to some degree. But I spent the last seven years working toward tenure, which in reality meant very little free time; most of my waking hours I spent in the lab doing research, or writing papers. When I wasn't teaching, that was."

Cat made a sympathetic noise. "Oh. I never thought of it that way. I always envied professors, thinking they had the easy life."

Something like a snort came out of Ben's nose. "Tell that to my family, who always complain I'm never around. It's getting better, though. Now that I'm a tenured professor, I expect by next year to be sitting on a private island sipping frozen drinks, while my teaching assistant does all my grunt work back here."

"Can I join you?"

Ben's face took on a peculiar expression. "You and me alone on a deserted island?"

"You never said anything about deserted. Besides, if we load up on Twinkies before we go, we won't have to worry about food spoiling, right?"

"Excuse me," came a voice from behind her. "I'm trying to get to the Hostess cupcakes."

"Oh, sorry." Cat pulled her cart out to the end of the aisle.

Ben followed her. "Who knew there'd be traffic jams in Giant at 11:30 on a Monday morning?" he joked.

"Ugh, now I'm near the fish." Cat pinched her nose. "I can't stand seafood."

"Me either." He took off with his cart toward the frozen food section, and she chased after him, laughing. "There, that's better," he said. "Nothing here but the smell of ... cold."

"You do realize you've stopped in front of the frozen fish section, right?"

Ben whirled around. "Ah. So I did. At least we can't smell it, however."

"Whoever thought of eating crab and lobster to begin with? Look, a creature with its own armor and pincers that can hurt. Let's eat it!"

Ben laughed. "I'm guessing someone who was very, very hungry. If I were a contestant on *Survivor* and it came down to starvation or squid, I'd go for the squid."

Cat wrinkled her nose. "I suppose." She paused for a moment, setting her finger against her lips.

"What?"

"I was debating whether in times of emergency, as you said, I'd rather eat clams or mushrooms."

"Mushrooms? Ick. Fungus."

Cat widened her eyes, a grin spreading across her whole face. "My thoughts exactly. Tell that to Eliza the next time she wants a pepperoni and mushroom pizza. *Who eats fungus?*"

"How do you feel about beets?"

Cat stuck her tongue out. "Eww. Disgusting."

"I agree. They rank lower than squid and fungus for me.

When I was a kid, my uncle bet me ten dollars I couldn't eat one slice of canned beets."

When he didn't continue, Cat prompted him. "And?"

"Oh, I ate it. It just didn't stay down. And my uncle reneged on the bet, saying my 'reversal of fortune' meant I hadn't succeeded."

Cat stomped in mock indignation. "That's unfair."

"Yes, so I remind him every time I see him. In my view, he still owes me ten bucks."

"I agree."

There was a pause after their chuckling died down. This was a natural point at which to part ways. She had other errands to run. Surely he did, too. "Well, at least if you and I ever were to eat together, we have similar tastes," she blurted out.

Ben glanced at his watch.

Guilt nipped at her for holding him up. "Sorry," she began, before he cut her off.

"How about right now? Wanna grab lunch? Chili's is right over there and I'm hungry now that I've deprived myself of my Twinkies." His words came out in a rush. "I wanted to ask you about your computer, anyway."

Cat hesitated. Was he asking her out on a date? She wasn't sure. For one thing, he was talking about her computer. Not exactly flirtatious banter. For another, it was a last minute offer. Maybe he felt obligated, given their conversation. And thirdly, he had a girlfriend. At least Cat thought so.

Maybe Eliza was right and she should ask him. But that would be awkward either way. If he hadn't meant it as a date, she'd be mortified that she'd assumed it was. If it were a date, she didn't quite know how she felt about that, either. On the one hand, she really enjoyed this Ben Cooper, from what she knew of him. He felt comfortable, familiar. On the other, that's exactly why he was a bit scary. She'd rather not think of things in terms of dating or not. Wasn't it much more pleasant just to enjoy someone's company?

"Um, sure. But I've got all this stuff in my cart."

Ben glanced down at the frozen dinners. "No problem. We're in the right place." He scanned the aisle, looking for the low-cal meals. "Here, I'll help."

She giggled as he started pulling items out of her cart and sticking them back in the freezers. She scooted around to the front of her cart to help him. "Let's make it a race. Last one with a box buys dessert." She threw him a wink.

"You're on," he called, reaching for several more boxes. "Only you've got me at a disadvantage." He whipped open another freezer door, searching for the proper spot.

"What's that?"

"You know where you got all of these to begin with."

A minute later, they were done, Cat claiming victory. She laughed out loud, her breath fast from the exhilaration of their goofy game. Other shoppers shot them disapproving glances, but she didn't care.

Ben gave her a formal bow. "I concede. 'Twas a noble fight, but you outfoxed me."

"I cheated," she admitted. "I knew I had five baked zitis in there. I grabbed them all at once."

"A general never reveals her wartime strategy."

"Aye, aye, sir." She gave him a mock salute.

He walked back over and retrieved his own cart. "Hey, let me get these few things, okay? They'll keep fine in the car. I'll meet you over there."

"No problem." Cat pushed her own now-empty cart to the front. She didn't even mind that she'd have to come back and get her groceries later. She couldn't deny the jauntiness in her step as she left for the restaurant. Bantering with Ben Cooper was fun.

A few minutes later, he slid into the booth across from her. "Hope that wasn't too long."

"No, no, you're good. I was debating what I wanted. I'm thinking a salad."

Ben raised his eyebrows. "What kind of lunch is that? Go for the nachos!"

Cat took a sip of her ice water, the corners of her mouth turning up as she did so. "Nachos and Twinkies. The foods of the gods."

"Darn right," he said. "At least once in a while."

"Fine. I'll eat one or two of yours, if you'll share. But I still want a salad."

"Deal."

After they ordered, Ben sat forward. "How's your Internet working? Any more problems?"

"You mean since my cat tried to derail the biggest sale we've ever had? Nope. It's working like a charm." *Was that disappointment on his face?*

"Good, good." He paused. "Do you guys have wi-fi?"

Cat swirled her straw in her glass. "Um, upstairs, yeah. Eliza set that up. I don't get how all of that stuff works."

"But not in the store?"

"No." Her eyebrows furrowed. "Why?"

"I was thinking it might draw people in. You know, like the coffee idea. More and more places offer free wi-fi, because they know people want to be on their gadgets."

"I run a bookstore, not a computer store."

"I know." He held his hands up. "It was only an idea."

"Would it cost extra?"

"Nope. You already have Internet. I could come over and

help install a router, if you'd like."

"Hmm. Eliza probably *would* like being able to work on her laptop while she's downstairs."

The waitress brought their nachos. Ben dug in with gusto, which tickled Cat for some reason. "I guess you do like nachos."

"Sorry." He dabbed at his mouth with his napkin. "I didn't eat breakfast, so I'm super-hungry."

"For shame, Mr. Cooper. They say that's the most important meal of the day."

"Who's this 'they' that everybody always refers to? I'd like to know who invested 'them' with such power?"

Cat shrugged. "Dunno. Anyway, yes to the router, if you have the time." She set a nacho on her plate. They did look good.

"Sure. I'm busy most of tomorrow, but could come by in the evening if you'd like." He scooped up another nacho and popped it in his mouth.

"Ooh, no, sorry. Tomorrow night's our first open mic Poetry Night." She rested her arms on the table and leaned in. "Wanna come?"

Ben stopped mid-bite. He shook his head. After he'd finished his mouthful, he said, "I'm, uh, not exactly the poetry type. Too emotive for me."

Cat gave him a cheeky grin. "Not even limericks?"

"Ha ha. Limericks, maybe. But ask me to go much beyond '*Roses are red, violets are blue*,' and you'll quickly learn, that, uh, er …" He paused. "Well, you'll learn I'm not a poet. As evidenced by my lame construction of that simple sentence."

Cat speared a piece of lettuce from the Caesar salad the waitress had just brought. "I can't look at you right now," she teased before taking a bite, throwing her nose up in the air.

"Okay, fine." He took a breath, looking her square in the eye. "How about this:

"Seafood's disgusting. Mushrooms are eww.
I'd rather have Twinkies. Nachos, too."

His eyes sparkled in merriment as he finished his impromptu poem. If the word could be applied to the travesty, that was. She brought her napkin to her mouth to cover it while she laughed. He was a riot.

"Thank you for interrupting me from grocery shopping," she said after a moment. "It's my least favorite chore."

"And here I was thinking you were going to resent me, because now you have to go back."

She waved a hand. "More excuses to order pizza. Eliza will thank you."

He settled back in the booth, having polished off his nachos. "Why don't you like grocery shopping?"

She hadn't expected such a direct question, though she should have, considering she's the one who brought up the topic. "Um," she said, fumbling. "To be honest, it's lonely. I'm buying for one. Sometimes two, if I'm getting stuff for Eliza, too. But mostly I watch moms with babies, or couples flirting over which kind of cereal to buy, or see girls around the same age as my nieces, and it makes me feel alone. More alone than I feel about anywhere else."

He studied her for a moment. "That makes sense." He sat up, taking a sip of his iced tea. "Where are your nieces? Local?"

"No. Ohio. My sister Marie and her husband live there. My mom moved there a few years ago, too."

"That must be hard. My parents live in Fredericksburg, but that's only ninety minutes away. And my sister is local."

"You're lucky."

"Ever thought about moving?"

Cat winced. "I have. But then I'd have to give up the bookstore. It's … well, it's one of the last links I have to my dad. At least it feels like that." After a pause, she added, "And I don't want to give it up. Most of the time, at least. I love it. Walking into the main room, with the wood and the fireplace and all those books, soothes me every time." She rubbed her hands up and down her arms. "Does that sound weird?"

"Not to me. I'm peculiar about my spaces, too."

"Peculiar. Not a word people generally want ascribed to them."

Ben shifted in the booth. "That's not what I meant."

She laughed lightly. "Teasing." She nodded in thanks as the waitress refilled her ice water. "So, what brought you to Charlottesville? Or did you grow up here?"

"Nah, Fredericksburg. Nice town. Of course the last place I wanted to be when I finished high school was in Virginia, so I headed to MIT for undergrad, then Carnegie Mellon for grad school."

"Holy cow. You must be brilliant. Even I know those are some of the top schools for computer science."

Ben looked down at his plate, but he couldn't hide the color spreading across his cheeks. "I don't know about that. Regardless, by the time I finished grad school, I was longing to be closer to home again. I got lucky when I got the position at UVa."

"Sounds more to me like they're lucky to have you."

He chuckled. "You're good for a man's ego, Catherine Schreiber. I can tell you that."

"Just giving credit where credit is due. So tell me more about your time here."

They lapsed into easy conversation, talking about favorite places in Charlottesville. He was fond of Jefferson's gardens on the UVa grounds; she confessed she enjoyed sitting on the downtown pedestrian mall to people-watch when she got a chance. They talked about good places to eat, movies they liked—*The Princess Bride* was a mutual favorite—books they didn't—why *was Moby Dick* so highly rated?

At one point, Ben's phone beeped. He pulled it out, checked the screen, and frowned. "I have to go," he said as he tucked the phone back in his jeans pocket. "I didn't realize it was already 2:00. That was a colleague, saying I have a line outside my office. I'm supposed to be there for office hours." He waived the waitress over and asked for the checks.

"It's 2:00?" Where had the time gone?

"Yeah. I took up much of your free day. I'm sorry."

"Nah, this was fun. Much better than wrestling with the dreaded checkbook."

He stood up. "Do you want me to get this?" He gestured toward the bill.

"No, don't be silly. I can afford a salad." Eliza would say if he offered to pay, it was a date. Cat was certain, however, he'd only offered because she'd stupidly referenced her checkbook.

She pulled out her credit card and set it on the table. "Thanks for a delightful afternoon."

"It was. And I have a dinner date this evening. Talk about feeling spoiled."

Okay. Definitely *not* a date. He's going out with someone tonight. Her mind pictured the redhead she'd seen him with before. *You could ask him about her.* The slightest of frowns crossed her brow before she smoothed her face into a pleasant smile. *Not on your life.*

"Business?" she heard herself say. She cringed inwardly.

What happened to not asking?

"No, thank goodness. Going to the American Shakespeare Center in Staunton, actually. I can't wait."

She stood up, using the excuse of leaning over to get her purse to hide her face from him. She knew it had to reflect the disappointment coursing through her.

"I'm free Thursday morning. Shall I stop by then?"

Clearly he hadn't noticed. Good. "Sounds great."

He flashed a broad smile at her. "I had a great time, Cat."

"Me, too." She walked out ahead of him, squaring her shoulders.

"See you!" he called as he drifted off toward his car.

"You, too."

You, too, her head echoed. *'Mushrooms are eww.'*

CHAPTER 9

"**D**ude, this is the poetry place, right?"

Cat looked up as a group of teenagers tumbled through the door. The one who had spoken was clutching a pack of papers in his hand. Tattoos snaked up the side of his neck, seemingly at odds with the thick-rimmed glasses he wore. Two girls behind him laughed in that self-conscious way teenage girls had. One had long blue hair and blue fingernails to match, and was garbed in a floor-length black dress. She had a pretty face, from what one could see under the heavy eyeliner and lipstick she wore. The other girl was dressed more plainly, in faded jeans and a ratty T-shirt under a black jacket, but had piercings in her eyebrow, cheek, and nose. *And probably tongue.*

"Yes, it is," she answered. "Head over there by the podium and find a spot to make yourself comfortable. We've got coffee and a few treats from the coffee shop across the street, so help yourself."

"Dude, free food!" said the other boy in the group, the one Cat hadn't noticed at first. He was skinny as a rail, but watching him dive into the food, Cat knew she'd be lucky if there were anything left over for the other people now coming through the door. A couple of college-age girls entered, followed by the elderly couple who had been in earlier. The man winked at Eliza, who was across the room pulling out extra chairs.

"I told you we'd be back," he said to Cat, a teasing glimmer in his eye. "C'mon, Myra, let's go get a spot next to the blue-haired girl. She looks interesting."

"Help yourself to coffee and snacks—while they last." Cat turned to greet the next party coming in, a group of older ladies wearing red hats.

"Welcome to the Treasure Trove," she said in greeting, "and to our first Poetry Night. We've got seats over there and a few refreshments, if you're hungry or thirsty."

"Oh, I shouldn't have any sweets," demurred one of the ladies, a plump little white-haired woman with a friendly face, as she made a beeline for the brownies.

Eliza sidled up to Cat. "Wow, did you think we'd get so many? There must be at least twenty people in here."

Cat grinned. "I know. This is wonderful. But I think the posse of teenagers may lay waste to the food before anyone else has a shot at it."

"Oh, don't worry about that," Eliza answered. "I can always run over and get more."

Cat nodded, looking around the room and then back toward the door.

"He's not here, is he?" Eliza asked.

"Who?" Cat ignored the butterflies in her stomach.

"Whadd'ya mean, who? Your guy, that's who—Grayson!"

"He's not my guy." She had to admit, she was disappointed not to see him. Any woman with hormones would be. But perhaps it was better; she needed to focus on the business at hand, not moon after a sex-on-a-stick twenty-something with whom she'd never have a chance, a chance she shouldn't want. "Anyway, I've gotta go open the floor. It's time to get started."

Cat crossed to stand behind the podium. "Welcome to the Treasure Trove's first Poetry Night! We're so glad you're here, and look forward to hearing what you have to share with us, whether it's original compositions, or some of your favorite poems. Anything goes, but let's try to keep it profanity-free, all right?"

"Aw, shit," she heard the tattooed boy mutter under his breath.

She went on. "I'm Cat Schreiber, and this is Eliza James, and we own the Treasure Trove. We hope you'll spread the word about us."

"Rah, rah!" Eliza called from the back.

"And now, without further ado, I turn the mic over to you." Cat looked out over the small crowd. Nobody came up. She waved them forward with her hand. "Come on, who's gonna break the ice? I promise we won't laugh."

"OK, dude, I'll go," said the boy with the tattoos. He adjusted his glasses and walked to the front. Cat moved off to stand at the side.

The boy gave what Cat assumed was intended to be a sultry look to the girl garbed in black and said, "Annika, this is for you.

"Your eyes so brown, your hair so blue.
Your bitchin' body and nose ring, too.
Your way of smoking your cigarettes,
These are things I'll never forget."

Cat glanced at Eliza, struggling to control the laughter bubbling to the surface. *I promised I wouldn't*, she told herself sternly as she bit down on her bottom lip. Briefly her mind wandered to Ben. His poem hadn't been much better. Eliza, who'd taken a seat next to her senior admirer, rolled her eyes, and then pointed toward the object of the poem, who sat as if enraptured, gazing at the boy with wide eyes and a happy smile on her face.

"At least someone's enjoying it," whispered a voice from behind her. Jumping, Cat turned to see Grayson standing there.

"When did you come in?" Her voice came out sharper than she had intended, from the shock of seeing him and having him stand so close to her. Damn, he smelled good, of a heady cologne that, thank goodness, he hadn't applied too heavily. She could feel the warmth of his body against her back. A shiver raced down her spine.

"I sneaked in while you were greeting the Red Hat Club over there. I was looking at a book while you were performing the opening ceremony."

She relaxed her shoulders and gave him a brief smile, as the boy at the front continued.

"*Your long, long tongue and soft sweet lips,*
The sexy way you swing those hips,
It's such a fuckin'—er, pardon me, friggin'—*thrill to be*
The dude for you, and you for me."

Upon finishing his poem, the young man ran back to Annika, who was watching him with hero worship in her eyes. "I told you I was gonna do it, babe," he said, and then kissed her.

After a minute, Eliza elbowed them from her other side.

"This a family joint, guys," she joked as they moved apart.

"The poem sucked, but points to him for getting such a reaction out of her," Gray said. "She'll be mooning after him for days now."

His eyes bore into hers, and she sucked in a breath. The man exuded sensuality.

"You think that's all it takes? Read a poem and we'll fall at your feet?"

"We'll see," he responded. "But the little Red Hat lady with brownie on her shirt is going next."

For the next hour, as they listened to everything from Shakespeare to long love poems about various pets, to what Cat could only call spoken rap, she was cognizant of Gray standing right behind her. As people spoke, he'd often whisper commentary into her ear, and the delicious feel of his breath on her neck sent the most delightful sizzles through her body. She was surprised, frankly, by the intensity of her body's reaction to him. There was no other word for it than lust. Sheer lust. And yet, oddly, she was also grateful for it. She'd felt dead inside for so long, had denied the sexual side of herself forever. Too messy to deal with. But now, it felt as if an undercurrent of electricity was racing between them.

She shifted positions, locking her arms over her belly. She longed to glance back at him, to see if it was all one-sided, this attraction. But she kept her eyes fixed firmly ahead. If she were wrong, she didn't want to ruin her delusions just yet.

Eliza looked over at her occasionally, once with a raised eyebrow, and once with a wink. *She obviously thinks there's something going on.*

A few people had already drifted out and others seemed on the brink of sleep, lulled in part by the warm fire blazing behind the podium and the soft candlelight Eliza had set up around the room, when Grayson walked up to the front. Cat noticed a group of young college women sitting in front of her begin elbowing each other. They tittered back and forth as Grayson spoke.

"I hope you like this one. It's always been one of my favorites, but lately I seem to be thinking of it more than usual," he said, his voice soft as he glanced at Cat. "It's called *Première Soirée—The First Evening*, by Arthur Rimbaud."

He began reading, his voice rendered all the more sensual by the fact that the words dripping off his tongue were in French.

He's reading in French? Cat glanced around. Did anyone understand him? It didn't seem to matter whether they did or not; one of the Red Hat ladies had begun fanning herself with her hand as Grayson read, and it was clear the other women in the room were falling under his spell, as well. Even Myra had turned to look at Gray with an admiring gleam in her eye. Her husband, noticing, elbowed her.

Cat chuckled to herself as she heard Myra retort, "Turnabout's fair play, Fred. Now let me enjoy the young man."

Gray paused, having come to the end of poem.

"This next one is dedicated to Cat, our fearless bookstore owner, for providing us with the space to meet tonight, and because we seem to like similar imagery," he said, his voice silky.

The college girls in front of Cat turned and peered at her. Her cheeks burned as she remembered which image she and Grayson had last been discussing together.

As he began to speak, all eyes returned to him.

"*Dip your fingers into my ink,*
Spreading my flesh across your page.

Smooth me, shape me, shade me darkly with your hands.
Take my mouth and paint it raw,
Dripping oil down across your brush.
Feel me rise under your pen,
My skin an extension of your touch.
Make me come alive, color my world, draw me
In to who you are.'"

Cat stood, transfixed. It was as if an electric current were flowing between the two of them. She winced. That's the kind of corny thing she'd expect Eliza to say.

While Grayson spoke, he kept his eyes, those startling, mesmerizing cerulean eyes, on her, barely glancing down at the words on the page. Several women in the room noticed, assessing her with disappointed looks on their faces. Cat broke eye contact with Grayson to note Eliza was watching her, too, looking back and forth between the two of them. Eliza sat back in her chair, smiling consolingly at Fred, who was looking morose now that Myra and all the rest of the women in the room were focused on the man behind the podium. The Goth girl, Annika, was leaning forward in her seat, as well, much to her boyfriend's dismay. *Not that I blame her.*

Cat's eyes were drawn back toward Grayson's, pulled as if by a magnet. His eyelids flared as she met his gaze again.

As he finished speaking and silence covered the room, Eliza hopped up. "Well, that concludes our first Poetry Night. I hope you all enjoyed it. Please come back to visit us during regular business hours, and be on the lookout for announcements about our upcoming events here at the store." Her bright, energetic voice broke the trance that had fallen over the crowd. She chatted with folks as they made their way to the door. After everyone but Grayson had left,

Eliza waved at Cat and bounded upstairs before Cat could stop her.

Grayson was in the back of the room, cleaning up coffee cups and moving chairs. Once they were alone, he stopped, fixing his eyes on Cat. It was a hot, piercing gaze. Cat moved toward him slowly.

"What did you think of the poem?" His voice was low, intense.

"Um, well, it was pretty … vivid," Cat mumbled. "Which one of your feminist authors wrote it?"

He stepped forward and ran his thumb over her lower lip. "I did. Yesterday. When I was thinking of you. Of how I want you to be thinking of me."

Cat swallowed. Grayson, this sex god, this unbelievably attractive, hot, seductive younger man, wanted her? *Her?*

Slowly, so slowly, he dipped his head and kissed her, a light kiss at first, a gentle tasting. After a moment he intensified the kiss, running his fingers through her hair as he ravished her mouth. Cat responded in kind, wrapping her arms around his neck, wanting to get closer to him. Her whole body felt enflamed, on fire.

He broke off abruptly. "I've been wanting to do this since I first saw you," he murmured, before swooping in to kiss her again. Cat ran her fingers through his hair as he moved his mouth across her cheek to her ear and down her neck, trailing soft kisses along the surface of her skin. Electric shivers raced up and down her spine and flamed out across her body.

"You have?" she panted. "Usually it's Eliza the guys go nuts for."

He chuckled as he pulled her into him, running his hands down her back. "She is beautiful," he conceded, "but I was drawn to you, pulled in by you. I can see the passion in you. I can feel it." He dipped to kiss her again. "You try to hide it, which is part of what makes you so irresistible. You need someone to bring you alive. You need me."

"Oh," she whispered. Then stopped talking.

He slid his hand down over her backside and pulled her hips full into his. She could feel how aroused he was. Emboldened, she slid her hands up under his shirt, marveling at the hot feel of his skin. He gasped, and then kissed his way down her throat to her chest. Slowly but skillfully he opened each button of her shirt, licking the skin as he exposed it. Cat grew wild with desire, wanting to devour him whole, wanting the heat of his skin against hers. She hadn't felt this way in such a long time and it was utterly delicious.

They fell together on the sofa in front of the fireplace, murmuring words of desire and sex. He moved his fingers over her body, following each place he touched with his mouth. Trembling, she allowed him to remove her jeans, watching with wide eyes as he unzipped his. After pulling out a condom from the front pocket, he tossed them aside.

"Is this what you want?" His eyes were deep, dark, seductive pools.

She didn't want to think. She wanted to feel. "Yes. Oh, yes," she panted, marveling at how her body had come alive again.

Quickly he tore open the condom package. "Me, too. God, me, too."

Rising over her, he shifted his hips between her legs, piercing her with his eyes, those intense, beautiful, impossibly blue eyes. He slid into her. *I can't believe I'm doing this; this isn't me.* And then there was no more space for thought—just joy and movement and bodies, and pleasure and release.

CHAPTER 10

"**Y**ou *slept* with him?" Eliza halted the rise of her coffee mug to her lips as she gaped at Cat with wide eyes. "On the couch in the *bookstore*?"

Cat ducked her head as several sets of eyes transferred to her from around the room.

"Geez, Eliza, say it a little louder, would you? I don't think the people in the kitchen heard," she muttered. "Besides, why are you so surprised? You're the one who's been telling me to get out there and get back into the game. *You* even said you'd sleep with him."

"Yeah," Eliza conceded. "But I kind of thought you'd only dip your toes into the water instead of going for full-blown skinny dipping on the first return to the pool. Did you use a condom, at least?"

"Of course," Cat snapped. She knew embarrassment fueled her reaction, knew that she shouldn't attack her friend because of her own actions.

What she didn't know was how she felt about last night.

Her body this morning occasionally sent zings reminding her of the previous evening's activities. It had felt fantastic at the time; there was no denying that. And she didn't feel guilty about the sex, per se—there was nothing wrong with sex, with physical pleasure. It was more that she'd broken her own cardinal rule about one-night stands. She'd never been one to go for physical pleasure over emotional connection. And that's what had been missing—true intimacy.

Even if Grayson called her, even if this went beyond one night, it still nagged at her how quickly she'd succumbed to his seductive ways. She'd done exactly what she'd mocked the night before. She'd fallen at his feet, ensnared by those poetry-reading lips.

Eliza looked past Cat toward the window. "Uh, oh."

"What?"

"I think Ben heard me, too. He's staring this way with a … a … I don't know … an odd expression on his face."

Cat pulled her sweater more closely around her and crossed her arms, determined not to check it out for herself. She hadn't noticed Ben was here. "What's it to him?" she grumbled. "None of his business, anyway."

She heard the shuffling of books and the sliding of a chair. She could feel the air stir as Ben passed their table. As he went, he gave a little wave to Eliza, who was facing him, but did not turn to acknowledge Cat. With a forceful shove on the door, he exited the coffee shop.

"See? I knew he was into you," Eliza whispered.

"*Now* you whisper? You couldn't have done that five minutes ago?" Cat took a sip of her coffee and brushed the hair out of her eyes. "And he just made it clear who he's really interested in, if anybody."

"Are you kidding? The light flirting; his dashing aid to a

damsel in distress when the computer died; the fact that he now comes in here every day when before it was only once in a while?"

"He does?"

"You haven't noticed?"

Cat drummed her fingers on her arms. "Yeah, well, if he does, I'm sure it's coincidental. He's taken, remember?"

"I'm not so sure." Eliza fingered the rim of her coffee mug. "He's all about you."

Cat had thought maybe, at their lunch. Until he'd mentioned his date, and Shakespeare. She hadn't told Eliza of her lunch encounter with Ben. She didn't know why. She eyed her friend. "What makes you say that?"

"Because I observe people, Cat. It's what I do. How else am I supposed to find my Wentworth?"

"Wentworth? I thought you were hoping for Darcy."

"Oh, I am. But *Persuasion*. So romantic." Eliza flicked crumbs off her fingers. "Although I hope my Wentworth and I wouldn't face quite the sad situation that he and Anne did, I suppose."

"I liked the movie version of that one," Cat said. She looked around the shop, glad the normal hum of conversation had resumed, and that no one was paying the least bit of attention to Eliza and her. "But you're wrong about Ben. You've practically talked to him more than I have." Except for that lunch, which for some reason, Cat wanted to keep as her own secret.

Eliza shook her head. "Nope. I've seen the way he watches you. With me, it's like I'm a friend—a kid sister. He's less sure, more nervous, with you."

"He's had the opportunity to ask me out and never has," Cat protested, not sure why this battle felt so important. He hadn't, really; after all, an impromptu sharing of nachos was not a date.

"Maybe he's been waiting for *you* to notice him and do so. Plus, he's heard you talking about other men in here. Hard to make a move after that."

Cat glanced at the door again, though Ben was long gone. She was mortified that he'd overheard Eliza, that he knew she'd slept with Grayson. But why? There were no connections between the two of them. She'd done nothing wrong. Had she?

She turned back to Eliza, determined to block all thoughts of Ben Cooper from her mind. "I thought you wanted to talk about Grayson."

Eliza's eyes popped back to Cat. "Oh, yeah. Sex. Deets. Spill. Now."

"Uh, no. This isn't one of your books. Let's just say … it was magnificent." She sighed as she remembered the feel of Gray's lips down her side. It had all been so dizzying, so electrifying. She hadn't felt so alive in years. She ran her hands over her thighs, remembering the feel of him, of those muscular thighs, those perfectly toned arms. Her skin erupted in goose bumps and she closed her eyes, reliving the scene in her head.

Eliza interrupted her reverie. "OK, fine. Ruin it for the romance junkie. Are you going to see him again?"

"We'll see," Cat replied. "Maybe I was a one poetry-reading fling for him."

"Would that bother you?"

"Yes, it would. In spite of what you've been hinting to the good folks in this coffee shop, I'm *not* the type to sleep around, as you well know. I don't know what came over me."

"It's called lust, girlfriend. But I know you're not. You're almost as old-fashioned on that as I am."

Cat smiled at her as her friend went on.

"In spite of the smutty novels and, I admit, a fair number of dates, you know I'm not going to get intimate with just anyone. Sex is more meaningful than that. At least for me." Eliza chuckled sadly to herself. "Geez, I really do belong in the nineteenth century."

"Are you going to ditch me now that I've allowed myself to be seduced by a virtual stranger?" Catherine teased.

"Not a chance, girlfriend. You're stuck with me. Besides, who knows what will happen?" Eliza glanced at her phone, checking the time. "What about Derrick, though? He called last night while you were, uh, otherwise occupied."

"He did?" Cat pursed her lips. "I've thought about it. I'm not interested. He's a nice guy, but he seems a little stuck. I mean, he's got the same job, the same friends, the same hangouts he's had since high school. It's one thing to be the quarterback when you're eighteen. It's another to be holding onto that when you're thirty-eight." She broke off with a snigger. "Listen to me! When did I become such a conceited bitch? As if I'm any less stuck than he is."

Eliza stood up and grabbed her bag. "I've got to get to class, but I get what you're saying. Too bad about Derrick, though."

Cat's eyebrows puckered. "Why's that?"

"He's got such a nice car."

On Thursday morning, Ben Cooper showed up as promised, router in hand.

Eliza clapped when he walked through the door. "Yippee! Now I can do online research while minding the store."

"Check Facebook, you mean," Cat sniggered. She smoothed her hands down the front of her navy blouse, inexplicably nervous.

Ben nodded at them both, heading directly to the desk. "This should only take a minute." He crawled underneath, rustling around with the cables.

Eliza shot Cat a questioning glance.

What? Cat mouthed. Okay, so he wasn't being effusive in his conversation, but he wasn't being rude, either. Maybe he had somewhere to be. Maybe this brusque attitude had nothing to do with her.

And maybe it did, part of her chided. Why did she feel guilty? There were no ties between Ben and her. He'd told her himself he had a date to dinner and a play. Why would it matter to him that she'd had a date of her own? *Not exactly a date. More like … a seduction.* She blew the hair out of her eyes. She hadn't heard from Grayson, either, which rankled. She didn't need grief from Ben Cooper.

After a minute, Ben backed out from the desk and hopped up. "May I?" He gestured to the computer.

"By all means." Cat crossed her arms, watching him.

"Thanks again, Ben," Eliza offered. "I'm so excited. What do we owe you for the router?"

Cat noticed his jaw tic slightly. It hadn't even occurred to her the router would cost something. Duh.

His eyes flew to hers, and then moved to Eliza. He grinned, his dimple showing, but Cat didn't think it quite reached his eyes. "On the house. I have plenty of extras." He clicked a few more keys. "There. Tell me if your laptop is showing available wi-fi."

Eliza pulled her laptop out of her backpack and fired it up. "Yup!"

"Good. The password is *Fungus*. You can change if it you want."

Eliza giggled, giving Cat an odd look. *Crap. She knows that's what I call mushrooms.* "No, *Fungus* is just fine, isn't it, Cat?"

"Yes, great. Thanks, Ben. This is very nice of you."

"No problem." He finally looked her full in the face. She couldn't read his expression at first, but then it softened, and he gave her what seemed to be a genuine smile. "Always happy to help out a Luddite."

Eliza cackled. "She *is* a Luddite. You're so right."

Ben winked at Eliza. "Part of her charm," he said, and then quickly tacked on, "Gotta scoot. Professorly duties call," as if he were embarrassed by his admission.

"See you, Ben," Eliza said.

"Yeah, see you." He turned to Cat. "You, too, Luddy."

Cat's cheeks stretched out into a wide smile as he walked out the door.

"Have you heard from Grayson?" Eliza asked a few days later, while opening a box of children's books.

Cat grimaced. "No. It's been more than a week, so somehow I'm thinking I won't be seeing him again. Oh, well. Live and learn."

Eliza sat back on her heels, peering at her friend. "You all right?"

"Yeah. I had hoped maybe for once some guy wouldn't screw me over. Guess that's what you get for, you know, being easy."

"Ouch." Eliza winced. "You're not easy and you know it.

Now Angela from my Dickens class—*she's* easy. She boasts about having slept with at least half the department, including several professors."

"Whatever. I feel stupid."

"Oh, honey, you're not stupid," Eliza said. "You're a woman with hormones. And a man as electrifying as that? I probably would have caved, too."

Cat hauled a pile of books from the box. "It was electric," she conceded with a pained grin.

She'd had so many mixed emotions since that night. On the one hand, it had been fantastic to feel her body come alive again. On the other, she'd jumped into bed with someone she didn't really know, and that didn't sit well with her conscience. Physical intimacy had always come hand-in-hand with emotional intimacy for her. It still did.

She'd hoped Grayson would call. But what had she been expecting, really? That they would start seeing each other? That they could have a future together? They had a love of literature in common, true, but she doubted much more. The man was probably a decade younger than she was, and on a different career path. Not to mention the fact that he was so absolutely delicious, Cat knew she'd never feel at ease with it; too many other women would constantly be trying to get his attention. He'd never want to be long-term with her when there were so many younger, firmer, sexier fish in the sea, would he? She had to admit she'd at least wanted the chance to find out, though.

Cat bit the inside of her cheek. She'd joked with Eliza about a fling, but her heart had reminded her every day for a week now that she wasn't the fling type. She exhaled loudly. Life had been so much easier before Derrick and Grayson had shown up. And Ben. Boring and unfulfilling, but easier.

Eliza stood up and pressed her hands against the small of her back. "Can we take a break and go grab something hot to drink? I'm freezing."

Cat glanced outside at the leaves falling from the trees. The brisk wind whipped up a pumpkin-and-mustard cascade of colors. She loved autumn, especially November. Something about the crisp, cool air always revitalized her.

"Sure, sounds good. Do you mind if we stop by Alderman Library, as well? Jill says I can finally pick up my book."

"Of course, but do you want to leave the store for that long?"

"Because we'd be disappointing all the customers?" Cat gestured around the empty store.

Eliza giggled. "I'm sure it will pick up this afternoon, Eeyore. I'll change the sign to say we'll be back in an hour."

They locked the door behind them as they exited. Since the library was only a few blocks from the bookstore, they walked.

"I'm glad we're going," said Eliza. "Jill texted me last night to say she wants to show me a copy of *Ackermann's Repository* she found. She says there's quite a dreamy duke pictured in it."

When Cat cocked an eyebrow at her, Eliza went on. "It's a famous British magazine from the Regency period."

"Ah. I should have known. You do realize your dreamy duke's been dead for two hundred years, right?"

Eliza elbowed her. "Spoilsport. Let me have my fantasy, will you?"

"Better you than me. I had the fantasy, I guess. And he hasn't called in a week." She gave Eliza a rueful grin.

"Ah, but you had him." Eliza winked. "That's more than I can say. It's been a long time. My Darcy needs to show up soon."

Cat linked her arm through Eliza's as they strolled across the brick walkway in front of the UVa Rotunda. Not too soon, Cat hoped. She couldn't imagine life without her best friend.

As they entered the library foyer, Cat paused. "Hey, you go ahead with Jill. I want to go find my old study carrel on the fourth floor and see if *Elvis* is still carved in it. I'll be down in a few minutes."

"Sure thing." Eliza poked her. "I had no idea you were such a vandal."

"I never said *I* did it." Quirking an eyebrow at her friend, Cat added, "But I never said I didn't."

As Eliza headed toward the elevator, Cat walked back to the old side of the library. Passing through the metal doors, the familiar smell of timeworn books assailed her. She breathed in deeply. *Geez, I'm as bad as my dad.* She moved through the stacks until she reached the spot in which she'd sat many an hour in school, reading Cicero while dreaming of a Romeo. *Yeah, those days are long gone.* She reached out and ran her finger along the bookshelf in her old carrel. *Elvis* was still inked across the edge of it.

"I have a sneaking suspicion you know who defaced this lovely university property," drawled a voice from behind her. She whirled and came face-to-face with Grayson. "Maybe I should turn you in. Put you in handcuffs."

"U-um," she stammered, not sure what to say. How could he look so damn *luscious*, standing there in a V-neck charcoal sweater and faded jeans, holding a volume in his hand? Sylvia Plath, she noted absently from the cover.

"It's good to see you, too." He moved in to close the space between them. "I've been thinking about you. In fact, I can't *stop* thinking about you."

"For over a week?" she said with a snort, stepping back in an effort to break the spell she seemed to have fallen under. Again.

"Sorry about that. I've been slammed with grading, plus my own dissertation chapter to finish." He set the book down on the carrel and leaned into her, his eyes entrapping hers. "I want to see you again, Cat."

She could feel his breath on her cheek. He trailed his fingers down her arm, gazing at her expectantly. When she didn't protest, he leaned in and kissed her. She gave into the kiss, marveling again at being in the arms of this oh-so-sexy man, in the library in which she'd spent hours, days, years, dreaming of future love.

And with that future had come heartbreak. And a heart-stoppingly beautiful man who had seduced her in her own store and then not contacted her again.

Anger flared up inside her. She pushed against him, breaking the kiss.

"I don't think so. I am *not* the kind of girl who'll sleep with you whenever you happen to show up!"

Gray frowned, running his fingers through his messy hair. "I said I was sorry. I've been busy. I guess I was lost in my own studies and didn't notice the time passing. Please, Cat."

He sounded sincere. But she wasn't interested in playing second fiddle again, whether to another woman or an intellectual addiction. He reached up to tuck her hair behind her ear, but she backed away.

"I've got to go meet Eliza and Jill," she said.

Gray picked up his book. "Can I come see you sometime? Maybe next week, after I get this chapter done?"

"Maybe." *What? No! Turn him down, you idiot!* She frowned. "Probably not."

His smile faltered and his eyes clouded for a second. Then he leaned in close, so close that she could see the darker blue flecks near his irises, and whispered, "I think I can get you to change your mind."

She closed her eyes, her hormones at war with her head. He chuckled, running his fingers along her chin. When her eyes flew open again, his face was an inch, maybe less, from hers. Taking her bottom lip between his teeth, he bit it gently, and then licked it in atonement. When she gasped, he took her mouth with his, his tongue ravaging the insides of her mouth as he pulled her flush against him.

He murmured something, some line about walking in beauty. *Byron.* She knew that poem, had loved it since a child. Suddenly, Ben's ridiculous poem from the other day sprang to mind. '*Mushrooms are eww.*' His brown eyes swam before her, accompanied by a wave of guilt.

She frowned. She had nothing to feel guilty about. It wasn't as if she and Ben Cooper *were* anything.

Grayson's hands moved down, cupping her bottom.

She and Grayson weren't anything, either. Not really. She pushed against his chest. "No. I don't want this."

He let her go. Backing up, he gave her a wink. "You're right. Here is not the place." His gloriously blue eyes darkened with desire, as a lop-sided grin spread across his face. "You're addictive, Catherine Schreiber. One taste is not enough."

He turned and sauntered off without another word.

She admired his legs in his jeans as he walked down the aisle. What had she just given up?

"Sex, dummy," she muttered as she walked toward the elevator. A young student looked up at her in surprise as she passed, overhearing her words. Cat blushed as she stepped into the elevator, but said again loudly, "Meaningless sex!"

Chapter 11

"**I** still can't believe you own this book," Jill said as she thumbed gently through the pages.

"I know, isn't it amazing?" Cat answered. She took the book from Jill's hands, goose bumps prickling her skin as she did so. *Odd. It's not particularly cold in here.*

She, Jill, and Eliza had sat down with a coffee drink in the café in the main entrance area of the library. "We can't stay long," she'd said. "But it's nice to have a few minutes with you."

She tucked the book carefully in her bag. Jill handed her the color copies she'd printed from the scans.

"Thanks so much for doing that for me, Jill. I know I could have taken it to Kinko's or something, or done it myself, but I was worried about damaging it."

Jill nodded. "Not a problem. Sorry it took so long. Since it wasn't official work business, I had to fit it in around other projects and keep others from noticing it, or everyone would have wanted to see it. Why'd your dad put it in such an ugly modern binding?"

"I don't know," Cat said. "He died before he could tell me anything about it."

Eliza squeezed her hand. "We think he was trying to keep it a secret," she piped up. "If you saw it on a bookshelf as it is now, you'd pass it right over, right?"

Jill shrugged. "Yeah, probably. Why would it need to be a secret? What does it say? I took a gander at the first page, but didn't get very far. My Latin is far rustier than yours, Cat—I only took those two semesters."

Cat pulled out the copy of the first page and read it. She didn't need to look at the Latin. In truth, she'd memorized the translation she'd written down that first morning.

"'In her hands she holds
The greatest power of them all.
The ability to create
That which all want but few attain.
Helped by God she writes the letters
And the Word becomes Flesh
Bringing Love to all who seek it.'"

"Wow." Jill's eyes were round and full. "Heavy duty. But what is it? Sounds Biblical." She took a drink of her Coke.

"Yeah, that's what I thought at first, too," Cat answered. "But the few stories I read before giving it to you all revolve around love in some way—and not in the Christian sense, but more in the Eliza-type-of-book sense."

"You're reading medieval smut?" Jill choked down a laugh. "Dang, my soda shot up my nose. Oww!" She reached for a napkin.

Eliza chortled. "Serves her right for all the grief she's given me about my reading choices that when she finds a centuries-old book, it's all about romance."

"What I find intriguing," Cat said, ignoring her friends' needling, "is that at the front of every story the illumination shows a woman writing. Isn't that cool? Many people think only educated men, and mostly men of the Church at that, served as scribes in that time period. Yet here this woman is, writing down these stories."

"Do you have any sense of the history of the book?" Jill asked. "Wanna leave it here and let us do some research?"

Possessiveness overtook Cat with an intensity that startled her. The book was hers. *Hers.* "Um, no, thank you," she said in as nonchalant a manner as she could muster. "I'm going to work with it a little while longer. If I need help, I know where to find you."

Good Lord, I feel like Gollum from The Hobbit, not wanting to lose my Precious. She needed to get a grip.

"OK, no biggie. I've gotta head back to work in a few minutes, but tell me about these guys Eliza tells me you've been seeing. A lonely single girl wants to know all."

"I'm still a lonely single girl, too," Cat said. "One date and one, erm, evening does not a lifetime of bliss make."

"Yeah, yeah, whatever. Start talking."

Cat briefly sketched out the details of Derrick and Grayson, but skirted over much of Poetry Night, and what had come after.

Jill regarded her with a cross of admiration and envy on her face. "You go, girl! What's your secret?" Jill said.

Cat shrugged. "I don't know. I just felt ready. I don't know why."

"It's certainly helped that three guys are suddenly chasing you," Eliza said.

"Three?" Jill echoed, raising her eyebrows.

"There are no three. There is no chasing," Cat scoffed. "I'm not interested in Derrick, and Grayson isn't truly interested in me, at least not as much as he's interested in his work. I was merely a—what do the kids call it these days?—a booty call to him." Under her breath, she added to Eliza, "And as to the third, we've already discussed that."

Cat fell silent, taking a sip of her coffee as an excuse to avoid further discussion. Why *were* guys like Derrick and Grayson pursuing her? It didn't make any sense, given the dearth of male attention in the last six years. Eliza's undergrad roommate, Joy, whom Cat had met a few times, would probably say Cat was giving off different vibes to the universe, ones sending out a signal that she was available. Joy was into that stuff: reiki and chakras and auras, and all that.

Cat didn't know if she believed that, although it did feel like something had changed, something she couldn't quite put her finger on.

"I'd take a booty call." Jill sighed. "I'd take any call. Not exactly a happening social scene here in the bowels of the library."

"Right there with you," Eliza said, her thumb tracing the edge of the table. After a moment, her face brightened. "But I know someday, ladies, our princes will come."

Jill snorted.

Giving Cat a meaningful glance, Eliza added, "Or knights."

"I ran into Grayson," Cat confessed as she unlocked the door to the bookstore.

"What? Where?"

"When we were in the library. Right before I came down to you and Jill."

"And you didn't tell me? What happened?"

Cat told her of the encounter, and how persistent Grayson was. "I swear, he would have had sex right there in the stacks, if he'd had his way."

Eliza gave her an odd look.

"What? I wouldn't have done it."

"No, that's not what I was thinking."

"Then what?"

Eliza hung her coat on the hook behind the door, and then turned back to Cat. "It sounds like the story you wrote. You know, the smutty one."

"I know which one you mean." She exhaled loudly. Good God, it *did* sound like that story. "What's your point?"

"I don't know. I … it's weird, you know? First Derrick, the popular high school quarterback. Now this? Being seduced by a grad student in the library? At your carrel? Exactly like in the story you wrote?"

Cat stood rooted to the spot, gaping at her friend.

"Don't you see?" Eliza gestured toward the papers Cat had tucked under her arm. "What you just read at the library? 'She writes the letters? And the words become flesh?'"

Cat's eyes widened and her mouth fell open. "No. That's impossible."

Eliza said nothing, her eyes unusually serious.

"You can't be suggesting …" She waited for Eliza to speak. When she didn't, the words burst forth from Cat in a tumble. "You think the stories I wrote are … coming true? That Derrick, that Grayson … that they're men I *created*?" She wanted to scoff, to reject it all outright. But even as she spoke, her mind raced back to Derrick. She'd freaked out on her date with him because of the similarities, hadn't she? And now Grayson. Still, there had to be a logical explanation. There had to be.

Eliza shrugged.

Cat's eyes felt as if they might pop out of her head. She grasped her hair with her hands and stared at the ceiling.

"Have you finished reading the manuscript yet?" Eliza asked. "What does it tell you?"

"I only got about halfway through it before handing it over to Jill. She's had it since then, as you know."

Eliza crossed her arms and leveled a steady gaze at her friend. "Fine, work on it now. We have time; nobody's here. What does the end of it say?"

"You want me to skip to the end?"

"Horror of horrors to you, I know," said Eliza, "but *yes*, skip to the end! Maybe it reveals something, some sort of key to this situation."

There is no situation, Cat wanted to protest. But unease spread through her. Eliza wasn't saying anything she hadn't wondered, even if she hadn't admitted it fully to herself.

"Fine," she said, walking over to the register desk. She pulled Jill's photocopies of the book out of her bag and sat down, turning to the last page. "Can you grab me a Latin dictionary off of the shelf?"

As Eliza rushed to get the book, Cat pulled a pencil out of the pens and pencils jar. She started to translate.

> "'*From her beginning to her end,*
> *The power remains with she who has been chosen.*
> *Use it carefully.*
> *As you sow, so shall you reap.*
> *Give and receive.*
> *Write and believe.*
> *Love has much to teach you. Learn from it.*
> *And open your heart to what may be.*'"

The two women sat quietly, both staring at the ornate illustration drawn underneath the final words. It was of a woman with long, wavy brunette hair and gray eyes, seated on a throne-like chair and holding a book in her left hand, a quill in her right. She stared out from the page with a commanding gaze. Cat turned the book to the left and to the right. *I swear her eyes are following mine.*

"She looks like you," Eliza murmured, tracing her finger over the woman's face.

"Eliza, come on. She does not. This is insane." Except she did, in a stylized, medieval sort of way.

"Whatever you say. I'm rather fond of my theory, myself."

"Theory?"

"That you've been given the power to create the Perfect Man." She patted her friend on the shoulder. "Could you please make a Darcy of my very own for me? I don't ask for much. Just a duke. In England. Who's wealthy. With his own Pemberley. And who lives at the same time as Jane Austen, because I've always wanted to meet her, you know."

"Eliza …" A nervous giggle bubbled in Cat's throat. Her friend was putting her on. Right?

"Okay, yeah." Eliza exhaled heavily. "It's much more likely all my fanciful notions are exactly that—fanciful—and that you knew Derrick twenty years ago, and that Grayson is an odd coincidence. A … very odd coincidence. I mean, come on. Even *I* know my romance novels are just that—novels."

She tapped her finger against her lips. "But there's a side of me that has always believed in ghosts, always wondered about paranormal phenomena, always wondered if time travel was truly possible. And that side of me has tingles up and down my spine."

Cat set the book back on the end table. Eliza wasn't the

only one with tingles, but Cat wasn't about to admit that out loud. "You can have your fantasies. I'm going to stick to reality, which tells me the only logical explanation—the only *possible* explanation—is exactly what you said; I took something I knew of at the time and wove a stupid story about it. That's all. And Grayson certainly isn't the only grad student ever looking to get some tail."

Eliza giggled.

"What are you laughing at?"

"You, friend. I'm thinking it's *you* who can have her fantasies now, not I."

Eliza ducked before the pencil could hit her.

They both burst out laughing. After a moment, Cat sobered, chewing on a new pencil as she stared down at the manuscript.

"It's true that I don't know how to explain it. And that it seems weird to me, too." Not that some medieval book of love stories had anything to do with it.

"The Law of Attraction," Eliza said, snapping her fingers. "Maybe you've been attracting what you thought you wanted."

"I wanted a guy stuck in high school, and a guy anxious to score as quickly as possible? I need higher aspirations." She didn't dare mention wanting a computer scientist already spoken for. Eliza would have a field day with that.

"Well, you *were* thinking about them, right? I mean, having just rediscovered your stories and all. It's not so far-fetched that you put those vibes out into the universe and got an answer back."

Cat rolled her eyes. "Are you going all new-agey on me?"

"Hey, Joy was always talking about what the universe gives us, and what we give the universe. Who's to say it isn't true?"

Cat mulled that over. It was a pretty feeble explanation.

Better than believing characters you wrote about years ago have come to life. Because that's *completely insane.*

Eliza ran her fingers along the top of one of the nearby bookshelves. "You could always test it, you know."

"Test *what?*"

Her friend peeked at her out of lowered eyes. "Whether the book and those stories you wrote are somehow connected to Derrick and Grayson."

Cat snorted. "Give it up, Eliza."

"It wouldn't hurt to try, would it?"

Cat stared at her. She was serious, wasn't she? Everything in Cat wanted to laugh out loud, to scoff at Eliza's ridiculous suggestion.

On the other hand, Eliza was right: Cat had nothing to lose. Plus, she'd delight in teasing her friend about this for years to come, suggesting a book was a magic matchmaker. With her mouth tipping up in a smug grin, she shrugged. "You're right. But how would I test it?"

"Write something into the stories that wasn't there before and see if reality changes."

"Brilliant. I'll do that. If only to prove to you that I, in fact, cannot break all the rules of human reality." She burst into uncontrollable giggles, at the same time as the door jiggled and a couple of college kids entered.

"But not now." She nodded toward the customers, attempting to regain her composure. "I know you have your evening seminar tonight, so let's, um, talk about this again in the morning, okay?"

"Sure thing," Eliza said as she grabbed her coat back off the hook. "I've gotta go talk with Professor Avery about my dissertation chapter, anyway." She cast a glance at the college students, who were chattering amongst themselves. "But I'm not letting you off the hook. First, the test. And then, my duke."

"Uh, Eliza? Prepare for disappointment."

Eliza winked as she opened the door. "We'll see."

CHAPTER 12

The next morning as they entered the coffee shop, Cat stopped short. Derrick was sitting in the corner—with the cheerleader. *Candy.* Sickly-sweet.

"I guess he got the message that you weren't interested," Eliza said.

The woman said something to Derrick, who turned and looked right at Cat. He gave her a little wave, said something back to the cheerleader, then stood up and began walking toward them.

"He's coming over here," whispered Eliza.

"Um, I can see that," Cat answered. Smoothing her hair back, she told herself she had nothing to be nervous about. Nothing to be nervous about. Besides the fact that Eliza thought she'd made this guy up. *Ha. As if.*

Derrick stopped a few feet before her, looking unsure about whether or not he should approach her.

"Hi, Derrick." Cat attempted to sound relaxed.

He rocked back and forth on his heels as if nervous, but

answered her with a smile. "Hey. Nice to see you. It's been a while. I figured when you didn't call …" He trailed off.

"Yeah." She paused for a second. "It wasn't you, it was me. I guess I'm not ready to be involved with anyone." *I'm such a liar.* She smiled politely at him.

"Derrick, did they call you something else in high school?" Eliza interrupted. "You know, like, did you have a nickname?"

Derrick frowned.

"Did they?" she persisted.

"Yeah." He squinted, confusion written on his face. "Ricky. I told Cat that."

"The girl that you dated? Abby? What did she look like?"

Derrick's eyes danced back and forth between her and Eliza. "You told her about Abby?" he said to Cat.

She shifted, crossing her arms across her chest. "Yeah. I'm sorry, was it a secret?"

Why was Eliza grilling him?

Eliza didn't give up. "What did she look like?" she repeated.

His lips narrowed. "A little like Cat, actually. Same color hair and grey eyes. Her hair was short, though."

"Buzzed in the back?" Cat broke in, unease snaking its way through her veins. She'd had her hair quite short in high school, a rebellion against the mullet from her middle school days. Looking at pictures from either era made her wince.

"Uh, yeah. Look, why are you asking me these questions? I just wanted to say hi and wish you well, no hard feelings."

"Oh, sorry," Eliza said, managing to sound flippant. "We were trying to figure out if we knew you or Abby back then."

"I don't remember either of you." He paused, his eyebrows furrowing. "Wait, didn't we go to different schools?"

"Yeah," Eliza said. "Guess we didn't know you after all. Oh, well."

Glancing back at Candy, who was starting to look impatient, he said, "I should get back. Cat, um, you remember Candy?"

"Yes," Cat answered, giving Candy a friendly wave and a wide smile to reassure her she had nothing to worry about. "Give her our best."

"Will do," he responded, before walking back to his table.

Cat remained rooted to the floor, smiling an unnatural smile.

Eliza yanked on her elbow, pulling her toward the counter. "Relax," she whispered. "You don't want everyone in here staring at us, do you?"

Cat clutched her abdomen. "I think I need to sit down. Will you get me my regular?"

"Sure."

Cat staggered toward a window booth, her stomach whirling. Her mind struggled to make sense of it all: the stories; Derrick being Ricky; Abby. But she couldn't. It was like she was in a lucid dream—aware of everything going on around her, but with everything and everyone feeling surreal. *Maybe I am dreaming. Maybe this is just one long nightmare.*

Eliza slid into the seat across from her, handing her coffee. "I had them add butterscotch, like you like."

"Thank you," Cat mumbled, absentmindedly taking a sip, grateful for the comfortably familiar taste.

Eliza took her fork and began eating the brownie she'd ordered. "Is that proof enough? I mean, come on. Derrick was called Ricky? His girlfriend was Abby? She looked like you, and even had the same hair?"

"Lots of girls had my same hair."

Eliza snorted. "If you truly thought there was nothing going on here, you wouldn't look so shell-shocked."

"So you believe I somehow magically created these men I've been dating?"

"I've decided it's within the realm of possibility," Eliza conceded.

Something raced up Cat's spine, but whether it was excitement or fear, she wasn't quite sure. It couldn't be. Could it? This was an awful lot of coincidences in a row. The book talked about turning words into flesh. But for her, a mere human, to have *created* Derrick? "You can't make people up, Eliza."

"Apparently *you* can, Cat," Eliza cracked, laughing out loud.

Cat choked on her coffee, staring at her wide-eyed. "How can you be so calm about this? This is *crazy*. You're claiming I've done something no one but God has ever done: created another human being. Beings."

"Other people have created human beings, Cat. There's just usually a lot more, um, physical pleasure in the process." Eliza's eyes sparkled. "But I don't think we have definitive proof. It is still possible, after all, that you *had* heard of Derrick years ago, and also heard about his girlfriend, and you wove it into your story. And, well, you're right; Grayson wouldn't be the only hot-blooded male ever to roam the library stacks."

"That's true." Cat's eyes brightened. "That could be true, couldn't it?"

"Sure. But let's test it, like we said last night. Change something in the story about Grayson and see if it shows up in real life."

"Fine," Cat said, chewing on her lip. "I'll change something. But it won't do anything." *It won't. The mere idea is insane.* "Plus, I haven't seen Grayson since the library. Who knows if we'll ever cross paths again?" She couldn't believe she was considering this. It was all so bizarre, so silly.

"Maybe not. But it wouldn't hurt to try." Eliza swirled her latte with her spoon, her lips pursed in thought. "I think you should change something minor, something not likely to affect your relationship with him directly."

Cat rolled her eyes, still not believing they were talking about this. "Like what?"

"I don't know, maybe his area of study? No, that would mess things up if he weren't quoting sexy poetry to you. Maybe something about his family?"

Cat hesitated for a moment. "I remember him telling me he was an only child. I could give him a sister."

"Yes!" Eliza said. "But how about making her a twin? That would be harder to chalk up to coincidence, in case you're misremembering him claiming only-child status. You always say your memory isn't the best."

Cat gave her a baleful look. "True," she conceded, then took a sip of her drink. "All right, a sister. What should we name her?"

"I think you should decide that, Cat. I'm pretty sure I don't have your magic powers."

Cat kicked her under the table. "Don't underestimate yourself. You certainly have the power to annoy me."

Eliza stuck her tongue out. "Right back atcha."

Setting her mug down, Cat said, "Okay, we've dawdled long enough. Let's go open up. I'll work on editing my, um, story during our lulls." *As if it's going to do anything. Hah.* She looked out at the cold, gray rain that had begun. "Given the gloomy weather, we might have a lot of lulls. Nobody likes November rain."

As they stood up, Cat noticed Candy glaring at her from across the room. Cat tossed her another wide smile.

"Think of what I could do to her man if I really could change people," she said to Eliza with a chortle. "The power. The sheer power. I could make him stupid. I could take away his hair. Heck, I could make him gay!"

"Sure, your highness. Or holiness. Or whatever I should call you. But remember, as Spiderman said, 'With great power comes great responsibility.'"

"As my sister would say, 'Screw that!'" Cat retorted. "What good is this alleged ability if I can't give a guy blue hair and three eyeballs?"

"Oh, my goodness, I've created a monster. And monster, thy name is Catherine!" Eliza shrugged on her jacket, looking out the coffee shop's front window as she did so. "Hey, check out the limo."

"What limo?"

Eliza gestured toward the window, through which the Treasure Trove was visible. "Earth to Cat. The limo that just pulled up in front of our store."

"Oh, yeah. That limo. Wonder why it's there? That's not a parking spot."

"Maybe when you have a limo, you don't care."

They watched as a sprightly older gentleman hopped out of the driver's seat, opened an umbrella, and walked around to the right side of the vehicle. He pulled open the back door, and a tall, elegantly dressed man stepped out, accepting the umbrella from the driver. The man paused to adjust his suit jacket before he started walking up the stairs to the bookstore.

"Holy cow, he's going into our store!" Eliza exclaimed.

"Not unless we're there to unlock it. C'mon, let's go." Cat grabbed her friend by the elbow and pulled her out the door.

After opening their own umbrellas, the two women walked as quickly as they could across the street. As Cat reached the bottom stair, the man, who had been inspecting the hours sign, turned to come back down, a disappointed expression on his face.

"We're here," Cat called, taking the steps two at a time. "We ducked across the street for a mid-morning pick-me-up. Sorry!" As she reached the top of the stairs, she fumbled in her pocket with her right hand for her keys, while holding her coffee and umbrella in the left.

"Here, let me help you," a melodious voice said. Cat looked up as the man took the umbrella from her hands. He had folded his own umbrella under his arm, and did the same with hers, then took her drink.

Ralph Fiennes. He resembled a young Ralph Fiennes. *The English Patient* Fiennes, not Voldemort Fiennes. She stifled a giggle as she imagined this impeccably groomed man with no nose.

He looked at her, a curious expression on his face.

Eliza, who'd just reached the landing, gave him an impish grin. "Hi! Sorry about that."

He glanced at Eliza. "It's not a problem," he replied, as Cat opened the door. Taking hold of the edge, he ushered them through. Following the women in, he continued, "I'm just glad to find you here."

"What's with the limo?" Eliza said. Cat elbowed her subtly. Eliza ignored her, keeping her eyes fixed on the stranger.

"The university hired that for me," he said as he handed Cat back her umbrella and drink. "I've been guest lecturing at the Darden business school. I asked the driver to stop here on the way back. I promise I don't usually drive around in limousines."

"Well, welcome to the Treasure Trove," Cat said brightly as Eliza hung up their umbrellas behind the door. "How may we help you?"

"I'm William Dawes. I'm looking for the Dawes family Bible I saw advertised online this morning. It said your store listed it for sale yesterday."

"I remember that one. I did that listing," Eliza broke in. She shrugged off her jacket and hung it next to the umbrellas. "It has all those beautiful old photographs in it."

"Yes. Roger Fenton did those portraits for my great-grandfather's great-grandfather."

"Roger Fenton?" Cat asked.

"Do you know of Mr. Fenton? He was a childhood friend of my great-great-great-grandfather, William. Family legend has it that Fenton invited Will and his family to pose for portraits so that he could refine his technique before he photographed Queen Victoria and her family. William's wife added those portraits to the Bible sometime after that."

"You know your ancestors back to the early nineteenth century? In England?" Eliza interjected, her eyes wide.

"Yes, ma'am," he replied politely. "We can trace our family lineage back to Henry VIII's time. Or at least my grandmother can. She's been the family historian for years."

He looked over at Cat. "She's the one who donated a box to Goodwill years ago that she thinks must have had that family Bible in it. She'd wrapped it in a blanket to protect it, and somehow the blanket ended up in the wrong box. Grandma was traumatized to discover it was gone. That's why I'm here: to retrieve it."

Cat frowned. "That Bible is a first-edition Regency Bible, featuring plates by Richard Westall. My father found it at an estate sale over twelve years ago."

The corner of William's mouth cocked up in a wry smile. "I take it you don't believe me, Ms. …?"

"Schreiber. Catherine Schreiber. And it's not that I don't

believe you, it's that the Bible is worth a small fortune to a bookseller like me."

"Oh, I'm prepared to compensate you for it. My grandmother would give anything to have it back in the family's possession. I've been searching for it for her for years."

Cat relaxed.

Eliza, to her right, was practically bursting with excitement. "What did this great-great-whatever grandfather do, Mr. Dawes?"

William turned to her. "Something with railroads, I believe, Ms. …?"

"Eliza James." Her voice lost some of its enthusiasm.

He cocked an eyebrow at her. "You sound disappointed?"

Eliza gave an embarrassed little laugh. "I'm sorry. I was hoping he was an earl or a duke, or something like that."

Catherine blew her bangs out of her eyes. "Eliza loves anything that's to do with the Regency period. Especially the peerage."

William adjusted the cuff of his suit jacket. "Actually, William's father *was* an earl, if I remember correctly. But William was the youngest son of four, so no title for him. Sorry."

Eliza gazed at him raptly while clasping her hands in front of her. "A real earl? Wow."

Catherine laughed, disrupting Eliza from her fantasies. "Did this earl run off with a governess, Mr. Dawes?"

"Uh, no. At least not to my knowledge." His eyebrows crinkled in confusion.

Eliza elbowed her friend. "She's just teasing me about my reading genre of choice, Mr. Dawes. Ignore her."

William reached down to pet Elvis, who was weaving in and out of his legs.

"Nice cat. We had one like him when I was a kid, a Maine

Coon. Einstein," he commented, scratching the cat behind its ears. "Anyway, may I see the Bible to ensure it is indeed the one for which I've been searching?"

"Sure thing. Give me just a moment." Cat turned to walk to the back storage room where they kept their online inventory. *A man who doesn't dangle prepositions. A modern rarity.*

After locating the Bible, Cat reentered the main room to find Eliza and William chatting. Eliza was twirling a tendril of her hair around her finger in the way she did when she found someone attractive.

Oh, my. Now that Eliza knows he's related to the peerage, there's no hope for him. Cat gave a little snort as she held the book out to William.

They turned toward her. Eliza frowned, then turned crimson as Cat raised an eyebrow at her. *Yeah, she knows what I was thinking.*

William gingerly took the Bible into his hands and opened the cover. "Yes, here's my great-great-grandfather as a baby. And here's his mother, Rebecca, with my great-great-great-grandfather on their wedding day in 1867." He looked up at Cat, excitement radiating from his face. "This is wonderful."

"Happy to be able to help," Cat answered.

"I'd like to offer you five thousand dollars for it."

"Five thousand?" she gasped. "But it was listed for half that."

"I know, but you have no idea how happy this will make my grandmother. It's obvious you have taken excellent care of it; I see no sign of damage whatsoever. It's the least I can do."

"All right," she answered slowly. That, plus the *Pooh* book sale, would cover expenses for at least a couple of months, and let her keep on the high school girl, Emily, whom she'd hired over the summer to help out now and then. Her muscles relaxed as tension eased out of her body.

"And dinner. I'd like to take you to dinner."

"Me?" she squeaked in surprise. Hadn't he been eyeing Eliza earlier?

Eliza grimaced, but gave her friend an encouraging nod. "At least this time you didn't have to endure nearly drowning to secure an invitation."

William cocked an eyebrow.

"Never mind," Cat replied to the silent question. "Um …" She hesitated. He was definitely Fiennes-like, a truly handsome man. But out of her league. She eyed him head-to-toe. His suit had probably cost as much as the Bible. She wouldn't be surprised if it was Armani, or Dolce and Gabbana.

He took out his checkbook. "If you are not interested, I understand," he said. "Will you take a personal check? I can provide ID."

"Yes," Cat answered. "Yes, we will take a check."

As he was writing out the check, Eliza grabbed her elbow and pulled her to the side. "You didn't write any more stories that I don't know about, did you?" she whispered hurriedly.

"Uh, no. Don't think so."

"Because he seems like he'd be right out of one."

Cat sighed. He rather did.

William pulled the check free from the checkbook and extended it to Cat before she had a chance to answer Eliza. Walking back to him, she paused. She shouldn't let the Grayson debacle keep her down. Plus—not that she believed any of this magic book stuff—it was nice to know that no man resembling this wealthy, well-mannered, attractive gentleman before her appeared in any of the papers from that box.

"And yes," she blurted out as she took the check. "Yes, I will go out to dinner with you."

He smiled. "Thank you, Catherine. How is Saturday?"

"Saturday's good," she replied.

Eliza beamed at her.

"Wonderful. I'll pick you up here at 5:00 p.m. I'm looking forward to it." Settling the Bible under his arm, he strolled out of the store, closing the door behind him.

Cat raced to the window, watching him open his umbrella before descending the stairs. *Why would a man such as that be interested in a small-town bookstore owner like me?*

"You're sure you never wrote more stories?" Eliza called from behind her.

Cat exhaled. "Seriously, Eliza? Are you going to claim every man I run into now is one I made up?"

Eliza's eyebrows puckered. "You don't need to take that tone. And no, of course not—I know perfectly well you are an amazing catch and any man would be lucky to have you. It's just, well … three in a row?"

Tingles ran up Cat's arms. Eliza was right; it *was* odd to receive so much male attention after such a long drought. But to say she had magical powers connected to a medieval manuscript?

Before she could say anything else, Eliza enveloped her in a giant hug. "Whatever the reason," she said, "you deserve it."

Cat's eyes welled up as she returned the hug. "So do you, Eliza. So do you."

"Oh, I know." Eliza sniffed as she stepped back. "My time will come. I trust in that. I think it's your time, now."

Cat thought of Derrick, and Grayson. And William. And Ben Cooper.

Ben. She hadn't seen him in the coffee shop since the time he'd overheard her confession about Grayson. Just remembering that brought heat to her cheeks; talk about mortifying.

It was strange, how frequently she thought of Ben. Why *did* he pop into her mind so often, especially when he had a girlfriend, which rendered him strictly off limits? It didn't make sense.

Maybe it was that he reminded her a bit of her father. Her dad had always been quick to offer help whenever he could. Ben's easygoing, relaxed personality was reminiscent of Frank's. He and Ben even seemed to share a similar sense of humor. Luddy, indeed. She could totally see her father calling her that. Yes, that had to be what drew her mind back to him again and again.

Except her feelings weren't exactly familial when it came to Mr. Cooper, if she were honest with herself. Which she didn't want to be.

Lost in her own thoughts, Eliza's voice startled her. "I'm going to go unpack that new shipment. And maybe ponder more about what kind of hero I'm going to have you write for me." She spun in a circle, ending it with a hop, before she bounced toward the back.

Cat laughed. "Fantasize away," she called after her friend's retreating form. "No matter what I write, that's what they'll remain. Fictional fantasies."

Eliza merely waved a hand back at her.

At least in Ben's case she was sure it couldn't have anything to do with any fantasies she'd written. Not that she truly believed the others did, but still … She knew without a doubt that a love story centered around a computer science professor had never crossed her mind. She snorted as images of computer nerds flooded her brain. Until a certain jeans-clad backside suddenly chased those images away.

She traced her finger along the raindrop paths on the window.

No fantasies until now, that is. Great.

Chapter 13

"Package for you, Cat," Eliza called out, as she breezed into the apartment the next evening, dropping a rectangular box on the side table.

Cat wandered out from the kitchen. "From whom?" she said, munching on a carrot stick.

"I dunno. There's no return label on it." Eliza hung up her coat, and then reached down to pet the cat. "It's not heavy, so I don't think it's books. Open it. Open it!"

Laughing, Cat picked up the box. "I will, I will." She pulled off the brown paper packaging to reveal a white box with a designer name emblazoned across the top.

"Versace?" Eliza squealed. "Are you serious?" She hopped up and down in her excitement. "Open it already."

Cat slid her fingers under the edges of the lid and removed it. Nestled in tissue paper inside was something black, with a small note card on top of which was printed in a crisp, clean hand, *Saw this and thought of you. Looking forward to Saturday—Dawes.*

Dawes? He signs a personal note to a date as Dawes?

Cat pulled the fabric out of the box.

"Ooh!" Eliza clapped her hands. "It's a little black dress. Shake it out. Hold it up!"

Discarding the box, Cat smoothed the dress down across the front of her body. It *was* gorgeous, she conceded, a form-fitting black sheath rendered elegant rather than overtly sexy by the black lace netting that ran across the upper bodice and formed long sleeves.

Eliza sighed, running her hands down her abdomen. "What I would give to be able to wear a dress like that. It wouldn't forgive my, um, tummy. Or these hips. You, however, will look beautiful in it. Go try it on."

"I don't know, Eliza."

"C'mon, just try it."

Reluctantly, Cat headed to her bedroom and slipped the dress on. Much to her surprise, it fit her like a glove. It was more revealing than anything she would normally wear, that was for sure, but she had to concede she looked *good*. She twirled around to check out her backside as Eliza walked into the room, laptop in tow.

"Cat," she gasped. "I looked it up on the Internet. That dress retails for over fifteen hundred dollars."

"Are you serious? Oh, my Lord, who *is* this guy?"

"Wait, I'll Google him." Eliza typed quickly on the keyboard. "Here he is. Oh my God, girlfriend, he's a bigwig. Listen to this:

"*William Dawes VII, partner with his father, Mr. Bill Dawes VI, in Dawes Wealth Management, has announced the acquisition of Bluebird Software for fifty million dollars. William Dawes V made millions in the stock market in the 1930s and 1940s through his investments in the General Dynamic*

Electric Boat Company, which crafted submarines for the U.S. Navy.'"

Cat interrupted her. "Where are you finding this?" she demanded, moving around to read the screen.

"It's right here in Wikipedia." Eliza looked at her with wide eyes. "This guy is *loaded*, Cat."

"Uh, the five grand he paid for a Bible didn't tell you that?"

"Well, yeah. I just didn't think he was *this* loaded."

"Should I propose tomorrow, then?"

Eliza gaped at her.

"Oh, good Lord, I'm kidding, Eliza. This is not a romance novel, and one dinner doesn't mean we're destined for each other." She moved to shrug out of the dress. "I don't think I should accept this. This is all a little too *Pretty Woman*-ish."

"Oh, Cat." Eliza threw her hands in the air. "You look fabulous. Accept it. Wear it. If not for him, then for me." She flopped down on the bed.

Cat laughed. "All right. For you, darling," she said in an overdone French accent. "How about we go grab a bite to eat after I change? I hear that new Chinese place over on Fourteenth Street is pretty good."

"Yeah, sounds good. I'll call Jill and Shannon."

"Great. Just don't tell them about the dress, okay? I'll never live it down."

"So what's your secret, Cat?" Shannon asked before taking a bite of Tso's chicken.

"Secret? What do you mean?"

"Oh, come on. Jill's filled me in on all the details. You

haven't had a date in, what, years? And suddenly you have three men hot after you?"

Cat shifted in her chair. "I wouldn't say *hot* after me."

Jill broke in. "Uh, I would. Given Eliza's retelling of poetry night? *Hello*."

Cat glared at Eliza across the table, who at least had the grace to blush as she quickly popped a spring roll into her mouth. "You *told* them?"

Since Eliza was chewing, Cat turned to Jill. "She *told* you?"

"Yeah," Jill retorted. "You weren't giving enough details over coffee."

"Wouldn't you want us to tell you if something that exciting happened to one of us?" said Shannon.

"Shannon, you're married. You have two kids. Something like that had better *not* happen to you," Cat pointed out.

"Ha, thanks for the reminder. Scott knows I adore him. But back to my question: what's your secret? Inquiring minds want to live vicariously. And Jill needs a date, too."

Jill frowned at Shannon. "Well, yeah, I would like to meet someone," she admitted as she picked at her fried rice. "Rare books are fun and all, but they don't keep me warm at night."

Cat picked up her water glass to sip from it. "In all honesty," she said, "I have no idea. You know I'm not looking for anyone. It's been as much a surprise to me as to you."

Eliza piped up. "And they've all been hot. You should *see* the grad student. And the date for this Saturday—he's super-rich."

Cat kicked her under the table.

Eliza let out a small yelp. "Oh, come on, Cat. Don't most women dream about those kinds of men coming to sweep them off their feet?"

"I don't know about most. We know you do, Lizzie, what

with your reading genre of choice." Cat was grateful Eliza hadn't blurted out her theory about the medieval manuscript; she didn't want to have to think about that, much less explain it to their friends. She paused for a moment. "Maybe I did want that when I was younger. Before, you know …"

The three other women at the table nodded. "We get how hard that was for you, Cat," Shannon said. "But not all men are like that. Look at my Scott."

Cat had to agree with that. Shannon had snagged a man who was devoted to her and their kids, and the other women at the table openly admitted envy when watching them together. "Maybe," she conceded. "I have to admit, it's been kind of fun."

"I'll take an order of that kind of fun," Jill quipped. "But for now, tell us about Saturday. Where are you going?"

"No idea. He's picking me up at 5:00."

"Five? Isn't that kind of early for a date?"

"Believe me," Eliza broke in. "If you had met the guy, you'd go on a date no matter what the time. I think he's Cat's knight in shining armor."

An image of Ben waving his imaginary sword, slaying Internet dragons, popped into Cat's head. Maybe Eliza had been right; maybe Ben had truly been interested. Jeez, did she think every man she saw wanted to bed her? Besides, He. Had. A. Girlfriend.

"Hey, isn't that Ben over there?" Eliza exclaimed. She leaned into the table and lowered her voice. "He's with a woman."

Jill and Shannon turned at the same time to check out the back corner where Eliza had surreptitiously pointed.

"Stop it, you two, he'll notice," hissed Cat. Her shoulders tensed.

"Who's Ben?" Jill asked. "You've got *another* guy in the mix?"

"No, I don't. He's a professor here at the university who came over and fixed our computer system one day, that's all," protested Cat, even as her ears started to burn. She took a deep breath. She had to admit she was curious. But unless she turned completely around, she wouldn't be able to see him, and doing so was out of the question. That didn't stop Shannon and Jill from glancing again and again, though.

"Ooh, I think she's his girlfriend," Eliza said.

"Told you he had a girlfriend." Cat smirked at Eliza, attempting to ignore the mixed feelings that statement aroused.

"No, it's a different woman, not the one we saw in the coffee shop."

Wow. The guy gets around. Cat whipped her head around without thinking, her eyes locking instantly with Ben's. His brow furrowed. She turned back to the table, determined not to look again. Her stomach knotted.

"She just put her hand over his on the table," Eliza said. "Now she's laughing at something he said, and he's smiling at her. And now … Oh, crap!"

"What?" Cat whispered.

"He's looking over here. I think he saw us staring at him." Eliza waved.

Cat focused on the fried rice in front of her. "Now what is he doing?" She was careful not to move her head in his direction. Goose bumps raced up her arms, but she didn't know if they stemmed from tension or excitement.

"Well, he and his date are getting up. I guess they're done. No, wait. They're coming our way."

Great. No big deal, Cat. He's just a friend, anyway.

After a few seconds, Cat heard that deep voice at her side. "Good evening, ladies. Enjoying a night out, I see?"

Cat turned and looked up at him. His eyes fixed on hers. She could feel her friends turn to focus on her, as well. She stared up at him, her gaze dropping from his eyes to his mouth. Anything to avoid this discomfort.

Nobody said anything. "Yes, we get together at least once a month," she finally answered, feeling lame. Why weren't her friends talking? "How are you? We haven't seen you in the coffee shop in a while." Ugh. She shouldn't have brought that up. Now he would know that she'd noticed.

"I've been busy. May I introduce my friend, Li Mei? She's a first-year computer science professor here at the university."

Of course she is, thought Cat, an odd stab of jealousy piercing her side.

"Mei," he continued, "this is Catherine and her friend Eliza. They own the bookstore across from The Grounds, that coffee shop I told you about. And these are …"

"Their friends, Jill and Shannon," interjected Shannon. "It's nice to meet you."

"Hello," Mei said in a soft, shy voice. "It's nice to meet you, too."

Ben gently placed his hand at Mei's elbow. "We're off to see a movie. It was nice running into you. Enjoy your evening."

"Yes, you too, Ben," Eliza answered. "Hope to see you again soon."

He just nodded, glancing once more at Cat before heading out the door.

Jill exhaled slowly. "C'mon, tell us the truth. Is there something there?"

"No—" Cat started.

"—Yes!" Eliza asserted.

"No, there isn't," Cat insisted. "Besides, you can see he has a girlfriend."

"That doesn't always mean anything," Jill said.

"It does to me."

"Fine, you're right," Jill answered. "Tell me more about the grad student guy in the stacks, then." She dipped her head and arched her eyebrow. "You know how books are an aphrodisiac for me."

They all laughed. As Eliza started describing Grayson, Cat couldn't help but look out the window, trying to catch a glimpse of Ben as he drove away.

CHAPTER 14

ey, Cat, it's 4:40," Eliza called from the other room. "You'd better hurry up. Daddy Warbucks is going to be here in twenty minutes."

"He's *not* Daddy Warbucks," Cat hissed under her breath. Although now that she knew how wealthy he was, she did feel like Little Orphan Annie in comparison.

"What do you think?" she asked a short while later as she walked into the living room. "I feel awkward in heels. You know I never wear them."

Eliza looked up from her latest book and gasped. "Oh, my gosh, Catherine Schreiber, you are *gorgeous*!"

Cat twirled around to show the dress and her hair, which she'd pulled back in a simple chignon. She was head-to-toe in black: black dress, black hose, black shoes, and she'd opted to wear the silver and sapphire hoop earrings her father had given her years ago. With her hair up and jewelry on her body, and even a little eye make-up on, she *felt* gorgeous. It was a nice feeling, one she hadn't experienced in some time.

"Do you think the heels are too much? I splurged on them at Nine West."

"They're no Manolo Blahniks, but they'll do nicely."

"Mano-whats?"

"Are you serious?" Eliza twirled a piece of hair around her finger. "I know you're not much into fashion, but did you never watch *Sex in the City*?"

Cat wrinkled her nose. "Nah. Not my style. I'm more a *Bones* or *Castle* girl."

"In any case, you look great, Nine West heels and all. Just don't fall over."

"Don't curse me!"

The doorbell rang. Cat nervously adjusted her skirt and checked to ensure she had her phone in her handbag. Peeking into the mirror in the entryway, she brushed her bangs out of her eyes, and then opened the door.

"Wow." William stood in the doorway, eyeing her appreciatively. He pursed his lips and let out a breath. "You look fabulous. Even better than I had imagined you would in that dress."

Cat's face warmed with the compliment. "You don't look so bad yourself, sir."

He was clad in a well-fitted black suit with a slate blue sweater vest underneath, a long black coat over one arm. The other arm was behind his back, but he brought it forward to present her with a single white rose. "I thought this would express my gratitude that you are having dinner with me."

Cat took the rose. He was grateful that she was going out with him? It should be the other way around.

"Hello again," called Eliza from the background. "It's nice to see you, Mr. Dawes. Here, let me fetch a vase for that."

Walking over to Cat, she took the rose from her hands.

"You two have fun. And don't forget your jacket, Cat. It's getting a bit nippy out there."

"Thanks, Mom," Cat teased, but shrugged into her black Lands' End coat, wondering if it was a sin to cover Versace in such a way.

Outside a limo was waiting.

"A limo? Again?" She gave him a teasing grin.

He shrugged. "I decided this was more comfortable than a taxi for getting back and forth from the airport."

"Airport?"

"I live in D.C. It's quicker to fly than drive. At least when you fly privately."

"You live in D.C.? And you came all the way back here for a date with me?"

He grinned. *Wow, he had a sexy smile.* "You're worth it."

Cat didn't know what to say to that, so she opted for silence.

The driver had hopped out upon seeing them and now held the limo door open for them. He helped Cat get settled inside—not an easy feat when one wasn't used to a form-fitting dress and heels. William seated himself beside her.

"You said privately. Are you a pilot?"

"No, although I've taken a few lessons. My pilot, James, is very capable, though. You'll see."

I'll see? Surely we're not flying somewhere tonight? Rather than pepper him with additional questions that would reveal how out of her depth she was, she took a deep breath and nestled back into the seat.

"Ooh, it's warm," she exclaimed before she could stop herself. *God, he must think I'm a complete ninny.*

He ran his hand along the seat edge. "I know, isn't it great? Whoever invented seat warmers in cars should be awarded the Nobel Prize."

The lights of Charlottesville passed by as they rode. They asked each other simple questions about their families. She learned he was the oldest of four, with two middle sisters and a younger brother, all of whom worked in what he referred to as the family firm. He was so attentive and comfortable to be with that she shared about the loss of her father, and how she missed her family out in Ohio.

They passed Hollymead Town Center at the north end of town. "May I ask where we are going? Most of the restaurants I know are back that way."

"Sure," William replied, as the limo turned onto Airport Road. "I thought I'd take you to this Italian place I like. Sound good?"

"Yes, I love Italian."

"Good. It shouldn't take us too long to get there, maybe forty-five minutes by plane."

"By plane? We *are* flying?"

William chuckled. "Yes, as long as that's good with you. The restaurant's in Harlem."

Cat clasped her hands together, excitement pulsing through her veins. "Harlem? As in New York? You're taking me to New York City? *Tonight*?"

The limo pulled up to the departures entrance and the driver stepped out to open the door. As William helped her from the car, she gave him a spontaneous hug. "This is going to be so great. I've never been to New York."

"I'm glad you approve of the plan." He held her close for a brief moment before stepping back. "I hope you enjoy being with me, as well."

Her cheeks prickled in embarrassment and she bit her lip in chagrin—she hadn't meant to act more excited about the city than the date.

"No worries," he reassured her. "I'm excited, too. It's been a while since I've been to the city for anything other than business."

Less than an hour later, they were ensconced in yet another limousine, heading from LaGuardia west into the city. It was hard not to act like a kid peering into a candy shop with her nose against the window. William had been telling her how his grandmother had burst into tears upon receiving the family Bible back last week, but broke off to start playing tour guide as her eyes darted everywhere.

"It's dark. What are you expecting to see?" he kidded her gently. "But on our left is St. Michael's Cemetery, burial place of Scott Joplin. And now, a bunch of interstate and buildings here and there."

Cat laughed.

"And now," he continued, "a very long bridge over water."

She elbowed him.

Realizing that there wasn't much to see beyond headlights and taillights, she turned away from the window and asked him about his work. "What exactly *is* wealth management?"

"People pay us to tell them how to invest their money."

"Really? Sounds—"

"—Boring, I know. Sometimes it is. But I have a head for figures." He shrugged. "And it makes my dad happy to have his kids working with him."

"He must be proud of you, and you him." Envy stabbed through her at all the time she'd lost with her dad.

"Yes, that's true. I'm lucky there. On the other hand, all my siblings are married, and my younger brother is about to become a father, so in some ways I feel as if I'm missing out."

She could relate to that. "Haven't met that special someone yet, huh?" she asked in a teasing voice.

He paused before answering. "It's hard to know if someone likes me for me, or likes me for, you know." He gestured around the limousine.

She nodded. "Yeah, that makes sense."

"That's one of the reasons I wanted to have dinner with you. It was clear you had no idea who I was."

"Okay, but the Bible and the dress and the clothing you wore tipped me off that you weren't exactly in the poorhouse, William."

"True. But most women pursue me because of my name."

"Don't sell yourself short, Mr. Warbucks. You're pretty easy on the eyes."

"Mr. Warbucks?" His mouth tipped up in amusement.

Catherine wanted to melt into the seat. "Um, that's what Eliza calls you. She Googled you."

"Ah, so you *do* know who I am. Glad to see a mercenary gleam is still absent from your eyes. And Mr. Warbucks amuses me, as it would my oldest sister. She always tells me I should run an animal shelter, because I want to take care of all the stray cats and dogs I see. They're orphans, right?"

Hmm. Am I just a stray to him? I do feel kind of like a mutt sitting with a purebred at the moment. She shook the thoughts off, reminding herself that tonight, at least, she was Cinderella at the ball. If tomorrow she were sitting in pumpkin remains wearing tattered rags, so be it. For now, she was going to enjoy herself.

The limo eased over to a corner. "We're here," William announced.

Cat glanced out the window, expecting some sort of large, glamorous nightspot cordoned off by ropes. Instead, a cozy-looking dining nook nestled at the bottom of an unassuming apartment building. It was painted a rich tomato red, and had large white letters across its top illuminated by small spotlights. She liked it immediately.

"Joey's? Is that it?"

"Yes, ma'am. Finest Italian cuisine in the city."

"Great, I'm famished."

"I am, too. Glad you brought an appetite."

After helping her from the car, William spoke briefly to the chauffeur, who nodded and drove off.

"He'll be back when we call," William said, presenting his elbow to Cat.

Arm-in-arm, they descended the few steps to the door, which an impeccably dressed older gentleman opened. He spread his arms in a welcoming gesture upon recognizing William. "Mr. Dawes, nice to see you again."

"Thank you, you too, Joey. It's been too long." He turned to Cat. "Joey, this is my friend, Catherine. Catherine, Joey, owner."

"It's nice to meet you, Catherine. Come in, come in; get settled."

Cat stared at the man. He seemed familiar. As they entered the restaurant, it struck her—he'd been in that mob show on HBO. She had to stop herself from gawking at the first famous actor she'd ever seen in person, so she turned to survey the room. It was small, holding maybe eight or ten tables, but was packed with people. At the bar, a man wearing a flashy gold vest waved at Joey and Will, and then went back to mixing a drink. The walls were covered with photos of celebrities, people she presumed had eaten here over the years. The smell of cigar smoke was in the air—not her favorite, but she'd manage, because she loved the music emanating from a black jukebox over in the corner, and it was clear everyone here was having a raucously good time.

Will led her to a small table covered with a white tablecloth nestled between two high-backed, darkly stained wooden booths. "I hope this place meets with your approval. The meatballs here are to die for," he said as they sat down.

"Are you kidding? I love it! It feels so homey. And I love that the Christmas lights are up already, although it's not even Thanksgiving."

He chuckled. "They're up year-round. Part of the charm, I guess."

Joey pulled up a chair and told them about the evening's specials. "Wine?" he asked after taking their orders.

"Actually, it gives me headaches, unless it's sparkling," Cat answered. "So I'll just stick with water."

"We've got Cristal." Joey raised his eyebrows toward Will.

"Sound great, Joey, thanks."

Cat continued to people-watch. She couldn't wait to tell Eliza about the thick Brooklyn accents surrounding her. At the table next to them, three men were engaged in an animated conversation about the Yankees versus the Mets. In the back, men in suits looked to be in serious but congenial negotiations of some sort.

Her eyes returned to Will. "Are they Mafia?" she whispered.

He leaned in over the table and lowered his head, as if confiding a secret. "If they are, better not to ask."

She gulped. "Good advice."

Two glasses of champagne later, Cat was quite tipsy, in spite of having eaten a huge amount of the best Italian food she'd ever had. Chatting with William came easily, almost as if they had known each other for months instead of a few hours. That's what she'd always wanted: someone with whom she was completely comfortable from the start, instead of having to worry about dating etiquette that she'd never mastered anyway.

Or having to worry that she'd made him up. She fought back a snort. She wasn't going to think about that manuscript right now. She was going to enjoy this date. Starting with more champagne.

William chuckled as her hand wobbled in its effort to get the glass to her mouth. "Maybe we ought to opt for dessert over Cristal for now?"

She grinned sloppily. "I'm sorry. This stuff is so good I just want to quaff it."

"First of all, kudos for working 'quaff' into a sentence. And second, may I say that I've never heard anyone refer to Cristal as 'stuff' before? I like it. I like you. No pretense about you."

"Wait a minute. Are you saying that this is *the* Cristal champagne? The stuff that Puff Daddy or P. Diddy—or whatever his name is now—likes to *bathe* in? Isn't it, like, super-expensive?"

He shrugged. "I can handle it. And I don't know if the bathing rumors are true, but if they are, what a waste of a delicious drink."

She scrunched her nose. "Think about the bubbles. Wouldn't it feel odd to have those bubbles tickling you in, you know, all your private places?"

Will's gaze dropped to her mouth before his green eyes rose and pierced hers. She swallowed and set the glass down. "Yeah, maybe I've reached my limit."

He reached across the table and caught her hand before she removed it from the glass. "I was just entertaining the thought of …"

He cut himself off, looking down at his own plate and smiling briefly. "Never mind, I shouldn't finish that. But tell me, Catherine. Why is such a lovely woman as you not married? Or at least not involved with someone?"

She gulped again. "I could ask you the same thing, Mr. Rich-Man-In-A-Limo," she teased. She enjoyed the feeling of his warm fingers over hers. The noise level had risen as well-fed guests indulged in numerous drinks of their own, but it felt as if they were the only two people in the room.

"I was engaged," she admitted. "Six years ago. Then my fiancé decided one woman wasn't enough for him."

Bitterness crept into her voice. "He'd had a girlfriend up in D.C. on the side for months. I didn't find out until our wedding day, the day he stood me up at the altar. What a cliché, right?

"I didn't know why he didn't show until later, when the hotel called, saying housekeeping had found a note left in our intended honeymoon suite. When I read it, I learned about Stacy." Cat practically spat the name. "He said he was in love with her and they'd run away to Vegas to elope."

She paused to fortify herself with another sip of the champagne. "It was the most embarrassing moment of my life, standing there in front of all those people—my family and his family, *our* friends—not knowing where he was or why he wasn't coming, my whole world crumbling at my feet. And he didn't even have the decency to break it off beforehand, to spare me the public humiliation."

Her eyes welled up with tears.

William let go of her hand and stood up. Her stomach flipped. Was he leaving because she'd blabbed all that to him? Why had she blurted all of that out?

He moved to her side of the booth, gathering her in his arms after he sat down. *Oh, oh. I really am going to cry.*

"I'm so sorry that happened to you, Catherine." She liked how he called her Catherine, rather than Cat. "You certainly didn't deserve it, any of it."

He sat back but remained with his hand holding hers,

facing her. "And I know how you feel."

Her eyes flew to his. "Wh-what?"

"Yes, I do. Well, I wasn't left at the altar. But my college sweetheart, with whom I was together for four years, decided my best friend was better in bed than I was. Or so she told me when I caught her with him in our condo. In our own bed." He shook his head in disgust. "Do you have any idea how emasculating it is to be told someone else is a better lover than you are? In fact, I can't believe I'm admitting that to you now. Must be the champagne."

Cat could read the pain on his face, though he acted nonchalant. "I'm sorry, William. She sounds awful."

He squeezed her hand. "It was a long time ago. I've had years and lots of practice since then." He wiggled his eyebrows in a lascivious manner.

Cat broke out laughing. The lightened mood was just what she needed.

"You seem pretty fantastic to me, Mr. Dawes." She gestured around the room. "I feel downright spoiled tonight."

"I like that about you, Ms. Schreiber, that a simple meal in a low-key restaurant can make you feel that way. It's a nice change from the women with whom I'm normally surrounded."

"Don't forget the limo," she added mischievously.

"Ah, yes, well, who could forget a limo? Speaking of limos, it's about time for us to go. We've got a plane to catch."

"What, no Broadway show?" she teased. "It is my first time in New York, after all."

"*Annie* was sold out," he shot back.

At her puzzled glance, he said, "You know, the little orphan girl. Daddy Warbucks?"

Cat laughed. "I do hope you know I was kidding about the

show, William. I don't want you think I'm anything less than thrilled with this date. It's been fabulous. An absolute dream. In fact, I keep waiting for the clock to strike midnight."

"No dream. But it *is* past eleven. We should go—I know you need to work in the morning."

"It's *how* late? I can't believe we've been here so long. It's felt like five minutes."

William stood, offering his hand to help Cat out of the booth. "I hope that means you've been enjoying yourself as much as I have."

She grabbed his hand and smiled as he pulled her up close to him. For a moment, she was sure he was going to kiss her. He stepped back, however, saying, "Don't forget your bag."

Disappointment flooded her veins. As she picked up her purse, she could hear her cell phone ringing. Ignoring it, she gathered her coat and walked with Will to the front door, pausing on the way out to thank Joey for a wonderful meal. He shook hands with them both, letting them know they were welcome back anytime.

At that moment her phone rang again. *I should have put it on silent.*

"It's all right if you want to check it," William prompted. "I don't mind."

"Well, I do. But I guess I'll see who it is."

She pulled out her phone. Both calls had been from her sister. Why would Marie call so late at night? Not only that, but she had called a number of times before. The noise in the restaurant must have kept her from hearing the ring. Worry crept in across her brow.

"It's my sister. Would you mind if I called her back? She's been trying to reach me, so I feel as if I should check in. I'm sorry."

"Of course, go ahead," he answered.

"Thanks," she said as she started dialing.

Her sister answered on the first ring. "Cat? Where the hell are you? I called you at home, but Eliza said you were out. I've been calling your cell for several hours, but you didn't answer. Why didn't you answer?"

"I'm sorry. I've, um, been on a date. What's wrong?"

"It's Mom. She's been in a horrible car accident."

CHAPTER 15

Cat nearly dropped the phone. Panic rushed through her. "Mom? Mom's been hurt?"

"Yes! A pickup truck sm-smashed into her as she was leaving the Target parking lot. She's broken some bones and they're worried about her brain."

Cat could tell her sister was crying.

"You need to come to Ohio right away. She's in surgery right now, but they're not sure she's going to ma-make it. She's at OSU, at the We-Wexner Center. How soon can you get here?"

Closing her eyes, Cat clutched the phone to her ear. *Mom. Oh, my God, Mom.* "I'll be there as soon as I can, but I don't know how long it will take, Marie."

"Just h-hurry, please. She needs you here. *I* need you here."

William's face radiated concern as she hung up.

She stuffed the phone back in her purse, a million thoughts racing through her head. "My mom's been in a car accident. I've got to figure out how to get to Ohio. I need to get to Ohio."

"Not a problem. We'll fly there directly. Tell me where you need to go," William said as the limo pulled up.

"Really? You'll take me there tonight? You'd do that?" Her eyes filled with tears of gratitude.

"For what else is having a private jet any good than being able to rescue damsels in distress?" he quipped as the driver opened the doors for them.

With the mention of damsels, Cat's mind jumped to Ben Cooper. *What's wrong with me? My mom's fighting for her life. I'm with someone who seems to be absolutely wonderful in every way, and I'm thinking about a guy back home?* She groaned.

"I'm sorry to hear about your mother," William said as they settled themselves in the limo. He pulled her in to lean on him, fixing his arm around her shoulders. "We'll get there as quickly as we can. I pray that everything turns out all right."

"We need to go to Columbus. I need to go to Columbus. Mom's at the Wexner Center, Marie said."

"That's an excellent hospital. I'm sure she's in great hands there."

Cat grew silent, tears streaming down her face. William rubbed her knuckles, but she hardly noticed. *What if this is it? What if I lose my mom, too? I can't lose my mom. Please, God, don't take my mom.*

She closed her eyes as the miles passed by.

"Holy shit, you're here. You're *here*! How did you get here so fast?" Marie shouted, leaping up off the hospital bench as Catherine raced into the waiting room.

"How's Mom? Is she okay?" Cat fought to catch her breath.

"She's out of surgery now. The surgeons said everything went well—better than expected, actually—and they were able to release the pressure on her brain." Marie rocked back and forth on her feet. "She's sedated and they'll keep her that way for a while, but they're much more positive about her situation."

Cat exhaled loudly, sinking into the seat beside her. "Oh, thank God."

William strode into the room to Cat. "I parked the car. How's your mother?"

"She's out of surgery. Doing well so far," Cat answered, turning toward him. "Thank you so much for bringing me here. I will never be able to repay you. Never."

Marie inspected him, open curiosity on her face.

"Oh, I'm sorry. Marie, this is William Dawes. William, my sister, Marie."

Marie gave him a brief nod before looking back at her sister. "How did you get here so fast?" she asked again, her forehead wrinkling in confusion. "Charlottesville is at least six hours by car. Flying takes at least a few hours. You got here in one. How is that possible?"

She turned to William. "And no offense, but why are you here?"

Cat had to laugh at her sister. "You and your numbers obsession. Yes, I got a great flight. A really great flight: William flew me here in his private jet. That's why he's here."

"Private jet?" Marie gasped, her jaw dropping open. "Are you serious?"

"Yes, ma'am," William answered. "I'm happy to have been able to help at a time such as this."

"Yes, thank you, thank you," Marie stammered. She turned back to Cat. "Have you known each other long?"

"Not exactly. We were on our first date."

Marie eyed them up and down, taking in the stunning dress and William's suit. "Must have been some date."

A nurse came out into the waiting room and addressed Marie. "Mrs. Bachman? Your mother is out of the recovery room and resting in her own room now. She's sedated, but you may see her if you'd like."

Marie and Cat turned to follow the nurse. As Marie walked through the doors to the patient rooms, Cat paused, looking back at William.

"It's all right, Cat. Go be with your mother." He took a step toward her. "Do you want me to stay? I'll wait here if that is what you need."

Cat gave him a wan smile. "No, William, you've done enough. More than enough. Go ahead and head home. I'm sure I'll be here for at least a few days. Thank you so much for a lovely date, but especially for getting me to my mother. I can't tell you how much that means to me."

"Glad to be able to help," he replied. "And I look forward to a second date. If you're interested, and after your mother is better, of course."

"Thank you. I'd like that."

"Shall I call Eliza for you?"

Oh, God. Eliza. The bookstore. "The store. Eliza can't run it on her own. Crap." She chewed on her lip, trying to figure out what to do.

"Let me take care of it, Catherine," William replied. "I'll hire temporary staff to help out."

"I can pay them. I'll pay. The store can afford it for a little while."

"Don't worry about that. You stay here for as long as you need and trust that things back home will be fine."

She eyed him. "Why are you doing this all for me? You hardly know me."

"True," he answered. "But what I know, I like. A lot. And what good is having wealth if you can't help others? It's more meaningful to me to know I'm helping you in a real crisis than it is to drive you around in fancy cars or buy you dresses. No matter how sexy you look in them."

At his words, she crossed her arms across her torso. She wasn't used to men calling her sexy; it had been so long since she'd felt that way. "Well, thank you, Mr. Dawes. You certainly are playing the role of Prince Charming tonight. A woman could hardly ask for anything more."

He gave her a courtly bow. "At your service, ma'am. Now go see your mother. You've got my cell number. Let me know if there is anything else I can do."

She nodded, her eyes moistening with tears.

Stepping forward, he kissed her lightly on the lips. "Until we meet again, my Cinderella." Then he turned and walked out the door.

Cat gasped at her mother lying against the hospital bed. Her left eye was swollen grotesquely shut and was a livid black and blue, her head bandaged on the left side over her ear. Her left arm was wrapped in a cast from her wrist up past her elbow. Although blankets covered her lower torso, Cat could see the edge of a cast on her lower leg, as well. It was eerie to see her mom lying so still and lifeless, her skin, with the exception of the area around her eye, alarmingly pale.

"She's really going to be okay?" Cat whispered to Marie, who stood holding her mom's right hand. "She looks awful."

"Yeah, she does." Marie's voice caught. "And hell, I hope so."

Cat walked around and hugged her sister. "She'll get better, Marie. She has to. And we'll help her. We'll help."

Marie nodded, her red-rimmed eyes meeting Cat's. "How long can you stay? I need you here, Cat. I need you. Roger's working long hours and the girls have some gacky, snotty thing they picked up from school. That's why they're not here now."

"I'll stay as long as I can." Cat thought briefly of the store, and Eliza, and everything back home. *I have to trust it will all work out. Somehow it will.* "In fact, why don't you go home and get some rest? I'll call you when Mom wakes up. Promise."

Marie sniffed and nodded wearily. "OK, sistuh," she said, using their term of endearment for each other. "Thank you."

"Ca-Ca-Catherine?"

The small voice roused Cat from her fitful sleep on the hospital room chair. She glanced at the clock: 6:10 a.m.

"Mom? Mom!" She jumped up, crossing to her mother's side.

Her mom tried to smile, but winced instead.

"It's fine, Mom, just relax. You're in the hospital. You were in an accident."

The older woman raised her right hand to the left side of her head, touching the bandage there. Tears filled her one open eye. Cat squeezed her left hand lightly in reassurance, mindful of the cast. "You're going to be fine, Mom. Everything's going to be fine."

With a quick knock at the door, a man with salt-and-pepper gray hair and a gentle face strode into the room. Given his white coat and stethoscope, Cat presumed he was the doctor. "Good morning, Mrs. Schreiber. I'm glad to find you awake."

He turned to Cat. "You must be her daughter? I see the resemblance." When Cat eyed her mother's bruised and battered face, he added with a grin, "I don't mean in her current condition."

"How's she doing, Doctor …?"

"Lancet. George Lancet. Remarkably well, all things considered. She sustained a broken elbow and fractured her wrist. We thought at first her ankle was broken, but X-rays show it's merely badly sprained, so it's in a restraining boot for now. As far as her eye, although it looks as if she was in a nasty bar fight, it should heal just fine. The eye itself wasn't damaged, just the area right below it. And we've seen no further swelling in the brain, which is the best sign of all."

Grace Schreiber glanced back and forth from the doctor to her daughter with her one good eye.

"We'll keep her here for a few days, of course, to ensure no complications and keep her pain under control, but hopefully all will be smoother sailing from here on out."

Cat breathed a sigh of relief. "Thank God."

"I'll check back in an hour or so."

"Thank you, Doctor," Cat replied.

After he left, she turned back to her mom, who'd already drifted back to sleep. Cat rubbed her mother's hand. "I love you, Mom. Thank you for not leaving me."

Marie shuffled into the room a short while later, a Diet Coke in hand. She looked exhausted. "How's Mom?"

"Sleeping, thank goodness. Dr. Lancet says she's going to be fine, though. Eventually."

"Thank God." Marie plopped down in a chair next to her sister. She blew her bangs out of her eyes, and then sipped her soda. After a moment, she poked Cat in the side. "So. Tell me about this William. He seems like a prime catch."

Cat rolled her eyes. Marie had always been far more into dating, and had had more boyfriends, than she had. It didn't surprise her that her sister would want to know all the details. Immediately. "Maybe," she said. "But let's not count chickens—or husbands—before they've hatched. We've been on one date. A grand date, I concede, but just one."

"That's more dates than I've heard you had in six years, sis. I'll take it."

Cat chuckled. "I know." She paused. "Although I've had dates with two other guys in the past month."

Marie nearly dropped her soda can. "*What*? Spill the beans!"

Cat told Marie about Derrick and Grayson, casting glances at her mom every once in a while. These were stories she didn't want Grace overhearing.

Marie's eyebrows went up at Catherine's careful retelling of Poetry Night. "Sounds like you got to act out a scene from one of Eliza's trashy novels right in your own living room."

"Sure, if you don't count missing out on the happily-ever-after part. Believe me, it was great, but that kind of great seems like the only thing Gray's interested in. Or talking about poetry. But mostly combining sex and poetry."

"I can think of a few women who'd like that combination. Myself included." Marie pumped her eyebrows up and down, making Cat laugh out loud. "Not that I'd cheat on Roger, but as good a husband as he is, he doesn't spout poetry at me. Ever."

"You're telling me accountants aren't hopeless romantics? I'm shocked. I could totally see Roger as the next Lord Byron."

"Lord who?" Marie said. "Kidding. Of course I know who Byron is. Mom would kill me if I didn't."

Cat chewed on her lip. Telling Marie about Derrick and Grayson had been fun, but she knew she'd only revealed half the story. Should she tell her of the medieval manuscript, and her own stories? Her hands suddenly felt clammy. *Marie will think I'm nuts.*

"Do you, um …" She hesitated. "Do you remember those stories I wrote?"

"What stories?"

Cat bit her lip. Doubt crept back in. Maybe she shouldn't mention anything to Marie. No need to give her sister fodder for years of future ridicule.

She was almost grateful when a moan wafted from the hospital bed, and Marie jumped to their mother's side.

Thank God. Maybe she'll forget I ever said anything.

Chapter 16

"**I**sn't it great to be home?" Marie exclaimed, as she wheeled their mother through the front door of her modest home a few days later.

Grace winced as the wheelchair bounced over the doorframe into the living room. "It's going to take me a while to get used to this chair," she said. "You know I like my independence."

Marie and Cat grinned at each other, rolling their eyes. If there was one thing they knew about their mother, it was that.

"It won't be for long," Marie reassured her. "Just until your ankle heals a bit more."

Grace held up her casted arm with a rueful expression. "This one's going to take a lot longer, though."

"Maybe," said Cat, "but at least it's your left side. You can still write. And the physical therapist you're seeing at the hospital is kind of cute. What was his name? Luke?"

Grace snorted as Marie wheeled her into the kitchen. "Yes, that's what makes such a dreadful accident okay. A cute guy half my age."

"At least this house is fairly wheelchair-accessible, not that I ever thought about it before," Marie said, changing the subject. Cat glanced around the Cape Cod. The hallways were surprisingly wide, and thankfully the master bedroom was on the main floor. Two bedrooms were upstairs, but one served as a playroom for the grandkids when they came over, and the other was mostly used for storage.

"Marie, you'll have to help your sister clear out the second room upstairs so she has a place to sleep. I was sorting through boxes and I'm afraid I left it in a mess." Grace yawned. "I'm exhausted. Would you help me back to my bedroom? I need to rest."

"Sure thing, Mom. Hey, Cat," Marie said, "go on up. I'll be there in a few minutes."

Walking up the stairs, Cat paused as she passed by a ledge full of pig figurines. Her mother had made the mistake of telling the family she liked pigs—they reminded her of growing up in Iowa—so every year she received at least one as a gift from one well-meaning family member or another. Cat's favorite was the dancing Elvis Pigsley. She picked it up and held it in her hand. "Thank ya, thank ya verra much."

Setting him back down, she walked into the bedroom. Her mom hadn't been kidding. Boxes were strewn over the floor, the bed and against the back wall. Cat moved a few off the bed and sat down. She looked up at the space over the desk and saw a framed photo of her mom and dad on their wedding day. She stared at it for some time, admiring and envying the enraptured expression on her dad's face as he'd beheld her mother. She knew their marriage hadn't been perfect; she remembered arguments now and then, not to mention the time they'd vacationed as a family in Florida and her parents hadn't spoken to each other the entire trip. But he'd been devoted to her, and Grace to him.

Marie popped her head in from around the stairwell. "How long do you think you can stay?"

"A week, at most. I have to call Eliza. When I talked to her the day before yesterday, she said the woman William sent over was very helpful. But I need to get home soon. Christmas season is the busiest time of the year for us. And I need all the business I can get."

"I'm sorry we spent Thanksgiving in the hospital." Her sister crossed the room and sat down next to her on the bed. "But it's nice to have the family together again, even if not under ideal circumstances."

"Wait—what? We missed Thanksgiving?"

Marie laughed. "Uh, yeah. It was yesterday. Didn't you notice they served Mom turkey and mashed potatoes?"

"Ugh. Sorry. The days have all been a rush since Mom's accident."

"But we have a lot to be thankful for, don't we?"

Marie leaned down and pulled the lid off a box. In it were remnants of their childhood: artwork and report cards and trophies, the latter mostly for Marie. Cat had never been the sporty type.

"Oh, wow," Cat said. "Who knew Mom saved all this stuff?"

Marie let out a harrumph. "It's a good thing Roger took the girls over to his parent's house for the day. We're going to be here a while." She picked up a misshapen clay pot. "I'd so rather be hitting the Black Friday deals."

Cat's eyes widened. "Oh, God. It's Black Friday. Listen, is it all right if I call Eliza? I need to check in and see how it's going."

"Of course." Marie continued pulling items out of the box as Cat dialed the phone.

"Treasure Trove Booksellers, how may I help you?" answered a deep voice.

Cat frowned. "Ben?" she said, confused.

"Yes, this is Ben—how did you … Oh, Cat, is that you?"

"Yes, it's me. Why are you answering the phone? Where's Eliza?"

"Busy ringing up a customer. It's been crazy in here today."

Cat could make out voices murmuring and the door opening and closing in the background. "Eliza, it's Cat," she heard Ben call.

"Here she is, Cat. Good talking to you. I hope your mom is doing well," Ben said.

Eliza's voice came on the phone. "Hi, Cat!" she said in a cheerful voice. "How's your mom? How are you?"

"We're well," Cat answered. "Mom's getting better every day, and the doctors say she should make a complete, if slow, recovery."

"That's great. Hold on." Cat could hear her directing someone to the History section.

"It sounds busy in there."

"It is! It's been a great sales day so far. Thank goodness Ben's been here all day helping."

"Ben's been there? All day?"

"Yeah, the woman who's been here most of the week called this morning to say her son had food poisoning— from the turkey, they think. Most of their family got it. Anyway, she couldn't come in today. I called Emily, but she's in Pennsylvania visiting grandparents. I didn't know what I was going to do. Oh, hold on."

Cat heard muffled voices and then Eliza came back on the line. "Ben saw me at the coffee shop right before I was going to open up—I figured I needed to fortify myself with caffeine if I was going to be here all day by myself. Once I told him about Judy's son, he insisted on coming to help me. He even called his girlfriend to cancel their lunch plans."

"Wow. That's very … nice. Extremely nice."

"I know! Our knight to the rescue again. And he's great with the customers—chats them up and everything. I'm sure we've made a few extra sales because of him today."

"Wow," was all Cat could think to say.

"When are you coming home? We're doing fine, but I don't know when Judy will be back, and I told Carol I'd cover for her lit class on Thursday."

"Wednesday at the latest. Can you last that long?"

"Of course. You take care of your mom."

"Thanks so much, Eliza. You're the best. Hey, may I talk to Ben for a moment?"

"Sure. Tell your mom I'm thinking of her, and say hi to your sister. Enjoy the time away if you can. Hold on, I'll get Ben."

Cat heard her call Ben's name.

"Hello again," came his voice a moment later. "Happy Thanksgiving! I hope your mom is doing all right. Eliza filled me in on the accident."

"She is, thank you. She's banged up, but the doctors expect her to make a full recovery."

"That's wonderful. She's lucky."

"Definitely. Listen, I want thank you for helping Eliza today. It's certainly not something I would have expected you to do, especially since it sounds like you already had plans."

"It's no big deal. I could see the panic in Eliza's face and I was happy to be able to help her out. To help you out."

"Well, thanks again. I truly appreciate it. Seems as if you're always getting us out of one jam or another."

"Anything for my damsel in distress," he quipped, then amended quickly, "I mean, damsels. You know, both you and Eliza. I like helping out women. I mean people. Damsels. Or maybe even guys."

Cat put her hand over her mouth to keep from laughing at his sudden babbling.

"Yeah, I should go," he continued. "There's a line at the register."

"Great, Ben. Thanks again. I owe you big time. Maybe when I get back I can buy you coffee. Although that would hardly be adequate for what you're doing. So maybe coffee and a muffin," she joked.

"That's not necessary, but I wouldn't say no to a date with you, either. I mean a morning date for coffee. That kind of date. Between friends. A coffee date."

Cat giggled. She would have thought he was flirting with her, except of course he was involved with Mei. "Perhaps you've had enough coffee for today, Mr. Cooper. I'll see you next week, okay? And thanks again."

She hung up the phone.

"Who's Ben?" her sister asked, clearly having eavesdropped. "You haven't mentioned any Ben."

"He's a computer science professor at the university. He helped fix our computer, and now I guess he's helping Eliza today in the store." *And I had lunch with him once. A two-hour lunch.* She kept that information to herself.

"So not another guy hot after you, huh?"

Cat suddenly imagined herself locked in a torrid embrace with Ben, like on one of Eliza's romance covers. Where had that come from? She looked down at the floor, praying Marie wouldn't notice her cheeks, which burned so hotly Cat was sure they were fire-truck red. "What, three isn't enough?"

A snarky expression sneaked across Marie's face. "Not in my day. But let's get back to it. I still want to hit Toys-R-Us today."

"We all have our priorities."

Marie threw the clay pot at her, missing by a mile. The pot shattered as it hit the floor. "Yeah, no great loss there."

"Marie, I'm worried about leaving Mom here alone. I know you'll help as much as you can, but you've got stuff of your own to do, and I'm going home in a few days. I can't afford to stay longer, but I hate to leave when she's still so far from recovered."

"We'll figure it out. Maybe we'll hire a nighttime aide. I can be here most of the day while the girls are in school."

"A nighttime helper? You think Mom will go for that? I doubt it—she's too independent for that."

"Well, yeah. But maybe this time she'll listen to reason."

"Yeah, maybe," Cat replied. "When her Elvis pig flies."

Marie snorted. She picked up some more papers out of a box. "Ha. Here's my paper on Stonehenge I wrote in seventh grade." After a minute, she said, "Hey, that reminds me. What were these stories you mentioned?"

Dang. I was hoping she'd forget. "Oh. Um, Mom sent me a box of stuff she found up here. There were a few in it." Cat didn't mention the manuscript.

"And?"

"And what?"

Marie rolled her eyes. "And what was in the stories?"

Cat toyed with the edge of her shirt. Why had she brought this up? "They were … love stories."

"Love stories?" Marie hooted with laughter. "Like the kind Eliza reads?"

Cat wanted to punch her. "Yeah." She closed her eyes.

"Ooh. Are you serious? Can I read one?"

"They're not here. They're in Virginia. Forget I ever said anything."

"Not happening, especially since you're being so cryptic about it."

Cat heaved a big sigh. Might as well tell Marie everything; she knew her sister wouldn't drop it until she did. "Dad never showed you a medieval manuscript, did he?"

Marie gave her an odd glance. "Uh, no. What does that have to do with love stories?"

The words tumbled out of Cat's mouth. She told her sister about the manuscript, her translation of it, the stories, and the coincidences with Derrick and Grayson. Marie just sipped her soda, saying nothing. When Cat had finished, she crossed her arms over her chest, waiting for her sister to respond.

"Yeah, you're nuts," Marie said with a devilish grin. "But I always knew that."

Silence stretched out between them.

"That's it? That's all you have to say?"

"What is there to say? You don't believe it's true, do you?"

"No." Cat's scalp prickled.

Her sister stared her down, just like she'd done when they were kids. "You can't *truly* believe there's an iota of a chance you made these guys up? Seriously? You really are nuts."

"Maybe," Cat muttered. "Maybe I am."

"Come *on*, Cat. You may like those weird sci-fi fantasy shows on TV, but this is real life."

"I don't like sci-fi. I like *Bones*. And *Vampire Diaries*. They're *not* sci-fi."

"Tomato, *tomahto*, sister. There are no vampires in real life, and you can't write someone into being."

Cat nodded. "Yeah. You're right. Stress must be getting to me."

Their mother's voice rang from below. "Girls? I need your help."

Cat and Marie raced down the stairs to their mother's bedroom. "Mom? You okay?" Marie asked.

"Of course. I just can't get the lid off this pain medicine one-handed."

Marie took the bottle and opened it. "I'll get you some water. Meanwhile, why don't you ask Cat about her dates?"

Cat snorted. "Thanks a lot."

"You're dating someone, Catherine?" Her mother looked at her with interest.

Cat shifted, blocking her arms over her chest. "Not exactly dating. I've gone on a few dates. Nothing serious."

"Don't count yourself out. Maybe this gentleman is the one."

"Which one, Mom? She's been dating three!" Marie proclaimed as she reentered the room.

Cat mimed stabbing Marie in the head. "That's true, but the first two, at least, didn't work out."

"Then tell me about the third. I assume he's the man who brought you to Ohio?"

Cat scowled at her sister.

"*Of course* I told her about William," Marie said. "It's not every day your sister shows up in a fancy dress with a jaw-droppingly handsome man. In his own plane."

"Point taken," Cat conceded. "His name is William Dawes, Mom. I met him when he came into the store looking for an old Bible—the Regency one Dad found that one time, remember?"

Grace nodded impatiently, clearly more interested in Mr. Dawes than the book.

"We went on a date last week. The night of your accident,

actually. That's why he ended up bringing me here, as Marie so kindly told you."

"He's rich."

"And that's what's important?" Cat glared at her sister.

"Well," Marie said with a huff, "if you're going to fall in love, nothing wrong with falling in love with someone with money."

"If Roger had no money, would you love him less?"

"Of course not. I'm just saying it doesn't hurt."

"Fine. Anyway, Mom," Cat continued, "there's a lot more to William than his money. He's kind and generous. He made me feel safe in the middle of a horrible situation. He's sent over help for the store while I'm here, and has told me not to hesitate to ask for whatever I need." She fidgeted with her ear. "Not that I would take advantage of him; you know I'm not like that. But he's like a modern Prince Charming. What girl wouldn't fantasize about being taken care of like that?"

"A feminist one," sniped her mother.

"One can be a feminist and still enjoy a man's attentions, Mom," Marie countered.

Grace swallowed and sipped some water, nodding in acquiescence. "Definitely true. I adored your father. And he never once acted like we were anything less than equals."

Her gaze grew thoughtful as she studied her daughter. "You know, that Prince quip reminds me of that story you emailed me shortly after your dad died, when you were visiting Aunt Kate. Do you remember?"

CHAPTER 17

Catherine stood rooted to the spot. A story? She'd sent her mother a story? She could feel the blood drain from her face.

Her mother didn't seem to notice. "You wrote about wanting your own Prince Charming to sweep you off your feet," she continued, "lavish you with great things, and treat you like a princess. You called it *Caterella*. I remember the title because it was so you: half-humor, half-literary. I figured the rest of it was your way of wading through the grief after the loss of your dad, by creating this fantasy of a man who could whisk you away from all the pain, out of reality and into the glamorous life."

Grace set her cup down on the nightstand. "It never sounded like the real you, that pining for a man. I'd forgotten about it—but I remember saving the email because you also told stories about your dad that I wanted to hold on to. I think it's out with the photo albums. Maybe you girls can find it."

Cat's breathing accelerated and her heart pounded. Was this what a heart attack felt like?

Grabbing her elbow, Marie pulled her into the hallway. "Relax," she whispered. "Seriously. You don't need to freak Mom out."

Cat clutched her elbows, holding her arms against her stomach. She attempted to breathe in and out, in and out, but the air wouldn't come.

Marie walked to the back end of the hallway and bent down. She thumbed through the old albums housed on a bookshelf there. A moment later she held up a piece of paper. "Found it."

Cat approached her sister, taking the paper with a trembling hand. She scanned it, blanching further. "Oh my God. I said his name was Will. Marie, I said his name was *Will*!"

Marie grabbed the paper, reading for herself. "C'mon. You said he'd be named something wealthy and noble sounding, like William or Harry or Edward. You didn't say he *was* William. You must have been thinking of the British royal family."

They heard the sound of their mom's wheelchair and looked up to see her wheeling herself slowly down the hallway. Cat yanked the email back from her sister and stuffed it in her pocket.

"Did you find it?" Grace called.

"No," Cat said, as Marie raced to their mother's side.

"Mom!" she chided. "You shouldn't be out of bed."

Grace waved her off. "You guys were taking too long; I had to see what the problem was. I could've sworn it was in there."

She looked back and forth between her daughters, a perplexed expression on her face. "What's going on? Cat, you look a little green."

"It's nothing, Mom. She just needs something to eat. Can I make you a sandwich, Cat?" Marie asked in an extra cheerful voice, giving Cat a pointed look.

Realizing she didn't need to freak her mother out any more than she was freaking herself out, Cat forced herself to agree. "Yeah, Mom, nothing, I'm just tired. And thinking about Dad. I always miss him this time of year."

Grace seemed satisfied with her answer. "I miss him, too. Anyways, you know I think you deserve someone as wonderful as that fantasy guy, right, honey?"

"I know, Mom."

"If you want someone, that is. Women don't have to have a man to feel fulfilled."

Marie snorted from the kitchen. "She knows, Mom. You remind us often."

"Don't get me wrong, girls. I loved your dad. I miss him every day. But he wouldn't want to see you dependent on someone else for your happiness any more than I do."

Grace rolled herself farther into the living room. "Any chance we could put up the tree while we're all here as a family? You know that's my favorite thing about Christmas, especially when I've got my two girls with me."

"Sounds great," Cat said absentmindedly. Her brain felt fuzzy and nausea had rooted itself in her stomach. Three stories. Three men. It was too much to ignore now, though she desperately wanted to.

She took a deep breath as Ben Cooper's face flashed through her mind. Where did he fit in? Had she written a story about a computer science professor, too? One who already had a girlfriend? Closing her eyes, she clutched the back of the sofa for support. The manuscript, the stories. None of it made any sense. She had to ask.

"Mom, do you know anything about a medieval manuscript Dad had?"

"What manuscript?"

Cat pressed her hand to her forehead in a futile attempt to stave off the horrendous headache now pounding through her temples. "You sent it to me a few weeks ago—it was in with some other papers? It was wrapped up like a present, actually."

"I don't remember that."

Cat's shoulders slumped. "So you don't have any info on it?"

"I'm sorry, no. Is it authentic?"

"Seems to be. Never mind. I was hoping you'd know where he got it." So much for that. Pushing the thought of men—any man—firmly from her mind, Cat swallowed and squared her shoulders. There must be an explanation, but she wasn't going to think about it right now. She couldn't.

"Unless …" her mother said.

Cat's eyes flew back to her.

"There *was* something Grandma Schreiber gave to your dad a long time ago. When I tried to look at it, she motioned me away, saying it was a family secret. As if I wasn't family." Grace made a disgusted noise. "People always said Grandma was batty, so I didn't give it a second thought. Is that what it was? Some sort of manuscript?"

Cat nodded, suddenly sorry she'd brought it up, especially since Marie was now rotating her finger in circles near the side of her head. "Looniness obviously runs in the family," she said, pointing at Cat.

Grace ignored Marie. "You'll have to show it to me sometime. Unless you sell it. I bet it's worth a pretty penny." Wheeling herself over to the stereo, she pulled out a CD. After a minute, the familiar strains of *The Nutcracker* filled the room.

Cat was grateful her mother had lost interest in the subject, although it frustrated her to no end not to have more information about her dad's odd gift. Especially if it were a family heirloom.

As they put up the tree and hung the ornaments one by one, Cat tried to relax and enjoy being with her family again, doing the Christmas traditions they'd done since she was a baby. It pained her to think how much she was going to miss them when she returned to Virginia.

Maybe she should move to Ohio. But chasing after family wasn't any better than chasing after a man, was it? *How about being chased after by three men I created?* A nervous laugh escaped her, and Marie and Grace both turned around.

"Nothing. Nothing!" Cat held up the ornament she'd unwrapped. "I found the old Pac-Man ornament, and was remembering how we used to dance to *Pac-Man Fever*. That's all."

Marie raised her eyebrow.

"That's all," Cat repeated.

And I'm crazy. Absolutely nuts. Bonkers. Because I'm more and more convinced that the three men I'm dating, or was dating, were somehow created ... by me.

An hour later, as the three women were sipping hot chocolate in front of the tree, Cat's phone rang.

"Hello?"

"Hi, Catherine. It's William. William Dawes."

The room started to spin. Half of her wanted to hang up the phone; the other half wanted to drill him with questions in an effort to prove she either had or hadn't made him up.

She attempted to sound casual. "Oh, hi. How are you?"

"I'm well. I hope the same is for you and your mother. How is she?"

"Much better. She's got a ways to go, but she's back to her old self, at least personality-wise."

Grace gave her a sidelong glance as if to ascertain whether that was a positive or negative statement.

"I'm so glad to hear that. I would have checked in before, but the whole family came home for Thanksgiving at my parents' house, and then the office has been swamped."

"It's all right, William, I wasn't expecting you to. But I wanted to thank you again for all you've done for me, especially since you hardly know me. I truly appreciate it."

Maybe I didn't make him up. Maybe it really is all one big weird coincidence. He certainly sounds perfectly normal and not like a figment of my imagination. My apparently quite creative imagination.

"You're more than welcome, Catherine. It was my pleasure. In fact, that's why I'm calling."

"Oh?"

"I spoke with Eliza to check in on the store, and she mentioned you were returning to Charlottesville tomorrow. I asked her how you were getting there. She said she didn't know."

"I'm renting a car."

"May I send the plane for you? I won't be able to accompany you, as there is a shareholders' meeting tomorrow in New York, but the plane is yours if you want it. I'll be traveling with my father."

"*On his* plane?" Cat joked without thinking.

There was a small pause. "Well, yes. Listen, if you would prefer to drive, I'll understand."

"No, no, I'm sorry. I didn't mean to upset you. I don't usually rub elbows with folks who own jets. I was gauche, and I apologize." Her sister watched her as she fumbled for words.

"Don't worry about it."

"Anyway, um, sure. If the offer still stands, I accept. It would save me six hours of driving. And when you're driving through West Virginia, those hours are long."

"Not a fan of West Virginia?"

Cat was relieved that he no longer seemed offended. "It's definitely beautiful, but after a while how many more mountains and trees can one stand?"

William laughed out loud. "In any case," he said, "if you can be at the airport at 7:00 p.m., someone will meet you at the main entrance and escort you to the plane."

"Thanks again, William. It all feels like too much, but, um, they tell you not to look a gift horse in the mouth, so I'll take it." *Besides, if I've created you to be my savior, I might as well let you do the saving.*

"Wonderful. I'm still hoping you are interested in that second date. I've been thinking about you and looking forward to it."

"Yes, absolutely. That'd be great."

"Good. I'll talk with you once you're back home. Take care, Catherine."

"Thank you, William. You, too."

Grace spoke the minute Cat hung up the phone. "I take it that was your 'Prince'?" She hooked her fingers in the air, making mock quote marks to emphasize the word.

"Oh, Mom." *If you only knew. If you only knew.*

"I would say if he's sending a plane to retrieve you, the answer is yes," Marie said. "That's almost as good as riding up on a horse."

"I have to concede that." Cat raised her brows at Marie. "It's as if he's everything I've wanted a man to be," she continued in an exaggerated tone.

Marie snorted, waving her sister off with a hand.

"What are you two are talking about?" Grace demanded. Neither daughter answered her. "Fine. Whatever. Sister secrets." She looked at Cat. "I'm not glad to be injured, but I *am* glad you came. We miss you, especially at the holidays. Will you be back at Christmas?"

"I don't know. I'll try. I'm just glad you are okay and I have something to come back to."

"Honey, you always have somewhere to come back to. Even if only the memories in your head and the photographs on your walls." Grace gestured to the collection by the stairs. Cat swallowed after spying a picture of herself as a toddler with her dad, laughing with outstretched hands as she sat on his shoulders at some parade. Lord, she missed him.

"The people you love are always in your heart, whether you're physically with them or not," her mother added.

"Well, *that's* eerily maudlin. I think your pain medicines are on overdrive, Mom," Marie said, hopping up. "I say it's time to watch *Christmas Vacation*. Cat, you find the movie. I'll make the popcorn." She headed into the kitchen.

"It's in the cabinet over the stove," Grace called, wheeling herself after Marie. "Don't forget the butter."

I love them so much. Too bad I'm going insane.

CHAPTER 18

"God, it's good to be home. Thanks for picking me up." Cat folded Eliza into a giant hug. "Thanks for everything, Lizzie."

When Cat didn't release her right away, Eliza gave an uncomfortable giggle. "Everything okay?"

"Yeah. But I think I'm going to have to write that Grayson test now."

Eliza reared back, studying Cat's face. "Really?"

"Yeah. I'll tell you about it on the way home."

The two headed out the airport entrance to Eliza's car. Along the way, Cat told her all about her date with William, her mother … and about the email she'd written long ago.

Eliza took it all in stride—a far cry from Cat's reaction. Even now, in relating the details, the whole thing felt surreal, as if she were watching a movie, a film of someone else's life. She wished she could skip to the ending, to find out how it all turned out. Was she in a romantic comedy, or a horror flick?

Eliza gave her a knowing grin. "Told you so." Another street or two passed. "I still want my Darcy. In a story to outdo that Nicholas one, baby."

"It *could* all still be coincidence. Or, as you yourself, suggested, that Law of Attraction sort of thing. Marie agreed."

A scoffing noise was her only answer.

Later that evening, Eliza wandered into the living room to find Cat sitting on the sofa, bent over her laptop, staring at the screen. "Whatcha doing?"

Cat jumped, startled by the interruption. "Geez, you scared me."

"Who else do you think is running around in this apartment?"

"It's not that. I was just lost in this story. I'm trying to figure out what details to add about Grayson. I gave him a sister named Amaryllis. Isn't that a ridiculous name? She's a fashion model who's into insects—as in, she wants to be an entomologist."

Eliza wrinkled up her nose. "Bugs?"

Cat grinned. "I know. But there will be no mistaking it if Gray shows up with a bug-loving, twiggy sister named after a flower, right? And as ludicrous as that all sounds, I feel even *more* ludicrous for believing for a second this could be real. I feel idiotic for trying. It just can't be real. It can't." The grin left her face.

"That you created him?"

Cat rolled her eyes. "What else would I be talking about? *Of course* that."

"Sorry," Eliza said with a shrug. "I think it is real. And I think it'd be awesome to have such power."

Cat set the laptop aside for a minute. "But what of the potential repercussions?"

"What repercussions?" Eliza flopped down on the sofa next to her friend. "You get to create your own reality. You can have the Perfect Man you've always dreamed of. You can fix all your problems. Sounds ideal to me."

"Does it? Does it truly? I mean, I know everybody thinks they want the easy life, but …" Cat's fingers rubbed the keyboard. "It's been my fantasy for six years, or, if I'm honest with myself, even longer—at least since my dad died—to have the fairytale story that felt like it was ripped away from me."

"Um, Cat?" Eliza interjected. "Ryan was no fairytale hero."

"I know that now. I probably knew that then. I just wanted to believe so badly, to believe the stories in the books could be true, instead of the misery and suffering I see all around me. The misery and suffering you and I've both gone through." She ran her fingers through her hair, squeezing her eyes shut as if she could block it all out. "But I couldn't believe. Not anymore. I shut it all away. The pain. The longing. The hope."

After a moment, she opened her eyes and smiled at Eliza fondly. "So, yeah, it *seems* ideal to have everything just the way you want it, to be able to stop worrying about things so much. And yet, I don't know. It doesn't feel right to have everything handed to me the way it has been in the last month. It doesn't feel real, and I'm not sure it could ever feel real, could it?"

Eliza nodded, saying nothing. She grabbed Cat's hand and squeezed it.

With her other hand, Cat took a sip of the tea from the mug she had resting on the side table. "Maybe my mom is right," she continued, "and character-building experiences are what give meaning to our lives. You can't have a character-building experience without some struggle, without some challenge, right? Of course, whenever Mom tells me that when I'm in the middle of something crappy, I want to tell her to kiss off, but still."

"Excuse me, did you *really* just say a 'character-building experience?'" Eliza exclaimed with a laugh. "Isn't that exactly what you're doing right now? Building characters?" She gestured at the laptop.

Cat had to chuckle. "Come on, you know that's not what I meant."

"Maybe not, but it's still funny," Eliza said, chortling.

Grabbing a pillow, Cat bopped her lightly on the head. "What I want, if anything, dear friend, is a man of character—not a character of a man I've created. At least I don't think I want that. After all, it's disheartening to think the only reason Grayson wanted to sleep with me is because I wrote him that way—assuming I did, I guess. Not that it makes much sense otherwise that he'd be into a woman ten years his senior."

Eliza pursed her lips. "I get that. But just because you've created them doesn't mean you've controlled everything they've done, right down to the details, right?" She leapt up from the sofa, pacing back and forth. "I mean, look at Derrick. When you wrote about him, he was in high school. You didn't write anything beyond that, and yet here he is, having a life, wanting to date you, even though it's years later. And as to Grayson—first of all, stop underestimating yourself, Catherine. I know you consider yourself a Plain Jane, but you're wrong. And I'm not just talking looks. There's something about you that attracts others—when you let it. I think it's what drew me to you, too."

Eliza paused, gaping at her in mock horror. "Unless you're telling me you created me, too?" She snickered at her own joke, and then asked in a less certain voice, "You didn't, did you?"

"Oh, for Pete's sake, Eliza. Of course not."

"Well, anyway, you may have written about Grayson as a sex object, but that doesn't mean that's the only reason he's into you." Eliza stopped moving for a minute. "He's younger than you are. How does that work into this whole scheme, when you wrote about him years ago?"

"My sister pointed that out, too, as evidence *against* your theory. Rereading the story about him, I did describe him as being a perpetual grad student, so maybe that did it. Maybe that froze him in time ..." Cat trailed off. After a minute she shook her head. "We're being ridiculous. I think it's far more likely my sister is right and we'll discover a reasonable explanation for all of this."

"Sure. If you say so." Eliza's face fell.

"You think that would be *bad*?"

"I don't know. I'm still hoping you'll write my Mr. Right."

"Tell you what—if this experiment with Grayson works, I'll write you anything you want."

Half an hour later, as Cat and Eliza were watching *Vampire Diaries* in an attempt to block out the craziness of the past week, Cat's cell phone rang.

"Hello?"

"Hi, Cat, this is William."

"Hi, William. How are you?" Nervousness coursed through her veins. She wanted to believe this was a nice, normal conversation between two wholly human, wholly *not* supernatural adults. But the way the hair on her arms was standing up, she knew at least part of her suspected otherwise.

"I'm very well, thank you for asking. How is your mother?"

"She's doing much better. Her ankle is stable enough now

that she can hobble around wearing a protective boot, which has made her much happier."

"I'm glad to hear that. I hope she continues to feel better and recover quickly."

"Thank you."

"Listen, I'll be back down in Charlottesville next week while we're working on some investment plans for the UVa hospital. I don't want to be presumptuous, but I'm hoping you're still interested in that second date."

"Absolutely," Cat answered. "I'd love that." Even if she'd made him up, he *was* quite the catch, right? Given everything he'd done for her, she owed it to him to explore the possibilities further. As if that would be a hardship.

Eliza watched her, raising an eyebrow.

"Great," William said. "I promise, no limos this time. Unless you want one."

"No, no." She laughed. "A regular old car will do just fine. In fact, how about I drive?"

"Sure," William agreed. "That sounds like an adventure."

"Ha, ha. How's Saturday?" she suggested. "I can pick you up at 1:00."

"An afternoon rendezvous. I'm intrigued."

Had she imagined the innuendo in his voice? "Where will you be staying?"

"The Boar's Head Inn. Do you know where it is?"

"Yes, I do."

"Great, I'll see you then."

After Cat hung up, Eliza said, "Going out with Will again, huh?"

"Yup."

"And you don't mind that you created him?"

Cat glared at her.

"Well, you were just saying you didn't know if a fake guy would be what you wanted."

"We don't know that he's fake. Besides, if he were—and I'm not saying he is—he's the closest to what I'm looking for, so maybe I'd consider it."

"Because he's rich?"

Cat elbowed her. "I'm not shallow." Hesitating a second, she added, "Well, not *that* shallow. It's not that I want to be rich, but financial security sounds appealing to someone who's been battling to keep her head—and her bookstore—above water for the past ten years. And for all my talk about struggles making us stronger, well, William makes me feel safe, and whether it's feminist or not to say so, that's what I crave. Right now, at least. I'm sure my mother would be appalled."

"You don't know that, Cat," Eliza said. "You've always said how devoted your parents were to each other. I'm sure she wants that for you, too. You know I do. I want to see you open yourself up to love again. Your heart's been frozen for years; it's time you thawed it out."

"What fancy imagery." Cat sighed, wriggling around on the sofa for a more comfortable position. "You're right. I've been in limbo for a long time, not taking chances on anything. Now with all of this, I don't know what or who to believe any more. I feel like I'm walking on eggshells, not knowing what is real and what isn't. I mean, if someone overheard us talking like this at the coffee shop, acting as if bringing characters to life were possible, they'd think we were crazy. And maybe we are. Maybe I am."

"Don't pull out the straitjacket just yet. Let's wait and see if Amaryllis makes a grand entrance."

Cat half-laughed, half-sobbed. "Oh my God, I really am insane."

"No, insane is the Salvatore brothers continually working with Klaus when they *know* he's evil," Eliza said, pointing at the TV. "Seriously, would it be so bad if Elena became a vampire? At least then all these crazy efforts to keep her human could stop."

Cat laughed as tears slipped down her face. "You *do* know that this is a TV show, right? It's not real."

"Hey, if *you* can create sexy men, who's to say? A girl can dream. And Damon is so yummy."

"I like Stefan better."

"You would."

"What's that supposed to mean?"

"He's all about safety. Damon's all about danger."

"I like danger, too."

Eliza snorted.

"Okay, yeah, I don't. I don't want danger. A little intrigue, maybe. I'll leave the adventuring to you."

"Yeah, like I'm living on the edge," said Eliza, her voice bitter. "I guess I've been hiding out as much as you have, Cat."

They gave each other a long look. After a moment, Cat said, "Who would've thought a silly television show could lead to such introspection?"

"You're right," answered Eliza. "Enough of that. How about we go out for a pizza?"

Cat stood up and grabbed her coat off the hook near the door. "You're on. Heck, let's throw caution to the wind. Let's add breadsticks, too."

The next morning, the Christmas bells she'd tied on the front door jingled, and Cat looked up to greet the first customer of the day. Ben Cooper walked in, shaking off his umbrella. He wiped his feet on the doormat, and then searched the store with his eyes. Spying Cat standing near the Biography section, he broke into a grin and strode toward her.

"Hiya. It's great to see you again." His voice was cheerful. "How've you been? I hope your mom is doing well."

"She is, thank you." She ignored the sudden racing of her heart at his appearance, gesturing toward the window, through which they could see rain coming down hard. "I think you're the only person I know who could be so happy on such a glum day."

"Yeah, well, it isn't the rain that has me in this mood, I guess."

"What does? Do tell." An uncomfortable expression skittered across his face for a second.

"Uh … Christmas shopping. I need a gift for Mei, and thought who better to ask for help with that than you?" His eyes didn't quite meet hers.

"You guys are still seeing each other? That's great! I hope it's going well." *I'm not disappointed. I'm not disappointed. I'm not disappointed.*

She paused for a second. "Why would I have any idea what Mei would want for Christmas? I don't know her."

"Oh, um. She's interested in container gardening, whatever that is. Considering I have two black thumbs, I'm way out of my element here, so I thought I'd ask you." He ran his fingers through his hair, making the front stand up. *Cute.*

"Here, let's check over in this section and I'll see what I have."

Ben dutifully followed her across the room to a small section marked Plants/Gardening. Cat bent down to pull a title off the bottom shelf, then abruptly stood and whirled around, almost knocking Ben off his feet.

He reached out with both arms and grabbed onto her to steady himself. "Whoa there, you okay?"

She looked down at where he still gripped her forearms. She could feel the heat of his long, lean fingers against her skin. She studied them, noting the veins cording their way across the backs of his hands, the well-trimmed nails. She'd never thought a man's hands could be sexy, and yet that's exactly what flitted through her mind. Ben Cooper had sexy hands.

She raised her gaze back up. Good Lord, she was just a few inches from his face. And he was looking right at her. *Wow, his eyes are beautiful.*

She'd never really been a fan of men with brown eyes, though her father had had them—brown had always seemed rather plain, without the exotic hues of the blues and greens she fantasized about. But she was ready to revise that, staring into the chocolaty richness before her.

Their mouths hovered within inches of each other. If she leaned in, she could … *Whoa. Where'd that come from? You can't kiss Ben Cooper!* She worked to control her breathing, which had inexplicably sped up. She stared at him, wide-eyed.

For a second she was sure he wanted to kiss her, too. His grip tightened ever so slightly, and his eyes softened. Had he just rubbed his thumb over her arm? She sucked in a breath, unsure of what to do. Of what she wanted to do.

Ben gave her an awkward smile, dropping his hands as he took a half step back. This close to him, she could see a small mole to the side of his eyebrow, and had to tamp down the urge to reach out and touch it. Instead, she rubbed her arms where he'd been holding her, suddenly feeling cold.

"You okay?" he repeated.

"Yeah, uh, yeah. Sorry. I just realized I never thanked you for helping out Eliza on Black Friday. I should have called you right away when I got in yesterday. I'm so sorry. I've been, um, kind of distracted."

Her heart pounded. Her stomach raced. What was wrong with her? Her nose detected the delicious smell of coffee mixed with man—a heady, warm scent that had her wanting to step closer again.

"With your mom." He nodded in understanding. "Perfectly logical. In any case, it was no big deal. I was glad to help. Definitely a nice change from students complaining about their grades and planning for finals."

She didn't disabuse him of his notion that it was all about her mom. Because to clarify the alternative, the reality, the bizarre fact that she was wrestling with the possibility, the improbability, that she was bringing fictional characters to life, was not an option.

She dropped her eyes to his lips. She needed a break from the intensity of those chocolate eyes. Moving to his mouth wasn't much better, however. She wanted to reach up and trace those lips, to feel the hint of stubble she noticed along his jaw.

She took a step back herself, squaring her shoulders to ward off her untoward—and inappropriate—thoughts. "Still, it was far above and beyond the call of duty. May I pay you for your time?"

Ben crinkled his face, clearly perturbed. "No. No, I offered that as a service to a friend. We are friends, aren't we, Cat?"

"Of course we are. I'm sorry, I didn't mean to insult you," she answered. Taking a deep breath, she turned back around to the bookshelf. "But I do think there's something down here Mei might like."

She bent down and pulled off a book. "Here it is," she said as she handed it up to him. "*Container Gardening: An Easy Step-by-Step Guide.*"

Ben took the book from her hand, his fingers touching hers as he did.

She shivered, surprised by the contact. Had it been intentional? And why was she reacting this way? She wasn't the kind of woman who swooned over a man, was she? *Except that's all I seem to be doing lately, ever since this fall. Must be something in the air. Or my biological clock ticking. Or a certain manuscript.*

She looked up at Ben to ascertain if he'd noticed the touch. He was thumbing through the book, not looking at her, seemingly unaware of the unexpected cascade of emotions running through her.

For a moment, she wondered if she'd made him up, too. Was that why he was having such an effect on her? A snort burst forth from her nose. *Good Lord, I really do think I'm God now, imaging I've created everyone around me.*

Ben stopped his perusal of the book and looked at her, questions in his eyes.

"I'm sorry. Again. I'm a little, uh, stressed out. That wasn't directed at you."

He watched her for a few seconds. "Anything I can do to help?"

There was such genuine concern in his face that Cat suddenly felt the urge to cry. It'd been so long since anyone, except Eliza, had worried much about her. Her family loved her and wanted what was best for her, of course, but they were six hours away. Derrick hadn't asked her all that much about herself. Grayson had clearly had his eye, and his mind, on other things. William … William was wonderful, but maybe that was because she'd written him that way. At least she and he had gone on a date, and were planning another.

But Ben Cooper? She didn't know Ben that well. Not really. Why was he being so helpful?

"No. Thank you. You've done so much already."

He looked ready to say something else, but cleared his throat instead and looked down at the book in his hands. "This is perfect, thanks. I'm sure Mei will love it."

At Mei's name, Cat's insides spasmed. *He's taken. Remember? And you have William. Not to mention the bookstore.* She nodded.

Together they walked to the cash register. "Are you getting her anything else?" she asked as Ben fumbled for his wallet in his back pocket.

"I wasn't planning on it," he said, surprise evident in his voice. "This is what she wants."

"Sorry. It's none of my business. Lord knows I would find books a delightful gift from a boyfriend, but some women might feel it's, um, less than romantic."

Ben handed her his credit card. He paused a moment before answering. "We've only gone on a handful of dates, so I'm not sure she'd call me her boyfriend, but thanks for the tip."

"Candles are nice. Or jewelry. Does Mei like earrings?" Why she was persisting in this? And why was she so happy that he'd said he and Mei weren't serious? They still were something.

"I have no idea. I've never noticed if she wears earrings."

Cat touched her own ears self-consciously, fiddling with the blue sapphire earrings her dad had given her as a college graduation present.

Ben leaned around to peek at her ears, and then looked her full in the face. "Beautiful."

Cat stared at him.

"Those earrings, they are beautiful," he clarified.

"Thanks. They were a gift from my father."

He watched her a moment longer. "They suit you," he said simply. Their eyes remained locked until the door jingled again, breaking the connection between them.

A man walked in.

Cat gasped. "Grayson."

CHAPTER 19

Ben turned to assess the newcomer, and then glanced back at Cat. His face seemed stonier, more reserved. He picked up his purchase, his lips tightening before he spoke. "It was nice to see you again, Cat. Please tell Eliza hello."

"I will," she answered mechanically, not looking at him, still watching as Grayson sauntered toward her, a lazy grin on his face. The two men exchanged a quick glance as Ben walked out without looking back.

"Hi, Cat," Grayson said.

"Hi, how are you?" She stared into his gorgeous blue eyes. See, *those* were the kind of eyes that made her melt. Not chocolate. Chestnut. Sorrel. Mahogany. *Ugh, why am I still thinking about Ben Cooper's regular old brown eyes?* She smiled extra widely at Gray, as if to erase Ben's face from her mind.

Gray's gaze dropped to her mouth. She licked her lips nervously, and his nostrils flared. *Good Lord, he's like a stallion in heat.* She twisted her fingers together and shot him a grin, amazed to think she could elicit such a reaction in a man as model-handsome as Gray. It made no sense. Then she sobered.

Of course it didn't. Unless I wrote him to behave that way. What a deflating realization, to think that maybe the only reason this guy was attracted to her was because she'd created him to be so. Her smile faded.

Gray didn't seem to notice. "I'm great," he said. "Five more papers to grade and my second dissertation chapter to turn in, and I'm a free man. At least until mid-January."

"That's great."

The glumness she suddenly felt must have been evident in her voice, as Grayson reached out and touched her cheek. "Hey, you all right?"

"Yes. I'm sorry." *Geez, there I go, apologizing again.* She shook her head. "Nothing to do with you, Grayson. Just some things I'm, um, realizing all of a sudden."

He scrutinized her face as if trying to figure her out. After a moment, he said, "I'm here to find an anthology of Margaret Atwood poems. I love her *Variations on the Word Love*. Have you read it?"

"No, but I've read a few of her books. I loved *Lady Oracle*."

Grayson walked toward the poetry section, thumbing through the books. "Here it is. I think it's in this volume, at least: her poems from 1976-1986."

Cat followed him automatically, lost in her own confusion over Ben Cooper, these men and her writing and what it all meant. If it were true. Grayson was alone, after all; no sister in sight. Was that evidence enough *against* Eliza's notions—and hers, if she were honest—that she had created him, much less had any control over him?

"Shall I read it to you?" Gray's voice dipped seductively. His eyes trapped hers again and her pulse fluttered.

Was it possible, since nothing seemed any different, that Grayson's attentions had nothing to do with any stupid story, any silly manuscript, and were truly focused on her?

Cat hesitated for a second. She knew where it would lead if he read poetry to her: where it had led last time. She could feel the electricity between them, the currents flowing through the room. It was a different kind of magnetism than with Ben, but it was still powerful. Maybe Grayson wouldn't seduce her right this minute, in the middle of a business day. But soon enough. Did she want that?

No. Sex without love isn't worth it to me.

Eliza traipsed out of the back room, carrying a box of wrapping paper and ribbons. "I found the extra gift wrapping supplies," she called out before she spied Grayson. "Oh." She nearly dropped the box on the floor. "I'm sorry, I didn't realize you were busy."

"It's fine, Eliza. I was helping Grayson find a book he wanted. That's *all*," Cat said. She didn't know Eliza had been downstairs. Had her friend witnessed her interaction with Ben? Not that anything inappropriate had happened, of course. Outside of her own head, at least.

Eliza grinned. "Sure, if you say so, Cat." She turned to Grayson. "Hey, Grayson, how've you been? We need you to come to our next Poetry Night—you draw quite the crowd."

Gray flashed her a flirty grin. Cat was amused to see pink infuse Eliza's face. "I'd be happy to. When is it? I so enjoyed the last one." He turned his gaze back to Cat. She could feel heat rush to her cheeks. *Great, now I'm blushing.*

"Cat did, too," Eliza said. "I mean, we all did. But I think Cat especially appreciated how the evening turned out."

Cat wanted to sink into the floor. If she'd been standing closer, she'd have given Eliza a swift kick to the shins. Surreptitiously, of course. Or perhaps not. "We're still considering when to hold the next one," she managed to say. "Certainly not until after Christmas. Maybe January. That's one of our slowest months, so it would be good to draw more people in." She was babbling. She needed to stop talking.

"Not a problem," Grayson said. "Just let me know. I'd be more than happy to repeat my performance."

Eliza dropped the ribbon she'd been holding.

"Thanks, we'll be in touch." Cat's voice was a bit too cheerful in her desperate attempt to mask her embarrassment. "In the meantime, I've got to shelve more of our new inventory, so can I ring you up for the book?"

Grayson's eyes cooled at the obvious dismissal. "I'm just looking today. Still considering my options."

I bet you are. He had no idea what she could do to him. Or what she maybe possibly could do. She could make him dreadfully odiferous with enormous buckteeth. Or give him a painful boil on his neck. Maybe a nose that never stopped running. *Try then to work your wiles on women with your poetry quoting.*

She smiled smugly, feeling more in control of herself. Sure, it was crazy to believe she had such powers, but at least it took some of the power away from him.

Gray reached out and grabbed her hand, caressing her palm with his thumb. *Okay, less in control now. He's still damned sexy.*

"I hope to see you again soon, Cat." He pointed to the mistletoe Eliza had hung over the Romance section. "Maybe I'll catch you under that. Got to honor Christmas traditions, you know," he said with a wink. Then he turned and walked out the door without waiting for an answer.

"Can you believe how many of these gingerbread house construction kits we've sold?" Eliza asked Cat as they cleaned up the kids' section of the store the following Friday. They'd hosted a rowdy but fun group of kindergartners for Shiver Me Timbers Story Time that morning—temporarily renamed Shiver Me Gingers in honor of the season. Now they endeavored to get a big juice stain out of the area rug.

"I know, who knew they'd be a hit? I'm so glad you thought to order more of them while I was in Ohio."

"Actually, it was Ben's suggestion to get more. He noted that we sold six on Black Friday alone. He said a number of moms commented how nice it was to find a sturdy set that wasn't made out of candy and sugar. Especially since they're reusable."

"Not sure the kids will have the same reaction. But I guess I'll have to thank him … again." Cat's thoughts flew back to the near-kiss from a few days ago. *Had* it been a near-kiss? It'd seemed so to her, but perhaps she'd misread the situation.

"Yes, you do. He was so great." Eliza gave her a pointed look. "He asked me lots of questions about you."

Cat stopped scrubbing. "What kinds of questions?"

"Questions that told me I was right on the money about his feelings about you. He tried to be discreet, but …"

"He's with Mei."

"Yeah." Eliza frowned. "Yeah, he is."

"He came in last week and bought her a Christmas present."

Eliza held up her hands in mock surrender. "You're right. You're right. Clearly one can never have feelings for two people at once."

Cat's shoulders tensed. "Are you mocking me?"

"Of course not." Eliza bit her lip. "Just … no, never mind. Let's drop it."

Cat resumed scrubbing. Irritation brought a scowl to her face. Because obviously one *could* have feelings for two people at once. She herself had feelings for three, if she counted the physical desire Grayson sparked in her. Acknowledging that made her feel sick. She was different from her duplicitous ex-fiancé. Wasn't she? Having feelings was one thing; acting on them quite another. She snuck a glance at the sofa. Except she had acted on them. At least one of them.

But she hadn't actually cheated on anyone, she reminded herself. She'd gone out with Grayson after deciding Derrick wasn't for her. And she'd already put Grayson in the 'not again' category before going out with William, in spite of her stupid body reacting whenever he was near. Plus, she and William had only gone on one date; hardly enough time to consider being exclusive.

Although she'd finally acknowledged her silly attraction to Ben Cooper—to herself, at least—she hadn't pursued it. And he hadn't pursued her. She was in the clear, right? So why did she feel so guilty?

"Too bad," Eliza continued after a moment, oblivious to her friend's inner torment. Her mouth quirked up as she shot Cat a grin. "Because he's rather awesome. So funny. Kind. Helpful. And have you ever noticed his eyes? They remind me of hot chocolate. *I'd* date him if I could."

Cat sat back on her heels again and blew her hair out of her eyes with an exasperated harrumph. *Yes. Yes, I have noticed those eyes.* "Maybe you should tell him that. Don't let him having a *girlfriend* stop you."

Eliza raised an innocent eyebrow, obviously delighting in needling her friend. "I'm not his type."

"Good to know. Can we get back to cleaning?"

"Sure," Eliza said, spraying a juice spot with carpet cleaner.

"You know what else he suggested?"

"No, what?" Cat bit out.

"That we should have a Facebook page for the store. I can't believe we didn't think of that ourselves. You know I'm on there all the time."

"I'm not," Cat said. "It's all cat pictures and playing weird, fake farm games, and people hooking up with their exes."

"No, it's not. Besides, Ben's right; I see more and more businesses with Facebook pages. Seems to me like a good way to advertise for free."

"It's free to have a business page?"

"Oh, *now* you're interested?"

"If you're willing to set it up, sure. I'm so not techie."

"No problem, Luddy," Eliza said. "I'll work on it this evening."

The door jingled. Cat stood up to see Grayson removing a scarf from his neck, while the stunning woman next to him glanced around the store, a bored expression on her face. Cat took an immediate dislike to her, although she didn't fully understand why. Except maybe that this woman was tall and lean and absolutely gorgeous. And she had hooked her arm through Gray's in a possessive manner. A small spark of jealousy caught Cat off guard. She might not want Grayson, but apparently she didn't want anyone else to have him yet.

"Hi, Grayson," Eliza called out as she walked forward to greet them.

Oh, sure, Eliza, betray me by being friendly to this model-like creature. Cat crossed her arms. Wait, model-like? Cat studied her again. Could it be? Was that a sisterly rather than a lover-like grasp?

She followed after Eliza, pasting a smile on her face.

"Hi, Eliza. Hi, Cat." Grayson gestured to the woman at his side. "I'd like you to meet my sister, Amy. Amy, this is

Eliza James and Catherine Schreiber. They own this great bookstore."

Eliza's eyes whipped to Cat's. *Amy*?

Amy gave them the barest of nods before turning back to her brother. "Since when are you Grayson, Nick?"

The room started to spin. Nick? His name was Nick? As is Nicholas? She grabbed Eliza's elbow to steady herself, though Eliza didn't seem too stable at the moment, either.

Grayson glared at his sister.

Amy rolled her eyes. "I take it Nick didn't sound intellectual enough for a guy into poetry, so you're using Mom's maiden name?" She sneered at Cat. "I guess it would impress some women."

Cat bristled even as she fought not to throw up.

"Amy?" Eliza broke in. "You're Gray's—Nick's—Gray's sister?"

Amy's face was like ice. "Um, yes. That's what he just said. Although I prefer to go by my full name, Amaryllis. Only Nick—I mean *Grayson*—calls me Amy."

Gray ruffled her hair. "That's what big brothers are for. I am older by seventeen minutes, don't forget."

"I thought—I thought you told me you were an only child?" Cat stammered, the blood draining from her face.

"What? No, I never said that." Giving her a confused look, he continued. "I'm sure I've told you about Amy—oh, pardon me, *Amaryllis*." He elbowed his sister.

Cat gulped in big breaths of air and clutched her arms around her belly. "I'm going to be sick."

"Gross. That's a sign we need to be going, Nick." Amaryllis edged away from Cat.

"Sorry, Cat. Hope it's not that stomach flu going around," Gray said, concern in his voice even as he, too, moved a few steps away. "We'll let you go. I wanted to show Amy your store before I take her over to my department. She's only in town for a few days. There's some sort of bug conference—"

"—Entomology conference!" Amy interjected.

"—over in Gilmer Hall that she wanted to attend."

Cat said nothing, but turned and fled to the back of the store, shutting herself in the storeroom. Eliza burst through the door a minute later, where she found Cat leaning over a bucket, dry-heaving.

"Cat, are you okay?"

Cat sat back on her knees, eyes red and hair wild. "I guess it's good I didn't eat breakfast," she gasped, fighting to catch her breath. "Are they still out there?"

"No. Amy was dragging Grayson out the door as I came back here. He did say to let him know if you needed anything."

They heard the door jingle again. "No! I can't go out there right now, Eliza. I can't. I can't!" Cat whispered, utter panic in her voice.

"Don't worry, I'll take care of it," Eliza said. She left for the front room. Cat could hear her greet someone—it sounded like a grandmotherly-type lady—enthusiastically.

At least it wasn't Grayson returning. Thank God for Eliza.

She sat on the floor of the storage room, struggling to control her racing thoughts. *It's real. It's all real. Or maybe what I should say is, it's fiction! All of it!* She heaved over the bucket again. *I made them up.* A maniacal giggle rose in her throat. How was that even possible?

She raised her eyes to the ceiling. "God, I'm not sure I believe in you half the time, but isn't creating people your arena, not mine? What is this? *What is this*?"

At that moment, Eliza hurried back into the storage room. "This calls for emergency coffee," she exclaimed. "Can you do coffee?"

Cat shook her head weakly as Eliza paced back and forth. "It's two in the afternoon. We can't close now."

"We certainly can." She grabbed Cat's hand and pulled her to her feet. "And we are. Because I can't face this without coffee. And cheesecake. Definitely cheesecake."

Eliza raced to the front of the store, dragging Cat along behind her. Cat's insides still churned. She barely noticed as Eliza flipped the sign to *Closed,* and herded her out the door and across the street.

Entering the coffee shop, Eliza said, "You need to eat something. Now."

Cat shook her head. "I don't think I can. I'll just have a drink."

"Fine, but I'm having cheesecake. Maybe even two slices." Retrieving their orders, they slid into their usual booth.

Cat stared blankly around her, holding the coffee with both hands without drinking it. "I'm going insane. That can't have happened." Her eyes fixed on Eliza with desperation. "Tell me that can't just have happened."

"If you're insane, then I am, too, Cat. Because we were both there and it did happen. You changed the story, and it changed reality."

"But, but … maybe he did tell me he had a sister and I forgot."

"Really? You're going to try to dismiss this *again*? How much proof do you need?"

Cat sank her head down onto her hands, gripping her hair tightly. She stared at the table. "I don't know. I don't know."

Eliza softened her voice. "I know you don't. I don't, either."

"Hey, Cat, Eliza. What are you guys doing here at this time in the afternoon? Is there a problem at the store?"

Oh, God. Ben's voice. *Not now.* She closed her eyes. Not now.

"No, no, everything's fine," Eliza said. "We needed a breather for a few minutes. We'll go back over soon. Can't stay away long in the middle of Christmas season."

A hysterical giggle escaped Cat.

"Is she all right?" she heard Ben say. Then he addressed her directly, putting a gentle hand on her shoulder and asking again, "Are you okay?"

She glanced up at him, her eyes rimmed with tears. "I'm fine, really. Just … just a tough day. I'll be fine."

Ben's eyes radiated concern. She could feel the warmth of his hand through her shirt. "Anything I can do?" he asked.

"No." She shrugged his hand away. His gentleness was making her eyes well up again, and she was afraid she was going to burst into tears right here in the middle of the coffee shop.

He looked stung, but gave her a small smile. "I guess you know how to find me if you need me. Take care."

He nodded at Eliza before walking to the other side of the room, where he sat down and opened his laptop. He was alone today. He didn't look her way.

Turning back to Eliza, she said, "Do you think you could cover the rest of the afternoon? I—I need to sleep. To sleep, and perhaps wake up where all of this makes sense, and where I know what is real and what isn't. Because I sure don't know right now."

"Of course." Eliza squeezed her friend's hand.

"Thanks, Eliza." She closed her eyes again. The manuscript. Derrick. Grayson. William. She couldn't take it all in. *Ben?* She opened her eyes and watched him across the room. Where did he fit in to all of this? Did he?

"Let's go," she said to Eliza, who was shoveling cheesecake into her mouth.

Eliza licked her fork before hopping up. "That'll prepare

me for whatever might walk in the door this afternoon, right?"

Cat just stared ahead, unseeing, as they walked out the door arm in arm. Right. Sure. Unless it were Fitzwilliam Darcy. Or Jane Austen herself.

Which, frankly, at this point wouldn't surprise Cat a bit.

CHAPTER 20

"oly cow. I zonked out for more than sixteen hours," Cat mumbled as she wandered out of her bedroom the next morning, clad in her fuzzy PJs. She yawned and walked over to grab a banana.

"Feel better?" Eliza asked from her perch at the breakfast table. She leafed through a magazine while munching on a bowl of milkless Cap'n Crunch.

"Ugh. How can you eat that stuff?"

"Are you kidding? Nothing better than breakfast with the Cap'n!"

"If you say so. And I feel much better, thanks. Still more than a bit mind-blown about all of this, and wondering if even right now, here with you, I'm dreaming or something, but yeah, better."

"Not a dream." Eliza set the magazine aside and concentrated fully on Cat. Mischief sparkled in her eyes. "Now that you've discovered your secret magical powers, what are you going to do with them?"

"You can joke about this?" How could Eliza be so calm

when everything in Cat was a chaotic swirl of emotion? Her dreams had been a tangle of male faces interspersed with Latin words, all swirling about her in a tornado reminiscent of the one out of *The Wizard of Oz*. In truth, she wouldn't have been surprised to wake up and find herself somewhere over the rainbow. That's how bizarre this all felt. If she clicked her red Converse shoes together three times, could she go back to a time and place when the world made sense?

"What else should we do? Have you ever been in this situation before?" Eliza sipped her orange juice. "My mom always told me 'Start as you mean to go on.' Since there are no precedents for this kind of thing, I say starting out with humor might just be the best approach. Because otherwise it's terrifying and overwhelming. And I'm not the one with superhero abilities."

"Superhero? More like black magic," Cat griped, reaching for a second banana. She wished she knew about the manuscript's origins. Had her ancestors been burned at the stake on account of this miraculous power? The thought was sobering.

"Do we need to add 'Turned herself into a monkey' to your list of professional accomplishments? 'Creator of Amazingly Sexy Men' isn't enough?" Eliza teased, gesturing toward the banana.

Cat waved the fruit toward Eliza. "Abracadabra! I turn thee into ... Elizabeth Bennet!"

Eliza burst out laughing. "I wish."

Cat slid to the floor and leaned back against the oven door. She fingered the fraying edge of her pajama shirt. "Seriously, Lizzie, what does this mean? What could it possibly mean? Why *me*? Why *now*? I wrote those stories years ago—if these men were going to appear, why not back then?"

Eliza rolled a Crunchberry between her fingers as she mulled that over. She shrugged. "I don't know. Maybe the universe was sad you've turned thirty-five and are no longer in the coveted nineteen-to-thirty-four marketing demographic, so it tossed you a bone?" She chucked the piece of cereal into her mouth.

Cat yanked a kitchen towel off the oven door and whipped it at her.

Ducking, Eliza went on. "Why was Greg in the Twin Towers that day? Why do some people win the Lottery and others don't? Why hasn't anyone ever invented the calorie-free donut?"

"Be serious, Eliza."

"I *am* serious, Cat. I learned long ago to stop asking why. I lost my husband when I was eighteen, my parents a few years later. I spent years asking, 'Why me?' One night, I asked myself, 'Why not me'? Life felt better after that, believe it or not."

Cat reflected on that. "But what could it possibly mean? Why would I—or anybody—be able to bring words on a page to *life*? What am I supposed to use that for?"

They both fell silent for a few minutes, lost in their own thoughts. A shrill meow broke the mood as Elvis stalked in, demanding his morning turkey.

As Cat hopped up to feed him, Eliza spoke again. "Maybe that fortune teller we saw over the summer was right. Maybe it's to get you to open yourself up to love again."

"Through a magic *book*?"

"Maybe. I'm choosing to believe it's true."

"You would." Cat gave her a lopsided grin.

Eliza threw a piece of cereal at Cat, hitting her square on the nose. After chewing another bite, she sat up straight and looked at her friend. "Wait. The fortune teller talked about a book."

"What?"

Eliza twirled her hair around a finger. "A book. Remember? She said, 'A book will reveal all, and bring to you all that you want, all that you need.'"

Cat's face froze. "Oh, my God. She did."

"You figured it was because she knew you owned a bookstore. But what if she was talking about the manuscript?"

"I didn't have the manuscript then."

A chill came over her. That's why these men were here now, and not before—she hadn't had the manuscript before. It *was* the manuscript that made all of this possible. Duh. *Oh, my God, if Dad could see me now, he'd say I was madder than the Mad Hatter.*

Except her dad was the one who'd given her the manuscript. He'd promised to tell her about it in his note. But then he'd died. The idea that she'd never know its history tore at her.

Eliza stood up, folding her hands in front of her face, resting her thumbs on her chin and touching her nose with her index fingers. "All three of these men are love interests, right?" she said after a moment.

"Were potential interests, maybe. Not are."

"Yeah, all right. Not Derrick anymore. And I take it not Grayson, either. But they all represented something you were looking for in love at one point, right? I mean, that's why you wrote those particular stories at those particular times."

"Yes. I suppose you're right." Cat leaned down to pet Elvis, who was meowing at her feet. "I wrote about Derrick in high school, when I felt like an outsider and longed to be part of the in crowd." She let out a big exhale. "He did try to make me feel that way on our date. Well, kind of. But I figured out pretty quickly that's not what I need anymore. I'm happier being weird little me."

Eliza nodded.

"And Gray—well, who wouldn't be attracted to Grayson Phillips?" Cat laughed sardonically. "He oozes sexuality. I wrote about him as an undergrad, stuck in the library for all those hours alone when I really wanted to be making out with someone. Anyone."

Eliza raised an eyebrow at that.

"Okay, not just *anyone*," Cat continued as she moved to the sofa, plopping down on it. Elvis immediately jumped up and settled on her lap, nudging her to pet him. "But you remember how that felt, right? Those coed days? The hormones?"

"If you remember, for much of my undergraduate time I was a grieving widow."

Cat stopped petting the cat and looked at her friend. That had never occurred to her, how different college must have felt to Eliza as a new widow. Cat, for the most part, had been carefree. She'd had her studies, her friends, the occasional short-term boyfriend, her dad. "Gosh, Lizzie, I'm so sorry."

"But not all of it," Eliza added. "By senior year I was feeling, er, frisky again. So yeah, I get it." She walked over and joined Cat on the sofa. "Why do you think you wrote about William?"

"I sketched him out when what I wanted most was a man to make me feel like my father had: safe, protected, loved, and supported. Maybe it wasn't so much a Cinderella fantasy as an aching for my dad." She stared unseeingly at the floor.

Eliza made a sympathetic noise.

"Fine, the Cinderella fantasy, too," Cat admitted, "but mostly security is what I craved. What I still crave, really."

She stopped, looking up at Eliza.

Eliza's eyes widened and she clapped her hand to her mouth.

"What?" Cat's voice was sharp.

"I just realized something," Eliza yelled. "You're Ebeneezer Scrooge!"

"Say what?"

"You're Scrooge! Being visited by three men: Derrick, the man of the past; ageless Grayson, the man of the present; and William, the man of the future. That's why the book brought these three guys to life; you're Scrooge, and the universe wants you to stop saying 'Bah, humbug' to love."

"I think you've reached your limit on the breakfast cereal, roomie," Cat said with a snort. Her head was swimming. *What about Ben?* part of her demanded. She'd never written about him, so why was he in her life, and often on her mind? "In the end, Scrooge rejected all those ghosts, you know. He changed himself, and changed his life. His future."

"True."

After a minute, Cat looked at Eliza again, horror etched across her face. "You said I was Ebeneezer. A fictional character. You don't really think *I'm* a character, do you?" Cat took in great gulps of air. "What if we all are? What if somewhere someone else wrote a story about us, and now we're alive because of them? Oh my *God*, Eliza."

Eliza sat back down on the sofa, grasping her friend firmly by the shoulders. "Breathe. Just breathe."

They both inhaled and exhaled for several breaths. After a minute, Cat gave a brisk nod. "I'm fine. Relatively speaking."

"I'd like to think if I'm a character in someone's novel that they'd have pity on me and give me a more fulfilling life than this," cracked Eliza.

Cat chuckled. "Yeah, can my author give me bigger boobs and an even bigger bank account?"

They both guffawed at that thought.

"Maybe you could do that for yourself, Cat," Eliza said once they'd stopped laughing.

"Seriously?"

Eliza nodded vigorously. "Of course seriously. If you've created these guys, who knows what else you can do?"

Both women were silent for a moment.

"Maybe it's not limited to just the romantic idea of love, you know?" Eliza ventured.

"There's only one way to find out." Cat jumped up and rushed over to the kitchen table, pulling a napkin from the center holder. Grabbing a pen from the nearby pencil jar, she scribbled down *Catherine Schreiber had enormous breasts and a checkbook balance to match.* Standing back, she peered down at her chest.

Eliza stared at it, as well. "Nope," she said after a few minutes. "No bigger."

Cat hiccupped a laugh. "Maybe the boobs were too much to ask for. I'll check the bank balance. Can I use your laptop?"

"Sure." Eliza gestured toward the computer sitting next to the sofa.

Cat walked over to it and opened a web browser, typing in her info. It only took about ten seconds until she said, "Dang, no luck there, either."

"Maybe you need to write a real story, not just a line on a napkin."

"Maybe." Cat paused. "I can't believe we're having this conversation, can you?"

"Eh, I've had weirder."

Cat raised an eyebrow.

"All right, not much weirder, but Greg and I did stay up all night once imaging in elaborate detail what it would be like to be a cockroach."

"Sounds like you'd been drinking too much tequila. Or reading too much Kafka."

Eliza giggled. "Maybe. We decided a cockroach's life might not be so bad. At least we knew we'd survive an atomic bomb. But we agreed if people started singing *La Cucaracha* every time they saw us, that'd be it. That song drove us nuts."

Cat rolled her eyes. "*We're* seriously nuts. Let's go grab a coffee and get the store opened. I'm thinking we'll get lots of Christmas shoppers today." She rubbed her hands together in anticipation.

"You do? That's unusually optimistic of you. Is there some event going on I don't know about?"

"Nope. I'm going to write an elaborate story about it while we're at the coffeehouse. What further guarantee do you need?" She headed toward her room to get dressed.

"Based on your chest, or lack thereof," Eliza called after her, "a much bigger one. Guarantee, that is."

Cat turned around, grabbed Eliza's latest romance off the back of the couch and whipped it at her friend. "Thanks a lot!"

"Anytime," Eliza sang out as she danced away. "Anytime!"

Fifteen minutes later, they were settled in their usual coffee booth, Cat indulging in another morning muffin. Worrying about calories seemed a trivial concern in the face of everything going on.

"Lizzie," she said, setting the muffin down. "Do you think I could write a story in which my dad doesn't die? Do you think I could bring him back?"

Eliza was quiet for a bit. "You could try, I guess. If you consider the consequences."

"What consequences?"

"I don't know. We don't know how all of this works. Based on our interactions with Gray and his sister yesterday, it seems once you change something about someone, the person doesn't remember their life any differently. So if you write a story in which your dad never died, maybe you'd never be the wiser if it came true." She nibbled at a chocolate chip cookie. "And what would that do to us? I wouldn't be living with you, right? If your dad were still running the bookstore, what would you be doing? You told me often before he died that you didn't see yourself selling books forever."

"Hmm." Cat fiddled with the stir stick for her coffee. "I'd like to think we'd have met in the same way, regardless. And even if *I* didn't remember, you still would, just like you and I knew yesterday that Grayson had never really had a sister, even if he didn't."

"True. I guess." Eliza ate the last of her cookie. "This is all so confusing. If I remembered, but you didn't, who's to say I could convince you to befriend me again?"

Cat couldn't imagine ever not being friends with Eliza. "It's a bizarre thought, isn't it? Kind of sad. Although I'm certain I'd be friends with you, no matter what. You're that awesome." She paused, brushing her hair out of her eyes. "But I have to try, Eliza. I have to try."

"Fair enough. Are you going to finish that muffin?"

"Nah, here, you have the rest." Cat pushed the muffin over toward Eliza. "I'm going to write a story about my dad never dying. And I'm going to put in it that we also win the Lottery. Anything else?"

"Let's see if those work, first."

Cat spent the next fifteen minutes sketching out the details in the spiral notebook she'd brought with her. With a smile, she put the cap back on her pen and closed the book. Gazing out the window, she said, "I'm ready to go back to the Treasure Trove now. Maybe when I walk through the door, my dad will be there. My dad could be there, Lizzie." She stared wistfully at the bookstore's front steps.

Eliza closed the novel she'd been reading while Cat wrote. Catching a glimpse of the cover, Cat snickered. "*Earl To Bed, Earl to Rise*? That's the title of your latest smut book?"

"I thought it quite catchy, myself. Wouldn't you want *your* earl to be able to 'rise' to the occasion?" Eliza said cheekily, standing up and gathering her to-go cup.

Cat raised her eyes to the ceiling.

"Look who's talking," Eliza said. "You've written about three men having the hots for you, in some highly descriptive detail, I might add, and you're chiding *me* about *my* reading material? I only read it, oh, Queen of Smut, I don't write it. Much less live it."

"Point taken," Cat muttered. "Point taken."

Cat bounded up the stairs to the bookstore, eagerly unlocking the front door and launching herself through the entrance.

"Dad?" She scanned the room. Running toward the back, she called out again. "Dad? Are you here?"

Eliza walked into the storage room after her. "I'll check upstairs."

"No, no, I'll go. If he's here, I want to be the one to find him." Cat raced up to the apartment. As she flung open the door, she called out, "Dad, it's Catherine!"

The only answer was a questioning meow as Elvis padded out to see what all the commotion was about.

Cat waited a moment. "Dad?" she said more softly.

But it was clear he wasn't there. She shuffled back down the stairs. Eliza stood waiting at the cash register, a hopeful expression on her face. Cat shook her head, a tear rolling down her cheek. Eliza's face fell, too, and she rushed to gather her friend up in a fierce hug.

"I'm so sorry. Maybe you need to give it some time?"

"I doubt it," Cat answered dully. "I wrote that he'd never died, and crafted an elaborate scene in which he was decorating the store with thousands of Christmas lights, the way he used to love to do. I dated it today, this morning, at 8:30."

She sighed, tears streaming down her face. "It's 8:43 right now. It didn't work." Waves of grief washed over her, nearly as strong as they'd been right after he'd died. She didn't want to acknowledge how much she'd pinned on being able to see him again. She knew how lucky she'd been to have a father as wonderful as her dad. She just wished she'd had him a little longer. Was that so much to ask? A few more years?

Eliza rubbed her back for a while, holding her friend. "I'm sorry. I know how much you miss him. I know." After a minute, she asked, "I guess it's too much to hold out hope we won the Lottery?"

Cat choked out a half-laugh. "I don't know. Let's see if there is a ticket in my wallet. If not, then nope."

Backing out of the hug, she pulled her wallet out of her

pocket and checked its insides. "Nope, no ticket. And like they say, 'you can't win if you don't play.'" She started to giggle.

Eliza watched her, concern etched across her face.

"I guess raising the dead is better left to sorcerers." Cat cackled harder.

"Do you need to go back to bed?"

"No, no," Cat replied, struggling to adopt a more sober demeanor. She wiped the tears from her eyes. "I'm just wondering what the frigging point is of this super-power, as you call it, if I can't use it for what I truly want. It's been fun to have some male attention, but I don't want love, Eliza. What I *want* is my dad back."

Eliza rubbed her back again. "You think you don't want love, but maybe it's exactly what you need. Ever consider that?"

Cat pushed away from her. "Romance isn't the only thing in the world. Wasn't that what you told me after Ryan left? That there was so much more to life than being in a relationship?" Her voice exuded bitterness.

"Yes. I did say that. Because you were my friend and you were grieving and in pain."

Cat looked at her with wary eyes.

"It's still true," Eliza continued. "There *is* a lot more to life than any single relationship. But wouldn't that 'more' be richer still if you had the right person with whom to experience it?"

Cat sniffed. "I'm sorry. I shouldn't have snapped at you. Some friend I am." She hugged Eliza again. "Sometimes I'm so focused on my own crap that I forget about yours. You seem so at peace with it."

Eliza rocked back on her heels. "I guess I am. Do I wish Greg had never died? Of course. But sometimes I wonder if we would have made it. We were so young. So very young."

Cat shoved her bangs out of her face. "Wait, are you saying you don't think love can last forever? You, the romance novel addict? Who's told me repeatedly that's what you want?"

"Of course I want that. I just don't think every relationship, or even every marriage, can achieve that. I'm holding out for one that can."

"How will you know when you've found it? Everyone wants that, but most marriages end in divorce."

"Not most. Fifty percent, and that number is going down," Eliza said. "I'll know when I find it."

Cat raised an eyebrow.

"I'll know. I believe Greg and I were destined to be together, but as the years have gone by, I've come to believe we were also destined to be apart. Like a flame meant to burn only briefly. I can't explain it. I've always felt as if that lifelong love is still out there, waiting for me. We just haven't found each other yet."

"You are an incurable romantic."

"Yes, I am, Ms. Schreiber. And proud of it."

The door jangled and a group of teenagers wandered in. "Shouldn't they be in school?" Cat remarked.

"On a Saturday?"

"It's Saturday?" Cat shrieked.

"Uh, yeah."

"Oh, no! I have that date with William this afternoon." She ran over to check her hair in the mirror next to the door. "You can still cover the store, right?"

"Sure thing. I wouldn't want to get in the way of you and possible true love."

CHAPTER 21

"So to where are you spiriting me off?" asked William, as he crawled into the front seat of Cat's Honda.

"Can you ice skate?"

William's eyes lit up. "Yes, I can. We skated on my cousins' backyard pond in Wellesley every Christmas. I love it."

He adjusted his long legs without complaint in the cramped space of the passenger seat. "I'm nowhere as good as my cousin's son, though. He's training for the Olympics."

Cat snorted. "I should hope you're not that good. I'm not sure I can make it around the rink without falling down—it's been years since I've skated. But I thought it sounded like a fun, low-key afternoon, so I'm glad you're up for it."

"Where's the rink? It's hardly cold enough for ice around here."

"There's an inside rink downtown."

"Great!"

Cat drove through Charlottesville, casting surreptitious glances at Will. He was definitely handsome, and whatever cologne he was wearing smelled heavenly. He caught her looking at him and smiled, placing his hand over hers on the gearshift and squeezing it.

"I'm glad I'm here today, Catherine. I enjoy being with you."

Cat smiled in return, but her smile slipped a little when she reminded herself he liked her because he had to like her. She'd created him that way. Or had she? Just because she said she wanted a certain type of man and they showed up didn't mean they *had* to like her. They could be into her of their own volition. Couldn't they?

A frown puckered her brow.

"Was that too forward?" said William, removing his hand.

"Not at all. I was trying to figure out how to switch to third gear without disturbing your fingers," she lied.

He smiled but kept his hand on his own knee. "I don't know many people who drive a stick anymore. That's a skill."

"My mom insisted I learn. I'm glad she did. One of the reasons this car was cheap was because the dealer said nobody wanted a manual transmission any more. It was the only way I could afford it."

"I could get you a car if you'd like," Will said casually.

"What?" Cat glanced at him in surprise, and then flicked her eyes back to the road. "You can't be serious. We hardly know each other."

"I know I like being with you, and I know I can afford it. It'd make me happy to give you one if you'd take it."

"Well, I won't. Besides, what's wrong with this Honda?"

"Nothing," William conceded. "If you don't mind very little leg room."

"It's cute."

Will wrinkled his nose. "Cute? Cute is not a characteristic one looks for in a car."

"It is if you're female, buddy. Or at least this female." She arched an eyebrow at him.

"Let me guess. You like Mini Coopers and Bugs."

"Why, yes, I do. My favorites are those tiny Smart Cars, though."

William shook his head in mock disgust. "Those things are death traps. One fender bender and the car would be totaled—and you along with it."

"Good thing I'm an excellent driver, then, because I still want one. Only not from you," she amended quickly.

He raised his hands in surrender. "The lady doesn't want me to buy her a car, I won't buy her a car."

"Such sacrificial gallantry."

"Like a knight in shining armor ... in reverse." His eyes crinkled in amusement.

Cat's mind flew back to Ben Cooper. Every time the word 'knight' came up, she thought of him, and his jeans-clad rear, in the bookstore. It was distracting, and annoying. She did not need to think of him when she was on a date with a modern-day Prince Charming. She gripped the steering wheel, determined to push thoughts of Ben far, far away.

She pulled into a parking space near the rink. "We're here."

William grabbed her hand and placed a kiss on the back of it. "I've been looking forward to spending time with you again, Catherine."

A Prince Charming who was completely into her.

He hopped out and strolled around the front of the car to open the driver's side door.

"This feels backwards," he noted, one side of his mouth tipping up.

Taking his hand, Catherine eased out of the car. "I'd say this feels pretty good."

William raised his eyebrows in pleasant surprise and tucked her arm into his. "In that case, lead on."

"Wow, you really *can* skate!" she said to him a short while later, as she edged her way along the wall of the rink.

William glided next to her easily. "You can hold on to my arm," he offered, extending his elbow.

"Not yet. If I fall, I don't want to take anyone down with me. I'm still getting used to this again."

"I wouldn't let you fall, Catherine. Ever." He gave her his best smile, shaking his elbow again.

She sighed inwardly. *He really is perfect.* So why did she feel tense? It's not as if she wasn't having a good time. She was. But something felt off. She frowned, closing her eyes briefly.

"Are you doing all right?" William asked with solicitous concern. "I can slow down."

"No, no, I'm fine. In fact, I do feel more secure with you."

"I'm glad to hear it. I'll always keep you safe."

Of course you will. Because that's the reason I created you, to keep me safe. She released William's elbow and grabbed his hand, lacing her fingers through his and clasping them firmly.

"I'm getting better!" she exclaimed, just before she lost her balance and started to stumble. William instantly yanked her back up, pulling her against him to keep her upright.

"See? Told you." His cheeks dimpled in a grin.

Cat stared into his green eyes, a green the color of grass in the springtime—not the brown of chocolate, thank goodness.

His face grew serious as he returned her gaze, and they

stopped in the middle of the rink. He pulled her into him, brushing his lips across hers. She relaxed into his body, looping her arms up around his neck. Just as William intensified the kiss, the sound of cheering from the skaters around them caused them to break off their embrace. He gave her a sheepish grin.

"Sorry," she said.

He touched his finger to her lips as if to silence her. "Don't be, Catherine. I don't mind an audience if it means I get to kiss you."

She laced her fingers through his once more and they made several loops around the rink. She enjoyed watching the families there: fathers teaching their daughters how to skate, sons showing off for their moms, and the occasional couple taking a spin around the rink, often hand-in-hand as she and William were. After an hour of easy conversation, several near falls, and lots of laps, she said, "How about some ice cream? There's a great place down about a block."

"Sounds delicious. I'm glad it's unseasonably warm outside. Ice cream in December isn't my usual thing."

Cat chuckled. "Mine either, but I have a craving for some with chocolate chip cookie dough in it, and I'm going to go with it."

"I like a woman who knows what she wants," he said as they made their way off the ice.

She almost tripped getting to the bench to change back into their regular shoes, and was thankful when William didn't notice. *Did* she know what she wanted? It was easy to get caught up in it when she was with him. But this was a fantasy. Would a man like William have taken an interest in her if she hadn't written him that way?

Just do as you said you're doing with the ice cream, and go with it already.

They walked down the Ped Mall. "My sister Caroline would love it here," William said. "She loves artsy stuff and antiques. I'll have to bring her down sometime to meet you."

Family? He wanted her to meet his family? A jolt of panic hit her out of nowhere. *I'm not ready for that. I don't belong in his world. Not really. Or rather, he doesn't belong in mine.*

"She'd love you," William continued. "You remind me of her, actually. Maybe that's one of the reasons I was instantly attracted to you."

He paused for a second as Cat raised an eyebrow at him. "Th-that came out wrong. I'm *not* attracted to my sister, not like that. I meant I feel comfortable with you because you're like her. Except that I'm captivated by you in a way that I'm not by her, of course." He blew out a long breath. "I'll stop talking now."

It thrilled Cat that she could fluster this man who walked with ease in the world of wealth and power. "I knew what you meant," she said with a grin. "But it was fun to watch you try to get yourself out of that one."

"Thanks a lot," he said wryly as they entered the small gelato shop. "Every man wants to act the idiot in front of their lady."

She snickered. At his confused look, she said, "Sorry. I was glad you didn't call me your 'old' lady."

William laughed. "Come on, you're not that old. What are you, thirty? Thirty-two?"

"Thirty-five," she said with a grimace.

"Hey, me, too," he answered, and then gave his order to the young man behind the counter.

That brought Cat up short. They were the same age? He ran a company, owned his own private jet, and travelled regularly all around the world. What did she have to show for herself at thirty-five? A bookstore that was failing, a car with nearly one hundred thousand miles on it, and a cat that ate too much.

She gave her order. Accepting her ice cream, she licked at it without tasting it, suddenly dispirited. Eliza, she reminded herself. She had Eliza. And Eliza would remind her that William was not out of her league, because she'd created him for herself. She should enjoy him. Of course that would be easier if she could trust that he liked her for her, not just because he was written that way.

"Shall we catch dinner, now that we've had dessert?" he asked before licking a bit of ice cream off his spoon.

"I can't. That's why I suggested the afternoon. I'm sorry, I should have told you. Eliza and I are hosting Santa Claus at the store this evening. In fact, I need to head back to get ready. Santa arrives at six o'clock."

"Oh." William looked nonplussed for a moment. "Okay, then. I'm glad to know, at least, that you don't have another date," he teased.

"Not with anyone over twelve, anyway," she quipped as they walked back out on the Ped Mall.

They strolled for a bit in comfortable silence before William asked, "Do you need any help?"

"Really?" she said, surprised. "You'd be surrounded by lots of screaming children, many with runny noses."

"Sounds delightful. I see why you want to host it."

"Ha, ha. I don't, except that it generates a fair number of sales. Give away a hot drink and candy canes, and parents usually feel guilty enough to buy something. We'll take it."

"That's the spirit of the season," he gibed as they reached her car. He opened her door for her. "You're not going to make me wear an elf costume, are you? Because I don't look good in pointy ears."

Cat laughed out loud as she slid into the driver's seat. "You're in luck, because we're all out of elf wear in your size."

She eyed him speculatively. "You might make a good Mrs. Claus, though."

CHAPTER 22

"**G**oodness, Eliza, I had no idea it'd be this busy. You should've called me."

"And ruin your date? I don't think so. It was only a couple of hours. Besides, Jill came in and helped out for a while. She left about ten minutes ago."

Cat took off her coat and hung it on the hook behind the door. Smoothing her hair back, she hurried to the desk to ring up a family's purchases.

"Don't forget that Santa is visiting tonight," she said to the dad. "Free hot chocolate!"

He nodded pleasantly, herding his children ahead of him toward the door.

"So nice to see a dad out with his kids, isn't it?"

"Yeah, it is," Eliza said, pausing from stuffing candy canes into a red bag trimmed with white fur. "Now spill the beans. How was the date?"

"I felt like Cinderella at the ball, marveling over this Prince wanting to dance—or skate—with me." She didn't mention her doubts to Eliza. Didn't mention Ben Cooper.

Didn't mention how hard it was to trust that a fantasy could be real. She wasn't going to think about all of that right now.

Eliza winked at her. "You deserve a Prince, darling." She moved to arrange the hot chocolate carafe and marshmallows on the table near the fireplace. "Think we have enough? Remember last year, when we almost ran out?"

"We'll be fine. If we do start running low on supplies, I'll send my Santa's helper out for more."

"Santa's helper?"

"Yes, William. He's coming over in a bit. He wanted to help."

"Wow. Now that's a dream come true: a man willing to put up with a room full of kids hopped up on sugar."

The door jingled. "Ho, ho, ho!" they heard, as in walked Santa Claus—or, as they knew him, Shannon's husband. It always amused Cat and Eliza that Scott, the skinniest man they knew, insisted on donning that big suit and scratchy beard every year. But he loved it, he insisted, loved seeing all the kids come in, even his own, who apparently hadn't yet figured out it was Daddy beneath all the red velvet and pillows stuffed into his belly.

"Hi, Scott," Cat called out.

"That's Mr. Claus to you, missy," he replied jovially. "Think we'll have a big crowd this year?"

"I hope so. Fifty-degree-weather doesn't generally put one in the Christmas mood, but then again, people are more willing to come out in it than they are in snow."

"True, true." Santa took up his seat on the couch, which they'd flipped to face away from the fireplace for this event. He adjusted his bowl full of jelly. "Let me know if there's anything I can do to help."

The door jingled again, and Cat looked up to see William

enter. He smiled, crossing over to kiss her cheek. "Hello, you."

"Hello back," she replied. This man treated her like a princess. But Cinderella had turned back into a regular old working girl at midnight. Gone were the riches, the atmosphere, the magic. *She got them back in the end, though*, Cat told herself firmly. No one ever said Cinderella felt like a pretender to her throne, right?

"Hi, William. It's nice to see you," Eliza called from the other side of the room, where she was arranging the children's books after an afternoon of kids playing with them.

"It's a pleasure to see you again, as well, Miss James," he responded with a wink.

The door chimed again. "Santa!" shrieked an excited little voice, as a girl about four shot through the door and raced over to his lap, her laughing mother following behind.

"And so it begins," whispered Cat to William.

For the next half hour, Cat was busy ringing up sales and helping people find books. She loved to see the store humming like this, and wished it would happen year-round. It felt more like it had when she was a child, hanging around with her dad on the weekends helping to restock shelves: full of life and energy and fun. She hugged her arms to herself during a slight lull in customers, praying she'd be able to keep it going.

She studied William. *What would he want if we were to get more seriously involved?* She doubted he'd be willing to live in Charlottesville, given his company's needs. She frowned. She hadn't thought about that, what she might have to give up to be with her Prince. Cinderella had escaped a bad situation, but Cat had a real life here, with people and places she loved. It was one of the reasons she hadn't followed her family to Ohio, although she missed them dearly.

I could just write him as having his company here in town, she reminded herself. That would work, wouldn't it? Only that felt unsatisfying. She wanted him to be with her because *he* wanted to, not because she'd created him to want her.

"This is a conundrum," she muttered under her breath. She had created the Perfect Man, and yet she didn't know if she could trust that he actually cared about *her*, Catherine Abigail Schreiber, rather than was just acting a part he didn't know he'd been cast to play.

"Cat!" called out a deep voice as the door jingled again. Ben Cooper walked through the door with a little girl of about six, decked out from head to toe in a Snow White costume.

"Hi, Ben," she replied in a friendly voice, ignoring the zing of excitement that raced through her upon seeing him. She looked at the little girl, who seemed familiar. Had Cat seen her before? "Who's this darling princess you've brought with you?"

"I'm Sthnow White," said the girl in a cheerful voice. "I'm here to sthee Sthanta!"

"She's my niece," Ben explained. "My sister's daughter. Martha is home with the flu, so I said I'd bring Alice today."

"Well, hi, Alice. I mean, Snow White," Cat amended. "You look beautiful! I'm sure Santa will be delighted to see you. There are a few children waiting ahead of you, but you can go right over there and get in line if you'd like. Eliza can get you some hot chocolate or a cookie."

"Okay!" Alice chirped, and ran off to the area near the fireplace.

Ben remained near Cat, studying her. Her insides flipped as her cheeks filled with heat. What was up with that? She was a mess today.

"Hello," a voice interjected. Startled, Cat looked over to

see William next to her, inspecting Ben with curious eyes.

"Hello," Ben replied, returning William's inspection.

"Ben, this is William Dawes. William, this is Ben Cooper," Cat said, feeling oddly uncomfortable. The men shook hands, giving each other a small smile.

"How do you know Miss Schreiber?" William asked in a pleasant voice.

"We met at the coffee shop. I'm a friend."

"Oh, yes, Cooper. The computer science professor who fixed the computer system here once, correct?"

Ben's eyes met Cat's. "Yes, the computer repair person," he said flatly.

He sounds hurt. "Oh, he's more than that." She smiled widely at Ben. "He's a good friend. And he's helped me a lot in the store, coming up with great ideas like our new Facebook page."

William regarded her with a thoughtful expression. After a moment he said, "I guess I have some competition, then."

Ben and Cat stared at him.

"No, it's not like that. He's got a girlfriend," Cat said.

William chuckled. "I meant in terms of helping you out." He reached for her hand. Ben watched them intertwine fingers, but said nothing, a hard-to-read expression on his face.

"Uncle Ben! Uncle Ben!" Alice called, "It'sth my turn, Uncle Ben!"

"No jokes about rice," he said to Cat as he walked over to take a picture of his niece.

"Cat, we're almost out of hot chocolate," Eliza called a few seconds later. She rushed over to her friend. "And there's still a lot of kids waiting."

"Don't worry, I'll go get some more," William offered.

Eliza breathed a sigh of relief. "Thanks, William. If you just take this extra carafe across the street, you can get some from the coffee shop."

He took the empty pot from her. "I'll be right back," he called, heading out the door.

Cat walked over to the edge of the room with her camera, wanting to take a picture of Santa and the kids to display in the store. As she was angling for the best shot, Ben and his niece approached her.

"Thank you for letting us visit today," he said. "Alice had a wonderful time."

Alice beamed, showing her candy cane and the hot chocolate mustache over her upper lip. "Look, Uncle Ben! You're under the mithtletoe!"

Both Cat and Ben glanced up to realize they were, indeed, under the mistletoe that Eliza had hung above the Romance section in which they were standing. Cat glanced quickly at the various covers of women with bosoms about to fall out of bodices, clutching intense, impossibly beautiful men. *Awkward.*

"You haff to kissth her, Uncle Ben. That's what the rulesth are!" Alice insisted.

"I'm not sure—" Cat began.

"Alice, no—" Ben started to say.

Alice's face fell. "You haff to, Uncle Ben. Mommy saysth! She makesth Daddy kissth *her* under the missthletoe all the time!"

"All right," Cat said.

Ben looked at her. "Okay?"

She nodded. "We can't disappoint a little girl at Christmas, can we?"

"I guess not," he answered.

Cat licked her lips, suddenly nervous. *Come on. It's just a quick smooch for a little girl. It doesn't mean anything.*

Ben leaned in and she closed her eyes. His lips brushed hers and she was surprised by their softness. She was expecting a brief peck, but Ben moved his mouth over hers again, and she leaned into him, too, wanting to get closer. He tasted delicious, like vanilla. When his lips, those surprisingly soft lips, opened, she responded in kind, winding her fingers up through his hair.

Suddenly all she could feel, all she could hear, all she could experience, reduced itself to this one kiss. She no longer heard the kids wailing near Santa, no longer remembered she was standing in a store in front of a multitude of people, no longer wanted anything but to deepen their connection, deepen this kiss, which thrilled her in a way nothing else had in a long time. Not William's kiss that afternoon. Not even Grayson.

With those unwanted thoughts of other men, she broke off the kiss and stepped away. Ben looked at her in shock, as if he, too, was caught unaware by what had just happened. Alice gaped at them.

"It was the mistletoe," Cat offered lamely, pointing up and giving Alice a wan smile. She touched her lips with her fingers, as if disbelieving the feeling that still lingered there. She'd made him kiss her, and he had a girlfriend. "I'm sorry, Ben."

He looked her full in the face. After a few seconds, he said, "I'm not."

Cat's mouth dropped open. "But Mei …"

She didn't know what else to say. She was surprised at how badly she wanted to kiss him again, wanted to get close to those chocolate eyes, wanted to wrap herself around him and not let go.

Ben opened his mouth as if to say something, just as William's voice rang out. "Hot chocolate's here!"

He closed the door behind him, pot of hot chocolate in hand. The kids cheered. William nodded over toward Ben and Cat, who still stood under the mistletoe, then set the carafe on the table. Turning, he walked over to them.

"See? That didn't take long. Did I miss anything?"

CHAPTER 23

"**Y**essth!" piped up Alice.

Cat eyed her nervously.

"I got to sthee Sthanta, and he told me I wassth on the nice lissth. My mommy will be proud!"

They all laughed, but Ben and Cat continued to cast furtive glances at each other, even as William settled his arm around Cat's shoulders. Cat was sure Ben's eyes narrowed at that.

Her mind whirled with a million thoughts, a million emotions. How dare he act jealous when he already had a girlfriend? She sucked in a deep breath. She'd kissed a man involved with someone else. Not only that, she'd initiated it. She'd never been the cheating kind; the thought of being the Other Woman had always made her want to retch. She'd sworn she'd never do that to someone. She knew the pain it caused all too well.

She frowned, looking up at William. They'd only been on two dates. They were hardly exclusive, but she was technically involved with someone else, too. How could she? How could *he*? She clutched her arms across her stomach, disgust at her own actions warring with the heady recollections of that magnificent kiss.

"Come on, Alice," Ben said to his niece after a moment, a sad expression flitting across his face. "I promised you dinner, and then I've got to get you home."

"Ooh! Can we go to McDonaldssth?"

"Um, how about we get pizza instead?"

"Ooh! Pizztha! Pizztha!" she chanted excitedly, jumping up and down.

"It's been … a pleasure," Ben said, his eyes dropping to Cat's lips. "A real pleasure," he repeated.

Cat was sure her face betrayed everything. William looked at her curiously. "Yes, it was nice to see you again, Ben," she blurted out.

"Cat? Can you get more cookies from the back?" Eliza called, as Ben led Alice out the door.

It was all Cat could do to keep her eyes from following him. "Sure thing, Eliza."

William rubbed her shoulder with his fingers before removing his arm. "I have to go," he said. "I've got to head to the airport. But I'll call you soon."

He dropped a quick kiss on her lips. "Thanks for the great date. And at least you got to make use of the mistletoe," he said, pointing up.

Cat choked on her laugh. "Yeah," she answered. *If you only knew.*

Ben Cooper's face danced before her eyes as she watched William walk out the door. As she went to retrieve the treats, she was stunned to realize how intensely she wished Ben would walk back in.

Late that evening, Cat and Eliza were sipping celebratory wine while cleaning up the remnants of St. Nick's successful visit.

"What do you want for Christmas?" Cat asked her friend.

"What?"

"What do you want for Christmas this year? Sorry I'm asking so late, but I've been so caught up in everything that's been going on with my mom and, well, you know, that I haven't thought about gifts for anyone yet. I need to get on that." *Yes, I need to focus on Christmas, and not on Ben Cooper. Or anything about Ben Cooper. Not his eyes. Not his mouth. Not the fact that he cheated on his girlfriend. With me.*

Cat knew some would argue it wasn't really cheating, a kiss under the mistletoe done at a child's request. But that hadn't been just any kiss. It was unlike anything she'd ever experienced, and one glance at Ben's face had told her he felt the same.

And then there was William. Kind, generous, unknowing William. Guilt and desire raged within her. *Nope. Not going there. Christmas. I'm focusing on Christmas. And Eliza.*

Eliza sat back on her heels, taking a break from scrubbing candy cane droppings out of the carpet. "I don't know. Let me think about it."

"Okay," Cat said as she picked up paper cups from around the room.

"Are you going to Ohio?"

"I don't think so. I'd love to see my family, but I was just there, and with Mom feeling so much better and us being so busy here, I'm thinking I'll go in January like I usually do."

"Don't you mind not being with your family on Christmas?"

"Not if I have you." Cat dropped the bag of cups into the large trashcan she'd pulled to the middle of the room. Pausing, she looked at Eliza. "You'll be here, won't you?"

Eliza gave a derisive snort. "Where else would I be?"

Cat jerked as if stung.

"Not that I don't want to be with you, Cat. I didn't mean it like that. You know how much I love you. I just wish that I had a family like other people. I'll be here because I have nowhere else to go. I haven't for years. An only child of only children parents, with no surviving family. Aren't I the lucky one?"

"Well, *I'm* lucky to have a friend like you. I don't know what I'd do without you." Cat walked over and bent down, enfolding her friend in a giant hug, releasing her only after several moments.

Eliza sat back again. Grabbing her glass, she took a big gulp of wine. Staring at the floor, she asked in a quiet voice, "Would you be willing to find out?"

"What?"

"Would you be willing to find out what you'd do without me?"

"What are you talking about, Eliza?"

"There's somewhere I want to go. If you'll help me."

Cat sat down next to her friend.

"I know what I want for Christmas, Cat," Eliza said. "Or rather, I know who."

Cat held her breath. She knew what was coming.

"I know it didn't work when you wanted to bring your dad back. So I know I can't bring Greg back. But it *has* worked for you to find love, or at least possible love interests, right? Maybe you can make that work for me." She looked at Cat earnestly.

"Eliza …"

"Just listen. Please. I know it might not work. I'm good with that. But I'm asking. For Christmas, I'm asking you to write a story in which I finally get my duke. A Regency duke."

Cat pressed her lips together. "You want me to write a romance for you in which you are with a real Regency duke? In England? Like, two hundred years ago?" She paused to sip her wine. "I mean, you've been talking about a duke for a while, but I thought you were kidding. Or at least aiming for one in this century."

"Yes," Eliza said in a solemn tone. "That is what I want."

Cat sat, nonplussed. "I think you've had too much wine, Lizzie."

"There isn't anything here for me anymore," Eliza cried. "I love you, and I enjoy the store, but I have no one else. No family. No husband. I'm twenty-nine years old, and my life is passing me by." She threw her arms up in the air. "I'm getting nowhere in finishing my doctorate degree, and I think I'm stalling because I don't know what to do when I'm done. I don't really want to teach. I don't want to have to write papers and go to conferences and all that. I definitely don't want to have to start paying back those grad school loans. What I *do* want is to immerse myself in nineteenth-century English culture, rather than have to make a career out of it. I want to *live* it."

"Eliza, even if time travel were possible, how do you know you'd truly *like* living two centuries ago? It's not all a Jane Austen novel, you know. You'd lose so many freedoms that you take for granted now. Like voting. And dressing in shorts. And pizza."

Eliza patted her belly. "It would do me good to give up pizza."

Cat snorted.

"And I know all that, Cat," Eliza continued. "But I don't just want to be in Regency England—I want to have a grand love story in Regency England. Seeing you with Grayson and William … Well, I've been really jealous. And it's made me realize what I want. I want a husband. I want kids. And I don't seem to be finding that here."

"You think it'd be like a romance novel."

"I think it could be, if you wrote it," Eliza said, nodding.

Cat swallowed. "I'm humbled by your faith in me, but I don't know anything about Regency England. How could I write an accurate story?"

"You don't have to do all the details—just something similar to what you wrote about William, only make it a duke for me." Her eyes beseeched her friend. "Please? Try it? I penned something myself after the Amaryllis debacle, but it didn't work. It's gotta be you."

Cat stared at her friend for a long time. She didn't think it would work, creating a love story for someone other than herself. In another time period, to boot. It was an absolutely nutso idea—but what if it did work? *Then I'd be on my own.*

Shame crept over her. It was selfish to want to keep Eliza for herself. And it wasn't fair, either, to want to hold on to her friend because she'd been afraid to move on in life and take on new challenges.

She took another sip of her wine. "Okay."

"You'll do it?" Eliza said, her voice wavering.

"Yes, I'll do it. I can't promise it'll work."

"I know. Oh, thank you, Cat! Thank you for trying."

"How do I get you back there? I mean, it's mind-boggling enough that I've created people to begin with—God, I can't believe how easily I say that now. But to throw time travel into the mix?"

Eliza studied her wine glass. "Let's throw a party," she said suddenly. "A Regency ball."

"What?" Cat nearly choked on her wine. "Here? Now?"

"Yes!" exclaimed Eliza, clapping her hands in excitement.

"We'll throw a Regency ball for New Year's Eve, and you can have my hero show up in the middle of it."

"But Eliza, New Year's Eve is just two weeks away, and we've got to get through the Christmas season."

"I know. But it doesn't need to be huge or fancy. A small group would be fine, maybe twenty or thirty people."

"How are we going to get that many people here on New Year's Eve?"

"Free champagne?" Eliza suggested.

"We can't afford that."

"I can. At least for one night. It'd be worth it to me if this works. Besides, as they say, 'You can't take it with you.'"

"That's for people who die, not for people who think they're traveling to a different century."

"Whatever. I'll still spring for it. Well, not Dom Pérignon or anything, but maybe those eight dollar bottles we see at Kroger."

Cat took another sip of her wine. "I guess Jill might come, but I don't know about Shannon and Scott. It's hard to find a babysitter on New Year's."

"We'll advertise it on Facebook," Eliza said. "On our page. That will bring people."

"Uh, isn't that what leads to those parties with, like, thousands of people you don't know?"

"Oh, yeah. Well, let's start with the people we know, and the people who've 'liked' our page, which is only a few, considering I just made it. We'll limit it to forty people total, and they have to RSVP."

"All right." Cat tucked her hair behind her ears. "I can't believe we're attempting this. What do you want me to write as far as your duke?"

"Uh-uh, I'm not writing it. *You* need to write it."

"But it's *your* guy. You've got to at least tell me what you're looking for."

"Fair enough," Eliza conceded. "But it's up to you to write how he gets here and what happens next. You can prompt me if I need to do something, but I don't want to know until after you've written it, because I don't want to mess anything up."

"No problem. Just give me some general ideas."

"I want him to be tall. And handsome."

"And dark? Like Hugh Jackman?"

Eliza wrinkled her nose at her friend's ribbing. "Yes, dark is good. Jackman is good. And …"

As Eliza spoke, Cat grabbed a notepad and jotted down notes, refilling her own wine glass several times as she did so. She frowned when the bottle ran dry. How had that happened? Eliza didn't notice, focused as she was on telling Cat all about Regency England, and dukes and viscounts and breeches, and something called a pelisse.

When Eliza had finished, Cat stood up and tried to toss the note pad on the register desk. She missed by about two feet. Giggling, she tottered over to the table and poured herself another glass from a different bottle.

"How much have you had, Cat?"

"Not enough, dear friend. Not enough. By the way, did I tell you I kissed Ben tonight?"

Eliza's jaw dropped. "You what? Where? *When*?"

Cat giggled again and took another big swig of wine. "I. Kissed. Ben. Cooper. On the lips. Tonight."

Eliza frowned in consternation. "I assumed the lips part, silly. When was this? Where was I? And *why* were you kissing him?"

Cat related the whole story, sipping her wine as she spoke. She didn't mention the intense guilt she still felt, didn't bring up Mei.

"I can't believe I missed all of that." Eliza shook her head. "Maybe that's when I ducked into the restroom." She grinned at her friend. "My goodness, is there any man lately who *isn't* interested in you?"

Cat paused. "Nope!" She wobbled over to the desk to set down her glass. "I'm irresistible."

"Must be nice," muttered Eliza. "So, what now?"

Cat stuck her finger up in the air and waved it back and forth. "No, no, no, we're not thinking about that right now. We're planning your duke. He shall be … the Duke of Earl. No, the Duke of Gloucester-Birmingham-shireton!"

"Okay, girlfriend. You've clearly had enough. Time for bed. We can plan in the morning. Or maybe the afternoon, considering the hangover I'm sure you're going to have."

Cat gave an exaggerated pout. "Aw. But I have such great plans. The Duke of Earl will arrive on a sleigh pulled by reindeer. And he will swoop in and stick you in his stocking and whisk you off to the North Pole."

"That's Santa, honey. And I'm not interested in living with a bunch of elves. Come on, upstairs. I haven't seen you this sloshed in a long time." Hopping up, she walked over and took Cat by the elbow.

Laughing drunkenly, Cat acquiesced and followed Eliza to the stairs. "I know, but Grayson … William … Ben … It's all too much. I need to drink more!"

"That's not the answer."

"But then I don't have to choose between being Cindercata and—wait, Caterella. No, I mean Cinderella—and being regular old Cat."

Eliza stopped halfway up the stairs. "What are you talking about?"

"William is clearly the Prince. If I marry him, I'm Cinderella. I own the glass slipper, and it's a pen," Cat said, speaking slowly, as if stating the obvious.

"You're getting married already, are you?" Eliza teased, helping her friend further up the stairs.

"We will if I write it so, right?" Cat retorted. "Because I can write anything. The pen is mightier than the, than the ..." She broke off. "Than the what, Lizzie?"

"Than the sword, but I'm pretty sure you're not planning on any duels anytime soon, are you?"

"Maybe. Ben has a nice sword."

"*WHAT*?"

"Ben has a nice sword. He waves it nicely. And he has such a nice mouth."

Eliza gaped at Cat. "You're telling me you touched Ben's sword?"

Cat gawked at her for a minute in confusion. "No, not *that* sword! Pervert. The one he used to slay the computer dragon. He's my white knight, you know."

"Wait. Now Ben is your knight? I thought it was William?"

"No, Eliza," Cat said with exaggerated patience, as they stumbled into the living room. "William is my Prince. *Ben* is my knight."

"Uh, all right. So which are you going to choose?"

Cat sighed heavily. "I don't know. I don't know that I have the choice. Ben's with Mei." At the thought of Mei, she winced. "But William's perfect, like he was made for me. Literally! William literally *was* made for me. I made him." Her eyes widened and she half-laughed, half-hiccupped.

Eliza helped her to her room, pushing her carefully onto the bed. Cat squirmed in an effort to get comfortable.

Eliza pulled a folded quilt up and over her friend. "I know

who's right for you, Miss Catherine. You just have to see it for yourself."

Cat nodded sleepily, too tired to respond. Princes, knights, and Snow Whites swam before her eyes.

Had the clock struck midnight yet?

CHAPTER 24

"Oh, God. I can't believe I drank so much. Why did I drink so much?" Cat nursed her coffee, wincing at the cacophony of sounds around her. "And why is it so loud in here?"

Eliza snickered. "It's loud in here because we're in a coffee shop and all these last-minute Christmas shoppers need their caffeine. You're the one who opened the second bottle of wine and basically finished it yourself. It wasn't my idea."

"I did? I don't remember that."

"Do you remember kissing Ben Cooper?"

Cat's face flooded with heat. She glanced around.

"He's not here," Eliza said. "I already checked."

Cat groaned. "What am I going to do, Eliza?" She took another careful sip of coffee, willing her stomach to settle.

"You're asking me for relationship advice? The woman who can't find lasting love to save her life?"

Cat gave a slight chuckle at that. "But we're fixing that, remember? Or rather, *I'm* fixing that. You reminded me this morning, and showed me my notes. Most of which I can read." She ran her finger over the rim of her coffee mug, and sighed. "I just don't know what to do about my own mess. I shouldn't have kissed Ben. *He* shouldn't have kissed me. He's dating Mei."

"Maybe not. She wasn't there last night."

Cat brightened at that thought. It's true, Mei hadn't been there. Nor had she been at the coffee shop the last time she'd run into Ben. Of course, that didn't mean they weren't still dating. She'd like to think he wouldn't have kissed her were he still involved; he didn't seem the type. Plus, there was her own mess with William.

But Cat wouldn't know Ben's relationship status unless she asked, and she wouldn't be able to ask until she saw him again. The idea made her stomach leap in a mixture of nervousness and excitement. "Should I call him?"

Eliza's jaw dropped. "Wait a minute. *You're* talking about pursuing a man? You, Catherine Schreiber?"

Cat reached over to smack her, then groaned when the movement intensified the throbbing in her head.

"I told you from day one he was interested in you," Eliza said. "You've just never been interested in *him*. And now you are, because of one kiss? That must have been one hell of a smooch."

Cat sat, silent for a minute. "I wouldn't say I haven't been interested," she admitted. "And it was."

She'd relived that kiss a thousand times in her head since she'd woken up. She may not remember all the events from the evening before, but there's no way she'd forget that. It had shocked her, the intensity of the connection, the way her toes had curled and her whole body had reacted from a mere kiss. It shocked her still, how much she wanted to kiss Ben again.

"What about William?" Eliza said, breaking into Cat's thoughts. "I know Derrick is history, and you're not interested in Grayson anymore, right? But I thought you liked William."

Cat sighed again. "Ugh. I don't know. Yeah, Derrick wasn't for me. I don't need to relive high school again, thanks. And I can't deny that the physical attraction with Grayson was anything less than, well, hot. But pretty words and sex are not enough for me and never have been."

Eliza dipped her head in agreement.

"William? You're right. He seems perfect. Too perfect." Cat clasped her head with her hands. "Isn't that pathetic? I somehow miraculously find—miraculously create—the Perfect Man, and he feels out of my league. He's too good-looking, too rich, too smooth, too everything. It's all coming too easily. Even Cinderella had to lose her shoe and turn back into a pumpkin."

"Cinderella didn't turn into a pumpkin. Her coach did."

"You know what I mean. He's everything I've ever wanted, and yet I don't know. I like him. I find him attractive. I think he would make life wonderful. We'd be living on Easy Street, Mr. Warbucks and I. But it feels … forced, not natural. I can't trust it. Knowing I created it means it doesn't feel genuine. It doesn't feel magical, Eliza. Not in the way I want it to, I guess. But that kiss with Ben—*that* was magical."

Eliza made a show of looking around. "Who are you and what have you done with my friend?"

Cat swatted at her, instantly regretting the sudden movement.

"I thought what you wanted above all, if you admitted to wanting anything, was safety and security," Eliza said. "What could be more safe and secure than a man you created to be exactly what you wanted him to be?"

"I know!" Cat exclaimed. "I'm so confused."

"Actually, I don't think you are. I think you're finally figuring it out."

They sat quietly, nursing their drinks, watching people come and go.

"Can we plan the ball now?" Eliza asked after a while. "I'm so excited! And if my duke never shows, well, I've always wanted to go to a ball."

Cat sat up straight, giving her friend a weak smile. Her head was killing her. "Sure thing. But you've got to help. I have no clue what a ball should be like. Is the bookstore big enough to host dancing?"

"Of course," said Eliza. "We'll move some of the book racks against the walls."

"I guess we can make the space work, but how are we going to find Regency-style clothing? I don't know what it would look like."

Eliza twirled her hair with her finger. "You watched *Pride and Prejudice* with me this past summer. Surely you remember the bonnets and Empire-waist dresses?"

"I guess," Cat conceded. Her eyes sparkled with glee. "I was more focused on Colin Firth."

"Who wouldn't be? But anyway, the drama department put on a stage production of *Emma* last spring. I bet they have some things we could borrow. I'll ask Galen." Eliza gazed dreamily out the window. "Ah, men in breeches and cravats."

"If we can get them to wear them," Cat reminded her.

"True. We can fudge some things; I don't care."

"Tell you what—you invite people today, and I'll work on sketching out your story in between customers. Hopefully I'll have an outline at least by tonight." She stood up and grimaced at the pounding in her head. "It's going to be a long day."

"It's going to be a *great* day," Eliza stated firmly. As the two friends walked back across the street to the Treasure Trove, Eliza said, "Cat? Can I ask one favor?"

"Sure, Eliza, anything."

"In my story, don't guarantee the outcome. Make it likely, but not destiny. I want to feel like it's real. Like you and Ben."

"There *is* no me and Ben," Cat protested. "But I get what you mean. I'll create the character, I'll create the opportunity, but I won't tell you too much, okay? You'll have to figure it out on your own."

Impulsively, Eliza hugged her as Cat struggled to unlock the bookstore door. "You're the best, Cat. The best. I'll never forget you."

Cat returned the hug, tears filling her eyes. "Back at you, friend."

"Catherine?"

"Yeah?"

"It's William. I wanted to wish you a Merry Christmas."

Cat rolled over and sat up, her eyes bleary. "Merry Christmas to you, too. The line sounds a bit crackly. Where are you?"

"Shanghai. My reception is so-so. I'm sorry I didn't get a chance to talk with you; we had something come up and had to fly out late last week. But I wanted to wish you a Merry Christmas. I haven't heard from you—is everything all right?"

Cat yawned. "Yeah. Sorry. We've been so busy in the store. What time is it there?" she asked, her voice groggy.

"Did I wake you? It's a little after ten p.m. here. I thought you'd be up."

She peered at her clock: 9:17 a.m. "Yeah," she muttered, scootching up onto her elbow and pushing her hair out of her eyes. "Eliza and I were up late last night planning our Regency ball."

"Your what?"

"We're, um, hosting a Regency-themed ball for New Year's."

"You're serious? A ball? As in waltzing? And deucedly uncomfortable formal wear?"

She could hear the amusement in his voice. "First of all, kudos to you for using the word 'deucedly' in a sentence," she said. "Second of all, yup."

"May I ask why?"

"It's a long story. Let's just say it's something Eliza has always wanted to do."

"If I'm back on the East Coast, I'd love to come. I can't imagine a better New Year's date than being with you, even if it means I have to don a waistcoat and breeches."

"Wow, Mr. Dawes. Kudos to you again for knowing Regency men's wear. And for the flattering statement."

"It's true, Ms. Schreiber. I can't stop thinking about you. I feel so drawn to you. I can't explain it, but that doesn't mean I don't like it."

Cat paused for a moment. *I get it. More than you know. You're drawn to me because you're made to be.* "Thank you, I'm flattered."

"Thank *you*, Catherine. You bring more pleasure into my life than I've had in a long time."

She shifted in her bed, seeking a more comfortable position. She sat up and self-consciously tucked her nightgown in between her legs. She could see snow outside the window falling in great clumps, and could hear Eliza banging around in the kitchen.

"You've been … great for me too, William." She hoped he hadn't picked up on her hesitation. She still wasn't sure what to do. She hadn't seen Ben since the Mistletoe Incident, and she was starting to wonder if she'd ever see him again. She'd called and emailed, but had gotten no response. Eliza had invited him to the Regency ball, but hadn't heard anything from him, either, as far as Cat knew.

"Have a Merry Christmas. I look forward to seeing you again when I come home—hopefully by New Year's."

"Thank you, William. You have a Merry Christmas, too. Goodbye."

"Goodbye, Catherine. Take care."

Cat sat in her bed, holding the phone, staring at the sheets. It was time to admit it. She'd created Mr. Perfect. He was all she'd ever wanted. At least ten years ago. Just as Grayson was what she wanted in college, and Derrick all she'd fantasized about in high school. But William wasn't whom she kept dreaming about, not whom she wanted to see walk into the coffee shop, not with whom she wondered if there were a real future.

She wanted more; she wanted someone real, who liked her because he chose to, not because he was written to. Someone with unexpected faults and unknown strengths. Someone who would challenge her and not give her everything she wanted, but with whom she could work for a future, together.

Who knew at some point the ability to create the Perfect Man would feel like a burden rather than a blessing?

Why did I invite him to the ball? Wait. She hadn't. He'd invited himself. But she hadn't exactly told him no. *If I don't want him, I shouldn't keep acting as if I do.* She put the phone back on the side table and groaned.

She wanted to keep him as an option, she admitted to herself. If Ben didn't work out, William was still the answer to all her prayers. Cat shook her head. Was she such a terrible person, that she would do that to someone? Guilt poured down over her like thick syrup, clinging to her every pore.

She stood up and crossed to the closet. She may have created these people, she chided herself, amazed at how easily she accepted that fact, but that didn't make them less real now than she was, right? They had feelings, lives, rights. And one right was not to be strung along by the likes of her.

She closed her eyes as she reached into the closet to pull out a sweater. She should call William back and put an end to things. She *would* call him back. But not on Christmas Day. She couldn't break up with someone on Christmas.

"Cat? You finally awake? I'm making us Christmas pancakes," Eliza called from the kitchen.

"Merry Christmas!" Cat shouted, pulling on the sweater and reaching for her jeans.

"Merry Christmas to you, too," Eliza sang in return. "Come see! Galen stopped by this morning on the way to his mom's house with all these costumes—I mean, dresses. We can have a fashion show today."

Cat walked out to see the couch draped with numerous different floor-length frocks. "On Christmas?" She fingered one of the dresses. "You really want to wear these? Do we have to wear corsets, too?"

"Yes, on Christmas." Eliza walked into the living room, spatula in hand. "He was on his way out of town and won't be back until after the New Year, so he wanted to make sure that we got the costumes. And no harsh corsets. They did wear stays, but nothing as restrictive as what you're probably thinking about. No *Gone with the Wind* struggles." She eyed Cat's chest. "You probably don't need them, anyway."

"And you probably need two sets."

Eliza threw the spatula at her.

Cat ducked, laughing. "I guess the pancakes are already done, since you apparently don't need that anymore?" She stooped to pick it up.

Eliza stuck her tongue out in response.

"Is this Gavin interested in you? A Christmas Day delivery seems rather above and beyond the call of duty."

"Galen. And no." Eliza's lips curled up in amusement. "If you'd ever met him, you would know I'm not his type. He wants his own duke, too."

"Alrighty, then." Cat cocked an eyebrow. "Do I need to write *two* stories?"

"Ha, ha. Maybe." Eliza picked up a gown and held it against her body.

"So many of these are white," Cat said.

Eliza nodded. "Yeah, they wanted to imitate the classical styles of ancient Greece and Rome. You can jazz it up with a shawl or spencer."

"What's a spencer?"

"A short-waisted jacket intended to show off the gown underneath. Here, like this one." Eliza held up a maroon example.

"You know your stuff."

"I'd better, if I'm going to have any chance on blending in once I'm there," Eliza said with a wink. "I've been cramming for my history test, so to speak. Thank God for the History section of the store."

"If you're there," Cat reminded her. "If."

Eliza poked her. "Think positively, Eeyore. And come eat some pancakes."

I am. I'm positive I don't want you to go.

"Have you heard anything from Ben?" Cat asked a few days later, as she sorted through the books they were marking down for post-Christmas clearance.

"No," Eliza answered, stacking paperbacks onto a rolling cart. "You could call him."

"I have. Twice. Emailed him, too. Guess it wasn't meant to be." She tried to act nonchalant, but in truth, it ate at her, his silence. He obviously hadn't felt the same way she did about that mistletoe kiss. She wished he'd say something, even if it were, *Leave me alone. I'm involved.*

Eliza peered at her friend. "I hope if he's who you really want that you'd fight a little harder than that."

"What can I do, Eliza? Run after him declaring my feelings?"

"Yes, that's exactly what you can do." Eliza bobbed her head enthusiastically.

"I could never break up another couple. You know that."

"Maybe you already have."

Cat blanched.

"But if you did," Eliza asserted, "it's because that couple wasn't supposed to be together. Just like you and Ryan were never meant to last—if you had been, he wouldn't have cheated."

Cat bit her lip. "I don't know if I believe that."

"You don't have to. The universe will work out the way it's supposed to. Including the parts that you don't get to control."

"You have more faith than I do."

"You'll see," was all Eliza said. Her phone beeped, and she hopped up to check it. "Thirty-seven! We have thirty-seven people coming now, Cat." Eliza clapped her hands in excitement. "Oh, I can't believe it's in two days. I just can't believe it."

Cat smiled as she set the last book on the cart. "I know. I'm excited, too, I'll admit. Once we close on New Year's Eve, Jill and Shannon said they'd come over to help arrange the room. Scott is bringing finger sandwiches and punch. Is that Regency fare?"

Eliza shrugged. "Close enough. For once I'm not focusing on the food."

"I guess not." Catherine wrinkled her nose in amusement. "Who else is coming?"

"Several of the Red Hat ladies, and even that cute older couple who were here for the poetry reading."

"They're on Facebook? I really am behind the times."

"No, no, no." Eliza grinned. "They stopped in yesterday to ask about the next Poetry Night, so I invited them."

"Good."

"I think the blue-haired girl is also coming, although I'm not sure she's still together with the poetry-reading guy. At least from what her profile pic on Facebook indicates—she's kissing someone else."

"That's a shame," Cat said. "His poem didn't do the trick, huh?"

"Guess not." Eliza examined the room. "I think we should put the iPod dock over there. It'd be nice to have live musicians, but once I found out the cost for a quartet, downloading music from iTunes became a much more appealing option."

"Yes, yes, we are nothing if not historically accurate," Cat said.

"I will be getting all the historical accuracy I need in a few days," Eliza stated with conviction. "For now, fudging the corners won't harm anything."

"Should we go over the plan one more time? Just in case some sexy dude in Hessian boots really does walk through the door?"

"Ooh, Hessians. You've been paying attention."
Cat winked. "Wait until you see his cravat."

CHAPTER 25

"We have to sing *Auld Lang Syne* at midnight," Eliza said, as she hung fake flowers on the fireplace mantel. "If I'm still here, that is."

"Okay," mumbled Cat, as she arranged food on the refreshments table. She wasn't looking forward to this 'ball' anymore. At best, she'd be entertaining a bunch of strangers late into the evening. Selling books was her forte; playing hostess was not. Besides, the only person she truly wanted to show up hadn't answered her three emails, or her two phone calls. It was painfully clear Ben Cooper wanted nothing to do with her, despite Eliza's claims to the contrary.

Eliza. Cat looked over at her friend. Exuberance shone in Eliza's animated face as she raced around the room, ensuring everything was just so. At worst, Eliza would disappear from her life. Forever. She pushed that thought from her mind. "You sure this is enough?" she called.

"At Almack's, they served day-old toast and dry pound

cake, with only tea and lemonade. People should be thrilled we're providing a little more."

"What's Almack's?"

Eliza rolled her eyes. "Never mind, my twenty-first century friend. Come on, it's time to go dress."

She grabbed Cat's hand and pulled her, giggling, toward the stairs. The two women raced up together. "We've only got twenty minutes until people are supposed to arrive. Not nearly long enough for our *toilettes* via Regency standards, but then again, we don't have lady's maids, either."

"At least you had your hair done, Eliza. It looks so elaborate with all those pins and curls. I don't know what I'm going to do with mine," Cat said as they walked into her bedroom. Two gowns waited on hangers over the edge of the closet door.

"You don't have to do much, just pull it up and leave some tendrils dangling down in front."

"Tendrils, eh? The things we do for those we love." She threw Eliza a smirk as she slipped her moss green gown off its hanger. The gown was in the high-waisted Empire style, gathered just below the bust with fine ribbon detailing and embroidery. It was quite beautiful, even to Catherine, who didn't care for dresses. And at least it wasn't white, as nearly all the other dresses were. She was grateful, too, for the long sleeves on this cold, chilly evening. Looking at her friend, who had pulled down a cream-colored silk gown with short sleeves and a very revealing bodice, she exclaimed, "Aren't you going to freeze in that?"

Eliza waved her hand. "I'll wear a shawl with it. Besides, do you think I'm going to be focusing on the temperature?"

Cat sighed. "Eliza, you do realize there's a chance—a strong one—that this won't work and you'll be back up here with me this evening, right?"

"Yes. I do. But in that case, what's the worst thing that could happen from wearing a revealing ball gown? I stand near the fireplace and maybe attract a new, more modern suitor."

"Suitor?" Cat grinned. "There's a word I haven't heard in a long time."

They studied each other in the mirror. Cat liked the way the green in her dress pulled out the red tones in her hair. She felt feminine, almost dainty. It was quite a change from her normal evenings in jeans and a sweatshirt.

Eliza's blue eyes sparkled and her cheeks glowed. She'd hung a strand of pearls around her neck, which emphasized her collarbones. With her hair up and those two pieces— *oops, tendrils*—hanging down in front, Eliza looked every inch the Regency lady. At least in Cat's view.

"We're beautiful," said Cat after a moment.

Eliza smiled. "Yes, we are. There's something to be said for emphasizing the feminine form, isn't there?"

"At least the boobs," Cat quipped. "They haven't seemed this perky in years. I actually have cleavage."

Eliza elbowed her.

"Look at us, Eliza. Really look at us," Cat said in a quiet voice. She reached over and grabbed her friend's hand. "I'd like to think that if we had lived two hundred years ago, we still would have been best of friends. You mean the world to me, and you always will, even if tonight is the last night we are together."

Eliza wiped a tear from her eye. She hugged her friend tightly. "I'm sorry for leaving you, Cat. I love you like the sister I never had. Thank you for understanding … and for letting me go."

Cat gripped her harder. "I'm not letting you go. I'll just

have to meet you in a difference place." Her shoulders shook as tears fell down her face. Backing up, she forced a smile. "If this works, that is. May I admit I'm secretly hoping it won't?"

"You may," said Eliza. "But if it doesn't, I know you were willing, and that means everything to me." She wiped tears off her own cheeks. "Thank goodness Regency women didn't wear mascara," she said, "or I'd resemble a raccoon right now."

Cat handed her a Kleenex. "C'mon, Miss Austen, let's go greet our guests."

Music flowed from the iPod placed discreetly on its dock in the corner: strains of Mozart and Beethoven. Candles illuminated the room from atop the bookcases, and a fire crackled merrily in the fireplace. About a dozen people had shown up already, and the array of Regency wear was quite amazing. Some had opted to borrow costumes from Cat and Eliza; others had decided to wing it with mixed results.

Cat particularly liked the blue-haired girl from the poetry reading, who was wearing a Goth-style dress that vaguely emulated Regency style, but was all black with blue lacings. When she moved, blue Chucks were visible underneath. Cat was impressed the teenager had shown up, instead of opting for whatever kids her age normally did on New Year's Eve. Eliza said the girl mentioned earlier that she was reading *Emma* for English lit, so perhaps this was her way of immersing herself in her studies. Cat could hardly fault her for that, considering the scheme she and Eliza had cooked up for the evening. She just hoped the girl didn't think she was getting champagne at midnight.

Cat glanced at the clock over the front door: 10:07 p.m. The bells on the door jingled and several members of the Red Hat Club walked through, bedecked in matronly Regency finery that made them look like suitable chaperones for the younger folk awkwardly dancing on the tiny dance floor.

Eliza worked her way around the room in her gorgeous creamy ivory silk ball gown that was embellished with embroidered ivy vines and small purple flowers down the front. Over her shoulders she wore a long green and purple shawl with matching flower design. She grinned broadly as she engaged in conversation with the various guests, her eyes flashing with excitement. *She looks right at home.* Cat's eyebrows furrowed. She didn't want to acknowledge what this evening might mean for her friend, and by extension herself.

"She's the belle of the ball, isn't she?" said Norm from her right side, startling Cat out of her reverie. "A real diamond of the first water."

"A real what?"

"Diamond of the first water," answered Myra, elegant herself in a modest long-sleeved floor-length gown of a maroon hue. Myra had a pink hat that rather resembled a small turban perched on her head, and was fanning herself with an elaborately painted hand-held paper fan. "It's what they always say about the heroines in my romance novels." She rubbed her husband's shoulder. "I guess he does sometimes listen when I tell him things."

"Always, m'dear. Always." He smiled at his wife, tucking her arm in his. "Thank you for hosting such a fine gathering," he said to Cat. "It's been a long time since we've wanted to go out on the New Year. Usually we're asleep by nine o'clock."

Myra hushed him.

"It's true!" he protested. "But once Myra heard you were

hosting a ball, she wanted to live out her Regency fantasy, so here we are."

"She's not the only one."

Eliza floated by, glancing for the umpteenth time at the door.

"I don't know if it qualifies as a true ball." Cat added. "We're rather cramped in here, and no one knows how to dance to the music much, but at least everyone is having a good time."

The door jangled again and Grayson strolled through the entryway, looking as if he'd walked right out of a Hollywood production of *Pride and Prejudice*. Dressed in all black with a gray waistcoat and fine top hat, he was impossibly handsome. He could give Colin Firth a run for his money. Evidently the other young women felt the same way, because silence fell as talking ceased momentarily. A group of female undergrads nestled near the fireplace openly ogled him. Grayson didn't seem to notice, crossing over the room to greet Cat. Norm and Myra gave her a knowing smile and moved off to partake of the punch.

"Hi, Cat. Quite the turnout you have here." He glanced around the room before fixing his intense eyes on hers. "I've been wanting to see you again. I hope you had a nice Christmas."

"Thank you, Grayson, I did. I hope you and your family did, as well," she said in a friendly but reserved tone. *Damn, he was an attractive man. Seductive. Sexy. And not what I want.* "You are looking very nineteenth century this evening," she added. "Well done."

"Do you like it?" he replied, cocking an eyebrow. "My sister knew a costume designer in NYC, so she Fed-Exed this to me when I told her I was attending." He slid his hands down the front of his waistcoat, drawing her attention to his lean midriff. Her eyes followed his hands, and when she returned her gaze to his face, he smiled in a suggestive way, having achieved his goal.

Cat shook her head. "Grayson, it's wonderful to see you again. I had a nice time—a very nice time—with you at our Poetry Night. But I'm seeing someone else." Kind of.

Gray's eyes cooled. "Oh," he responded. "Of course." He stood silently for a moment. "I'm good with not being exclusive. I just want to be with you again." He lowered his eyelids, giving her an intimate smile. "You're irresistible to me."

Stop giving me the smolder! Her insides quivered. *It's not you I want.* Tingles worked their way up her legs. *Well, not most of me, anyway. Stupid hormones. Stupid manuscript.* "I'm sorry, but that doesn't work for me."

Grayson started to move away.

Cat caught his elbow. "You're a great guy. You deserve someone more suited to you," she said feebly.

He nodded, and walked across the room toward the group of college girls. One of them flushed bright pink and giggled at the woman next to her, who just stared at Grayson, her jaw practically on the floor.

"*Who* is that?" asked Jill, who had come up behind her.

"That's Grayson."

"Wow. I can see what Eliza meant when she described him. He's gorgeous." Jill stared at him for a moment. Sighing, she said to Cat, "Do you know how hard it is to go to the bathroom wearing a dress like this? I feel like a stuffed sausage. I don't like wearing things this tight." She fidgeted with the dress, checking the back to ensure nothing had caught up in her undergarments.

"It's quite flattering, you know. It shows off your beautiful shoulders."

Jill started in surprise. "Really?" she said, adjusting the neckline.

Cat nodded.

A small smile crept across Jill's face. "Now if only it could attract a guy like him," she said in a self-deprecating way, gesturing toward Grayson. "But that would never happen."

"Don't rule it out." An idea flickered in Cat's head. "Maybe you'll find yourself embroiled in a torrid affair with him before you know it."

Jill sniggered. "I should be so lucky."

Eliza hurried over to Jill and Cat. "It's going well, isn't it?" she said breathlessly. Her eyes swept the room. "We must have fifty people here."

"No wonder it's so warm," Cat muttered. "I'm starting to wish I had your dress instead, Lizzie."

"I'm so excited." Eliza clapped her hands. "It's almost midnight. It's almost midnight!"

Jill wrinkled her eyebrows in confusion. "Do you have someone to kiss at midnight or something? What's with the giddiness?"

Eliza grinned. "I hope so. I really hope so." Turning to Cat, she added, "I'm sorry Ben isn't here, Cat. I was sure he would show up. William, too."

Cat closed her eyes. She was startled to realize she hadn't thought of William, hadn't noticed his absence. If that weren't proof she wasn't interested in him, that he wasn't the one for her, then she didn't know what would be.

She clenched her jaw. She'd sent an email off to William, after attempts to call him only rang through to voice mail, saying she needed to tell him something, but hadn't heard back. Guilt still enveloped her like a smothering blanket whenever she thought of him.

She *had* been checking the door every few minutes, however, hoping Ben would walk through. Considering he hadn't bothered to answer her, she wasn't surprised. *Figures right when I decide what—and who—I want, I pick the one who isn't interested back.* Why couldn't she have fallen for William? It's what she was supposed to do, right?

Oh, Dad. I wish you were here. I wish you could tell me about that manuscript, and help me get out of this mess of my own making.

Opening her eyes again, she saw Eliza scamper off toward Norm and Myra, who were beckoning her over. With a smile, Eliza let Norm escort her onto the dance floor, where they attempted a waltz. Norm was a decent dancer. The song ended and Norm led Eliza back to where Myra was standing, then extended his elbow to his wife. A second waltz emanated from the iPod, and Myra beamed at her husband as he led her through the steps.

Cat looked back at Eliza. Her friend was standing stock still, all color drained from her face, her eyes riveted on something at the back of the room. *Or someone.*

Cat followed Eliza's fixed stare. Her own jaw dropped. For there stood a man so elegantly clad, so utterly regal in appearance, that he put Grayson to shame. He wore a fitted navy blue topcoat with tails over a cream-colored waistcoat embroidered with blue and green flowers. Under the waistcoat, his high-collared ivory shirt hosted an elaborately fastened neck cloth—a cravat, Cat reminded herself—starched to perfection. Buff-colored breeches encased firmly muscled thighs.

Cat's eyes fell to his footwear. *Hessians. I bet those high leather boots are Hessians.*

Moving her gaze back up, she had to admit he was

quite a handsome man. Perhaps not in the model-sense of Grayson, but he had rich glossy walnut-colored hair tousled in charming effect, a bit longer at the neck than modern men wore. His face looked as if it had been chiseled from a Roman statue: fierce, powerful, commanding. A bit like Hugh Jackman, indeed. She crossed her arms in satisfaction.

The man walked a few steps into the room, his bearing suggesting a ready familiarity with controlling a crowd. Indeed, numerous eyes turned toward him and silence again settled across the room. At first, the man seemed utterly at ease, but as he surveyed the room and the people in it, his confidence faltered.

He fixated on the iPod in the corner, still playing the strains of the waltz. His eyes grew wide and his face paled. Wildly he stared around the edges of the room, taking in the numerous bookshelves. He moved his gaze up, noting the light fixtures. They weren't on, since Cat and Eliza had opted for candles and the fireplace for a more intimate feel, but he inspected them carefully. Headlights flashed outside the front windows, drawing his attention. With quick strides he started toward the front door, oblivious to the crowd around him.

Eliza, who'd stood frozen to the spot for several minutes, darted across the room and hooked her arm through his. He stopped, a baffled expression crossing his face.

"Hello. I'm Eliza, Miss Eliza James," she said to the man, who was staring at her as if she were an alien.

After a short moment, the man answered, "Mattersley. Deveric Mattersley." When Eliza just nodded and smiled, he added, "Duke of Claremont."

Duke of Claremont? Duke of *Claremont*? Cat's insides reeled. He was Eliza's duke. He was truly here. She'd done it.

The partygoers watched Eliza and the Duke with curiosity.

Deveric lowered his voice, but Cat could hear him ask, "Where am I? What is this place?"

Still smiling at him, Eliza steered him toward the back of the room, as Cat had told her to do. "This is a New Year's Eve Ball."

Deveric looked around blankly. "But it's March, and these are not the people with whom I was conversing. And you speak oddly, rather like an American."

Eliza turned to Cat, love and gratitude in her eyes, and mouthed, "Thank you."

Deveric hesitated for a moment, watching a woman put a small black rectangle to her face and touch something on it.

"Say cheese!" she shouted, and a flash went off.

"What the devil?" the Duke exclaimed, raising his arm in front of his face as if to shield himself from a second onslaught. Eliza ignored the woman, continuing to pull on Deveric's arm. She led the bewildered Duke through the door into the back room.

With a sinking feeling, Cat followed them, racing as silently as she could to the storage room door, which Eliza had left open a few inches. Cat peeked through, watching them. *Was this really happening? This couldn't actually happen, could it?*

"What are you doing?" she heard him ask in a dazed tone. "Where am I? This must be a dream. A bizarre dream, where music plays without an orchestra, and where lights flash by at inhuman speeds."

The sounds of people counting down the final seconds of the New Year floated, muffled, around the edges of the door. The guests cheered and blared horns as the clock struck midnight, and then the crowd broke out into an off-key rendition of *Auld Lang Syne*.

Without answering him, Eliza pulled his head down to hers.

"A dream," he murmured, as she fastened her lips onto his and kissed him, just as Cat had written Eliza needed to do. Cat watched as the man—the Duke—closed his eyes and returned Eliza's kiss. "A very satisfying dream, with my very own goddess to entice me."

He pushed Eliza back against the door and it shut firmly, leaving Cat standing there, dumbfounded. No more sounds came from behind the door.

After a minute or two, Cat walked over and looked into the main room, wondering if any of the guests were following this drama. No one seemed to have paid any attention to Eliza and Cat's exit—and the Duke's, she amended. They were all dancing and drinking the champagne Eliza had provided. Cat returned to the storage room. All was quiet. Closing her eyes, she opened the door. The room was empty. The only thing that remained was Eliza's shawl, draped across the floor.

Cat picked up the shawl and kissed it, holding it against her heart as her eyes filled with tears. She sat down, closing her eyes, her mind—and heart—a whirl of tumbling emotions.

About five minutes later, Jill entered the room to find Cat perched on the edge of a folding chair, staring at a piece of fabric in her hands. "Here you are," Jill said. "I've been wondering where you went."

Cat gave her a weak smile. "I'm sorry, I needed a breather."

"Where's Eliza?"

Cat sighed. "I believe she is with her duke."

"What?" Jill said. "That guy's name was Duke? What a bizarre name."

"No. It's Deveric."

"Oh, I thought you said Duke. Deveric is even weirder." Jill stuck her hands on her hips, tilting her head as she watched Cat. "I didn't know she knew anybody like that. He was something else, wasn't he? Not as good-looking as that Grayson guy, though."

Cat just nodded.

"Are you coming back out? You'd better grab a glass of champagne before it's all gone."

"I guess. You go ahead. I'll be there in a minute."

"Sure, no prob."

As Jill exited, Cat closed the door to the storeroom and leaned against it. Tears spilled down her cheeks. She couldn't believe it had worked. Her best friend was gone. Truly gone.

Her heart lurched at this new reality. Things would never be the same. And as happy as she was for her friend, grief, big and black, gnawed at her edges.

Cheering from the main room intruded, reminding her she had a store full of guests just a few feet away. Tomorrow she could bury herself and hide away, but tonight she still had hosting duties to perform.

She pasted a smile on her face as she wiped away her tears, readying herself to return to the party. With a final glance around, she said a quick prayer for her friend. "Godspeed, dearest Eliza. May you get the happily-ever-after you've always wanted."

CHAPTER 26

A few days later, Cat sat in the coffee shop alone, staring morosely into her cup of coffee. She took a sip, watching traffic creep by outside, edging through the snow that had fallen the night before. She pushed the hair out of her eyes, determined not to let the tears that threatened fall.

Whenever the door jangled, she looked up, hoping Ben would walk through. She'd emailed him one more time last night, deciding looking desperate was better than never having any answers.

Eliza had reassured her on the morning of the ball that Ben would return, and that it would all work out. "I know how interested he was in you, Cat. Seriously interested. There must be a good explanation for his silence."

"Yeah, like the fact that I got him to cheat on his girlfriend? Or maybe that he never wanted to kiss me to begin with, despite your claims to the contrary?"

"Ever the pessimist, darling. Ever the pessimist."

Cat had grumbled at that. "I wish I'd never found that manuscript, Eliza. I wish my mom had never sent it to me."

"Truly?"

"What good has it done? I was perfectly happy without a man. Any man. And now? Now I've had a one-night stand. That's so not who I am, Lizzie. Now I've found the perfect Prince Charming, but I've acted more like the wicked stepmother than Cinderella in stringing him along. And now, maybe because of all of that, because of all of those other men, I've lost my chance with Ben Cooper, who seems like a genuinely good guy, one who might have been Mr. Right."

"Scratch the might-have-been, missy." Eliza had tapped her on the head with the fan she'd been fiddling with. "Besides, do you think if you hadn't found the manuscript, and learned what it meant, that'd you'd have been anywhere close to being open to something with Ben?"

Cat frowned. "What do you mean?"

"Oh, come on. You saw him that morning in the coffee shop, the morning you said you found the book, and immediately rejected him out of hand. I remember."

"He was with a woman."

"That wasn't the reason, and you know it." Eliza walked over and sat down by her friend, who was slumped despondently on the sofa. "I think you owe everything to that manuscript."

Cat's snarl had given her opinion of that statement.

"No, really," Eliza had insisted. "You said it sent some sort of spark through you—that it woke you up. Remember how surprised I was that you agreed to go out with Derrick? I think we can thank the book for that. And if you hadn't gone out with him, and Grayson, *and* William, you wouldn't know what you *weren't* looking for. The book led you here, to this point."

"What point is that? Misery Lane?"

"No. To knowing that, for you, what is real is more important than any fantasy. And to being open enough to risk getting hurt in the pursuit of that." She hugged Cat. "You're not hiding anymore, Cat. And neither am I."

Cat had given a bitter laugh. It had rather felt as if she were hiding, sitting on that old sofa in their apartment.

She looked around the coffee shop again. Eliza had been right. She wasn't satisfied anymore with the same old day-in, day-out, lonely grind of the bookstore. She wanted more. *Thank you, Eliza. And thank you, Dad.*

Cat closed her eyes and listened to the steady hum of activity around her. She worried about Eliza, hoping that all had gone as—well, as written—but wondering if it were possible that something had gone awry. The worst part was that she'd never know. She didn't even know if she should file a missing persons report, because what would she say? Woman disappeared with strange man, who may or may not have been from another century?

And truth be told, she was lonely. Desperately lonely. It was clear now how much she had used Eliza to fill the gaping holes in her life. Maybe that's why Eliza had stuck so close to her for so long, because her friend knew she was only living half a life and needed someone there to push her, to get her to move beyond books, beyond the store and start living again.

She pulled out her cell phone and dialed her mom's number. Maybe she should give up the store's ghost and move to Ohio. There wasn't much holding her here, especially now that Eliza was gone and Ben Cooper had disappeared off the face of the Earth.

"Hello?"

"Hi, Mom, it's Cat."

"Oh, hi, Catherine. It's so nice to hear from you. Everything okay?"

"Yes, Mom, fine," she lied. "I just wanted to check in and see how you're doing. How's the leg?"

"Much better. And though it hurts like the Dickens, I'm starting to be able to bear a little weight on my arm, like the physical therapist wants me to."

"I'm so glad, Mom."

"Are you coming to visit soon? We missed you so much at Christmas, but I was glad to hear the store was busy. I've assumed you're making your yearly January sojourn here, but I haven't heard you mention it."

"I don't know," Cat said. "Eliza is, um, visiting a friend in England and may be gone for a while, so I have no one to watch the store for me. Emily's back in school, and I wouldn't expect her to work full days, anyway."

"Oh." There was a brief pause. "You could ask that nice William fellow to help out, like he did last time."

Cat pinched her eyes shut.

"Seems to me he'd be happy if you did. I think he is fond of you, Catherine."

"Uh, yeah, I guess he is, Mom. But I'm not interested." Cat winced. She knew what was coming next.

Her mother sighed. "I just want to see you happy, Catherine. That's all."

"I know, Mom, I know. I'm working on it. I promise."

Cat ran her fingers through her hair as she thought of the kiss she'd shared with Ben. If only she could write it so that he'd at least come and talk to her.

Except that was exactly what she didn't want. Oh, she wanted to talk to him, but it had to be of his own free will. She didn't mind setting up other people's love stories, but she had to know for herself that she was wanted for who she was, not because she'd created someone to want her. At least in Deveric and Eliza's story, she'd managed to sketch it out so that they both had a choice.

She turned her attention back to the phone. Her mom was still talking.

" … and Marie says he's a nice fellow. Divorced, so who knows the story there, but he has a darling little girl who's about four. And he attends the same church as Marie and I do. Let me know if you'd like to meet him."

"In Ohio?"

"Well, yes." He mother gave an irritated snort. "You could always open a bookstore here in Columbus, you know. At least you'd be around family."

"Thanks, Mom. If and when I ever decide to ditch the Treasure Trove, you'll be the first to know."

Grace sighed in resignation. "But it's not yet, is it?"

"Nope. Not yet. Bye, Mom, I gotta go. It's almost time to open the store."

"Bye, honey. I love you."

"I love you, too."

Cat sat for a while longer, rubbing her thumb along the edge of the phone, mulling over her choices. She hoped William would call her back. It wasn't fair to have him think she was an option when she knew he wasn't the one she truly wanted.

Anxiety curled up her spine and down through her fingers over the potential repercussions of giving up someone who offered her the safety and security she'd always craved. But she wanted more now. She didn't want the fantasy. She wanted something less certain, more challenging. She wanted something real.

She wanted Ben Cooper.

Later that afternoon, as she busied herself working on paperwork for tax season, the door jingled. She looked up to see the UPS deliveryman wheeling in a large box on his dolly.

"Do you want it over here?" he asked, pointing to his usual delivery spot in the front room.

"Actually, I'd like you to put it in the back storage room, if you don't mind."

Cat didn't know why she wanted it away from view, but something about the package had put her on edge. As the deliveryman moved the box past her, she noticed it had a customs form attached to it. She hadn't ordered anything from overseas. Her skin started to tingle.

"There you go," said the UPS guy, as he pulled the dolly back out the door.

"Thanks," Cat called after him, before racing to the back room.

The box was very large, and, as she discovered when she tried to move it, very heavy. No wonder he'd needed a dolly. She was impressed he'd gotten it up the stairs. She examined the customs label. It had been shipped from London. The return address was stamped care of Barclays Bank.

With shaking fingers, she took out her box cutter from her back pocket and carefully sliced through the packaging tape. Opening the large flaps, she discovered a beautiful wooden chest sitting inside, nestled among thousands of packing peanuts. Cherry wood, she surmised, as she emptied some of the peanuts into a nearby trashcan, and of high quality. The chest looked old, yet well preserved. Painted on the top was a delicate oval chain of ivy and purple flowers. Cat sat back on her heels and stared at the chest. The pattern was the same as the pattern of flowers that had been embroidered down the front of Eliza's gown and on the shawl she'd been wearing the night she'd disappeared.

Breathing slow, deep breaths, Cat fought to remain calm. This chest was from Eliza. It had to be. But how? Only days had passed since she'd last seen her friend—or hundreds of years, depending on how one reckoned it. Either way, the chances of her getting a chest to Cat from England seemed remote. Yet here it was. Reaching in with both trepidation and anticipation, she tried to open the lid. It wouldn't budge. *Great, Lizzie, send me something I can't get into.*

Sliding her hands carefully around the sides of the chest, she found nothing. Perplexed, she sat back again. The chest was too heavy for her to remove from the box, but she wasn't sure what else to do. Determinedly, she cut away as much of the cardboard as she could and dispensed with the remaining packing peanuts.

The chest sat on four solidly carved feet, which raised it about four inches off the ground. On its front in the center was embedded a heart-shaped lock. Cat ran her finger over it, thinking it looked familiar. Where was she supposed to find the key? She reached her arm under the right side, feeling the underside of the chest. Her fingers grazed the edge of an envelope. With excitement, she pulled the envelope free. It was addressed to *Catherine Schreiber* in a flowing hand, a hand that belonged to Eliza.

Cat ripped the envelope open and pulled out the letter. Unfolding it, she read, *Use the key from your necklace.*

Necklace? Cat reflexively groped her neck. *I don't wear necklaces.* She sat down in consternation, wondering what Eliza could have been thinking of. A minute later, she jumped up and raced up the stairs.

Charging through the living room, she skidded into her bedroom and ran over to her dresser. Opening the top drawer, she pulled out the jewelry box her mother had given her when she was twelve. There, nestled inside, was the *You Are the Key to My Heart* necklace Eliza had bought her to commemorate their trip to Vegas the summer after they'd met. Eliza had spied it in the casino gift shop and announced it was so kitschy that Cat had to have it. She hadn't cared that it was 22K gold, and thus expensive.

"What else are these slot winnings good for?" Eliza had said with a shrug. She'd bought one for herself, as well: the same gold chain with a key and a giant heart-shaped locket on it. They'd put photos of themselves inside the lockets, joking they were like Chandler and Joey on *Friends* with their 'Best Buds' bracelets. Cat, not much of a jewelry person to begin with, had eventually tucked hers away for safekeeping in her childhood jewelry box, where it had sat, forgotten. Until now.

Had Eliza been wearing the necklace the night of the ball? She hadn't seen anything on Eliza's neck, other than the pearls. Then she remembered Eliza had converted her savings into jewelry and sewn it into the hem of her gown—"I'll need some sort of back-up money in England," she'd said by way of explanation. Cat knew now why the lock on the trunk was familiar—it was made from Eliza's locket.

Running back down the stairs, she entered the main room at full speed. An older lady standing off to the left side called out, "Oh, there you are, dear. I was wondering if anyone was here today."

Cat pulled up short, breathing heavily. In her excitement over the chest, she'd forgotten that the Trove was open for business. Her eyes darted to the back room, but she walked over to the woman, trying to calm herself.

"Hi there. Sorry about that. Welcome to the Treasure Trove. How may I help you?"

"I want this biography of Benjamin Franklin for my husband," the woman answered, holding up a thick volume. "He's always admired Mr. Franklin, and this is a perfect anniversary gift for us. I'm so glad you have it in stock."

"Wonderful." Cat headed to the register to ring up the sale. Benjamin Franklin. Benjamin Franklin Cooper. Was there anything that didn't remind her of him these days? "Is there anything else I can help you with?"

"No, that's it. Thank you, dear. You have a fine store here. I will be happy to come back again. It's so much more personable than that huge one over on Barracks Road."

"Thank you," Cat replied with a genuine smile. "I do love it here."

"I can see why. It's beautiful and homey. You can tell you've invested your heart into it."

At the mention of heart, Cat's thoughts once again went to the necklace she had tucked in her pocket. After the customer made her way out the front door, Cat scrambled back to the trunk, dropped to her knees, and fitted the key into the lock. It opened easily.

I can't believe it.

A stack of letters tied with a ribbon lay in the left side of the trunk. The top one—and presumably all of them—was addressed to her. In the middle were several collections of books. They, too, looked quite old by the style of their bindings, but were in immaculate condition. Cat held her breath as her fingers ran along the spines. They were grouped in volumes of three, each bearing the same title, each group bound by string. She read the titles: *Sense and Sensibility,*

Pride and Prejudice, Mansfield Park, Emma, Northanger Abbey, Persuasion.

"Oh my God, oh my God," Cat repeated to herself, over and over. Eliza had sent her original editions of all of Jane Austen's works. Cat knew that the books had been published at the time not as a single work, but in three separate volumes, since lending libraries had preferred that.

Carefully pulling *Pride and Prejudice* out of the pile, she noted the uneven edges of the pages. Uncut, they called that in the book world. These volumes were uncut, and in the original covers, or boards. The rarest of first editions. Removing the string, she opened the front cover of the first volume. There, in clean, careful hand, below the printed line indicating the books had been written *By A Lady*, was signed, *Jane Austen*. Cat gasped out loud.

Autographed copies? Eliza had acquired autographed copies of first editions of Jane Austen's works? Cat lifted out each title and inspected the inside covers. Each of the books bore Miss Austen's signature handwritten in ink, except for *Northanger Abbey* and *Persuasion*, which made sense, since they hadn't been published until after Austen's death. Reaching again into the chest, Catherine discovered a second set of first edition Austen titles. These were not autographed, and were bound in handsome leather rather than the thinner, more cardboard-like covers of the first set, but were in the same pristine condition as the first.

Tears filled Catherine's eyes. She pulled out the first letter and opened the sealed envelope.

Dearest Cat, it began. It was definitely Eliza's handwriting, but looked a bit wobblier than in the previous note. It was dated 1854. Cat read on:

There is so much to tell you, and indeed the letters I've included detail my life each year since I left you. Suffice it to say after a few initial bumps (and one serious consideration at using the 'escape clause' you built for me), my Deveric and I settled into one long, glorious love affair. I owe it all to you, dear Cat, whom I've missed more than words can say. But I've taken great pleasure in knowing your life was still yet to come, and in knowing that perhaps I could ease it for you, as you did for me. Here are two collections of Miss Austen's works, one to sell and perhaps one for you to keep if you wish. My daughter, Rose, is gathering the works of Mr. Dickens for me now. I hope you will also find them here, although I believe my time is drawing short on this earth and I will not know if the collection is complete or not.

I have left for you photographs of my family. The one from 1842 is a daguerreotype from Mr. Beard here in London. The latest one, from 1853, was done by Mr. Fenton himself. I'm sure you will remember Mr. Dawes referencing him. I made sure to seek him out.

It may well be a shock for you, dear friend, to see me at such an advanced age, but I wanted to prove to you the truthfulness of my new 'time' of life, and to show you my beloved husband and glorious children and grandchildren.

Rose has promised to entrust this trunk to our bankers, with instructions to have it delivered to you at the appropriate time. I know it will be viewed as an odd request, but that is the beauty of being quite rich, dearest Cat—one can get away with doing eccentric things. Which is lucky for me, as I've been known to break out into my rendition of Wake Me Up Before You Go-Go, even at this ripe old age of seventy-one.

With much love, ever your bestie, Eliza

How strange it was to read such formal prose from her friend. At least she referenced Wham, so Cat knew for sure it was her. *Could there have been any doubt? Who else would send me something like this?*

Cat set the letter aside and carefully lifted out the bundle of cloth on the right side of the trunk. She had at first thought it was empty space, or maybe more books, but now she discerned the outline of frames through the material. She glanced quickly at what lay underneath the frames: several Charles Dickens books, including *A Tale of Two Cities* and *David Copperfield*. If her father could only be here now. It was unbelievable. A true treasure trove.

Sitting back on her heels, she removed the linen cloth from the frames and found herself eye to eye with Eliza. This must be the 1853 image, because it was clearly Eliza, only much, much older. She was still beautiful, and happiness shone in her eyes, although the portraits, as so many of that period did, showed no one smiling.

Next to her stood a tall man exuding pride, who had his arm clasped firmly around her waist. Deveric. In front of them, seated on a fancy sofa, were six adults—had they really had so many children? Maybe some were spouses, as there were three men and three women. Below them, on the floor, clustered eight children, ranging in age from toddler to teenager. Cat peered at their faces, marveling that these were all real people, that that was really *her* Eliza. But it was. It was.

Setting the photo aside, she found the older daguerreotype beneath it, again showing Eliza and her family, slightly younger. Cat ran her finger over the glass, touching her friend's face. *I hope you were happy, Eliza James. Truly happy.* She examined the large pile of letters waiting for her in the trunk. *I so look forward to reading about your life.*

Picking up the daguerreotype again, she felt a bump behind the edge of the frame. Flipping the frame over, she discovered a small oval wrapped in paper. She removed the paper and found herself staring at a painted portrait of her friend exactly as she had remembered her, although bedecked in jewels, including a stunning sapphire tiara tucked neatly into her elaborately coiffed hair. Turning it over, she found a piece of paper attached to the back that read *Eliza James, Duchess of Mattersley, 1814. R. Westall.*

Exhaling slowly, Cat surveyed the collection before her. She could scarcely believe that she was now in possession of autographed copies of Jane Austen's works. Leave it to Eliza to figure out a way to help Cat financially from two centuries ago.

It was too much to take in—all of it. Derrick and Grayson. William. The Duke. Time traveling. *What's next, werewolves and vampires?*

Tears ran down her face as she marveled over everything that had happened in a few short months. Her best friend was gone. And it was clear from the items in front of her that she was never coming back. Cat reached into the trunk and pulled out the stack of letters. Each had her name and a simple date written across the front. It was apparent Eliza had written her at least once a year, but often much more. *There's enough here to fill a novel. How ironic.*

The front door jingled, startling her out of her reverie. *Oh, yeah, I'm running a bookstore and we're open.* Hopping up, she quickly set the pictures back into the trunk and closed its lid, then walked out to the front of the store, wiping the tears from her cheeks.

"Cat?"

She looked up to see Ben Cooper standing in the entrance.

Chapter 27

"**A**re you okay?" He gestured to the trails running down her face.

"Fine, fine." She pasted on a fake smile. "How are you? Long time no see." She couldn't believe he was standing there, in front of her. It'd been nearly three weeks. He hadn't answered her phone calls, hadn't responded to her emails. Why had he shown up now?

He ignored her attempt at small talk. "You don't seem fine."

Cat burst into tears. Ben hesitated for a second, then strode toward her, drawing her into his arms. She stood there, clinging to him, her body spasming with the strength of her sobs. He didn't say a word. He just held her and stroked her hair.

"She's gone. She's g-gone."

"Who's gone?"

"E-Eliza. She's in England with her duke. And she's not coming b-back!"

Ben pulled back so he could study her face. "What are you talking about?"

Cat sobbed harder. Ben guided her to the sofa and helped her sit down.

"Give me a second," he said, crossing to the front door. Cat heard him latch the door, then watched as he flipped the sign from *Open* to *Closed*.

Striding back to her, he sat down and reached for her hand. She launched herself into his arms and let the tears come. Ben continued to stroke her hair, not saying anything. Eventually her sobs died down and she sat with him, staring into the fire that she'd started earlier that morning.

"I'm sorry," she said, sniffling. "I'm sorry."

"It's okay," Ben said simply. That made her cry harder. Reaching over, Ben grabbed the box of tissues off the side table and handed them to her. "Do you want to tell me about it?"

She wanted to ask him where he'd been. But she figured she might as well tell him everything. It wouldn't matter where he'd been if her story drove him away now.

Wiping her nose, she nodded. "I do. I really do. But you won't believe it."

"Try me."

For the next hour, Cat talked, uninterrupted, telling Ben every detail about the medieval book, and Derrick and Grayson and William, and Eliza and her duke. He continued to run his fingers through the back of her hair, but his body tensed as he listened. *Not that I blame him. At least he hasn't called the psych ward.*

When she fell silent at last, Ben didn't speak. She sat up and looked at him. He was watching the fire, an impenetrable expression on his face.

"You don't believe me, do you?" she said in a soft voice.

He turned to look at her.

"Not that I blame you," she added hastily. "I wouldn't believe me either."

"I have to admit, this was not what I was expecting when I came in here today," he conceded, his lips narrowing.

At that, she raised an eyebrow. "What did you expect?"

Ben shifted uncomfortably on the couch. "I, um. I don't know."

"*Do* you believe me?"

He fixed his eyes on her again, glancing away after a minute. "I don't know."

"Why didn't you come to the New Year's ball?" Cat said, desperate to keep him from walking out. She brushed the hair out of her eyes and reached for another tissue. "I thought maybe you were angry with me about, you know, the thing. And Mei."

"The *thing*?" he said. "That's what you refer to that kiss as—a *thing*?"

She shuddered at the anger in his tone.

"And as for Mei and I. We were already done. I broke things off with her after I bought the book for her. After I realized …" He stopped, shaking his head. "It was never a good fit."

"I'm sorry," she offered lamely.

Ben regarded her for a long moment. "I'm not."

She sniffed again. "You don't think I'm nuts for telling you I created all these people? That a book has given me this strange power?"

"You've been under a lot of stress." He shifted away from her a bit. "Maybe you just need some sleep."

Anger stormed through her. "I wish," she muttered. She wanted to snap at him, at the incredulity written across his face. Did he think she was lying? That Eliza was really sitting upstairs? Or maybe he was considering whether she'd offed

Eliza and hidden her body somewhere. Bitterness ate at the back of her throat.

She took a deep breath. It had taken her weeks to come to terms with all of this, she reminded herself, and she was the one directly involved. She's the one who'd translated the book and knew now what power it granted. Had claimed to grant, she'd first thought, until she experienced everything first-hand. No wonder he seemed to be debating whether to run out that door or not.

"Assuming it were all true—and I'm not saying it is …" Breaking off, he peeked at her again. "Are you telling me that I'm a literary creation, too?" He paused. "Because if I am, couldn't you have given me a smaller nose?"

She let out a sob at that. She could hardly believe Ben was doing just what Eliza had always done, trying to cheer her with humor in the midst of all this chaos. "No, you're not. You appear to be one hundred percent real."

"That's a relief. I guess." He ran his hands along the tops of his legs. "Because I'd hope you'd make me more exciting than I really am. You don't see many middle-aged unmarried computer science professors as the hero in a story, do you?"

Cat laughed. "I don't know. You've saved the day for me more than once."

Ben exhaled. "Cat. This is a lot to take in. And I wasn't in the best headspace before I got here today. Can we … Can we both get some rest and come back to this later?"

Cat frowned as he stood up. "But I have proof. Let me show you the medieval book. And Eliza's letters. Come with me to the back room," she said, grabbing onto his hand.

He wrested his fingers free. "Not right now. I'm sorry, Cat, but I need to prepare for this evening's lecture. And honestly, I need some time to think."

She stood up, tears welling in her eyes again. "All right. Okay."

He cupped her face with his hands. He didn't say anything, just studied her for a long while.

"I'll see you soon," he finally whispered, before turning and walking out the door, leaving Cat standing alone in the middle of the bookstore. She watched him go, wishing beyond anything that he would turn around and come back; come back and hold her again and tell her everything was going to be fine, tell her he believed her and that he would never leave her. But the shrill ring of the telephone interrupted her fantasy, drawing her back to the reality that she might never see Ben Cooper again. Just like she'd never see Eliza. Or her dad.

Ignoring the telephone, she left the *Closed* sign on the door and trudged up the stairs into her bedroom. Climbing into her bed, she burrowed as deeply as she could under the covers, wanting only to forget it all and not think about tomorrow. Elvis jumped up next to her with a curious meow, as if to ask her why she was in bed in the middle of the morning. He settled down with a contented purr against her side.

She ran her hands over his fur, grateful for the small amount of comfort he gave. Then, with thoughts of Eliza and Ben swirling in her head, she fell asleep.

A week later, Cat sat in her usual booth at the coffee shop, nursing her butterscotch latte. She had brought over the first few letters from Eliza, but hadn't yet opened any more of them, feeling somehow as if she left them untouched it wouldn't be real, and that Eliza would come sailing in any minute, chattering about how she shouldn't eat the cake but ordering it anyway.

Or maybe Ben would walk through the door.

That was the more realistic expectation, even though she hadn't heard a thing from him. At least she and he were still in the same century. She watched the door, but the only person to open it was a harried-looking mom struggling to push through a stroller, in which a small girl of maybe one or two was pitching an enormous fit.

"Here, let me help you, ma'am," a familiar voice said. The woman flashed a grateful smile, and then tilted her head flirtatiously at the impeccably dressed man who held the door for her.

William. William is here.

She hadn't tried to call him again. She probably should have, but she'd left two messages, and besides, she was, frankly, a mess.

"I'm glad to be of help," he responded to the woman, bending down to hand the little girl the teddy bear that had fallen by her feet. The girl stilled, chewing on the bear's ear and watching him with wide eyes. Standing up, he turned and looked toward Cat's booth. Seeing her there, he broke into a wide smile and walked over. The mom watched him go, an air of disappointment on her face.

"Hello, Catherine." He slid into the booth across from her. "I was hoping to find you here."

"William." Cat wished she were wearing something other than her ratty old sweatshirt. She'd stuffed her unwashed hair up into a sloppy bun. "What are you doing here? I wish you'd told me you were coming," she said, trying to adjust the bun briefly before giving up.

"I wanted to surprise you," he answered. "We just got back in from London, but I had my pilot fly me here instead of D.C. I needed to see you." He gave her a warm grin.

"I, um, would have tried to look a little nicer," she mumbled, wanting to sink below the table.

"You look beautiful, Catherine. You always do."

Cat chewed her lip as William reached for her hand across the table. "I've missed you," he said. "I'm sorry I wasn't here with you on New Year's Eve. We ended up having to stop in London for a few days to finish up some business on that end. I hope the party was a success."

"It was. Did you get my messages?"

The briefest of frowns crossed his face. "I did. The traveling and time changes threw me off. Besides, I figured the best way to talk with you would be in person."

Cat looked down at the letters strewn across the table. She wished he'd just called. She'd never been good at confrontation. Perhaps breaking up with someone didn't have to be confrontational, but it made her throat catch just thinking of it, when he was standing right in front of her, looking so hopeful.

He followed her eyes. "What beautiful script. Letters from an old relative?"

"A beloved friend," she answered. His eyebrows furrowed in question, but she ignored it.

"How's Eliza? I expected to see her here with you. I know this is your morning routine."

"She's ... fine. She's, um, gone to England for a while to visit ... family."

"Where in England?"

"Um," Cat said, fumbling. "London."

"I can't believe I missed her there. Not that London is exactly

294

a small town, I guess." He chuckled. "Have you ever been?"

"No. I've never left the States."

"We shall have to remedy that. I'd love to take you to England. I can show you our family's ancestral estate. I'm sure Uncle Edward wouldn't mind."

Cat gawked at him, once again reminded of the immensity of his power, wealth, and prestige. "You have an estate in England?"

"*I* don't," he answered. "But the Pierfield Estate has been in the family for centuries. Entailed to a distant elder male, however, so not part of my immediate family's holdings."

"Sure, sure, okay," she mumbled.

"You'll come?"

"Um, no. I meant, well, no. No, I won't come, William." She extricated her hand from his.

His face fell. "Too busy at the bookstore?"

"No. I mean, yes, I can't leave the bookstore, but no, that's not why." She swallowed hard. "I can't see you anymore, William."

His face creased in hurt. "Wow," he exhaled after a minute. "May I ask why? Have I done something to offend?"

"No, no," she said quickly. "Nothing at all. You're perfect. In fact, too perfect."

He gave an exasperated sigh. "That's ridiculous." He rubbed his forehead as if in pain. "This doesn't make any sense. I thought that you—that we—had a wonderful time together."

"We did. Truly. An amazing time. And I'll always be thankful for your help after my mother's accident."

He looked at her, trying to read her face. "You're telling me that you don't wish to see me anymore because I'm *perfect*? You're giving me the 'It's not you, it's me' line?"

Cat nodded, feeling miserable. "I guess I am. I don't feel

like it's right for us to be together," she said, adding softly, "At least not under the circumstances."

"What circumstances?" he asked. "Is there someone else?"

"Um, uh, just … never mind." Her tongue tripped over her words. "I'm sorry. I'm not the one for you, William."

"You mean I'm not the one for you, Ms. Schreiber," he said, a chill entering his voice. Standing up, he gave her a measured look. "It's been nothing but a pleasure," he finally said, a tinge of sadness evident in his tone. "I wish you luck in your future endeavors, whatever they may be. And, Catherine?"

"Yes?"

"If you ever need anything, please don't hesitate to contact me."

"You will find your great love," Cat burst out. "I promise. She's just not me."

He stood up, adjusting his coat. Leaning down, he gave her a peck on the cheek. She shot him a small, sad smile, then returned to staring at the table. Turning to leave, he bumped into someone standing behind him.

"Excuse me," William said. "Oh, it's you. The computer scientist."

Cat's eyes flew up, meeting Ben's. *How long had he been standing there? Had he heard much?* She couldn't read his face.

"It's you. The rich CEO," Ben replied dryly.

William regarded him for a moment, then turned back to peer at Cat. Looking between the two, he gave a wry grin, raised one eyebrow, and told her, "Good luck." Before she had time to react, he walked out the door.

She looked up at Ben. She hadn't heard anything from him since he'd left the bookstore the week before. She'd tried to give him space, knowing that everything she'd said was overwhelming. She still felt overwhelmed by it all. But last night she'd grown desperate, worried he'd decided she was insane, and that she'd never hear from him again. So she'd taken pictures of the two portraits of Eliza, as well as Eliza's first letter, and emailed them to Ben.

He remained standing a few feet away from the booth. "Did I interrupt something?"

"No. No, not at all. I was wishing William well. I told him goodbye."

Ben's body language relaxed, although he still didn't sit. "You broke up with him?"

"I guess so," she said. "If you can count two dates as a relationship."

"Well, they sounded like pretty phenomenal dates, from what you told me."

"True. Almost the complete Cinderella fantasy," she admitted, taking a small sip of her coffee. "But I'd prefer that most dates not end up with my mom in the hospital. The plane turning into a pumpkin would have been better."

"Maybe. Although riding in a large orange gourd at thirty thousand feet probably wouldn't end well, either."

Cat laughed. She gestured to the other side of the booth. "Join me?"

He settled in. "I feel like I'm taking Eliza's spot," he said, as he set his coat to his side.

Cat gawked at him.

"I mean here in the booth," he amended, seeing her stunned expression. "No one could take her place in your life."

"I love her," Cat said after a minute. "Not love-love her," she clarified.

Ben gave her an amused grin. "I knew what you meant. Not that there's anything wrong with that."

Cat chortled. "You're quoting *Seinfeld*, aren't you?"

"I am the master of my own domain." He waggled his eyebrows.

"I loved that show," she said, trying to gain control of herself, but the giggles continued to come. She knew at least half of them were from nervousness, from wanting Ben to stay, from wanting everything to work out. Somehow.

Ben watched her, a soft look on his face. "You're really done with Mr. Rich Pants?"

"Yes."

"But if what you told me is true—and believe me, I'm still struggling with it—then isn't he your Mr. Perfect?"

Cat nodded. "He's Mr. Perfect, alright."

Ben stared at her in confusion.

"He's just not Mr. Perfect-For-Me."

He watched her for a long moment, and then stood up.

Is he leaving? He's not leaving, is he? Tell me he's not leaving!

But he offered his hand instead. "Come on. Let's go for a walk."

Cat eyed the snow outside.

"Or do you have to go open the store?"

"No," she said. "I decided yesterday I'm taking a week's vacation. You know, mental health days. Although in my case, I may need years."

"Come on, then." He picked up her coat and handed it to her.

"In mid-January? It's freezing outside."

"Don't worry. I won't make you go far. There's something I want to show you."

CHAPTER 28

"The Rotunda? We're going to the Rotunda?"

"Yes," answered Ben, taking big strides. "I hope that's all right."

"Of course." Cat struggled to keep up with him. "I haven't been in there in a long time. Plus, it will be warm." She pulled her coat more tightly around her. "It's darn cold for Virginia right now."

Reaching the south side Rotunda steps, Ben stopped for a moment to look down the expanse of the Lawn. "Isn't it breathtaking?" he said.

Cat nodded. It truly was a gorgeous sight, one she'd taken for granted, having lived in Charlottesville for so long. "Yes." Her teeth chattered. "Can we go in now?"

Smiling, he linked her arm in his and escorted her down the few steps to the entrance. Once inside, they strolled at leisure, taking in the various rooms. Ben was mostly silent, making an observation here and there about the furnishings, but Cat didn't pressure him, figuring he'd eventually reveal why he had brought her here.

They climbed the curved stairwell to the Dome Room, passing by a few other tourists chatting with each other. At the top, Ben stopped and turned to the window. It was the same view as before they had come in, looking down the Lawn at the Pavilions and student rooms, with a glimpse of Old Cabell Hall at the far end. From up high, though, it was even more impressive, especially framed through the large white columns of the Rotunda's back entryway.

"Wow," Cat said.

"Yeah," replied Ben. "Wow." He took a deep breath. "This was my brother's favorite view."

Cat nodded. "I can see why."

Ben dipped his chin in curt affirmation. Cat could see a sheen of tears in his eyes.

"I'm so sorry, Ben," was all she could think to say.

"I didn't come to the New Year's Eve ball, Cat, because I was with my family, marking the anniversary of my brother's passing. He had cancer—an aggressive pancreatic cancer—and it was on New Year's Day of last year that he lost the battle."

He remained staring out the window, not looking at her, one single tear rolling down his cheek. "He was so young. Twenty-nine. He had his whole life ahead of him. But he's gone."

Cat slipped her hand in his and squeezed it. "I know some of that pain. I miss my dad every day."

He pressed back in acknowledgment. After a moment, he went on. "Wash was an architect. He loved buildings. He had begun working for a big firm in Richmond the previous year, and was so excited."

Ben took in a deep breath, still gazing blankly down the Lawn. "But he couldn't figure out why he was so tired. He was losing weight. And then …" He broke off, fighting back a sob. "Then he admitted he'd been having some abdominal pain for a while, but had been ignoring it." Ben snorted. "That was Wash, never wanting to go to the doctor for anything. When my mother finally convinced him to go—badgered him into it with guilt, rather—the cancer had spread."

Cat let go of his hand and enfolded him instead in a hug, mindless of the glances from passing strangers. Ben grabbed her, clinging to her much as she had clung to him in the bookstore when she was pouring out her grief over Eliza. He didn't say anything more, just held her. Finally he stepped back.

"Thank you." He reached for her hand again. "But I didn't bring you here to express my grief, deep as it still is." He led her over to one of the rows of chairs in the middle of the room and encouraged her to sit down. He took a place next to her.

"My family," he said, "is not a religious one. Sometimes we'd go to the Lutheran service when we visited the grand-parents on the holidays. But that was it."

He broke off for a minute, casting her a brief glance. Cat smiled in encouragement, and he went on. "My brother went so far as to declare himself an atheist." He paused again. "But on the night before he died, New Year's Eve, I was alone with him in his room. He'd been slipping in and out of consciousness for most of the previous few days, and was more out than in that day. We knew the time was near. But late that night—maybe around eleven thirty, I don't know—his eyes flew open. When he saw me, the most beatific smile spread across his face and he said, 'Ben, I saw God. I saw God.'"

Ben turned to Cat as if to gauge her reaction. She put her arm around the back of his chair, stroking his shoulder.

"I didn't know what to make of it. I don't know what I believe myself. But he was utterly convinced, Cat. He said his pain was gone, and that God was calling him home. He told me Grandma forgave me for stealing that twenty dollars from her cookie jar when I was thirteen. No one else knew that. No one. I didn't even think my grandmother knew it."

He glanced at her again, and then went back to staring at the floor. "He closed his eyes at that point, but said with conviction, 'I'm at peace. It's okay to let me go. God is with me.' It was the last thing I heard him say. When he lapsed into unconsciousness again, I paced the room. I didn't know what to make of it. I didn't know what to think. The next morning he passed away. He was smiling when he died, Cat."

She rubbed his back, unsure of what to say.

"My brother changed his entire sense of reality, or at least *my* entire sense of reality, in one day. I still struggle with it. I'm a computer scientist, for Pete's sake. My brain thinks in blacks and whites. I expect logical explanations for everything. It's hard for me to accept things that I can't understand. But my brother …"

He broke off. "When you told me your story, everything in my brain screamed, 'She's nuts. This woman is nuts.' It still does," he admitted with a wry grin. "A part of me said, 'If my brother the atheist can have a Paul on the road to Damascus moment …' But the rest of me, the rational side of me, couldn't accept it."

He ran his fingers through his hair. "Then you sent me that email, with those pictures. I'd accuse you of Photoshopping them, but given your, um, Luddite tendencies, I knew that wasn't remotely likely. I knew you had to be telling the truth."

Cat moved her hand from his shoulder and laced her fingers through his. "I'm so sorry, Ben, for the loss of your brother. I can tell you loved him very much."

His eyes welled up again at her words, but no tears fell. They sat in silence for a while longer, watching people come and go.

At length, Cat whispered, "I'm so glad you came back."

"Me, too." He stood up and reached for her hand, drawing her up with him. "I don't suppose I could buy you a cup of coffee? You know, like a normal, regular interaction between two non-crazy people?"

"Coffee? You're a man after my own heart." Realizing what she'd said, she bit her lip. "Um, I didn't, I mean ..."

"It's fine, Cat. Unlike Jack Nicholson, I can handle the truth."

The tender look on his face made Cat melt. She'd nearly missed this, this connection with Ben. If she hadn't tried again, if he hadn't come back ...

She knew there were no guarantees. She knew they were only at the beginning, although she hoped it was the beginning of something big, something long lasting. But she was okay with that. The not knowing wasn't nearly as terrifying as it would have been just a few months ago.

Images of Grayson, William, even Derrick, danced briefly across her mind. She was grateful to them, for what they'd taught her, and for what they'd brought her. They'd brought her clarity on what she really wanted. Guilt hit her in the gut over William, but she set it aside. She knew how she could make it up to him. Now was not about William. It was about Ben. Ben, who was running his fingers gently through her hair.

She laced her own fingers through his thick chestnut hair and drew his mouth down to hers. This time, there was no hesitation. He engulfed her in a fierce embrace, his lips meeting hers eagerly. She ran her hands around behind his neck, holding him to her. This kiss felt magical. Not magical in the sense of the medieval manuscript. Not even in the sense of the surprised passion they'd shared under the mistletoe.

But in the sense of connectedness, of completeness, of the sheer rightness of it.

After a moment, they broke off. He set his forehead against hers, and they stood that way, savoring each other. Cat couldn't have said if there were others in the Dome Room with them; to her, it was as if they were in a place all their own.

"Coffee," he murmured. "Before we make a bigger spectacle of ourselves by making out right here on the floor of the Rotunda." His mouth quirked up in a suggestive grin.

"Whatever would Thomas Jefferson think?"

"Eh, I'm pretty sure he'd root me on. I wouldn't be surprised to learn he'd engaged in scandalous behavior a time or two in this building."

"For shame, Benjamin *Franklin* Cooper, suggesting such a thing of one of your illustrious colleagues."

He poked her. She laughed.

Linking her fingers through his, they walked down the stairs together.

"Let me see if I get this right." Ben turned to the barista. "Vente latte, skim milk, with a shot of butterscotch. Unless you want something else, of course," he added hastily, looking back at Cat.

"No, no." Her lips turned up in a grin. "That's exactly right. How did you know that?"

"I, well. I've watched you with Eliza for some time in here."

"Like a stalker?" She started humming *Somebody's Watching Me*.

Panic crossed his face. "Well, uh, no, I mean …"

"I'm teasing, Ben. I'm flattered you know my order."

He breathed a sigh of relief. "How do you know that Rockwell song? I thought I was the only one who still loved all those cheesy seventies and eighties hits."

"Are you kidding?" Cat retorted, leading him to her usual booth. "*Wildfire*? *The Piña Colada Song*? I'm so there."

As she sat down, she started singing *Brandy (You're A Fine Girl)*. Ben joined in on the chorus, their voices blending in harmony together. Several customers frowned at them, but Cat didn't care.

Ben set his coffee down, reaching for her hand across the table. "I have to ask. You've never written about me, right? Because I'd still like that smaller nose."

Cat's cheeks burned.

Ben's eyes grew wide. "You *have* written about me. I thought you said I wasn't one of your characters?"

"You aren't! You aren't," she reassured him. "But I did write about you once, to test it."

Ben's face relaxed, and his eyes took on a teasing gleam. "Did it work? Did I used to have blond hair or something?"

Cat fidgeted with the handle of her coffee mug. "Uh, no."

"Good. Blond isn't my color. But that red on your cheeks has me dying to know. What *did* you write?"

Cat took a quick sip of coffee, avoiding his eyes. "It was after the mistletoe night. I wanted to make sure it was real, that you were real. I needed to test if I could, uh, write you the way I wanted." She stopped, but Ben waited, saying nothing. "So I wrote a scene in which you walked into the bookstore and declared you were madly in love with me and couldn't live without me."

"Oh, great," said Ben. Cat's eyes flew to his, which were crinkled in amusement. "So now when I *do* do that, you won't believe me."

"Yes, I will. I mean, no. I mean …" She broke off, flummoxed by the turn of the conversation.

Ben laughed heartily. "It's all right, Cat. I'm touched that you'd try. More than touched, actually." His thumb rubbed over her fingers. "But why didn't you go for the nose?" he added, lightening the mood.

"I *like* your nose."

"That would make one of us. I've tried to convince myself that if I had a smaller schnoz, the ladies would flock to me."

"Oh, I don't know." Cat smirked. "You know what they say: big nose, big hands, big …"

Now it was Ben's turn to flush. "Ms. Schreiber," he said with mock severity. "Are you alluding to, well, to what I think you're alluding?"

"A lady never tells." She batted her eyelashes at him. "But as long as we're playing this game, what should I change about me?"

"Nothing."

"What?" she burst out. "You're kidding. I'd kill to have Eliza's looks."

"Eliza's beautiful," Ben admitted. "But you're pretty much what I've always wanted."

"What?" Cat said, stunned.

"You are. You're gorgeous, for one thing. But more importantly, you're funny. You're intelligent. You're loyal. I've envied your relationship with Eliza; the closest I ever came to that was with Wash." He swallowed. "You're emotionally expressive in ways I'm not."

"God, I know," she broke in. "I wish I could control that better."

"I don't. It's refreshing, at least to me." He brought her hand to his lips and kissed it gently. "I've felt drawn to you, since the day I first saw you in the book store."

"You have?" Cat's eyes went wide. She pulled her hands back from the table. For a moment, she panicked. Oh God, what if she really *had* written about him at some point years ago? What if? *No*, she told herself sternly. *You wrote that scene in the bookstore and it didn't happen. You did* not *create Ben Cooper.*

Eliza had told her after the Grayson-Amy debacle that it was possible for a man to be interested in her, to want her, to love her for exactly who she was, not because she'd written him that way. "I promise," her friend had said.

Cat took another sip of coffee, fighting to accept that Ben was exactly who he was—not one of her creations—and that he was into her.

She suddenly realized what he had said. "Wait. The first time we saw each other was in the coffee shop."

He ran his hands along the tops of his thighs, exhaling. "Not exactly."

"What?"

"It was earlier in the fall. My sister brought Alice to the Treasure Trove for some sort of story thing. I met them there, as we had plans to go to lunch."

Alice? Alice had come to Story Hour? No wonder the girl had looked familiar.

"You didn't notice me when I came in, because you were so involved with the kids. You had an eye patch across your eye, and a stuffed parrot on your shoulder, and you were reading in a rather impressive pirate accent. Something about whether or not pirates ever took baths." He reached for her hand again, clasping it in his, resting both on the top of the table. "I was hooked. I wanted to know more about this woman. It's not every day you meet an adult wearing a stuffed parrot as a fashion accessory."

Cat ran her thumb over his. "Eliza always said you were

interested in me. I didn't believe her, especially since you were with a woman the very first time I saw you."

Ben's brow wrinkled. "I was?"

"Yes, a tall, reddish-haired woman. You gave her quite a hug when she came over to you."

"Reddish-hai—that was my sister! Martha. We met for coffee that day because she needed to talk. An argument with her husband, Jack."

"Your sister." Not a girlfriend. "And Shakespeare?"

"Shakespeare?" His brow furrowed.

"You know, the day we ate lunch together. You told me you had a date that night, at the Shakespeare Center."

"Oh! Yeah. No, not a date in that sense. Martha took me with her. She'd really wanted to see *A Christmas Carol*, but Jack had no interest. I've always liked Dickens myself."

Cat sucked in a breath at the mention of *A Christmas Carol*. Scrooge. Eliza. Those other men. Ben. He'd been single. If only she'd asked. Then again, he hadn't asked her out, and he *had* acquired a girlfriend soon after. "Okay, but when you started dating Mei, I assumed …"

"Cat, when I heard that you were dating those other men, I figured I had no chance. I don't look like a Grayson. I'm not wealthy like a William. It's not as if women fall all over me."

"Why not? You're pretty darn cute."

He choked on the sip of coffee he'd just taken. "Uh, thank you. I'm not quite sure what to say to that. Computer scientists seem to be less in demand than, say, firefighters. Or doctors. Or …"

" … Dukes and earls?"

He ran his finger along the rim of his cup. "Yes. Dukes and earls, indeed. So when Mei asked me out, I said to myself 'Why not? Give it a chance. You might not get another.' But it was clear to me pretty quickly that while she's a sweet lady, she wasn't the one for me. And it wasn't fair to her to keep pretending she was."

They stared at each other.

"What now?" she asked.

"Now," he said, "I'm hoping you'll let me take you on a date. A real one. Although I'd be lying if I didn't admit I'm feeling intimidated again, given what you told me about Mr. Dawes, at least."

"I'd like a date." She took a last sip of her coffee. "Don't worry about Dawes. Or any of them. Because the person, the only person, I'm interested in is you."

She smoothed her hair back from her face with her free hand. "Getting everything you think you wanted isn't all it's cracked up to be, you know. I never thought I'd feel this way, but a little mystery, a little uncertainty, a little less-than-perfect feels so much more exciting than getting my dream man." At his raised eyebrows, she grimaced. "Wait, that came out wrong."

Ben gave her a tender smile. "No, I get it. I'm no Prince Charming. I'm full of faults. People claim I'm a pessimist, although they're wrong. I'm a realist. I'm not good at sharing how I feel. I can't have foods touch each other on my plate. And I can be overly frugal."

"Frugality is a fault? That's news to me." She rubbed her fingers over his again, enjoying the feeling of warmth, the sense of connection. "But guess what, Ben? I don't need Prince Charming. I'm no fairytale princess, either. I take people for granted far too often, including Eliza. I tried to fill my emotional holes with books instead of people. I'm not fond of going out in cold or hot weather. I'm not good with change. And apparently I'm clueless about noticing when a man is interested in me unless he states so directly."

Ben nodded. "So we've agreed we're each quirky. I can live with that."

"Me, too," she answered with a grin. "But first, can I show you what I wanted to show you before?"

Ben stood up and shrugged on his jacket. "Lead on, fair maiden. Lead on."

An hour later, they sat in the back room of the Treasure Trove, immersed in Eliza's letters. Ben occasionally picked up the two photographs and the portrait, scrutinized them, and then set them back down. They had pulled out all the books and discovered that indeed most, if not all, of Dickens' works had been added to the trunk.

"These have got to be worth a fortune," Ben commented at one point.

"I know. But I'm not sure I can bring myself to part with them, especially since they're from Eliza."

"Do you have to?"

"Not yet," Cat said. "Selling the Bible to William and finalizing the sale on that *Pooh* book have me set for a little while. But I'm still working on paying off the second mortgage and loans my dad took out to keep the store afloat and send me to college."

She leaned back on the chair in which she was sitting and blew the bangs out of her face, clutching a group of letters in one hand. "To be honest, I'm trying to figure out if I want to keep going. In the business, that is. Without Eliza here, I have no extra help, no breaks, no one to take over when I go visit my family. I have Emily sometimes, but her schedule is limited, and of course the less I pay someone else the better I do."

Ben was silent for a minute. "I could help."

"What?"

"I could. On the weekends. Maybe some evenings. I have teaching and research obligations, but I love this store. You and your dad obviously put your hearts into it. I love how passionate you are about books, how you work to draw in the community to engage them in reading, especially kids. Too many kids go around these days with their eyes glued to a screen, rather than their noses to a book." He snorted. "Some might say that's ironic for a computer science professor to say, but it's the truth."

Cat nodded. "Thank you."

Ben swallowed nervously. "I guess maybe that's putting the cart before the horse. Or carriage, as Eliza might now say." He gave an uncertain chuckle. "I didn't mean to put pressure on you before we've even officially gone out once. I want to help. And to be perfectly honest, I want another excuse to be near you."

Cat's insides glowed. She set down the letters she'd been holding and stood up, crossing the short distance to his chair. She dropped herself into his lap, giggling at his surprised expression. Smoothing her fingers over the hair that had fallen across his forehead, she leaned in and kissed his nose, then his cheek, then his chin, before coming back to his mouth. He returned the kiss with enthusiasm, his fingers snaking up under her shirt to rub the bare skin of her lower back.

"Thank you," he said when she broke off the kiss. She didn't get up, though, instead settling herself against him. His arm encircled her and his fingers stroked lazy circles along her hip.

He cleared his throat. "I have to ask," he said. "I know why I want to be with you. I've shared that today. But I can't help but feel insecure, knowing you can create the perfect guy for yourself. Who am I compared to William, or Grayson? Or anybody you could dream up?" He glanced away, as if embarrassed to have revealed such insecurity.

"You are the man who made my toes curl when you kissed me under the mistletoe, Mr. Cooper." She slipped her finger under his chin and pulled his face back to hers gently. Smoothing her fingers down his cheek, she went on.

"You may say you're no Prince Charming, but you are the man who slayed my computer dragon. You're the man who stepped in to help without being asked or wanting acknowledgment, numerous times, and you did it because that's who you are, not because I wrote you to be that way. You are the man who understands my love for this store, and for my dad, and for my friend Eliza."

She leaned in and peppered his face with small kisses. "You are the man who intrigues me, the man about whom I'm dying to know more. You are the man who makes me laugh the most. You are the man who knows mushrooms are not food, they're fungus. And you are the man whom I truly believe likes me for me. Not because you have to—not because I created you that way—but because, for whatever reason, you want to. If I've learned nothing else from my experiences this winter, it's that that is more precious than anything else."

Pausing for a moment, she added, "I've spent years choosing the safe and known over the unsure and the unknown. But I'm finding I like not knowing how the story is going to end with you. I'm willing to accept the risk, and knowing that has made me feel so much more alive than I've felt in a long time. Plus, you have incredibly attractive chocolate eyes."

Ben's gaze grew soft. "That's quite a speech, Ms. Schreiber."

She leaned in and kissed him gently, then again. "Well, you're quite a character, Mr. Cooper."

CHAPTER 29

"What do you think?" Ben said a week later, stepping back to survey his work.

Cat eyed the coffee counter he'd installed across from the fireplace, complete with a shiny new espresso machine. "Who knew you were such a handyman? I thought you professor types were all brains, no brawn."

"Oh, yeah, lady? Get a load of these guns." He struck a variety of ridiculous bodybuilder poses.

Cat cackled with delight. "You constantly surprise me, Mr. Cooper."

"That's a good thing, right?" He winked at her.

"Absolutely." She gazed at him warmly. "Absolutely."

It had been an amazing week. They'd spent nearly every moment together, reading Eliza's letters, discussing plans for the store, sharing details about themselves. Cat showed Ben the manuscript and her translation of it. She even showed him the original stories she'd written, but only after he begged to see them. She was sure her cheeks had burned hotter than a blazing furnace when he'd asked to read Grayson's story last night.

He'd only gotten a little ways into it before his own cheeks betrayed a startling amount of color. Setting the story down, he'd said, "You know, I don't want to know any more about this fellow. Performance anxiety and all that."

"Well, there's only one way to allay those fears, right?" She'd been shocked to hear the words come out of her mouth. In spite of her one-night stand with Grayson, which she'd decided had to be due in part to the manuscript's influence, to the pull of her original story, she wasn't the type to rush into anything physical. But it didn't feel like rushing. Not with Ben. It felt good. It felt right.

Ben had raised an eyebrow at her, uncertainty etched across his face. She'd grabbed his hand, pulling him up from the sofa. Without a word, she led him into her bedroom, closing the door behind them. Elvis had meowed in protest from behind it, but they'd ignored the cat.

She'd kissed him ever so briefly, before stepping back and biting her lip. "I, um, really haven't been with that many people. In spite of, you know, what happened with Grayson. That's not who I am."

Ben reached for her, pulling her back to him. "It's not any of my business, how many people you've been with," he said, stroking her back. "It only matters than I'm with you now. I'd be lying, though, if I didn't admit that makes me happy to hear."

"Did you and …?"

"Mei? No. I've only been with one other person, actually." He coughed. "Hence at least some of the anxiety."

"As you said, what's past is past, and it doesn't matter. What matters now is the future."

"And right now. Because I don't want to rush through right now." He ran his finger down her cheek. "Not when I'm here with you."

Cat glowed at his words. Reaching up, she pulled his head down to hers, letting her mouth move across his. He returned the kiss, softly at first. Then his lips parted and his tongue sought entry. She opened to him, and he groaned against her, an exciting, intoxicating sound.

Backing up, she found the edge of the bed and fell onto it, pulling him with her. She enjoyed the feeling of his full weight on her as he continued to kiss her, rubbing his fingers along her cheek and through her hair.

"Oh, Cat." He kissed his way over to her ear, nibbling at the lobe. "You are so beautiful. So amazing. So … everything."

Her heart flooded with emotion. This felt so different, so much deeper than what she'd had with Grayson. That had been physical passion; this was emotional connection. She ran her hands up under his shirt, over the planes of his back. The warmth of his skin sent sizzles through her, and she pushed up against him, wanting to be closer, wanting more.

"Can we go slowly?" he'd whispered. "I want to savor this. Savor you."

"Yes." There was no need to rush, no need to hurry with Ben. He wasn't going anywhere. She felt secure in that, which surprised her. After Ryan, she wasn't sure she'd ever be able to trust again. But Ben was different. Ben wasn't Ryan. This all felt different, richer, deeper. She felt treasured.

"Yes," she breathed again, as his head dipped to her neck. His lips pressed against her skin, touching her collarbone, then the spot where her shirt buttoned. He looked up at her, seeking permission with his eyes. She nodded, and he released a button, then another.

She ran her hands over his back again, and then reached down to clasp the edges of his shirt, pulling it up and over his head. She tossed it to the floor, running her hands over his warm skin, loving the feeling of the hair on his chest, so masculine, so different from her own.

"Ben." Her breath was coming more quickly now, and she reached up to pull his mouth back to hers, savoring the taste of him, the way they blended together.

He flexed his hips against her once, twice, before fumbling with the buttons of her shirt. Slowly, patiently, he worked his way down, dipping to kiss the skin as he exposed it. Finally, he separated the two halves of the shirt and spread them open. She could feel his eyes on her, soaking in the sight of her.

He ran his fingers over the softness of her stomach, and then up, up, over her ribcage, to cover one of her breasts, which was still enclosed in her bra.

"So beautiful, dearest Cat." His thumb flicked over her nipple, and she bucked.

"I have a secret," she said, giving him a playful smile.

He arched an eyebrow. "Oh?"

"This is a front-hook bra." Reaching up, she unhooked the clasp.

Tenderly, almost reverently, he opened it, his eyes widening as her breasts were revealed.

She could see the desire writ across his face, and it set her on fire.

His hand hovered over her breast. "May I?"

She was touched at his carefulness, at his seeking permission. He wasn't here to take, to dominate. He was here to share, to take each step with her. "Please," she breathed, and his hands closed over her. Each touch, each caress had her body flaming, desire spreading from her breasts to every other part of her.

He took her mouth in a fierce kiss again, this one expressing every bit of his passion. She returned it full-force, reaching for the front of his jeans. But he moved down before she could touch him, his lips marking a trail down her throat to her chest, to her breasts. When he took a nipple into his mouth, she nearly exploded off of the bed.

She reached again for him. "Slow is all well and good," she managed to utter. "But you're driving me mad."

He raised his head and gave her a devilish grin. "Good," he said before pressing his full chest against hers. "Because you do the same to me."

She breathed in the heady scent of him, reveling in the feel of his skin against hers. She ran her fingers along his sides and over his back. They lay that way a while, sharing kisses and caresses. Eventually he rolled off of her, to the side. She froze for a moment, thinking he was leaving, but his hands dipped lower, under the waistband of her jeans.

He gave her a questioning look.

"Yes." She kissed his chin. "But only if I can take off yours, too."

His eyes jumped, nervousness creeping across his face, but he nodded.

"You and me," she'd whispered. "Nothing to fear. This is right. This is good. This is you and me, Ben."

His pupils had flared, a smile flitting across his face. Sitting up, she'd reached for his jeans, unfastening the button and undoing the zipper before slowly pulling them down, taking his boxers with them. Divesting the clothes onto the floor, she'd turned back to look at him. Damn, he was sexy. His legs were muscular, more so than she had expected, and her hand reached out to touch his thigh. He closed his eyes at the feel of her fingers.

"So muscular." She echoed her thoughts out loud as her fingers traced their way up to his hip.

Ben exhaled sharply. "I … run."

Before she could touch anywhere else, he reached over and pushed her back down on the bed. "My turn," he said, reaching for the button on her jeans.

For a moment, Cat had doubts. She wasn't as fit as he was. Her legs, while slender, had cellulite. Would he be turned off? She closed her eyes as his hands pulled, moving the jeans and undies down, down, down. Self-consciously, she slung an arm across her belly.

She could hear him breathing. "Open your eyes, Cat," he said. "Please."

She did. He ran a hand along her hip, and then pulled her arm away so that he could take in all of her. "You are beautiful. Beautiful."

He dipped his head to her stomach, pressing small kisses to it before moving lower, lower.

Cat ran her hands through his hair as he reached the most intimate part of her, clutching him to her as indescribable emotions raced through her veins. His touch, his fingers, his tongue felt oh-so-good. She trembled and shook as her body raced ahead, longing, seeking, questing for that peak.

"Oh, God, Ben!" Her world exploded into a thousand different colors, a thousand exquisite sensations. Her skin tingled and throbbed as pleasure flooded every inch of her. "Ben," she murmured again a moment later, reaching for him.

The look in his eyes nearly did her in again. He moved up, settling himself between her legs. "Do you have …?"

"Yes. In the side table drawer. But don't you want me to?"

"God, yes," he panted. "But not now. I can't. The time for slow is definitely over."

She grinned as she reached over and grabbed a condom, thankful Eliza had insisted she have a few on hand, though

Cat had thought there was no chance she'd use them. Opening it, she quickly sheathed him, delighting as her touch made him groan.

"Oh, Cat," he whispered against her mouth as he found entry. "I can't believe … finally … Cat!"

She clung to him, holding him tightly with every part of her body. Every nerve ending felt as if it were on fire, her brain overflowing with emotion and need.

"Ben," she breathed into his ear as he began to move, slowly at first, then faster and faster. "Yes. Yes. Ben."

His hands moved up to cup her face. "Cat." His eyes bore into her, and when she wanted to close hers, when it all felt too intense, he said, "No. Please. Stay with me."

And she did, gray eyes locked on brown, as they fell into shattering communion, together.

They'd lain snuggled into each other, chest to chest, legs entwined, for hours. Talking.

Cat had marveled that she could feel so comfortable naked in bed with a man, chatting about everything from *Monty Python* (turned out Ben loved *The Holy Grail* as much as she did) to Elvis Presley, painful middle school experiences, to long-term dreams. And yet she did.

After another session of passionate lovemaking—for that is what it felt like, lovemaking, not merely lust sating—they fell asleep, not rising until Elvis's shrill meow from beyond the bedroom door had informed them they'd overslept his feeding time.

Hearing the cat's meow as he wound himself around her feet brought Cat back to the present. Ben was tinkering with the machine. She openly ogled his jeans-clad derriere, knowing what was hiding inside now.

Trying to tame her errant—and dirty—thoughts, she

turned to survey the store, worry creasing her face. "Do you really think it's wise, selling coffee in here? We can't compete with the shop across the street. What if people spill it all over the books?"

"You spill it, we bill it," he said as he wiped the counter clean. "Although now that The Grounds has sold out and is becoming a Starbucks, I think you'll draw in people who want a more local feeling. Like me."

He walked over to her and brushed a piece of hair out of her face. "Plus, think of the amount of money you will save on your morning coffee alone."

"True. That's got to be enough to fund an entirely new section devoted to romances with trysts between fictional and real characters."

He raised his eyebrows.

She poked him in the side. "I'm not joking. Since I've been given this power to create love interests, why not put it to good use?"

"Makes sense to me," Ben said. "From what I've heard, romances are huge sellers. If you happen to become a rich and famous romance author, who's to complain? But if you never sold a thing, you'd create the possibility of happy endings for a lot of people. Sounds good to me."

Cat crossed her arms over her stomach. "On the other hand, isn't that exactly what I didn't want? Someone who *had* to love me, because I'd created them to do so?"

"Yes, but you knew that you had created them," he reasoned. "Other people won't. You could pen some novels and see what happens. You said you didn't guarantee the outcome for Eliza, and you rejected the love interests you'd created for yourself. Thank goodness." He dropped a kiss on her mouth. "Maybe the endings aren't as fixed as you think."

Cat chewed her lip, debating. "Well, it would certainly make Eliza happy, after all those years I teased her about her genre of choice."

"But would it make *you* happy?" Ben bopped her lightly on the nose with his finger. "You've made Eliza happy—isn't it time for you?"

"Yes," Cat said after a moment, thinking about Jill and Grayson. About William. She had been planning a story for him already, ever since she'd told him he would find his love. She owed it to him. "Yes, I believe it would."

She walked over behind the new drinks counter and surveyed the room. "I love this place," she sighed. "Not just because it was my dad's. But because it's mine now. Truly mine."

Ben brought out the photographs and portrait of Eliza from the back room. "Shall we hang these on the wall over the fireplace? That way it will feel as if Eliza is always here with us."

Cat nodded. She liked how he said 'us' without seeming to think about it.

The door jingled and the blue-haired girl from Poetry Night and the New Year's ball walked in with what must have been her new boyfriend, given the way he hung on her. His hair was a vibrant purple.

Ben and Cat looked at each other. "I've always wanted purple hair," he whispered just loudly enough for her to hear. "I hear it gets all the ladies."

"Sweet, an espresso machine! Now I don't have to go across the street to read," the blue-haired girl exclaimed, racing to the counter. Ben walked behind it. "A double, please," the girl said.

"No problem, milady," he replied, whipping up the drink.

After paying for it, the blue-haired girl took the drink and crossed over to the couch, dropping into it. "I love it here. Don't you, Ace?"

The boyfriend sat down beside her. "Sure. Very retro."

"Told you the coffee would be a hit," Ben said to Cat.

Cat eyed him. "How do you know how to make espresso like that?"

"I have many hidden talents." He shrugged. "I've had a machine like this at home for a year."

"And yet you came into the coffee shop almost daily?"

Ben shuffled his feet. "Well, yeah. My office is sterile. Some of my colleagues, too, but don't tell them I said that. I wanted more varied human interaction. And then," he added, his eyebrow quirking up, "I came for the delightful scenery. You know, the one that showed up every day at around eight."

Happiness spread throughout her body.

"Listen, I have to teach class in half an hour, but there's something I wanted to ask you."

"Okay."

"You know that date we haven't been on yet?"

Cat laughed. "You don't count it as dating when we've spent so much time together, reading Eliza's letters, examining that medieval book, and talking about everything under the moon? Or after last night?"

He gave her a quick kiss. "As much as I've enjoyed every minute of that—and I have, *especially* last night—no, that's not a date. But I know where I want to take you."

"You do? Where? Tonight?"

"No, not tonight. And you have to be willing to close the store for a few days."

"Now I'm intrigued. What do you have planned? Please don't say camping, because I can tell you right now, I am not an outdoorsy girl."

"I figured that out when you complained about walking to the Rotunda. No, what I want to know is," he continued, getting down on one knee. "Catherine Schreiber, will you go to Florence with me?"

Cat nearly fainted when he dropped to the floor. "You scoundrel." She pushed him hard enough in the shoulder that he fell over, laughing.

"I thought I was your white knight," he retorted, clutching his sides.

"Who told you that? I never told you that!"

"Eliza did. She told me not to lose hope."

"She *did*?" Cat gaped at him. "When? She never said anything to me. That stinker."

"Back in November, when I was helping out on Black Friday. That stinker loves you very much. And I can see why."

He propped himself up on one elbow. "Seriously, would you feel comfortable going to Florence with me? I have a conference there the second week in March. We could get separate rooms in the hotel if you wanted."

Florence? Ben Cooper is inviting me to Florence? As in Italy? She thought of the pictures hanging in her room, of the Duomo and the Ponte Vecchio. The Uffizi. For so many years she'd longed to go there, to fall in love there. *Dad, if there were ever a sign, this is it, don't you think?*

"I hardly think that will be necessary." Pouncing on him, she kissed him with great fervor, only breaking off when the sound of clapping intruded.

She and Ben looked toward the couch, where the blue and purple haired couple was applauding them.

"Epic," the boy said. "Old people making out. This place rocks."

Laughing, she stood up, pulling Ben to his feet. Out of the

corner of her eye, Eliza's portrait caught her attention. She could have sworn her friend's smile had grown a little wider.

"That's right, Eliza," she whispered. "This story is about the bookstore owner and the professor. And we're making it up as we go along. Can you believe it?"

"I can," Ben said. And he leaned in to kiss her again.

EPILOGUE

"**W**ho knew so much mail could pile up in a week?"

"Who cares? Let's go to bed."

"Good Lord, you're insatiable, Mr. Cooper. A week in Italy, every night together, wasn't enough?"

He laced his fingers through hers. "It will never be enough. But that's not what I meant. I'm exhausted. I could blame it on the long flight, but …"

She cocked an eyebrow at him. " … But?"

"I'm not sure *I'm* the insatiable one."

She threw the envelopes she held in her hand at him, laughing at his startled expression. As the envelopes fell to the floor, the handwriting on one of them caught her eye.

"Hey, that's from my mom. Since when does she send letters? She's more into email than I am."

"I think *anyone* might be into email, or texting, more than you, my luscious little Luddite."

She bent down and picked up the envelope, ignoring his

gibe. She pulled out the folded paper within, and opened it to reveal a second, smaller folded piece of paper. She looked at her mother's writing.

Dear Cat, the note read. *I found this when Marie and I were cleaning out the upstairs. I don't really know what your father was talking about, but since it mentions a manuscript and you'd asked about one, I thought you might be interested. Love, Mom.*

Cat sucked in a breath as she unfolded the second piece of paper.

"What is it?" Ben walked over to her.

"Something from my dad." She held her finger to her lips as she began to read.

Grandma Schreiber says manu handed down thru family. Origins not known—somewhere medieval Germany, maybe 13th cent. Can create love, create people (!), according to Grandma. Only for certain female members of the family, every 2nd or 3rd generation, @ 25. Must be guarded carefully, kept secret. Ancestors killed over it, died for it. Only told me b/c her health is frail & doesn't think she'll live to see Catey to 25. Only C will understand, Grandma claims.

Grandma's nuts, but I'm writing it down, as she said. Guess I better encourage Catey to learn a little Latin.

A tremulous smile broke over her face, even as her eyes filled with tears.

Ben's brow creased. "You okay?"

"Yes. Yes. Fine." A tear fell down her cheek. "Just one final gift, one final treasure from my father."

She cradled the paper against her chest. *Thank you, Dad.*

Looking at Ben, she held out her hand. "He loved me," she said, as their fingers intertwined.

Ben's eyes softened. "He's not the only one."

Reaching up, she smoothed her other hand through his hair, pulling him closer. The rich chocolate of his eyes melted her heart, and she knew the love there was mirrored in her own.

She touched her lips to his. "Here's to our own happily-ever-after, Mr. Cooper. Right after that nap."

He laughed, catching her up in a fierce hug. "Agreed, Ms. Schreiber. Agreed."

COMING FALL 2015:

A Matter of Time—Eliza and Deveric's story.

An excerpt from *A Matter of Time*

It is a truth universally acknowledged that a woman who's just traveled across an ocean and back two hundred years in time might find herself in a bit of a pickle. Unless that woman discovers herself to be trapped in the arms of a man in possession of a good fortune … and in want of a wife.

Eliza giggled out loud as that bizarre perversion of Jane Austen's opening line to *Pride and Prejudice* flitted through her mind. She looked down at the man in whose arms she was trapped. He was half-sitting, half-leaning on a settee sofa, but appeared to be passed out cold. His arms, however, held her firmly, and even as she tried to shift to survey her surroundings, he clutched her more fiercely.

Peeking out over her left shoulder, Eliza could see she was in a library of some sort. Not a public library, but rather an old-fashioned personal library, like the ones she'd always read about in her beloved romance novels. The walls were paneled in heavy oak on one side, with built-in bookshelves lining the other. Those shelves were filled with volumes of books in what looked to be antique bindings—only in new condition.

Turning her head to look to the right, she saw a large, heavy, ornately carved desk, covered with papers. A real inkstand sat on the top of the desk, and next to it, several quill pens. An old clock ticked forlornly from the wall behind the desk.

She couldn't see the entryway into the room—she presumed that was behind her, but thought she could hear distant strains of a violin and the low murmurings of conversation from somewhere fairly close by.

She closed her eyes again. It worked. It really worked.

The man shifted beneath her, but didn't relax his grip. Eliza's eyes flew open again as the enormity of her situation hit her.

"I'm trapped in the arms of a Regency duke. A duke my friend Cat created for me. A real duke," she whimpered, panic rising in her throat. She surveyed the room again, her eyes wildly leaping from object to object.

"And if the furnishings here are any indication, I'm in Regency England itself. Two hundred years ago. Oh my God. Oh my *God*!"

ACKNOWLEDGMENTS

"No man is an island," said John Donne. The sentiment is equally true for authors. This book would not exist had I not received assistance and support from so many people.

To Kary, for her constant support, help at all stages from brainstorming to beta reading to revisions, and especially for being such a wonderful friend.

To the Shenandoah Valley Writers, and especially Tamara, Rebekah, Taryn, and Deb. Every writer needs a community, and I'm so blessed to have found this one.

To my cousin Joy, for being my very first beta reader and avid cheerleader. And for having told me all those years ago that I was a writer.

To Jeanine, Johanna, Heather, and Teresa for beta reading and providing invaluable feedback.

To Joy Lankshear of Lankshear Design, for designing the amazing cover, and formatting the contents. My book looks so much better because of your efforts.

To Tessa Shapcott, my editor, for helping to shape Cat's story into the best it could be (or at least the best I could make it). Thank you for holding this nervous debut author's hand.

To my kids, for putting up with mom's need to escape to the Writing Cave to work.

And to Brett, without whom none of this would be possible. You're my everything.

About the Author

Don't tell her mom, but Margaret Locke started reading romance at the age of ten. She'd worked her way through all of the children's books available in the local bookmobile, so turned to the adult section, where she spied a book with a woman in a flowing green dress on the cover. The back said something about a pirate. She was hooked (and still wishes she could remember the name of that fateful book!).

Her delight in witty repartee between hero and heroine, in the age-old dance of attraction vs. resistance, in the emotional satisfaction of a cleverly achieved Happily Ever After followed her through high school, college, even grad school. But it wasn't until she turned forty that she finally made good on her teenage vow to write said novels, not merely read them.

Margaret lives in the beautiful Shenandoah Valley in Virginia with her fantastic husband, two fabulous kids, and two fat cats. You can usually find her in front of some sort of screen (electronic or window; she's come to terms with the fact that she's not an outdoors person).

Margaret loves to interact with fellow readers and authors!
You may find her here:

Blog/Website: **http://margaretlocke.com**

Facebook: **http://www.facebook.com/AuthorMargaretLocke**

GoodReads: **http://www.goodreads.com/MargaretLocke**

Pinterest: **http://www.pinterest.com/Margaret_Locke**

Twitter: **http://www.twitter.com/Margaret_Locke**

Interested in being the first to know about Margaret's
upcoming releases, or hearing about other insider
information not shared on her website? Sign up for her
newsletter! **http://eepurl.com/bitrp1**

What did you think of *A Man of Character*?
I would so appreciate it if you'd leave a review on
Amazon (**http://bit.ly/AManOfCharacter**) or
GoodReads (**http://bit.ly/GR-AManOfCharacter**).

Word-of-mouth is still the best way for indie authors to gain
readers, and the online version of word-of-mouth is reviews.

Thanks so much!

CPSIA information can be obtained
at www.ICGtesting.com
Printed in the USA
LVOW03s1622070517
533600LV00001BA/9/P